Also by D.L. Darby

SIRENS & STILETTOS

SLAY, BABY. SLAY.

SERIAL KILLER BOOK CLUB
BOOK TWO

D.L. DARBY

- Spousal abuse
- Spousal SA
- Spousal abuse while pregnant
- Mentions of abuse to a pregnant woman
- Mentions of abortion
- Attempted SA - not by MMC
- Murder
- Blood and gore
- Stalking
- Pregnancy
- Breaking and entering
- Dismemberment
- Abduction
- Isolation
- Assault
- Attempted murder
- Threats
- Gun violence
- Spousal homicide

- Explicit death scenes
- Paranoia
- Loss of autonomy
- On-page vomiting
- Explicit sex scenes
- Body Worship
- Consent
- The dick jerky returns

"Fetish" – Selena Gomez feat. Gucci Mane

"Words Are Worthless" – Sleep Theory

"Gravity" – Sleep Theory

"Can't Resist" – ORGAVSM

"Cry Me A River" – Diana Krall

"Pony" – Ginuwine

"Breakthrough" – Tie Die Sky

"Forever in Love" – Kenny G

"I Was Made For Lovin' You" –

YUNGBLUD feat. Dominic Lewis

"Afterglow" – Sleep Theory

"Fukai Mori" – Do As Infinity

*For all the little death darlings who need a golden retriever
to help you bury the bodies*

New Year's Eve

Despite being the city that never sleeps, the thundering footsteps that echo in the alley drown out the New Year's Eve nightlife—the blaring horns of midnight taxis, the cheers from the partygoers in the club, even the blood rushing in my ears like a tidal wave.

She knows she's being hunted. Knows exactly who's on her trail. Still, the Shadow Siren runs as if she might escape this time. As if there isn't a chain-link fence waiting to cut her flight short.

Maybe once she could have climbed it.

Not now. Now, she's trapped. Nowhere to run. Nowhere to hide.

I stop as she takes heavy breaths, watching the way her heels stutter against the pavement. Ahead, her silhouette is caught in the sickly glow of a lone bulb that shines just over the dumpster on the other side of the barricade.

We've been playing this game for years, I never imagined she'd let herself be cornered.

She's too clever. Too stubborn.

Too fucking perfect to make a mistake like this.

Her chin-length wig flashes neon as she spins, taking in her surroundings, and scanning for a route that doesn't exist.

Fight or flight.

Except this time, she has more than herself to think about.

Fitting that *now*—of all times—she finally faces the weight of her choices.

Labored breaths. *In. In. Out.*

I can taste her panic in the air as I close the distance, one toe of my Oxfords in front of the other, casually stalking through the puddles and the stale stench of desperation that clings to this city.

"There's nowhere to go." My voice cuts through the night, and she flinches as she whips around. "It's over."

Each step herds her closer to the light.

Closer to the truth.

I already know. I see the swell beneath her dark trench coat, the curve of a stomach that wasn't there before. I see the silvery scar tracing her cheek.

The chain rattles as she presses against it, hazel eyes burning with feral terror.

As if I'd ever harm a hair on her head.

Or our child's.

Still cloaked in shadow, I let a dark chuckle slip free.

I've dreamed of this moment—catching the infamous serial killer before me.

Fantasized about prying open the façade, stealing the woman's heart, and keeping it in a glass box.

Right beside mine.

Together. Where they've always belonged.

One last stride, and the orange glow spills across us both. Face to face.

Bunny and her Hunter.

The devil and her devoted demon.

"Time's up, Little Rabbit," I murmur. "Looks like I've finally caught you."

"HARDER." My throaty request fills the small room, candlelight flickering across the walls.

Fingertips dig deeper. A thin sheen of sweat slicks my skin. A cool sigh ghosts across my shoulder blades.

My back arches when he hits the spot I need him most. "Oh, fuck. Right there! Don't stop. Right there—harder!"

"I don't want to hurt you." The only other soul in the room sounds genuinely frustrated as he tests my body's limits.

He's almost got me there. I can feel it—feel him digging in, winding that spot tighter and tighter until—

"Fuck!" The knot finally gives, and I melt into a puddle beneath Mateo's very skilled fingers.

"Do you always have to make our sessions sound so sexual, Buns? I swear the girls think I give you a happy ending." He eases up on the muscle beneath my shoulder blade, working out a much smaller knot that collapses almost instantly.

"Happy ending, indeed." I sigh contentedly.

"What's got you so wound up?" He laughs, heading for a warm towel so I can wipe the oil from my body before I get in the sauna. I hate being slippery.

"Work's just been... tough lately." Tough is an understatement—but it's an inconvenience I accept willingly.

It's not like I have to work. Turns out, killing my abusive husband came with a mountain of life insurance. Technically, I'm set for life. It's not like being an investigative assistant is my dream job. It's just something I'm good at. Something to fill the hours.

Definitely not because of a six-foot-two, dark-haired detective with whiskey-colored eyes and cheekbones sharp enough to cut glass. A dick who lives to turn my life into a perpetual inferno of tension, lust, and animosity—especially when he keeps requesting me on his cases.

And it *certainly* has nothing to do with the fact that said detective asked for another woman's number right in front of me today, fully aware it would piss me off.

"Boss putting you through the wringer? I haven't seen you with this many knots since..." Mateo winces before finishing the thought. He doesn't realize my life actually got a hell of a lot easier after Nathaniel's death.

"It's fine," I assure him. "And yeah. It's just been... tense. Physically demanding."

I don't elaborate. My job at Metro PD is fun—I

don't even feel like it's work half the time. And while Detective Dick, a.k.a. Hunter Remington, and I may have a tangled past, present, and likely future, that job isn't the kind of *work* I meant.

But it's not like I can admit my second job involves killing men who abuse their wives. Or admit that I currently have a five-ten sack of shit chained in my basement—kept alive purely so I can take my frustrations out on him.

Mateo leaves while I gather my things, waiting outside with a glass of cucumber-lemon water and a wink. "Same time next week?"

"You know it."

I toss my stuff into a locker and grab my sauna-safe AirPods. I always pick a locker close to the sauna so I can listen to an audiobook while I'm in there. I'm behind on my buddy read with my best friend—and fellow serial killer—Dove, and she expects me to be finished before we meet at the bar later.

The sauna is empty when I slip inside. Eucalyptus-scented haze clings to my skin, instantly melting my muscles as I settle in the corner closest to the door.

My ears fill with the voice of a queen fighting for her kingdom—and the lover she can't have. I chose it because the dynamic mirrors mine a little too well.

A chance meeting with a forbidden love is followed by a tragic accident. The rest of the duet is her pushing him away while he refuses to give up on her.

Literally my life in a nutshell.

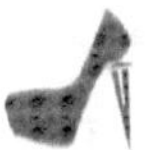

"I THOUGHT you said you didn't need any cocktail waitresses?" I lift a brow as the girl in question nearly faceplants ducking behind the bar. She glances around to see if anyone noticed, missing the puzzled glare I'm pinning her with.

I turn back to my favorite bartender—Alex—who also happens to own *The Tipsy Taco*, the unofficial watering hole for cops and reporters alike. He avoids my eyes, his creamy cheeks flushing pink.

"We've been getting busier." He shrugs, pouring electric-blue liquor into a shaker. His wavy sand-colored hair flops over his forehead as he sneaks another glance at the clumsy blonde.

It's her first night, and she's already spilled drinks twice. I know how hard it is to weave through a crowd with a tray, but I'm five-foot-two. Vixey, Alex's new girl, has to be pushing five-nine. She should have the advantage.

"What's got you in a mood?" Dove murmurs at my side, sliding over two tequila shots.

"Oh, you know. Just Detective Dick being his normal self today." I toss it back. The burn slides down my throat, settling warm and low in my belly.

I glance at my best friend's perfectly painted face. We're polar opposites. Where my clothing consists of black leather with the occasional pop of color, Dove Carroway lives in pinks and whites. Her hair is big, blonde, and bouncy. Mine's raven-dark, thick, and falls in a glossy sheet to the middle of my back. She's all porcelain and cream; I'm sunkissed gold. We're salt and pepper personified.

Though on the inside, we carry the same darkness. It's why we bonded when our paths crossed chasing the same target. Dove likes to kill men who prey on children. I prefer men who abuse their wives—our life experiences shaping our adult extracurriculars.

A shrill cackle snaps our heads toward the pool tables lined up near the bathrooms. Dove and I sigh in unison.

Hunter—the bane of my existence. And Wrenley—his best friend, Dove's work rival and current obsession—surrounded by a pack of bachelorette-party blondes.

A leggy woman wearing a glowing veil presses against Hunter's chest as she snaps a selfie. Her friends shriek, marking something off a paper list before scattering. The bride hangs back, her French-tipped claws hooked into his crisp white shirt.

"You know, Ryan said he wasn't coming tonight. Maybe we should just go…" Dove suggests.

Ryan's a cop at Metro PD, and Dove's on-again, off-again hookup. Judging by the way she and Wrenley keep sneaking looks at each other, he's about to get kicked off her roster.

Hunter's eyes snap to mine, so very aware of my attention even half a room apart. His whiskey-colored gaze narrows, daring me to cross the bar and stake a claim I have no right to. He leans closer to the woman, focus never leaving mine as he gives her that famous panty-melting smile.

This is what we do. A game we both keep losing, yet still play after three years.

My teeth catch my bottom lip, worrying at the permanently dented spot from nights like this. Watching him. Wanting him. Hating that I do.

"No, it's fine. Besides, I know you'd rather be checking out the blond hottie." I smirk at Dove, the motion crinkling the gold foil stars scattered over the scar at the high point of my left cheekbone.

"Oh, you hush." She swats my arm, glancing around to ensure no one heard me. "I'm not checking him out!"

"Uh huh. You've eye-fucked him twice since we sat down." I grab another shot, snagging a plump lime wedge to chase it.

"I think you're deflecting. Everyone in here can feel the tension between you and Detective Dick." Her bright blue eyes sparkle with mischief. I roll mine.

"She's right. Your pheromones are making me uncomfortable," Alex chimes in with a laugh.

His biceps flex under his red-and-black flannel, and for a split second, I wish I could be into him instead of the dark-haired devil who rents too much space in my brain.

"Shut it. You don't even know what you're talking about."

He does, though. Alex has heard every messy detail of our love lives. It's why he's our favorite bartender.

"I think you guys would make a cute couple."

Vixey appears on my other side, smiling as she reaches for a row of drinks. She's almost as bubbly as Dove, but I don't know her—and I don't appreciate her acting like she knows me.

I open my mouth to set her straight, but the highball glass she grabs catches the lip of the bar and tumbles—straight into my lap.

"What the fuck!" I jolt upright as icy liquid splashes over my vinyl leggings, dripping onto the floor.

Slowly, I lift my head, eyes narrowed, lips turned down, my gaze locking with Vixey's wide, honeyed look of horror. A visible shudder racks her body, her bottom lip trembling.

"Oh my god. I'm so sorry." She fumbles for napkins, trying to pat me down. Thankfully, my pants are water-proof. Doesn't mean she isn't testing my patience.

Alex tosses me a clean rag with a wince. "Sorry, Buns."

"At least you're wearing these pants," Dove says, snatching the rag to help. She flicks Vixey a pointed look that clearly says *leave.*

I take it from her before anything splashes onto her taffy-pink skirt. "At least I'm wearing black," I grumble. "Alex, I expect the next round to be on you." I flash him a saccharine smile, lips tight with sarcasm.

To his credit, he doesn't argue, just lines up shot glasses and reaches for the Patrón. I toss the damp rag aside and let my gaze drift back to the pool tables. The bride's gone. Hunter and Wrenley are mid-game.

Hunter checks his watch, then pulls out his phone

from his back pocket, and I can't help but wonder if he's made plans with the woman whose number he asked for earlier. The thought carves a hollow pit in my chest, filling it with adrenaline and anxiety.

We're not together. He can do whatever he wants, as I so often remind him.

It shouldn't be this difficult—love. You meet, you fall, and you vow to spend the rest of your life together. It's simple.

Only it's not.

Love is riddled with stipulations and expectations. A ring comes with rules that, rarely, both people follow. And even when you make a promise, you still find ways to break it.

Love makes people crazy. It rewires them. You can't promise to be the same person a year from now—let alone twenty.

Love hurts, even when the pain isn't intentional.

And the deeper you get swept up in all the pomp and circumstance, the more likely it is to utterly destroy you.

"Earth to Bunny." Dove's bubbly voice cuts through my spiral. "Hello! I'm trying to break you out of Detective Dick's snare, missy. You shall not let him dickmatize you." She even chants the last part like she's trying to hypnotize me herself.

With a sigh, I flip my hair off my shoulder. "Sorry. You have my full attention."

"Thank god. Don't make me—" Her words are drowned out by the crash of glasses shattering across the floor.

Our attention whips around to see Vixey, wide-eyed and sheepish, clutching an empty tray to her chest. If this were an anime, there'd be a giant sweatdrop sliding down her forehead as her fingers toy with the 90s-style tattoo choker around her neck.

"Third strike, you're out?" I mutter. Dove grins. "Five bucks says she doesn't make it till last call."

Dove releases a giggle, though she tries her damnedest to suppress it. Alex just glares as we clink our shots together. "Can you two be nice? It's her first night. Give her a break."

An hour later, I'm pretty sure he regrets saying that. If Vixey keeps it up, he'll be out of glasses before the night ends.

My head swims with too much tequila and not nearly enough tacos. After another, admittedly unnecessary, jab at Vixey, Dove pushes my shots away from me. I scowl past her, heat simmering under my skin, sharp and irrational. At the pool tables, Wrenley and Hunter are now surrounded by another set of women.

Fucking badge bunnies.

Desperate women who get off on cops and haunt their usual hangouts.

My friend grabs my shoulders, trying to convince me to leave and go sing karaoke, but all I can see is Hunter. The way he keeps shooting me those molten glances, like he wants me to be hyper-aware of every move he makes.

I am, you asshole. So painfully aware.

While Dove signals for the check, I slip off my stool. The alcohol hums through my blood, lending me a boost of false confidence. I'm vaguely aware of Dove calling out and trying to get me to stop, but I'm locked on target: a brunette reaching for Hunter's phone, probably to slide her number in.

Hunter sees me coming. He goes still, as if I'm the predator and *he's* the prey.

We both know better.

"I wouldn't bother with this one," I lilt, sliding around the brunette to insert myself between them. I flick her hand away and lean back against Hunter's chest. "He's already obsessed with his own *personal* rabbit."

The woman rears back, brows pinching as she looks between us. "Uh... sorry. I didn't realize he was taken."

"I didn't either," Hunter murmurs, amused. His fingers brush my waist, grazing the strip of skin between my crop top and pants.

I slap his hand away and bare my teeth at her. "Bye now."

She sniffs and retreats. Her friend's gone, too. Across the table, Wrenley's glaring at where Dove and Ryan, who wasn't supposed to come tonight, are talking at the bar. His mouth is set in a hard line. I'd bet twenty bucks he wants her just as badly as she wants him.

Idiots.

Hunter's laugh pulls me back. He's grinning like the smug bastard he is. "Finally staking your claim, Little Rabbit?"

"You're gross," I say flatly as he sets down his cue and grabs his beer.

He takes a slow pull from it, eyebrows raised, while I

hiss, "First the woman this afternoon, then the bride, now whoever that floozy was." I wave at the cluster of women who've already latched onto new prey.

"Admit it, Bunny, it makes you wet to see me flirt with other women." His grin is pure sin. He leans down, voice dropping to a heated whisper. "Just say the word, and I'll take you home right now. Or we can keep this up until you're dripping and begging for it."

I plant my palm on his forehead and push him back. Air stirs between us, carrying CK One and the scent that's uniquely *Hunter*. "Please. We both know I'll never beg you for it."

"You have once before. You will again." His certainty nearly distracts me from wondering what, exactly, he means.

Almost.

"The way I see it, you have two options." Hunter retrieves his cue, uncaring that Wrenley has abandoned the game to bother Dove, now sans Ryan, at the bar. He lines up another shot like I'm not even there, smoothly knocking the orange ball into a corner pocket. "Option one: give in and give me what I want." The blue ball disappears into the side pocket. "Or option two: keep up this torturous foreplay, watch me flirt, and get yourself off thinking about my tongue between your legs when you're home alone later."

He grins—wolfish, devastating—as another ball sinks.

"Well, *Hunter*, if your tongue didn't come with the risk of an STI, you might've had a chance of getting in my pants tonight." I lace the words with every ounce of sass I have.

His face twists. Just the implication makes me queasy, too.

"Okay then, Bunny. Option two it is." Disgust fades into a lazy grin. "Don't worry—I'll think of my *own personal rabbit* when I jerk off in the shower tonight."

The final ball flies into a pocket. Heat flares up my neck, down my spine, pooling low as he stalks toward me —slow and certain, like his namesake.

"Get over yourself, Detective Dick." I fold my arms. "It won't be you I'm thinking of later."

He chuckles, dropping the cue and bracing one arm on the table behind me. My nerves spark as he leans in, all taut muscle under a stretched white shirt. Dark, styled curls flop across one eye. My fingers itch to push them back then trail down the short beard framing his mouth.

This man can turn me to putty in seconds.

He knows it. I know it.

But he wants the one thing I can't give. And he won't give me anything else until I do.

"You'll try not to think of me later, Bunny," he whispers, sliding my hair off my shoulder. His gaze lingers on my lips, hand drifting down my jacket to skim my waist, scorching every place he touches. "But you will. You'll think about my mouth on yours. My fingers stroking the parts of you that are begging to be touched again. Parts only *I* know how to reach."

My hands catch his forearms. My body tilts into his, molten heat gathering between my thighs. "Hunter..."

"That's right, Little Rabbit. *Your* Hunter." His lips brush my neck. "And one of these nights, you'll stop denying us what we both want."

Then—air. Cool and sudden, as Dove barrels in.

"He called me a wanton slut! Can you believe the fucking nerve of that asshole?" she shrieks, looping her arm through mine and dragging me off.

I go, though my eyes stay locked on Hunter until the door closes behind us. His jaw ticks as the distance grows, eyes heated as our words replay in both our heads.

Every part of me screams to stop. To turn around. To run back to him.

Which is exactly why I keep walking.

Because Hunter will give me the world if I just ask. Ours is a twisted, reversed kind of love story—he's the one begging for forever, and I'm the one who can't commit.

Deep down, I know he'd never hurt me.

Once upon a time, though, I thought the same about my late husband.

And I ended up bashing his face in with a rump roast.

THREE YEARS AGO

"DON'T GO all rogue in there. Your job is to watch, collect information, and get the hell out. This isn't hero hour, and if you do something stupid to fuck up my investigation, I'll make sure you never make detective. You'll have a point of contact. They'll find you. Don't let me down, Remington."

Adrenaline rushes through my veins as I disconnect the call, the fear of failure pressing down like lead on my shoulders. But I was born for this—the thrill of the chase, the hunt. It's why I've advanced through the program so quickly. Narcotics doesn't even have room for me, but this is what I've been working toward since the day I joined the Metro Police Department.

Hard work and determination, Hunter. No fucking distractions. Just hard work and determination.

I pull at my collar and shove my phone into the

pocket of my jeans. It's early evening, the sun just starting to dip behind the skyscrapers of the Manhattan skyline. The strip club isn't bustling yet, so I grab a gyro from a halal cart two blocks over and bide my time. The scent of spiced lamb hangs in the warm summer air, trailing behind me as I head toward my destination.

This wasn't supposed to be a one-man job, but the douche they paired me with has failed every chance he's had at making detective. A few well-placed words were all it took to convince my sergeant I could handle it alone—with only my contact on the inside, whoever that may be.

I double-check that my fake ID is in the right place in my wallet and that my badge is hidden from sight. I had to shave my beard for this assignment, my baby face aging me down to early twenties when it's not hidden beneath week-old stubble. It's not going to do me any favors with the ladies, but I'm a scrawny shit with glasses and a love of smooth jazz—it's not like I'm getting anywhere with them anyway.

Which is exactly why I blend in. No one notices the skinny guy in the corner. Eyes are always on the muscled men who look like they might pose a threat.

Case in point—the bouncer barely glances at my card or me when I hand it over, despite my half-hearted comment that I've heard the chicken wings are the best in the city. Just trying to make polite conversation. No one actually comes to a strip club for the food.

The main room is dark—deep-colored walls and black tiled floors. Neon lights in shades of pink, purple, and blue serve as the only illumination. It takes my eyes a few seconds to adjust as I make my way to the bar, order a whiskey, and brace my arms on the glossy black marble countertop while I scan the room. Rows of liquor glow magenta from backlighting, framed by neon signs shaped like martini glasses and bubbles. Mini stages dot the main floor, the bases lit from below, surrounded by leather booths and black lacquer chairs.

Four women work their poles, costumes already half shed as groups of men throw crumpled bills. A few guys loiter at the buffet near the bathrooms—guess some people *do* come for the food. It's fucking disgusting that the wings are next to the shitter, but I can't imagine the kitchen here is much cleaner.

Nothing stands out as suspicious. No shrouded booths tucked away in shadows. No sharp eyes following me as I venture farther in. The bouncers inside stand like sentinels against the walls, arms crossed, watching the dancers with glazed-over eyes.

A woman approaches with an extra swing in her hips, her makeup thick enough to look like a mask while her tits threaten to burst from the red lace of her bra. "How about a dance, handsome?"

"Maybe later. I'm here for the show." I point to the main stage, where someone's adjusting the lights.

She shrugs and slinks off, leaving a cloud of powdery fragrance in her wake. She finds a new target quickly— the club's filling up, the air growing heavier with the stench of sweat and desperation.

I claim a table alone. Risky, isolating myself, but it'll make it easier for my contact to find me. The place is getting crowded enough that I doubt I'll sit alone for long.

Lights flicker on beneath my table, bathing the booth in a lavender glow. A few men turn their heads, gazes catching on something—*someone*—behind me.

I almost glance over my shoulder. Almost.

Then I *feel* her.

The air shifts, sharp and electric. The hairs on my arms rise.

She rounds the booth with the kind of presence that pulls gravity with it. Golden skin gleams in the phosphorescent lights, revealed in slivers between a two-piece leather set. Her breasts threaten to spill from the tiny top, while the brief-style shorts barely contain the curve of her ass. Understated makeup compared to the others, but her face is lethal—hazel eyes framed by thick lashes, pouty lips painted in a dark crimson, and high cheekbones that pop as she smiles at me.

She is the most breathtaking thing I've ever seen.

Swinging onto the platform before me, she balances her petite, hourglass frame on heels at least six inches high. A crowd starts to gather on the other side of the table as she sways around the pole, seductively whipping her long neon-blue wig and rolling her hips against the brass in perfect rhythm. Money rains at her feet, but for all the men watching, her gaze rarely strays from mine.

It momentarily blinds me. Distracts me from why I'm here—even if it helps my cover. Her attention makes me feel special as I settle back against the booth, sip my whiskey, and pull out a wad of cash. A delicate brow arches as her mossy gaze dips to the money, a slow, seductive smirk curling her lips.

I can't sit here and not throw money if I'm going to occupy her table. One performance won't hurt. Though it doesn't escape me that she's not stripping like the others.

Surely they wouldn't have my contact be a stripper.

She spins around the pole a few more times, flips upside down, her toned thighs and core suspending her in midair with sheer strength. As beautiful as she is, though, the fact that she isn't removing her clothes causes the men watching to lose interest and move on toward the topless dancers.

When it's just me, she sensually slides to her knees at the table's edge, crooking her finger. Like she's looped an invisible leash around my neck, I move forward, feeling like I've stepped off a cliff to freefall to my death.

Beauty like hers is deadly to men like me.

Up close, she's even more devastating. Freckles dust her nose and cheeks, gold flecks flash in her hazel eyes. Maybe it's the lights. But something tells me if I see this goddess outside this club, she'll be the only divine thing I ever worship.

She lowers her mouth to my ear. "I heard a hunter is looking for a rabbit to snare."

Well fuck me. She is one of ours.

The odds of seeing her again just multiplied by a fuck ton and the anticipation of those meetings has me high as a kite.

"The devil is looking for a new demon," I whisper back, finishing the code phrase.

The smile she beams when she pulls back is exquisite. "How about a dance, handsome?"

If it were anyone else, I'd numb myself to it. Let the intimacy wash over me without meaning. But when she slides off the platform and into my lap, *everything* in me goes taut and alive.

I start to lift my hands to her thighs when she shakes her head. "Nuh-uh. No touching."

But holy fuck does she touch me.

She moves slow, deliberate. Rolling her hips in a figure eight before grinding against my cock, which is fucking steel. Heat blooms low in my gut. My fingers stay welded to my thighs.

Standing, she turns and sinks her ass against my crotch, pressing her back to my chest as she keeps moving. Her arms loop behind her neck to pull my head down so she can whisper, "When we're done, go to the bathroom. The hall is dark, but there's a door at the end that's painted black, so it's harder to see. Make sure no one's watching."

I grit my teeth, trying to absorb her words while her scent—raspberry and jasmine, with a smoky vanilla undertone—takes over my senses, and it's all I can do not to blow my load like a teenager.

Her mouth brushes my neck. "It's okay. It's natural. Don't worry about offending me. I'm flattered. And you're easy on the eyes, which helps."

A whoosh of air drains my lungs as she resumes her

dance. "Take the stairs down the hall. A guy will tell you you're lost. Ignore him. Say you're looking for Gus. If he asks who sent you, tell him Larry—and that you wanna hit the jackpot. The rest is easy. Buy the shit and get out of here."

My nails bite into my thighs—not just from restraint, but from the thought of what's coming. There's always the risk they'll make me take a hit to prove I'm not a cop. But the last thing they want is doped-up guys harassing their girls.

As if reading my mind, she glances back, smirking. "Don't worry. They won't ask. They're too stupid for that."

She rolls her hips again, and this time I don't stifle the groan. "Okay, now you're just being mean."

She laughs low and leans over me. "I have to make it look real."

Sweat beads at my hairline. Fuck, I want to touch her. Grab her hips and drag her heat over me until she breaks.

"Meet me afterward." The words slip out before I can stop them.

She freezes, then arches a brow. "Oh, honey. If you cave that fast, you'll never make it."

"There's no way in hell I'd let any other woman get this close tonight." I straighten, careful not to touch her, but it brings our faces closer as she lowers herself until our groins press together again. "Meet me later." I nearly beg, the pleading tone causing her to blink.

"Why?" Her sexy lilt is genuinely filled with confusion as she cocks her head.

I lean closer, noses brushing. "Because I need to touch you. I need to know what your skin feels like under my fingertips." My mouth skims her cheek, nudging her wig back so I can whisper, "And if you let me, I'd like to worship you on my knees."

She takes a sharp breath and scrambles off my lap. We stare at each other as something silent passes between us. It was a bold request, though by the way her chest heaves, and her thighs press together, I don't think I was completely off in thinking there's chemistry between us.

This is the most alive I've felt in a long time, and that's saying something, all things considered.

One moment, she looks like she's considering it. The next, she grabs the discarded cash next to me and walks away without another word. I watch as she's swallowed by the crowd. I don't care about the money.

It's the best three hundred bucks I've ever spent.

My only regret is that I didn't get her name.

"Go home, Remington. You did good today. You can handle the rest of the paperwork tomorrow." Sergeant Kressler's deep baritone booms at my side.

My eyes never leave my computer as my fingers fly. "Thanks, Serge. I'm almost done. I'll make sure it gets finished tonight."

He claps my shoulder. "That's my boy. See ya Monday, kid."

It takes longer to finish the report than it should. My thoughts keep straying to the woman at the club. My body coming alive to the memory of her writhing over me, thinking about all the ways I'd like to take her *under* me.

Another hour passes before I'm able to print it out. By now, the lights in the office are low. Only a few guys sit at their desks. It's that odd hour between the day and night shift where the whole place is eerie like a graveyard.

Turning to grab the papers from the printer, I whirl back around when a loud thud sounds behind me. Sitting square in the middle of the worn-down pedestal desk is a rolled stack of money. And when I look up, the hazel eyes I haven't been able to forget are staring back.

"You know, I honestly thought about keeping it. But I decided you suffered enough through the dance." Her voice is pure sex without the music muffling it.

I flash her my best smile, sitting back in my chair. "I'd hardly say I suffered." I offer my hand. "Hunter Remington."

"Bunny Jones." She smiles and shakes it, a silky sheet of raven hair spilling over her shoulder as she leans in. She's dressed in black from leggings to a leather jacket hanging off one bare shoulder over a crop top. "I get it now. The *hunter* is looking for a *rabbit*..."

"And did this particular rabbit get caught in the snare?" I take off my glasses and set them between us. I'm not a moron, I know I have no game. But considering the woman of my dreams sought me out even though she had no reason to, I have a little hope.

Bunny arches a brow and props a hip on my desk, leaning forward as her voice lilts, "This little rabbit never gets caught." She winks and hops down, spinning on her stilettos—not the stripper ones—and saunters off. "See ya."

I blink, releasing a laugh that follows after her. "Wait, that's it?"

She stops and half turns with her hands on her hips, face lit up with amusement. "What do you mean, 'that's it?'"

My mouth hangs open while I search for something to say. I scrub a hand through my hair before putting my glasses back on to see her better. "I thought... that maybe..."

Bunny cocks her head, eyeing the other men in the room. No one wants to be caught checking her out, their heads snapping back to their paperwork. She sashays back, climbing on top of my desk as easily as she hauled herself onto the stripper platform earlier. I freeze, caught off guard as she presses into my space and balances on her knees.

"What? Did you think I'd let you take me home and eat my pussy when I have absolutely no idea who you are? What type of woman do you think I am, Hunter?" Her question drips with honeyed sex, and the crudeness of her words has my cock springing to life behind my zipper.

Bunny is bold.

It makes me want to be, too.

I plant my palms on either side of her, rising slowly. She leans back as I hover over her, our lips a breath apart. "One who likes a man who can never get enough to eat."

I dip my head to kiss her. I don't give a fuck that there are coworkers who will no doubt be talking about this tomorrow. I don't even care if it gets back to my sergeant.

After all, I'm networking.

Bunny giggles and slips away. "In your dreams, handsome."

Then, quicker than I can comprehend, she spins and lowers herself with graceful fluidity, walking away without so much as another word.

This time I let her go, watching her swing her hips purposefully until she's through the door and out of sight.

"Bunny..." I murmur her name like it's a goddamn prayer. "Oh, Little Rabbit. Game on."

The writing mass of flesh on the floor screams against the tape over his mouth—long, strangled notes, like music to my ears.

"Honestly, I'm jealous you can breathe through your nose well enough to keep carrying on like this." I cross my arms and lean back in my chair, kicking out my foot to drag my stiletto over his stomach. Blood wells from the neat slice made by the small blade hidden in my heel. It's enough to earn another round of screams, but not enough to seriously injure Oliver Wright—yet.

"You know, men like you really piss me off. Not only do you cheat on your wives, you put them through the emotional wringer. Gaslight them into thinking they're crazy when they ask why you're spending another night in the city, why your work shirts smell like cheap perfume. And then, because it makes you feel like a man, you hit them when they press the issue."

Oliver's breathing intensifies, chest heaving as I rise. His beady eyes track me while I step over his hips. He bucks against the chains bolted into the concrete, and my lips curve in a vulpine smile. "Regretting those decisions now? You sick fuck."

Tears brim. A high, pinched squeal rasps against the duct tape as I bring my heel down on his dick, aiming for a testicle and avoiding anything vital so he doesn't bleed out.

Blood spurts, spattering my bare leg, a skitter of revulsion crawling over my skin.

I know better than to skip the plastic suit when I play with my victims. But it's been a day, and it's made me sloppy.

I've been avoiding Hunter since our last run-in, but staying away physically doesn't stop my obsessive scrolling. He isn't active on socials much, but there's a recent tag he had to approve from some random girl who works at the coffee shop by work.

As Oliver squeals, the photo flashes in my mind. You can't see Hunter—just a blurry man across a candlelit table while she holds a glass of wine. But he let her tag him. Why do that if it isn't him?

It sounds like Oliver tries to scream *you fucking bitch*, snapping me out of thoughts about the man I desperately want but can't have.

You can have him. He just has stipulations—and you don't want to abide by them.

I sigh. "You're right, Ollie. I am a fucking bitch."

As I'm about to sink the bladed heel into the other testicle, my phone buzzes in my pocket. "Saved by the bell." I glare down at him as I fish it out and see it's Dove. "Hi, Love Dove."

"Hi! Are you busy? I'm still wound up from earlier. Let's go dancing!" Her chipper tone pleads, and I eye the man on the floor. He glares back, nostrils flaring with every breath, still struggling against the bindings.

"Want to take out your frustrations on some food instead? I'm already partaking in a meal." Dove and I have been friends long enough for her to read between the lines. Since Wrenley basically declared war on her by putting salt in her coffee this morning, I have a feeling killing a man who deserves it will soothe her more than a remixed Dua Lipa track.

"Oh, that sounds way better than dancing! I'll bring Fang so the boys can hang out. I'm already dressed up, so maybe we can still go dancing afterward?" Fang is her Chinese Crested. The *boys* are my Pomeranians, Yasha and Maru—affectionately named after Inuyasha and Sesshōmaru from one of my favorite animes.

"We'll see how you feel after dinner, my little dumpling slut."

There's a beat of silence. "Did you just call me a dumpling slut?"

"You said Wrenley called you a wanton slut, but all I can hear now is wonton slut. You know... like the dumpling? And now it's stuck in my head."

She snorts. "Now I kinda want dumplings too... dammit! I hate him!"

"Well, come take it out on my ham."

We hang up after she says she'll be here in twenty. Perfect. My heart's not really in it tonight. I'm too preoccupied with Hunter's date. I hate that he still has this kind of hold on me after all this time.

I look down at the man between my legs. "Ollie, I don't know how to break this to you, but we're having company, and the little spitfire on her way is much more brutal than I am."

He thrashes. I sigh, bored, and turn away. "You men should really stop pissing off women. We are way more creative with revenge, you know."

I consider ripping off the tape to give him a breather while I wait for Dove, but then he starts keening again and I change my mind. My wreck room is in the basement, tucked behind a door disguised as a shelving unit of random junk. No one would hear him... but *I* would, and I'm not in the mood.

I hit the lights on my way out, leaving him in the dark to stew. Upstairs—after removing my shoes and scrubbing the blood off until my flesh looks raw—I open a dating app. My babies greet me with playful yips, jumping at my calves, begging to play. They were fluffed and puffed this week, their silky coats sliding through my fingers and calming my nerves.

"Maybe Auntie Dove will bring you boys some treats," I coo. My bestie likes to turn her victims' privates into jerky for our pups. I'm not complaining—as long as she labels the bag and keeps it in the dog drawer instead of my pantry.

I'd have to kill her if I accidentally ate human penis jerky.

While I wait, I scroll mindlessly. If Hunter can go out and have a good time—even though he refuses to do that with me unless I give him my mind, body, and soul—then I won't feel guilty about finding a hot guy to take me to dinner.

It doesn't mean he gets anywhere near my kitty, even if she could use a workout. Lord knows she has cobwebs. The last time I had sex was years ago, and it ended with me losing my heart and fleeing the state for half a year. Traumatic and romantic all wrapped into one. I haven't been able to bring myself to sleep with anyone since.

My heart knows what it wants. It's my head that won't get on board. And while Hunter loves to perform patience, the fact that he's taking out other women isn't helping his case—no matter how hard the stubborn thing beating in my chest tries to convince my brain otherwise.

"SHE'S A FUCKING MENACE, Hunter! The most goddamn infuriating woman I've ever had the displeasure of knowing. The stylist said it's going to take at *least* four fucking sessions before my hair is back to normal!"

I bite my knuckle to keep my laughter from bubbling up. "Well, you *did* start it by putting salt in her coffee. Did you really think she wouldn't retaliate?"

A large man steps in front of my table, blocking my view. I cluck my tongue, shifting right, then left to get eyes back on my target.

Dude, get the hell out of my way.

"I didn't think she'd go crazy and put hair dye in my shampoo!"

I'm about to reach over the table and physically move the guy when he finally steps aside—completely unaware he was obstructing my line of sight. Relief washes through me as my target reappears, laughing and chatting it up with her date.

If she'd disappeared in that short window, I would've had to murder someone tonight.

As it is, my fingers itch to curl into fists and smash them into the man occupying my rabbit's time. He's basically a carbon copy of me—tall, olive skin, similar build, even the same style of dark, wavy hair.

Bunny has a type. And that type is *me*.

It should be me sitting there with her. Me putting that smile on her face. Me taking her home to fuck her within an inch of her life tonight. And it sure as hell *won't* be the douche who—

He brushes her knee. Dares to touch her exposed, naked flesh. Bunny's mossy eyes flick down to where their skin connects, a flash of hesitation sparking before she smothers it under her usual seductive stare. Her lips curve in a luscious grin as she lifts her gaze to his. It's flirtatious—and, as far as I'm concerned, a green light for the bastard.

Fuck. That.

"Why do I get the feeling you're not listening to a word I'm saying? Tell me you didn't follow Bunny after work and are now stalking her and her date." Wren's exhausted tone filters through my phone. I can picture him pinching the bridge of his nose. "You're a detective, Hunter. You know stalking is illegal."

"Who said anything about stalking? Not my fault they ended up at the same place I decided to grab dinner tonight."

Except it is my fault. Because I *did* follow Bunny after hearing her nonchalantly mention—*loudly*, I might add—to Heather in the forensic lab about where her date was taking her. She wanted me to come. Otherwise, she wouldn't have ensured I overheard.

Bunny is just as good at trapping me in her snares as I am her.

"Jesus, Hunter. You two really do have issues." Wrenley sighs as I abandon my dinner and push through the crowd toward them.

"Don't we all?" I murmur. My friend is definitely not without his own troubled problems. "Talk later."

I hang up before he can reply, sliding my phone into my pocket just as I reach Bunny and her date.

"Well, fancy running into you here, Little Rabbit."

Her eyes flick up. There's no shock, no annoyance—almost... relief. I thrust my hand at the man sitting across from her, deliberately angling my body so he has to pull his hand off her knee.

"*Detective* Hunter Remington. Bunny and I work together."

I can feel her silently begging me to intervene, even if she doesn't realize she's doing it—her knees caging me where I stand between her legs.

"Chad Drake." He shakes my hand, sizing me up before flicking a glance at Bunny.

"Of course your name is Chad." I laugh, not caring that it's rude. "Well, I hope you had a good evening, *Chad*, but I think it's time for you to leave now."

Bunny's knees press infinitesimally into my thighs. "Don't be rude, Hunter. You're the one who doesn't belong here right now."

Her saccharine lilt drips with playfulness. This poor guy never stood a chance. She knew I'd hunt her down tonight. Knows I'll never let another man take her home. Honestly, I think she counts on me showing up at this point.

Because at the end of the day, Bunny knows she's *mine*.

I rest my arm along the outside of her thigh, pulling her leg snug against my waist as I continue my silent standoff with my doppelgänger. Up close, the flaws are obvious—patchy beard, too much product in his hair, and eyes the wrong shade of brown.

Why go for Temu's knockoff when you can have the handcrafted original?

"Don't be silly, Little Rabbit." I don't break eye contact with Chad, who's looking at me like a fly in his wine. "You made sure I knew where you'd be so I could save you from a night of boring, meaningless conversation—and take you home to have hot, mind-blowing foreplay that'll leave us both with blue balls. Well, I'll have blue balls. You'll probably get an orgasm out of it, because I'm feeling generous tonight."

"Hunter!" Bunny smacks my ass, though amusement cracks through her dramatized scolding.

A smirk tugs my lips as Chad Drake—what kind of fucking name is Chad Drake anyway?—throws up his hands and slides off his bar stool. "Yeah, I'm out. Sorry, babe. You're hot, but not hot enough for these kinds of games."

Bunny huffs, affronted, as I cock my head and narrow my eyes, letting my words cut him as he retreats.

"She's hot enough to play every game in the damn universe... even if you lose every time."

Chad snorts and mutters, "Weirdos," as he disappears.

"Well, that was uncalled for." Bunny crosses her arms, and I finally turn fully toward her, pressing closer, using the arm looped around her thigh to pull her into me.

I don't care that we're in the middle of a crowded restaurant. I don't care that this caveman move probably has her soaked and that she's likely ready to make a mess all over the glossed oak stool she's perched on.

"Was it, though? Can you look me in the eye and tell me you didn't want me to crash your little show?" I push her hair behind her shoulder and cup her neck, my thumb nudging her chin up so she has to meet my gaze.

"I don't know what you're talking about." Her smile is sweet, but her gold-flecked green gaze darkens—like the forest floor at sunset. "You take women out all the time, Hunter. What's it matter if I get my rocks off with a stranger?"

The thought of her *getting off* with anyone else makes my blood boil. My grip tightens. My other hand slides to her waist, brushing the smooth strip of skin between her black skirt and lavender top.

"I haven't taken a woman out in years, Bunny. What are you talking about?"

She rolls her eyes, though her body melts into my

touch as I trace my thumb over her skin. Her words drip with sass. "Please. Some badge bunny tagged you in a photo when you took her to dinner."

There's a crack in her tone—a trace of hurt buried under her practiced delivery. It's annoyingly adorable.

It also turns my cock to granite.

Without warning, I lift her off the stool, sliding her down my body until her stilettos hit the floor. Neither of us speaks as I toss cash on the counter, grab her hand, and lead her out through the crowded space.

New York summer nights are humid and stifling, but nothing compares to the heat radiating from Bunny as I round the ancient brick structure and pin her to the wall. I have over a foot on her, so I brace my hands above her head and bend close.

"Listen to me, Little Rabbit. I have no idea what you're talking about. But your sass is lighting a fire in my cock that only your pussy can put out. So if you're done accusing me of bullshit that never happened, admit you're mine already so I can take you home and fuck you in the most disrespectful way imaginable."

She pushes at my chest, making space between us as she digs into her purse. My cock throbs painfully against my zipper as she swipes through her screen, finds what she wants, and holds it up. "See? She tagged you. So don't lie to me."

"Are you fucking kidding? Bunny, I don't get on social media. I didn't see any tags—but I can promise you that isn't me. I'd have to be fucking stupid to take out a badge bunny when I'm completely enamored with *you.*

And you *know* that." I push her phone away. She knows I'm not the kind of guy who would accept tags on photos, even if I *were* active on my profile.

Her defiance falters. She sags against the wall, gaze dropping to the dirty asphalt. The city hums around us as she chews her lip. I straighten and cradle her cheek, my thumb brushing the tiny red foil hearts that decorate her skin.

"Tell me you're mine," I whisper the request into the shared space between us, imploring her to give in already. Give in to this *thing* between us that sparked so long ago and never extinguished. "You have been in nearly every way imaginable—except the way that counts. Give me your consent, Bunny."

"You have my consent, Hunter. You've always had it. That isn't the issue and you know it." Her tone is stiff as she lifts her chin. Unshed tears cling to her thick lashes as her brows pinch and her voice cracks. "You just can't have my heart."

It feels like the organ in question takes a hammer to mine, even though this isn't the first time she's said it. She's scared. I know. She went through hell. No matter how hard I try to convince her otherwise, she's terrified of being shattered again.

Which is exactly why I press a chaste kiss to her forehead. "One day you'll give it to me. Until then, I can wait."

"Hunter..." She fists my white button-up and drags herself against me. "Just take me home."

It physically hurts to shake my head. I peel her hands

off my shirt and lead her to the curb to hail a cab. "I want all of you, Bunny. Not just part of you."

I don't tell her the truth—that it terrifies me to take her to bed without the promise of commitment. It's not that I'm the type who waits for marriage—we've had sex before.

It's because the last time I took her to bed, I woke up alone.

And then she disappeared for the better part of a year, taking my heart with her.

"Hey, did your Iconic reset? Mine changed my settings on its own, apparently. I know they're new and still working out bugs, but it's irritating as fuck."

Wrenley ignores me, eyes glued to the brunette he's chatting up. He oozes charm on a regular day, but it's starting to grate on my nerves with how he's carrying on—like he plans to take her home.

My attention drifts across the room to where Bunny stands at the bar, no doubt waiting for Dove to show up. It's rare for her to grace us with her presence without that short bundle of pink fluff she calls her best friend, and when she looks up and catches me staring, the corner of her pillowy mouth tips like she's just won a round I didn't know we were playing.

I hip-check Wren out of the way and sink the nine ball into the left corner pocket. "Anyway... some badge bunny tagged me in a photo, and the stupid app let her. She works at the coffee shop around the block from the department, and when I went in for a drink, she claimed she meant to tag a different Hunter."

Wren snorts and finally looks at me. "Sure, she did. I'll bet you got an earful from *your* Bunny, didn't you?"

The brunette clings to his side like a leech. Her friend —a willowy blonde who's probably giving herself a headache with all the lash-batting she's been doing at me —sidles up with a sultry smile full of sinful promises. Ignoring her, I move to the side to make another shot.

I couldn't care less that it would take nothing to have this woman on her knees, sucking my cock in seconds. Hell, both of them look ready to be taken out back by the dumpster, and they'd still make us come with a smile —accommodations be damned.

There's nothing I hate more than a desperate woman.

That's rich, considering you'd sell your soul for the woman who keeps refusing you.

"She certainly wasn't happy about it..." I glance at Wren, but his attention has already drifted. I follow his gaze and spot Dove.

Where my girl is all dark leather and sex on stilettos, her friend is spun sugar in pink—sweet enough to give you cavities and a stomachache if you overindulge.

Wren's been permanently nauseous since he met her, though it's taken weeks for the idiot to diagnose his metaphorical ailment. He still won't get out of his own damn way when it comes to the little sucrose sweetheart, though I suspect it's because she resembles his mother—a monstrous woman I hate with every fiber of my being.

He starts toward Dove, then freezes when Ryan—an officer who's had an on-again, off-again sexual situationship with her—walks in.

My gaze darts between Dove and Ryan's awkward encounter and Wrenley trying to wrangle his attention back to the brunette, clearly fighting the urge to storm across the bar and wedge himself between them.

"For what it's worth, I don't think he's spoken to her since that night," I state calmly, referencing a couple weeks back when Ryan and Wren went at it in the men's room over Ryan's crude comments about Dove.

"I don't care." He shrugs and rounds the table to take his shot after I miss. "She can do whatever the hell she wants."

Rolling my eyes, I watch Ryan brush Dove off and disappear. Both women look confused. I almost laugh. Wren warned Ryan to stay away, proverbially marking Dove as his after Ryan implied she'd be fine being shared by his buddies.

So why won't he claim her? No fucking clue.

"Sure, she can. You'd let her waltz out of here with anyone tonight, wouldn't you?" The women beside us scowl, unhappy we're discussing someone else. I ignore them. "Is that what it'll take to make you admit how you feel?"

"I don't have... *feelings*... for her," he mutters, pouring another beer from our nearly empty pitcher.

"Oh, but you do. You're attracted. You're intrigued."

"Don't you find this conversation ironic?" he bites out.

"Not at all." I clap his shoulder. "I have no such delusions. I'm in love with Bunny, and I'll tell her—and anyone else—exactly that. But if you play stupid games, you win stupid prizes. If you don't own your feelings, you'll lose her to someone who will."

He scoffs, causing the head on his beer to fly through the air. "Who? Ryan?"

"Anyone." I glance toward our women, now surrounded by tequila shots. Patrón is water to them. I'm not convinced they could survive without it. I often wonder how they function after drinking so much. "She's a catch, Wren. Stop letting the fact she's better at your job than you are get in the way."

He hums, pretending not to care. I'm about to push when a man drops onto the stool catty-corner from Bunny and strikes up a conversation before she can even blink. My hackles rise as Bunny meets my eyes across the room. One delicate brow arches—a dare to interrupt.

I drain my beer and grimace as Wrenley sinks the eight ball. "Next round's on you, Hunt."

"Yeah, yeah. Rack 'em again."

AN HOUR LATER, I'm about to lose my shit. Bunny's practically in the guy's lap, letting him murmur in her ear while she watches me over his shoulder.

It *would* hurt—especially since she knows how I feel.

If the roles were reversed, I'd be a dead man. But sometimes I think this is what she needs to get off.

It's like she wants me to go caveman and claim her in front of everyone. I'd gladly do it—except she won't surrender the one part of her I want most: her heart.

Any guy would be lucky to have even an iota of her time, but that's not enough for me. Bunny hurt me once. I swore I'd never let her do it again. But damn if she doesn't press my buttons to get a rise out of me.

My cock is the only thing that should be rising when it comes to you, Little Rabbit. Not my anger.

I'm seconds from ripping the guy's head off when Dove hops down from her stool, blue eyes set on Wrenley. She looks like she's giving herself a pep talk as she makes her way over to us. Meanwhile, he's murmuring to the brunette—too low for me to catch.

"The bubblegum princess is heading straight for you," I announce.

He barely turns before Dove reaches us and blurts, "Do you wanna get out of here?"

She looks hopeful, nervously smoothing her velvet pink dress as she waits for his answer. I want to smack Wren with my cue when he wraps an arm around the brunette's waist and pulls her close. "Actually, we were just about to leave."

Fucking hell. You dense dope.

Dove looks like she might be sick. I feel for her. She mustered the courage to ask him out, and he rejected her —even though I know the idiot would like nothing more than to take her home and lay her out like a candy buffet.

"Right." Her voice cracks. Out of the corner of my eye I see Bunny watching the wreck, ignoring her own guy. "I'm sorry. That was stupid of me to ask. Have a good night, Wrenley."

Wren's spine snaps straight. Dove's face flushes as our eyes meet for a second before she turns away.

I like Dove. As Bunny's best friend, I think of her as a future sister-in-law.

And I don't like seeing family hurt.

"What the fuck is wrong with you?" I drop my cue on the felt. Wrenley's frozen, looking like he wants to go after her but needs a boot in the ass.

Wish granted, fucker.

Before I can think, I'm storming after Dove. My brain is two steps behind my body, which has gone on autopilot. Sometimes a grand gesture is the only thing that gets things moving again. Wren and Dove are at a standstill, just like me and Bunny.

Even though it's the craziest idea I've had in a while, and there's *absolutely* a chance it will backfire spectacularly, I reach for Dove. She must see Bunny's bewildered expression, because she turns to me, confusion etched into her pretty features.

"Bunny, I'm sorry for what I'm about to do." I can't look at my little rabbit. She's about to get pissed enough to kill me. I cradle her best friend's face, praying to whatever god is listening that this will force Bunny to admit how she really feels. "Dove, just fucking go with it."

Then I press my lips to hers.

<u>Bunny</u>

Icy tendrils wrap around my chest, slowly climbing into my esophagus and turning my insides into a frozen wasteland.

Shock isn't a strong enough word to describe what I'm feeling. No—watching Hunter kiss Dove is more like a punch to the gut that steals the air from my lungs. It's betrayal and rage, despair and realization, all warped into a bomb of disturbingly potent jealousy that blasts violent shrapnel straight into my heart.

I feel the blood drain from my face with each agonizing second that ticks by. Dove squeals against Hunter, preparing to shove him away. But I can't sit around and watch any longer.

Like a scared rabbit, I flee. I vaguely register Dove crying out after me, but all I can think about is escaping the bar and going home. The crowd parts easily as I push through, tears blurring the city lights into hazy spots as I hurriedly hail a cab. Thankfully, it only takes a few seconds before I'm secured in the back seat, numbly reciting my address before I let the tears fall.

"Rough night?" the cabbie asks, his rasp suggesting a lifetime of smoking. He's an older gentleman with a big, bushy mustache and thick caterpillar brows that raise when I huff a laugh.

"I just watched my—" I cut myself off because Hunter isn't *my* anything. "Never mind. Yeah... it was a rough night."

My phone dings with an incoming message.

I know she means well and that it wasn't her fault at all, but part of me is irked she didn't push him away sooner.

Dove is my best friend, and I *know* neither she nor Hunter would ever do me dirty like that... but there's always been this nagging *what-if* in the back of my mind. Sometimes when they interact, I feel like if I weren't in the way, there could be something there. Dove's mentioned multiple times that she thinks he's hot, and he's always winking at her and calling her "doll"... which is ironic given her serial-killer pseudonym is the Baby Doll Killer.

What I just witnessed was an amalgamation of most of my worst fears coming to life: Hunter giving up on me. Him finding happiness with someone else. That someone else being a woman I know.

Logically, I know it would never be Dove... but Hunter is wanted by so many women...

Sometimes I wish I could get out of my own way.

But every time I even dare imagine the possibilities—

of a life with him—I remember Nathanial telling me I hung the damn moon as far as he was concerned. And it didn't stop him from lashing out whenever he thought he needed to put me back in line.

Hunter wants me. All of me. He's repeatedly proven he'd pick me over anything... over anyone. And I want him. Fuck, do I want to see what life has to offer us. No one gets me the way he does. No one has come close to making me feel the way he can.

And lord knows no one can make me come the way that man can when he makes my kitty purr. She doesn't even perk up in the general vicinity of a gorgeous, interested man. She only wants Hunter Remington.

So why the hell can't my brain and heart just cooperate?

"Take it easy. A nice relaxing bath and a good movie should do the trick," the cabbie says in a fatherly tone. I make sure to give him a generous tip.

I haven't even made it to my front door before the screech of tires has me spinning back to the street just in time to see Hunter hand a wad of cash to his cab driver. Some sense of relief courses through me, though I'm unsure why. I'm angry with him—showing up here unexpectedly after what he did will only lead to us fighting.

Which usually leads to *other* things that tangle the threads of our very twisted web even further.

As he approaches, all I can focus on is how his lips seem swollen and his whiskey-colored eyes flash with heated annoyance. "Those two are fucking idiots. You know it, I know it, and they know it. Was what I did okay? No. I'll be the first to admit it, but in my defense, I blacked out from sheer aggravation."

I blink.

My lips part, though I'm not sure what to say to his outburst. Before I can utter a word, he continues.

"I'd like the record to show that what I did kicked their asses into gear." Hunter saunters toward me like a big cat stalking its dinner. I don't even realize I've been retreating until my back hits the door and the knob digs into my spine. He continues his advance until we're toe-to-toe, bracing his arms on either side of my head just like at the restaurant. "Problem most likely solved... for now, at least. So I'd like to fix *this* one now."

My brows knit, my heart rate kicking up as his amber gaze darkens and drops to my mouth. "There's no fixing what you did, Hunter. I'll never be able to unsee your lips on hers."

I surprise myself with breathless honesty. Hunter's raised brows and look of shock say he's surprised, too. "Bunny..."

"Why are you here?" My resolve hardens as I spin and shove my key into the lock. "Please leave."

Shrill yips and sharp yaps grow louder as I enter the house and shut the door behind me. Neither of my dogs goes into attack mode when Hunter's foot crosses the threshold. As a matter of fact, he leans down to scratch each of them behind the ears, and they bombard him with happy air licks as he dodges their kisses. "Hiya, boys."

"Why are you being nice to him? He sucks," I chastise them, throwing my keys into the entry bowl and shrugging out of my jacket.

"Not yet, but I will be." Hunter doesn't allow me a moment of reprieve before he reaches for my hips and backs me against the wall.

My stupid heart skips a beat, and I funnel all my ire into a glare that usually makes my victims cower. Hunter smiles softly, almost as if laughing at a silent joke. His skin is warm as he slides a thumb over the red foil hearts that decorate my scar.

"You don't get to just show up and expect me to forgive you." I glower, though my hands find his forearms.

"There's nothing to forgive, Little Rabbit." His tone is leading, a longing inflection that begs me to contradict him—to show any ounce of my true feelings.

But he's right. He's not mine. I have no claim over him, even if it's what he wants.

Still, my heart shudders at the nickname he gave me when we first met. Outwardly, I've always pretended to hate it, but secretly, I love when he uses it. At first it was our thing—the first secret we shared. When he started using it in front of other people, my heart soared to hear him claim me so publicly... even when I was the property of another man.

Sure, I spend many nights a year killing nasty men who abuse their wives. I killed my own husband after months of him beating me. I am a strong, independent woman who can take care of herself.

But nothing makes me melt into a pliable mass of goo like Hunter calling me Little Rabbit.

"You kissed her, Hunter. Right in front of me."

"Think of it as me doing us an act of service." He grins, full of boyish charm, and for a moment he looks like the man he was when we first met—the one with wayward curls and glasses who made fun of guys who lived in the gym.

The man whose heart I broke.

Hunter pushes my hair back and cups my neck as his other hand drifts to my waist so slowly it leaves goosebumps in its wake. "Aren't you sick of listening to them bitch and complain about each other? They need to fuck and get it over with."

While I agree with the sentiment, I don't agree with his method of thawing the ice between our two friends.

"Besides..." He leans down to nuzzle his nose against mine. The scent of candy from Dove's lip gloss clings to his mouth, and I want to devour him simply to replace her taste with my own. "You don't want to be with me... remember? So why do you care that I briefly kissed Dove?"

It's a trap. Hunter knows damn well why I care—he just wants to hear me say it. "You sexually assaulted my friend."

He scoffs before nipping my bottom lip. "I wouldn't go that far. But I'm here to atone for that mistake."

Arousal pools in my underwear, and I rub my thighs together to keep it from leaking. My skirt brushes the tops of my thighs, and Hunter lights my body up like a candle. It won't take much for the mess he's creating to become obvious.

Hunter's teeth graze my skin as he sinks to his knees. His height puts his head level with my stomach, and he smirks as he slides his palms up the back of my legs before dropping his gaze to my leather-covered kitty. Hunter doesn't know the definition of slow as he delves forward and grips the hem in his teeth, speaking around the material. "Consider this a freebie for my earlier sin. You get to see stars, I get blue balls as penance."

Coiling my fingers in his hair, I tighten my grip, and force him to look up at me while my skirt is still bunched in his mouth. Blood heats my cheeks as his fingers find the straps of my thong and pull it down my legs, never breaking eye contact. I don't miss that he pockets the soaked undergarment—he has a proclivity for stealing my underwear after he gets me all hot and bothered.

We say nothing as he pulls my zipper down, inch by slow inch, until my skirt pools around my ankles, and he helps me step out of it before flinging it aside. At first it feels weird to be bare from the waist down, but when Hunter takes in the glistening mess on my thighs and licks his lips, the emotion evaporates, replaced by something headier.

I feel powerful. Adored. *Worshipped*.

"This isn't a religion, Hunter. I'm not a goddess, and you have to take me down from this pedestal you—" My breath flees, words forgotten, as he dives in and licks a slow path through my center.

In one swift move he lifts me, hitching both legs over

his shoulders, bracing my weight against the wall. A long groan vibrates up my core as he closes his mouth around my clit and softly sucks, his tongue sweeping the swollen bundle of nerves like a greeting to an old friend.

"You taste so fucking good." His fingers knead my thighs as he consumes me leisurely, like he has all the time in the world. Soft mewls escape my throat as I latch onto his hair and hold on for dear life while he fucks me with his tongue, treating my clit like a hard candy—rolling it between his teeth, sucking long and hard, then lavishing it soothingly. "I could eat this pussy every day if you'd just let me."

I open my mouth to tell him I will let him. I want this every night and every morning. I want Hunter to never stop cherishing my body like it's his own temple. To be consumed by this blaze that ignites whenever we're in the same room.

Even if it fucking terrifies me—even if it hurts—I want to burn.

My legs lock, toes curling in my stilettos. My entire body tenses with willpower, and I try not to dig my heels into his back as my orgasm rips through me like warm, rushing water spilling down my limbs. "Hunter!"

He hums his approval, continuing to lap at me, to kiss my pussy like he's ravished my mouth so many times. I tug his hair when he shows no signs of stopping even after the release ebbs. "I can't. It's too sensitive."

Hunter pauses long enough to say, "You'll be a good girl and give me another one, Little Rabbit. I want your taste branded on my tongue until the next time."

He plunges back in, massaging every intimate part of me with his lips, smearing my arousal over his short, trimmed beard—imprinting my smell and taste so he can go home and fuck his hand with my underwear later. I know that because he's told me many times that's what he does after our torrid encounters.

The thought overwhelms me with desire, and I beg him to give in to what we both want. "Hunter. Please. Fuck me."

A low, throaty chuckle reverberates up my core. "Tell me you'll be mine."

"Hunter." His name sounds like a petulant whine as I attempt to shimmy down his body. He only responds by gripping my thighs tightly and pulling me wider. His hips buck as mine undulate against his face, another orgasm coiling in my lower belly.

"Surrender your heart to me and I will fuck my soul into yours." He stops, waiting for my response, the lower half of his face gleaming as his eyes shine with longing—years of pent-up yearning thickening between us like a heavy, scorching blanket.

Tears prick my lashes. My impending orgasm edges back. Hunter senses my body language and breathes out a sigh of disappointment before his tongue slides back up to flick at my clit. The tears fall hot down my cheeks as my head hits the wall and my eyes roll back when I come again.

Hunter groans, sliding his mouth down to lick me clean before setting me back on my feet. He keeps his grip on me as I wobble, untangling my fingers from his hair to grasp the wall for support.

"You're wrong." He winds his arms around me in a hug, laying his cheek against my stomach.

Confused, I rake my fingers through his tousled hair, trying to reshape the careful style I roughly undid. "What?"

"You said you're not a goddess, but you're the most perfect deity I've ever implored." His tired tone drips with melancholy as he presses his forehead against me like he's actually praying.

My heart seizes. It's a sharp prick that launches a tennis-ball-sized bubble of uncertainty into my throat.

"Your logic is terrifying, Hunter." My tone is light, a wavering chuckle. I can't have a serious conversation naked from the waist down in my foyer, my dogs watching curiously down the hall, while the man who just worshipped me sighs and presses a chaste kiss to my belly.

"I know, but you're still giving me hope. Until you specifically tell me to *stop* pursuing you, I'll never give up until you're mine, Little Rabbit."

SOAPY SUDS FLY through the air as I whirl around to face Nathaniel, remembering the restaurant Hunter recommended earlier. "Oh! I forgot—Hunter told me there's a place on Bleeker Street with great arancini. I know it's your favorite, so I thought maybe we could go this weekend?"

My husband raises a blond brow, arms crossed as he leans against the fridge and assesses me coolly. "Hunter, huh? You know... *Hunter's* been recommending a lot of places lately. As a matter of fact, Bunny, you've come home nearly every night this week talking about *Hunter*."

His umber eyes narrow as my cheeks heat, dread pooling in my gut like ice water. I turn back to the dishes, forcing a shrug, feigning nonchalance. "We've just been paired up for a lot of assignments lately. It's just small talk."

It takes everything in me not to flinch when the heavy heat of him closes in behind me. His tanned, meaty hands plant on either side of me, his gaudy gold-and-diamond wedding band glinting like a warning flare.

Danger.

I know better than to mention another man around him. Just working at all challenges his old-school ideals—if he knew the full extent of what I do, I'm sure he'd lock me up and throw away the key.

Nathaniel Jones does whatever—and *whoever*—he wants, whenever he wants. And I'm supposed to be the good little housewife who caters to his every whim, has dinner ready when he gets home, and pops out babies he can emotionally and verbally bludgeon into trauma-laced adulthood.

If I'd known that was what I was signing up for, I would've stayed at *Hooters* and waited for a real Prince Charming to sweep me off my feet.

Someone like Hunter Remington.

"I know that gleam in your eye you get when you talk about him, Bunny. You used to look at *me* that way." His tall frame curves over me, pressing me into the counter as he roughly nips my ear. "And don't think I haven't noticed the absence of your wedding band. You swore to me you'd start wearing it. Are you cheating on me, dear *wife?*"

"What?! No! I told you, I'm afraid to ruin it. Or lose it." My reply is breathless as he reaches down to hike up the skirt of my pink paisley dress. Only it's not from lust.

My body doesn't melt under his touch anymore. It locks up, like a trapped animal, brain scrambling for escape.

I'm about to remind him that even though it's behind closed doors, I know he's screwing his secretary—but my words die when his large palm wraps around my throat and squeezes.

"Why would you lose it if you weren't taking it off? Do I need to remind you that you belong to *me*?"

Tears sting my lashes as the sound of his zipper splits the air. His grip tightens before yanking me forward, forcing my head down as he rips my underwear aside and shoves himself roughly inside me.

No foreplay. No prepping me for his size. Just the sharp, stinging burn of him taking what he wants until my body betrays me and readies itself to dull the pain.

Nathaniel has always been sexually aggressive. It didn't bother me when we met—in fact, I liked it, at first. I've never minded a little biting, a little pinching, a handprint that lingers for a few hours.

Then the bites became tooth imprints.

The pinches left bruises.

The pulling once left a bald spot that's still growing back.

And lately? The handprints, though hidden, last closer to a week.

I've become one of those women.

The ones who know they should leave, but don't.

Who have the resources to put their abuser behind bars... but don't.

Because at the end of the day, I still love my husband, even if I hate his ideas of what marriage should be.

Nathaniel had a rough life, just like I did.

Only, instead of bouncing through foster homes, he had a dad who beat the shit out of him and his brother.

I understand his need for control. And I foolishly pushed him here by bringing up Hunter so many times.

Sweet, brazen Hunter—who always makes me laugh. Who's convinced he can get me to date him.

Because he doesn't know I'm married.

My husband has quiet affairs all the time. Hunter is the only man who's ever made me even consider doing the same.

"I don't want to hear you say his name again. Do you understand me?" Nathaniel grits out, tightening his grip on my throat as he shoves my head further into the sink until my hair slips into the soapy water. "I will not be made a fool of. Especially in my own house."

"I'm sorry." Despite the crushing pressure at my airway, I force the words out on a moan, trying to lace it with fake sensuality. Trying to make him think I'm enjoying it. It's rare for him to leave visible marks, but his grip promises bruises I'll have to hide.

"You will not embarrass me, Bunny." His words come in shuddering gasps, his cock twitching as he nears release.

I want to fight. To scream and demand to know why he gets to fuck whoever he wants while I can't even speak to another man. Why he married me if he never wanted a wife.

Instead, I stay still. Dissociated. Pliant and pleasing, while I think of another man's hands on me.

Gentler hands. Warmer eyes.

Curly hair, glasses, and a cocksure grin that promises a world better than this.

Then again... that's how it started with my husband, too.

Kinder. Gentler.

Nathaniel finishes, his grip loosening as he tucks himself back into his pants. He turns me around, clucking his tongue like he's scolding a child. He even looks sympathetic.

"Look what you made me do, baby. You made me lose my temper again," he coos, smoothing my wet hair back from my face.

"I'm sorry." It's become my motto these past months. He's always had a heavy hand, but nothing like lately. And it's my fault—for letting Hunter affect me.

Stupid. Sloppy.

"If you're sorry, then you'll quit working." His wide palm splays over my belly, making my insides roil as I swallow the bile that rises in my throat. "I think it's time we started a family, anyway. Don't you? That's what we talked about, right?"

Numbly, I nod as he wipes the tears from my face.

"You know I hate hurting you, Bunny. I love you and I want what's best for you. This Hunter guy..." He shakes his head, rubbing my biceps in what he probably thinks is a comforting gesture. "...he doesn't seem like good news. Always around. Always putting ideas in your head. I have half a mind to march down to the department and demand they keep him away from you.”

I blow out a slow breath. “He’s just given us some recommendations, Nathaniel.” I don’t mention that they were all places he said he wanted to take me.

Why should I feel guilty for entertaining Hunter’s flirting when my husband cheats constantly?

But the threat of him finding out what I actually do for the police has my claws coming out.

“And if you don’t want me working with him anymore,” I add coolly, “maybe be a little more careful with Heidi when you’re at the office.”

His hands still. My words land sharp, exactly where I aimed. But he surprises me.

“You’re right. I’m sorry.”

I blink.

My husband doesn’t apologize.

He *never* tells me I’m right.

Warm fingers trace my throat before he dips and presses a chaste kiss over the tender flesh. The words that follow make my stomach turn.

“I’ll be sure to keep my affairs better hidden from now on.”

Hunter

“Bunny Jones! Light of my life, stealer of my heart, my little anime-loving hellraiser. I watched that show you suggested—*Future Diary*... you are one twisted little soul, aren’t you?”

My lungs tighten as the woman of my dreams rounds the corner. She wasn't in the briefing we just had, though that doesn't surprise me. I've become acutely aware of her missing presence this past week.

It's been months, and still my heart does a little dance whenever I see her. She brightens my day without even trying. I never believed in love at first sight before, but actually getting to know Bunny just affirmed what my body knew before the rest of me caught up.

Little Hunter was ahead of the game. And why wouldn't he be? She's a fucking bombshell. But it didn't take long for my brain and heart to fall in line.

We're opposites in almost every way—and that's half the reason I can't stop orbiting her.

"Hunter Remington, bane of my existence. Purveyor of lurid delusions regarding us." She walks past, clutching a book to her chest as she heads for the exit.

See? Always such a ray of sunshine.

"Whatcha reading?" I swing an arm around her shoulders—hard to do when she's so short I have to dip my upper body—and pluck the book from her hands. The cover shows a faceless man and a pumpkin. It's not even close to Halloween.

"Only One Night by A.R. Rose." I blow a raspberry, scanning the blurb. "This guy looks like a stalker. So tell me... what's appealing about him?"

Snatching it back, she laughs and smacks my chest with her literary weapon. "It's a self-insert, which is hot. It's really good."

"What's self-insert?"

Color blooms across her cheeks, highlighting the freckles I'm obsessed with. I've made it my personal mission to memorize every constellation of them. I hope it takes me a lifetime.

"It means I can dream about a hot guy breaking into my house and having his wicked way with me." Her eyes spark as her brows jerk up.

Waggling mine, I tug her closer. A tangible heat flares between us as we come to a stop in the hall. "Would you like me to break in and tie you up, Little Rabbit? That can be arranged."

"In your dreams, Remington."

"Oh, yes. Definitely in my dreams, Bunny. But one day, you're gonna cave. Then they'll be reality. I'm too persistent to keep saying no to. Once I see something I want, I don't quit until it's mine."

The corner of her lips quirks despite herself—just as Ryan Jacobs, the officer who should've made detective with me, passes by and snorts. "Yeah, he does whatever he has to, to get it, too."

"Hey, it's not my fault you keep failing to make detective. Don't get mad because I said I could handle the job with just my contact." And thank god I did. If Ryan had been with me that night, I'd have never gotten my chance with this raven-haired goddess. He'd have either scared her with his abrasiveness or blown our cover by charging off while I was distracted by her.

Bunny, surprisingly, comes to my defense. "Honestly, Jacobs, I don't think you could handle the strip clubs.

One pretty girl looks at you and you'd probably blow your load in your pants. You seem like the type."

"Fuck you, Jones. I eat girls like you for lunch," he sneers, turning to leave.

It doesn't escape me that Bunny hasn't moved from under my arm as she calls after him, "Oh, please. Women of my caliber wouldn't let you dine on them if you were the last man on earth and it was the only way to get off."

"Damn, Little Rabbit. You're so mean. I love it."

My grin dies the moment I see her itch at the collar of her turtleneck. Her mass of satin-black hair is pulled up, giving me a clear view of the blue-purple mottled flesh peeking above the fabric.

Rage scorches my blood at the thought of someone daring to mar her skin. "What the fuck is on your neck, Bunny?"

She freezes, then forces a laugh, tugging the collar up. "Eh, it's nothing. Had a job go a little south, that's all."

Lie. Even if a customer tried, none of the joints she's been assigned to would've let anyone lay a finger on her.

I hook her arm and steer her out of the hallway, cutting through the sea of desks to the cramped office they stuck me in after my promotion. More like a supply closet than an office, but I'm not complaining. It's private.

"What. Is. Your. *Deal*?" she snaps, exasperated, yanking her arm free as I close the door.

"Let. Me. See." I reach for her collar—and a low, frustrated growl slips out when she recoils, glaring.

"Did you just growl at me? Are you serious right now?" Ducking under my arm, she heads for the door.

I'm faster. My arm locks around her waist as I yank the collar down and expose the bruises. My breath hitches at the clear fingerprint shapes. Something primal tears through me—dark, vicious, and utterly fucking livid.

"Who the fuck did this to you?"

"I told you! Someone got a little handsy on a job! Now let me go, Hunter!" She writhes against me, and if the circumstances were different—between her soft body grinding against mine and the way she snarls my name— I'd be hard as a rock.

"What job?" She's like a feral cat, squirming to escape, but I hold her tight, pinning her arms to her sides and locking her back to my chest. My chin rests on her shoulder. Raspberry and jasmine flood my senses. Her ponytail tangles between my mouth and her neck.

"Where were you, and who was there?"

"Hunter..." This time my name is a plea—and I nearly groan imagining her saying it for a different reason.

"Don't lie to me, Little Rabbit."

"Why?" The word leaks out on a shaky exhale. She turns her head, our noses brush, her gaze searching mine like she might find safety there.

"Because I will kill them." My voice is calm. Absolute. "I will obliterate anyone who dares put their hands on you."

Each second that passes steals a little more of my breath as the space between us disappears.

"You don't know me," she whispers, eyes shimmering. "Why do you care?"

I loosen my grip. I want her to come to me willingly—not because I've caged her. Bunny spins away, widening the gap between us. For one sharp second, I wish I weren't such an honorable bastard.

"I'm going to talk to my sergeant. This won't happen again. I promise you that." I rise to my full height, letting her retreat even though every cell in my body screams to hold her. Just hold her.

The thought of anyone hurting her—of anyone daring to touch her—has my fists trembling at my sides.

Someone is going to die for this.

Shaking her head, she draws a shaky breath. "I don't work for the department, Hunter. I'm a freelancer, of sorts. There's nothing they can do—"

"I don't care if you work for us or with us. I want you protected."

Something shifts in her face at my tone—wonderment, and something that looks dangerously close to heartbreak. "Hunter... we can't do... whatever..." She gestures between us. "...*this* is. I can't—I'm—"

"Remington!" The door bangs open. A senior detective storms in, eyes barely flicking to Bunny before motioning at the files on my desk. "You were supposed to be in my office five minutes ago. Move it."

"Yes, sir." I grab the folders, fixing Bunny with a hard stare before I turn to leave. "I'm a patient man, Little

Rabbit. And you seem like the type who spooks easily. So, we'll go at your pace. But this conversation isn't over. I want names. And the establishment."

Her hands plant on her hips as she lets out a sardonic laugh, hair whipping as she shakes her head. "You just don't give up. Do you?"

I catch her chin before she can turn away, forcing her to hold my gaze. "What can I say? I'm protective of the things I consider mine."

It's comical how big her eyes widen. "*Yours?* You barely know me."

"I don't need years to know what I feel. I know my heart knows yours. It skips when you walk into a room. I look for you even when I know you're not there. I know I love how your eyes light up when you talk about books. Your favorite color is lavender, and you hate pink—though I admit I don't know why. You want dogs named after your favorite anime characters. You love Lucky Charms and hate oatmeal. You have no patience for ditziness.

"And more than anything, I know I think about your sassy mouth—and what it can do—far too often when I go home at night."

I fucking love the way her cheeks flush, rosy against her freckles, illuminating her sun-flecked forest eyes. She licks her lips, and I swear I'd die for a taste.

"Most of all," I murmur, "I *know* you're interested."

"And what makes you think that?" she breathes, leaning in just slightly.

"Because if you weren't... then what are you still doing here?"

My eyes dip between us before flicking back up as realization sparks in hers—realization that I'm not holding her anymore. She could've left.

But she didn't.

Even her subconscious knows she doesn't want to.

Bunny jolts back, stammering, "I—you—"

"Remington!" A harsh voice filters through the door.

"We're inevitable, Little Rabbit." I shrug, turning to leave. "It might not happen as soon as I'd like..." I glance over my shoulder, memorizing the way her chest rises and falls, how she looks scared—but there's something else in her eyes.

Something I've become very familiar with.

Longing.

"But make no mistake... this is happening."

"It's crazy to think you can go from utterly despising someone to loving them so quickly. How does that even happen? How does one go from hating someone to loving them?"

"I loved her before I hated her... and unfortunately for me, the first emotion clawed its way back to the surface and burned every remnant of my hatred when she showed back up like she hadn't ripped my heart from my chest."

It takes me a moment to realize the tapping of Wrenley's laptop keys has stopped. I glance over the top of my MacBook to see him staring at me like I've grown another head.

"Oh. You were talking about you and Dove."

Wrenley huffs a laugh, scrubbing both hands down

his face as he sinks back against my sofa. "She's pissed at me. And I don't know how to fix it."

"Well, Bunny's always pissed at me for some reason or another."

Except when my head is between her thighs.

"Dove will get over it."

"Yeah, I thought she'd get over it too. But it's been days, and she's unwavering. Legit will not speak to me."

I turn back to my screen, sighing as I click through the crime scene photos. The Baby Doll Killer got gruesome with her newest victim, and though I won't admit it out loud, the images make my stomach pitch.

"These girls are going to be the death of me," I mutter.

"What was that?" Wrenley asks, breaking off his quiet rambling.

"Nothing. Just questioning my life choices over here."

"Why *have* you waited for Bunny all this time?" He shuts his laptop and reaches for his beer, swinging one arm over the back of the sofa. "She's hot, but she's... a lot. Clearly, she wants you, but she won't be with you. And she doesn't want you to be with anyone else. You've told me enough to allude to the fact that you have a sexual relationship that's everything *except* sex. What are you doing, Hunter?"

It's not the first time someone has asked me that.

Guys in the department.

Women in the industry who've been around long enough to know I'm not a nut they can crack.

My boss.

My parents.

How do I explain that I'm waiting for a woman who I know loves me—but won't admit it because her husband was abusive and did a fucking number on her?

It's Bunny's story to tell, not mine. And if anyone knew what he did to her... what he did for years.

What he did because of *me*.

And anyone who digs too deep could uncover the truth about what happened.

I can't have that.

I won't.

I'll go down for her if I have to.

Bunny's suffered enough.

So, I deflect.

"What are *you* doing, Wrenley? Dove looks just like your mother, so you can't decide if you want to fuck her or kill her. And I swear, if you hurt her, I'm going to have to look the other way when Bunny kills *you*."

He laughs and shakes his head, pinching the bridge of his nose. The deflection works—he forgets about my love life and dives straight back into the blonde bubblegum princess.

"I know. I hate it. I've never been so fucking gone for a woman before. It's bad enough she keeps showing me up at work, then we go home and she sucks my cock like she's trying to apologize—"

My beer nearly comes back up as I choke on a swallow. Between Ryan at work and Wrenley here, everything I know about Dove's sex life I've learned against my will.

"—and how the fuck do you stay mad after that? Of course I was going to blow up eventually. But it's almost like she wanted me to get angry. Like she was pushing me away on purpose." He waves his beer bottle in the air, punctuating his frustration.

"We're pathetic, aren't we?" The words slip out quieter than intended, but they still echo off the walls of my brownstone.

"Do you think they sit around and talk about us the same way?"

"Oh, I guarantee whatever they have to say is way worse."

<u>Bunny</u>

"Look, I'm not yucking anyone's yum here, okay? I just don't like it. Give me the drama and the angst and the pining! I don't want them to share her, I want them to fight over her!"

Slamming a carton of oat milk on the counter, I spin and fix my best friend with a deadpan stare. "You're denying her a chance to have multiple cocks at any given time from men she actually likes—who also know what they're doing?"

"She can have all the cocks." Dove lifts her phone, shifting our props around on the counter. "Hell, she can even have two at a time if the tension is tensioning and the men are throwing insults at each other while they fuck their way through the argument with her body as the mediator. I just don't like when anyone can use her at any given time and no one gets jealous. I need the chaos!" Dove exclaims, rearranging the book we're currently reading for an aesthetic photo for our Iconic profile.

It's the third time she's moved the decorations around.

Chaos, my ass.

"Sooo... cheating?" I spoon another bite of Lucky Charms and talk around the marshmallows. "She can be with them all, just not as one big happy family?"

"It's not cheating if it's not exclusive," she chirps, fluffing a sprig of pampas grass. "Like I said, she can fuck them all, but I need the drama and jealousy. Otherwise, for me personally, it's too fluffy, and I don't wanna read about it."

I glance around her place at the pinks and creams, the endless flowers and frills. Even though Wrenley basically lives here now, there's not a hint of him anywhere. It's warm and cozy and so very fluffy, because my best friend is a walking puff of cotton candy.

So the fact that she hates why-choose baffles me.

But I don't point out the irony as she rants about despising fluff while *literally* fluffing cream-colored decor for her shot.

"Well, we'll have to agree to disagree on that one." I slide my bowl toward her for the photo—her idea to spell *serial killer* like *cereal* has taken off way more than either of us expected. Once she's snapped a few pictures, I reclaim my breakfast before the cereal gets soggy. There's nothing worse than soggy Lucky Charms.

"How are things with your songbird?"

Dove goes uncharacteristically quiet, chewing her bottom lip as she debates answering. "We're not speaking at the moment," she admits finally.

The air goes heavy—storm-cloud thick, like an unspoken monologue is about to break. But just as she parts her watermelon-pink lips, her phone rings.

We both jump at the sound as it vibrates on her granite countertop.

Mom.

Dove silences it without hesitation, releasing a weak laugh that shakes her delicate shoulders.

"You'd think she'd get the hint."

"I thought you haven't spoken to her in years?" I follow her to the sofa, my dogs passed out in a puppy pile on Fang's oversized pink doughnut bed.

"I haven't. She's in therapy, and *apparently* her therapist thinks it would be a good idea for us to talk." Dove pinches the bridge of her nose like she's holding back a headache. "I told her I wasn't interested and that she needs to stop calling."

"Why don't you just block her number?"

Dove and her mom have always been a mess. Her dad died young, her mom fell apart, and Dove had to raise herself... which caught the attention of a very sick man who ended up being her serial killer origin story. When she was finally brave enough to tell the truth, her mother didn't believe her. They've barely spoken since.

"I don't know." Dove shrugs, looking smaller than

usual. "I suppose it helps the illusion I fed Wrenley about her visiting." Melancholy flickers across her face.

I hate seeing her sad, so I change the subject. "Yeah, I can't believe he even suggested watching Fang."

At the sound of his name, her Chinese Crested lifts his rainbow mane from the floof pile. He stretches, yawns, then hops up between us.

"He loves Wrenley, though, don't you, baby boy?" Dove coos.

I snort. "Fang likes men in general, Love Dove. I don't think Wrenley can hack it here. And don't get me started on what he said about the Shadow Siren."

"Oh my god, I never should have told you." She groans with a smile, letting her head fall back on the cushion. "You're never going to let it go, are you?"

"Nope." I pop my p. "Besides, what happens when he finds out?"

The corner of her mouth twitches. "I think he's catching on."

"He wouldn't be if you hadn't gone to his house! Why did you think that was a good idea? What happens if he tells Hunter?"

Panic wraps its chilled fingers around my ribs, searing the bone with a coolness that burns my insides.

"Dove, I can't... Hunter can't figure us out."

"I know." She lays a hand on my knee, gaze steady. "Trust me, Bunny. You're safe. It's okay. If Wrenley figures out it's me, I'll deal with it if things go sour. I promise. You have nothing to worry about."

"I'm sorry, Love Dove. I just... I'm not ready..."

Because who's ever ready to tell the man they love that it's them he's been looking for all this whole time, and not in a romantic sense?

Hey, you know how you've been chasing your tail trying to catch this killer? Surprise. It's me!

"Kill me now." I groan, throwing my head back on the sofa. As if sensing my distress, Yasha and Maru untangle themselves from the puppy pile and climb into my lap, forming a new ball of fluff over my thighs.

"It's fine," Dove repeats, still sounding utterly unfazed. "Wrenley is obsessed with the Baby Doll Killer. And even though we're not speaking right now, I'm honestly convinced he'd never do anything to hurt me—including keeping this secret. And it's not like Hunter is trying super hard. I swear he works harder at keeping guys away from you than trying to figure out the Baby Doll's or Shadow Siren's real identities."

She's not wrong. Hunter loves his job—and he's brilliant at it.

They haven't caught us because he doesn't want to.

Not yet.

And I can't figure out why. There has to be another reason. Something beyond us only targeting bad men.

Right?

Hunter remains unwavering in his pursuit of me, and there have been so many times I've wanted to spill my secret.

If he truly loves me... what would he do if he found out who I really am?

Would he accept it?

Understand me?

Or would his job outweigh everything he feels about me?

All I know is I'm so tired of keeping secrets from him.

So very fucking tired.

"YOU KNOW, for hating this place, she sure is coming around a lot lately."

Alex sets another beer in front of me, giving me a questioning look—like I'm supposed to know why Bunny has suddenly decided to bring her dates to the one place I frequent more than anywhere else outside of work.

"She doesn't hate this place," Vixey chimes in. "She just avoids it when she can't trust herself around Hunter."

Alex and I trade a look, both wondering how the tall honey-blonde has that much insight into Bunny's feelings. My girl isn't exactly her biggest fan.

"Is that so?"

Vixey shrugs, balancing a pitcher of beer and a stack of frosted glasses on her tray. "I'm observant. I don't understand it... You two seem to *want* to be together, and I don't think anyone understands what her hang-up is—

except maybe Dove—but it's just what I've noticed since I started working here."

She spins away without waiting for a response, clutching the tray tightly to her stomach as she weaves through the crowd.

Alex watches her go, lips quirking despite himself. When he catches me looking, the smirk drops and he shrugs. "What?"

Chuckling, I shake my head and sip my beer, gaze sliding across the bar to where Bunny is laughing at something another carbon copy of me just said.

Since I went down on her at her place, she's been avoiding me harder than usual. I'd be pissed about it, except when I went to leave, she almost asked me to stay—something she hasn't done in a very long time.

The vulnerability in her eyes that night burned into my retinas, a permanent screensaver every time I close my eyes and remember how she tasted on my tongue. So sweet. So perfect. So fucking mine that I have half a mind to do what I always do—interrupt her date, derail her plans, and make her remember who she really belongs to.

Only, tonight seems different.

Bunny seems to be enjoying herself.

Her forest eyes haven't searched for me. The rosy flush on her cheeks—the one only I can coax from her— has appeared more than once. And her body language screams that she'll let this fucker kiss her if he tries.

Doubt trickles through my bloodstream like a slow bleeder. The kind that doesn't seem deadly... until it's drained the life out of you.

Bunny Katherine Jones confuses the ever-loving fuck out of me.

I know what she went through with her husband was a nightmare, and I know she's terrified to give her heart away again. But deep down, she knows I'd never hurt her. And what's worse—she *wants* to be with me. It's just all the red tape on both ends.

She doesn't want to commit.

Even if I tried to make this work on her terms, I'd always be waiting for the other shoe to drop. Always wondering when I'd wake up to find her gone again— just like last time.

I wouldn't be able to submerge myself in a non-committed relationship with her...

And I'm afraid I'd come to resent her for keeping me dangling on the edge of a cliff, waiting for the moment she decides to step on my fingers and watch me fall to a gruesome death.

Okay... so maybe *I'm being a little melodramatic.*

At the end of the day, we're at an impasse.

Neither of us wants to move forward unless it's on *our* terms.

And neither of us wants to let go.

I check my phone—still nothing from Wrenley, who's upstate on a lead. Since he's been back in town, he's been my unofficial ear for all things Bunny, helping me stay grounded as we've fallen back into our easy friendship from childhood rhythm. But with him gone, my anxiety swells unchecked. No one to talk me down. No one to validate my growing frustrations.

Vixey flounces back to the bar, slamming her tray down and blowing a rogue curl out of her face. "She's so mean."

"Who's being mean?" I set my phone aside and glance around, ready to pick a fight if someone's upset her. Alex has a soft spot for the girl, and I could use the distraction. Maybe the "*she*" in question has a boyfriend I can verbally dismantle.

Vixey's amber eyes are glossy, her bottom lip trembling as she tries not to cry. "Bunny! She's never going to let me forget that I spilled a drink on her, is she?"

Ah. Wrong "she."

I have no interest in fighting with my girl tonight. I don't need to do anything that will push her into the arms of the douchebag she's entertaining.

I turn back to my little rabbit—who's watching us now with thinly veiled annoyance.

Interesting. Especially since she hasn't looked my way once since I got here.

Without breaking eye contact, I reach over and pat Vixey's back, savoring how Bunny visibly bristles as her gaze flicks from me to the distraught blonde.

"Bunny's a grudge-holder. Don't let her see you cry. She hates weakness and can smell fear from a mile away."

Vixey huffs a laugh, grabbing a cocktail napkin to dab at her eyes. "I just want them to like me."

"Bunny and Dove? Why do you care if they like you? Not that they aren't great girls—I love them both—but why does it matter so much what they think?" Alex asks as he reappears to make a round of fruity-looking shots.

"I don't know." Vixey shrugs, then fixes him with a melancholy look. "They just seem like the kind of women I want to be around... they just don't want me in their circle."

"You're still new, Vix. Don't let it get you down. Those two have been inseparable since they met, and I've never seen another woman breach their circle of salt."

"Isn't a circle of salt for keeping danger in?" I ask, trying to follow his logic.

"Or out," they reply in unison.

I realize I haven't stopped rubbing Vixey's back.

And Bunny's attention hasn't returned to her date, who's now glued to his phone.

Smirking, I lean closer—about to say something—when Vixey suddenly jerks away.

"Are you trying to get me killed?" she demands, wide-eyed, putting distance between us and nearly tripping over her own feet.

"I was trying to console you!"

"You are trying to make her jealous, and I'm just collateral. I don't think so, *Detective Dick*."

"Hey now, that's reserved for people who actually know me."

"I know you well enough."

A shrill ring cuts through the noise as my phone vibrates against the bar. The tone is reserved for work, pulling me upright. "Remington."

"Yeah, we got a body. Looks like the Shadow Siren's work."

Fuck.

It's been a while since she's struck—or at least left us something to find. "You sure it's her?"

"Small puncture wounds in the groin, feet, and hands. Stomach slashed. Throat crushed. Found him in a club near where the last victim was."

"Shit."

Across the bar, Bunny flips her hair over her shoulder, turning back to her date. He's off his phone now and inching closer, arm draped across the back of her chair in a way that makes my teeth grind.

"Send me the address. I'm on my way."

I consider asking her to come with—just to see if she'd choose me over him.

But I stop myself.

I'm already itching for a fight, needing an outlet for the jealousy burning holes in my chest.

The last thing I need is to get suspended for punching a man she clearly wants to spend her night with.

With one last glance, I push away from the bar, clinging to the fleeting flash of disappointment that crosses her face as I leave her behind.

<u>Bunny</u>

"Sorry about that. We just got a wave of new residents."

My date, Mark, tucks his phone back into the inner pocket of his suit jacket. He's dressed for a Michelin-star restaurant but didn't even blink when I suggested we come here instead. His apology sounds as genuine as it looks in his warm brown eyes.

"It's okay. Is everything alright?"

I'd be lying if I said I wasn't enjoying myself. He hasn't pressured me once all night. He's polite, steady, considerate—probably a great guy.

He's just not the one I want.

The one who made me see actual stars in my entryway with his tongue... and then left with my juices still glistening in his beard.

That guy is currently pissing me off. The least he could do is not flirt with Vixey of all people.

Mark swings his arm around my chair, leaning in. "Everything's fine. But I might have to cut the night short. I should really get back to the hospital."

He bites his bottom lip, eyes dipping over my face, tracing my freckles and the purple foil stars dusted across my cheek. "Why don't you come with me? I shouldn't be that long."

An incredulous laugh escapes before I can stop it. "You want me to come with you to the hospital?"

My gaze flicks across the bar just in time to see Hunter leaving.

I know why—and where—he's going.

I have half a mind to tell Mark I can't and run after him, just to watch them all scratch their heads and wonder how I pulled off killing a man in a private room of a strip club and slipped away unseen.

It's why they call me the Shadow Siren.

Well... they have since Dove graced me with the moniker, anyway.

Before her, I targeted easy kills in their own homes, none of them ever linked to a single perpetrator. It wasn't until my tiny death-demon best friend convinced me to niche down that it became more of an art.

A carefully crafted match.

A game of cat and mouse.

Another way to keep Hunter interested... even if he doesn't know it's me he's looking for.

"I know, that's awful, isn't it?" Mark hangs his head as he signals Vixey for the bill. "The last thing anyone wants is to sit around at the hospital while I do a consult."

"Maybe another time," I offer weakly. My mind's already out the door, chasing the only man I'd actually wait around for. "I had fun, though."

Vixey returns with Mark's card slip, giving me a wide berth as she drops it off, though I don't miss the quirk of her brow when Mark leans in and kisses my cheek.

"I did too," he says softly. "I'd like to do it again sometime."

I nod, mute. Not from anticipation... but because another man's lips haven't touched me in years. My body recoils at the contact, visceral and sharp.

Craving Hunter.

Wanting to get as far from anyone else as possible.

Later, tucked into bed with Yasha and Maru curled at my feet while season four of *Inuyasha* hums in the background, I drift off and dream of the day Hunter and I finally figure our shit out.

"ARE you seriously eating Lucky Charms right now?" Dove demands as she steps aside to let me into the hotel room.

After only a few hours of sleep, *Kiss From A Rose*—Dove's ringtone—dragged me from my slumber like her own personal bat signal.

Because my little troublemaker killed a cop.

Not just any cop either. Ryan Jacobs. Her on-again, off-again fuck buddy. Hunter's old partner, back before he made detective. Recently suspended for putting his hands on Dove when he pushed her out of the way because Wrenley got in his face and tried to start a fight.

One Wrenley lost miserably, and honestly, where I saw it before, I'm starting to wonder what the hell Dove sees in the guy. He's whiny and rude to her, and while he may be attractive, I'm not convinced he can handle my girl. She *needs* someone who can handle her.

She's a fucking handful.

Case in point: Ryan is currently rolled up in the hotel comforter on the floor like a sushi roll.

"What? I'm hungry." I spoon another bite of marsh-mallowy goodness into my mouth as I take in the scene. "Did you fuck Ryan before you killed him?"

"Why would you ask that?" Dove's voice pitches high

with nervous energy as she spins, grabbing the disposable suits from my bag.

I shoot her an *Are you kidding?* look.

"Because it smells like sex in here. How do you go from 'we're fucking' to 'oops, he's dead with multiple stab wounds'?"

She blushes, pausing to think about it—which immediately sets off alarm bells. "What happened, Dove?"

"It was him... at the door. We were both surprised... though I really should've known better, because who uses Thomas Hardy as an alias?"

She wanders toward the bathroom, talking more to herself than me. "So I tried to divert his attention and make it about sex, and it just didn't go the way I planned, okay? It's not a big deal. No harm. No foul."

"You gut him like a fish, Love Dove. What part of that is no harm, no foul?"

I polish off my cereal, drop the trash in a disposable bag, and knot it shut before tossing it into my duffel. "This is bad. It's one thing to get rid of a bad guy... but he's a cop. People are going to ask questions."

Briefly, I consider calling Hunter. I'm a little out of my depth on this one. Sure, we can dispose of him more easily out here, far from the city. Hell, we can dispose of him in *pieces*. But if he's ever found, things will get messy —fast.

And with his recent fight with Wrenley over Dove, all signs will point to them first.

"Wrenley knows!" she blurts, reappearing in her suit.

Silver tears line her lashes. Her bottom lip trembles.

My heart stops for a beat before thundering against my ribs.

"What do you mean, Wrenley knows?" My voice goes slow, dangerous, as I approach. I guide her by the shoulders to sit on the bed, careful not to trip over Ryan's body—now bleeding through the comforter and threatening to soak into the carpet.

Cleaning essence of Ryan out of a dingy hotel carpet was not on my bingo card tonight.

"He followed me." Her voice is hoarse, paper-thin. "He followed me and walked in during the whole thing."

Her gaze snaps to mine, pink-tipped nails digging into my forearms. "But I trust him. He's not going to say anything. I know he won't."

"What if he tells Hunter?"

Panic slices through me, cold and immediate.

If Hunter figures out Dove is the Baby Doll Killer, it won't take long to connect that I'm the Shadow Siren.

It's unfathomable. The thought of him knowing who I really am... what it would do to us. Would he put me behind bars? Wash his hands of me and let me rot with real criminals—even though I only kill men who deserve it?

Would Hunter finally give up on me?

Of course he would. He wouldn't have a choice.

He's the law. I'm a serial killer.

Not exactly a match made in heaven.

When Dove doesn't answer, I release a long sigh. "You're sure he can be trusted?"

She nods emphatically. "I swear, he's not going to say a thing."

"Wait a minute." I look from her, to the bed, to the bleeding human burrito on the floor, then back to her. "You fucked him, didn't you? You kinky little bitch. You fucked Wrenley next to Ryan's dead body."

"It wasn't *next* to it!" she yelps, springing to her feet and waving me off as she ties her blonde hair into a messy bun before tugging up her hood and adjusting her goggles. "Ryan was on the floor when it happened."

"Kinky. Bitch."

"Shut up." She glares down at the bundle of meat at our feet. "Now, how do you wanna do this?"

"Small pieces. Multiple bags. I need fertilizer, so I already prepped the pressure cooker. Hope you don't mind me stealing part of your boy toy for my flowers. I'll take the torso."

"Okay, sure." Dove nods, scanning the body with her hands on her hips. Then her face twists in disgust as my words register. "Wait..." She gags. "What?"

"Yep." I pop my p. "It's a thing. But imagine how long that would take—pressure cookers are small. Which is why I'll keep one bag for fertilizer, but we'll need to dump the rest separately on the way back."

I pause, trying to remember how many bodies of water are between here and the city.

"Actually, it might be better if you go upstate while I head back to the city."

"Whatever you say, Death Mommy."

She looks like she'd rather be anywhere else, and I bite

my tongue to stop from reminding her we wouldn't be in this mess if it weren't for her.

Rolling my eyes, I zip up my suit and secure my goggles before picking up my saw.

"Don't call me that."

"Pressure cookers?!" Hunter and I shout at the same time, sharing a look of horrified disgust.

Phillip Keels, lead detective for Homicide, nods as he refills a white mug that says *World's Best Uncle* in bright blue bubble letters. "Multiple. The whole basement was covered with them. Slow cookers, too. That's how he broke 'em down. Quick and then slow. Over and over. Buried the sludge out back."

His partner shakes his head, pulling a fresh mug from the breakroom stockpile. "It was like a garden of bones."

"Beautiful azaleas, though."

Hunter's whiskey eyes drop to the fried chicken leg between his greasy fingers. He sets it on the wax paper. "I think I'm gonna be sick."

"No stomach for homicide, eh, Remington?" Keels jokes.

"A pressure cooker?" Hunter repeats, barely a whisper. Glassy eyes, unfocused, like he's trying not to picture it and failing.

I pat his back. "There, there. Not everyone can handle the gruesome monstrosities of life. You're okay, big guy."

He slants me a look while the other men chuckle. "Oh, *you* can handle bones and body parts and sludgy gut fertilizer?"

I shrug, stealing one of his fries and drowning it in ranch. "Don't your parents own, like... a farm?"

"They don't slaughter animals!" Horror climbs his face. I swallow my laugh. My fingers itch to cup his clean-shaven cheek and cluck my tongue.

Sweet, sweet Hunter.

I really do adore him.

Sadness spikes, stealing my breath and reminding me I shouldn't be here. I'm supposed to be shopping for a dress for a gala in a few weeks for Nathaniel's company.

But like a moth to a flame, I ended up grabbing lunch with Hunter instead.

"If you're ever looking for more work, Jones, we could use you," Keels says. "I heard you're a master of disguise. I wouldn't mind—"

"No." Hunter cuts in, one word—rugged, resolute— reverberating through the room. "Absolutely not."

"You her keeper, Remington?" Keels looks between us, amused and a little pissed.

"What are you doing?" I hiss, trying to kick him

under the table discreetly. "It's fine," I state louder. "I'll think about it. Thanks, Keels."

"No you fucking won't," Hunter says to me, anger and stubbornness peppering his tone. The others file out, tossing him *stay in your lane, kid* looks. "I'll be damned if you put yourself in danger like that."

"You think Narcotics isn't dangerous? What do you think I do in those clubs—hold hands with the other strippers and sing *Kumbaya?*"

His face softens. He wipes his hands, then pulls off his glasses to rub the bridge of his nose. "Little Rabbit, it's not the same. I know you can take care of yourself, alright? I'm not trying to reduce you to a helpless woman, so simmer down and retract the daggers from your eyes."

Exhaustion threads his voice. It makes me feel a little bad. He's worried about me. I feel the same when he goes on jobs I can't tag along for.

"I know... but could you maybe not treat me like glass in front of them?" I gesture toward the door.

Instead of acknowledging me, Hunter swallows thickly, his gaze pinned to a spot on the wall. "I don't know what I'd do if something happened to you out there, Bunny."

"Hunter, we both put our lives on the line. It's what we do. It's who we are." We've said it before—the shared thrill, the clean high. Who needs the hard stuff when'n adrenaline does the trick?

He thinks about it, then sighs. "I know. It's why I love y—"

We both freeze. Neither of us looks at the other. His almost-word hangs like a storm cloud about to break.

We've known each other a little over six months. No real dates—only stolen moments at work. Hunter can't love me.

An ache blooms where he's carved himself a space, pushing my husband out inch by inch with every day we spend together.

Once upon a time, I'd never have entertained leaving Nathaniel.

Now, though... now I'm starting to think Hunter's right. We're inevitable, he and I.

I have to leave my husband.

I'm not being fair to Hunter. Or to Nathaniel. Or to myself.

Because even if we haven't crossed that line, we want to. *I* want to.

And even if he's firing the L-word way too early, my heart wants to hear it in a way it never did from my husband.

Marrying Nathaniel was transactional. Stability for me. Family-man optics for him. We were attracted. He was obsessed in the beginning.

But not one second of *that* felt like this moment with Hunter.

Hunter snaps out of it first, slipping his glasses back on. "Anyway. I just don't think it's a good idea. That's all."

He picks up his chicken again. I reach into the box and nab a leg.

"Hey! You said you weren't hungry!"

"I changed my mind." The tension thins as we slide back into easy conversation. He tells me about a jazz club he found, divides his food, and slides half to me like I didn't go to the restaurant with him and decide not to order.

And that's when it hits me.

I think I'm starting to fall in love with him, too.

I've never liked shopping. Growing up broke, bouncing from home to home with barely a suitcase, I learned not to get attached to material things—and to expect hand-me-downs, nothing new.

Nathaniel and I have been married for a few years, and I still can't get used to just... buying a new dress if I need one.

We're not rich, but we're comfortable—and he loves to dress to impress at these parties. He wants his higher-ups to *see* him. Pour me into a four-figure dress, himself into a tux that costs a month's mortgage, and voilà: respect.

"One day, we'll be rubbing elbows with the elites in this city. Just you wait, Buns."

I couldn't care less about elbow-rubbing with rich snobs. The fewer eyes on me, the better. I'm good at what I do—blending in, unseen. If my face starts showing up on page one, my job is over.

"That's a beautiful choice. Is it the right size? We have other options in the back," a saleswoman says from my periphery. Tall brunette, stunning blue eyes. I wonder if Hunter would think she's pretty.

I look down at the black gown in my arms. It's a simple mermaid silhouette—backless, buttery silk, thin straps, scoop neckline. Nathaniel prefers pink, but I'm feeling rebellious.

Plus, my upper body's bruise-free at the moment. Perfect chance to show a little skin. He loves parading me as a trophy at these things. I'll just have to be extra careful not to upset him for the next few weeks.

"Thank you. I'm sure this size is fine. I'm pretty consistent across brands." She takes the dress to prepare a room while I keep browsing.

My phone pings as I head to the back with two more options—both dark, as far from pink as possible. In the stall, I finally check it.

SERGEANT RHODES

> I forgot to tell you. I started that show you told me about. Hard no for me. He's like… what even is he? A monster? And she's a kid. Bride is literally in the title, so if it's going where I think, I'm gonna respectfully pass.

I stifle a giggle with my palm. *Sergeant Rhodes* is my code name for Hunter. Previews are off, and I delete our messages before going home, but I'm not taking chances. I've been careful not to bring him up at home. Nathaniel seems pleased.

He's even been gentler lately, which is everything I don't want and everything I need from him—even if I'd prefer he not touch me at all.

Get your shit together, Bunny. End things. Or stop seeing Hunter.

One option feels impossible. The other, unfathomable.

Contemplating the sticky mess I've found myself in, I slip into the first dress. Too tight. So much for being "consistent." It's too sparkly anyway. I rehang it and grab my phone to reply.

> You're missing out. I promise it's not taboo. He's actually pretty cute in an adorable puppy sort of way. She helps him learn human feelings. And he helps her learn magic.

The second dress is just as tight. "What the heck?" I mutter, trying for a side view.

Why did I try on a ball gown? I'm too short for a cupcake skirt—and already pushing it with dark colors. Nathaniel likes them painted-on, not hide a whole person under the chiffon. Not sure why I grabbed it.

SERGEANT RHODES

> *wrong answer buzzer sound* Next.

This time, I let a chuckle slip as I change into the last gown—the first one I picked. Mild guilt prickles. Hunter is watching anime for me, and I still have yet to listen to a single jazz track he's suggested.

Jazz is most definitely not my jam. But he's trying to enjoy my hobbies. I owe him the same.

I suck in to pull the side zipper carefully past my skin. Usually, sizing isn't an issue, but three tight dresses is... odd.

You just stuffed your face with fried chicken and fries. You're bloated.

Duh.

Deciding that's it, I change back and bring the black dress up front, texting as I check out.

Try Dragon Ball Z. It's a classic, and one of my favorites. But I swear, if you don't like it, keep it to yourself or I'll go Super Saiyan on your ass.

Once the gala's over, I'll start planning my escape. Nathaniel won't let me go without a fight. I need everything in place before I tell him I'm leaving.

Part of me thinks it's insane to do this for a man I barely know. The other part—the one that swore I'd never become like so many of my foster mothers—knows Hunter is just the catalyst.

This decision's been a long time coming.

SERGEANT RHODES

I just looked up whatever that means, and now I'm intrigued. Scared… a little turned on… but intrigued.

Intrigued. Turned on. Scared.
Me too, Hunter.
Me too.

PRESENT

"OH MY GOD! YES!" I animatedly wave my hands as I lean toward my date. "Finally! Someone who *gets* it. They wouldn't have found the Dragon Balls without Bulma's Dragon Radar. She's the most important character in the show, and I will die on that hill!"

Duane—my date for the evening—laughs, a full-bodied rumble in his chest that isn't directed *at* me but with me. His bun shakes on the top of his head, the pink scrunchie holding up his sandy-colored strands threatening to fall out with the movement. "I can get behind that. I'll defend that choice."

While he's not making my kitty meow by any stretch, I must admit I'm having fun. So much so that I nearly forget Hunter is across the bar, drilling a hole into the side of Duane's head with his heated gaze.

Part of me feels bad that I keep going on dates. The

other part enjoys watching Hunter squirm. On one hand... I'm lonely. On the other... Hunter nearly always interrupts my dates. It's like he can't help himself when he sees me with another guy. And while he still won't fuck me until I commit to him, he'll still fuck with my body until he makes me see stars.

Our logic is bewildering.

It's just a phrase. Just a simple, *"Yes, I'll be yours,"* even if I basically am already. But for some reason, it holds so much weight with him. It's infuriating.

"Okay, but what about mecha? *Gundam Wing* in all its glorious forms?" Duane asks. "Or do you not like the heavy action shows?"

"Eh." I shrug while draining the last of my tequila and soda. "I like *Full Metal Panic*. Does that count?"

"Gotta have that romance, huh?" He laughs.

"I guess so, now that I think about it. But *Dragon Ball Z* isn't a romance." My tone hardens in preparation for judgment.

Duane holds up his hands. "Hey, I'm not judging. Promise."

It's one of the things I hate most about telling people I like anime. There's always someone who wants to call me out for only liking shows with romance, or only watching the dubbed titles.

How about you mind your business and don't hate on me for something so trivial? People really have a way of making everything about them, like my personal show choices have anything to do with their lives.

Weirdos.

"Have you been to *Anime Claw*? It's this fun little place—"

"Oh my god! I've been wanting to go there! It looks so fun!" I can't hide the excitement in my voice. It's definitely a place that would be better with someone who'll appreciate it as much as I do. I thought about asking Dove, but she doesn't understand my obsession, and I want to enjoy myself—not have to keep explaining everything.

He checks his watch, eyes lighting up. "They're still open. Wanna go?"

"Heck yeah, I do! I'm just gonna run to the bathroom first." I'm already up and out of my seat before he can say a word, his chuckles drifting behind me as I make my way to the restrooms.

Two giggling women exit as I enter, leaving me alone in the small space. For a bar bathroom, it's impeccably clean. Alex takes pride in keeping *The Tipsy Taco* spotless, having someone clean up every hour. There's not even a drop of water on the vanity as I lean closer to the mirror to reapply my gloss.

The door opens, and my heart skips a beat when Hunter enters, locking it behind him.

Through the reflective glass, I meet his gaze, narrowing mine to show my incredulity. "What are you doing here, Hunter? This is the women's bathroom."

I press closer to the counter, relishing the way his eyes drop to my backside. My black leather skirt is short enough to give him a peek at what's underneath, and he sounds like he's holding back a groan as he asks, "What are *you* doing, Bunny? Your date looks like Dove's doppelgänger."

"He's a nice guy. What's it to you?" I slip my gloss back into my pocket and turn to face him. His erection is already prominent against his dark pants, and the fact that he locked the door behind him is telling. We could get into a lot of trouble for whatever it is he has planned —and he knows it.

Yet, he steps toward me, heavy heat in his amber eyes. I cross my arms, lifting my chin to show him he doesn't intimidate me.

"I'm done." When there's barely any space between us, he stops, hands in his pockets, his expression carved from stone. "You win."

Adrenaline spikes like a bad drug, and I try to keep my fear from showing. My fingers dig into my arms, anchoring me so I don't spiral into the dark reality where Hunter decides he's finally finished with me. "And what did I win?"

Hunter withdraws a hand from his pocket and smooths his thumb over the teal foil star covering my scar. It's a warm and familiar touch that always grounds me, always makes my heart stutter. But tonight, it's almost as if I can feel his goodbye in that same gentle stroke.

"You don't want me. You've made that painfully clear for years. I think it's time I let you go, Little Rabbit."

No.

Of course I want you, you idiot.

It's me who's the fool. How could I expect him to keep playing this game? He was bound to lose interest. I'm surprised he lasted this long. I haven't been fair to him at all. I go on dates in front of him, get pissy when he so much as smiles at another woman, and it always ends the same way—him giving me an orgasm and going without, because he's convinced that if he sleeps with me without commitment, I'll leave. And I don't blame him.

We want each other, but we don't trust each other.

Hunter and I were doomed from the start.

Even so, I try to make light of the situation, to pretend his decision doesn't gut me. "What, you can't handle watching me take home strangers anymore?"

It's a lie, and he has to know it. *Right*? Hunter has to know I haven't slept with anyone since him. Haven't let another man touch me because the only touch I crave is his.

He breathes out a laugh and braces his hands on the counter on either side of me, leaning down until our noses almost brush. "Take home whoever you want. From now on, just know that I'll do the same."

I think I'm going to be sick.

Stepping back with a smirk—an honest-to-god, not-trying-to-get-a-rise-out-of-me smirk—he says, "Have a good night, Buns."

"Wait!" Whiskey eyes go wide as I launch forward, curling my fingers into his belt to stop him from leaving me.

Whatever it was I thought he came in here to say or do, this isn't it. Anxiety floods my bloodstream, my breaths coming in heavy pants as I scramble for words. Hunter gazes down at me with so much hope, his chest still as he holds his breath and waits.

I pull him back, and his arms remain at his sides. "I don't want serious. I can't *do* serious, Hunter."

Even though what we've been doing *is* as serious as I can give. He has every part of me—except the one crushing piece I keep under lock and key.

My fingers deftly unlatch his belt as I lick my lips, letting my desire bleed into my gaze.

"What *do* you want then, Bunny?"

I undo his pants before releasing him to hop onto the counter, reaching for him once I find my balance. Hunter lets me lead, steeling himself from touching me as I pull his zipper down and palm his throbbing cock.

"No strings."

The words leave my lips in a whispered plea. I'm begging him to play by my rules. I don't want to lose him.

His cock twitches in my hand as I pull him out, and I drop my gaze to take it in. I lick my lips again, thinking about how he'd feel inside me. In my mouth. In my body. In my soul.

'Surrender your heart to me and I will fuck my soul into yours.'

The words he spoke to me all those weeks ago replay until he says, "Too bad."

What he says contradicts his actions as his fingers trail up my thighs to grip the sides of my underwear. "That's just not my thing. But you know what? I'll make an exception, just this once."

Elation blooms in my chest as he pockets the lacy lilac garment. Then his lips are on mine as he says, "Consider it a goodbye fuck."

Disappointment pierces my heart. As quickly as the anticipation of him finally coming around to my terms settles in my bones, it vanishes.

But those thoughts blur and dissolve as he touches me between my legs, finding me warm and wet and wanting him.

"Hunter," I moan his name as he rubs my arousal over his length before sliding the crown of his engorged cock up and down my center. So fucking slowly. Torturing me. Torturing himself.

"All this time, you could have had me, Bunny." He angles himself against my clit, brushing the swollen bundle of nerves with each pass. "Now you'll only get a taste of how good we could have been together."

If this is a punishment, consider me a very naughty girl.

Hunter grips the back of my neck, forcing my gaze up.

Twisting my fingers in his hair, I draw him down, done being a scared little rabbit when it comes to him. I'll remind him exactly how good we *are* together. He'll be hooked again. He won't care about me verbally handing my heart over.

It's all in the power of the pussy.

"You're the one who won't be able to resist more

than a taste." I kiss him gently, savoring the way his lips feel on mine. "You've hungered for me for years."

Hunter presses into me, his cock sliding in just until I part around him. It burns. It's been so long since something this size has been inside me—his cock was the last thing to breach my walls.

"Here's the thing, Bunny." I whimper as he presses in another inch. "I'm done wanting a woman who doesn't want me. You want my cock, you'll have it." I squirm as he reaches the halfway point. He's taking his time, making sure he doesn't hurt me. Even when he's trying to be a big badass, Hunter's still a softie at heart. "Once. Just like you said."

"I said no strings." My thighs tense as I angle my hips, trying to urge him the rest of the way. I'm desperate to feel all of him, nearly ready to come from this alone.

Hunter digs his fingers into my thighs to hold me still. Even our first time in years, we're still fighting for dominance—who sets the pace and the circumstances. "And I said that doesn't work for me, Little Rabbit. You think I'll keep pining for you after this? I think I've proven my willpower is impeccable. This is it for us. So take it how you want it, Bunny. Because you won't get it again."

It's a dare I gladly accept. He relaxes, willingly handing me the reins. I don't just take them—I wrap them around my wrist and *pull*.

Fingers tightening in his hair, I pull him down and smash my lips to his. My feet tense on his backside as I grip him from behind, pulling him into me until he bottoms out. Hunter fucks me with deep strokes as our mouths battle—every second, every movement so familiar, like we never stopped. Like it hasn't been two whole years since he's been inside me.

"Hunter," I whimper against his lips as he angles my hips to go deeper. My hands grab him everywhere, pulling him as close as possible, wanting to feel all his hard muscle against me.

"Fuck, baby. Such a greedy little slut for my cock, aren't you?" His teeth drag down my neck, sinking in, anchoring himself as he tenses inside me.

With every stroke he rubs against my clit and I tighten around him, priming for release. Burying my face against his neck, I try to stay quiet as I warn, "Hunter, I'm coming."

In response, he picks up his pace, teeth digging harder into my flesh. I bite him back to stifle my moans as the wet slap of our bodies reverberates off the bathroom walls. I squeeze him to me as I come, my pussy milking his cock as he follows me over the edge.

"You're mine, Little Rabbit. Do you feel that? That's me marking you as *mine*."

I feel it—every hot rope that splashes against my walls, every pump of his hips as he keeps fucking me, every stroke of his thumb against my clit as he works me toward another climax. "You can try to keep running. But next time, it'll be *you* who comes to *me*. *You* who can't handle the thought of me making another woman feel this way."

Jealousy rears its ugly head as he speaks. Just the

insinuation that he's ready to do this with someone else has me claiming his lips once more—marking him with my mouth, my tongue, my teeth as he pulls another orgasm from me.

You're mine. But I don't have to say it, because he knows. Just as he knows I'm his.

Our kiss slows with his thrusts, yet Hunter doesn't disentangle himself from me. His cock remains sheathed even when our lips part. Smiling, I soothe his scalp, massaging it with my fingers to ease the ache from how hard I was tugging his hair.

"Are you really telling me you'll be able to stay away after that?" Now that he's finally given in, we can move forward. What we just did proves we work without labels and without pledges.

"I told you, Bunny. I think I've proven my resolve is steel. You don't have to worry about me pressuring you for a relationship anymore. I'm done."

My heart drops into my stomach. My body turns cold even though his warmth is still pulsating inside me. "Hunter..."

"You'll figure it out. You don't want to be with me." He gives me one of those breathtaking, melancholy smiles. His tone is firm yet gentle as he smooths my hair and cups my cheek. "You've told me a million times, and I've never listened. I'm listening now."

No. No, you have it all wrong.

"That... that isn't... Hunter, you can't—" I can't form a coherent sentence as I fight tears, clinging to him harder when he tries to step back.

"I can. You know why? Because you're mine, Little Rabbit. Whether you want to be or not. You've been mine since the moment you gave me a lap dance at the strip club, and you know it. Now you're going to go out there with my cum dripping between your legs. And later, if you take that lucky bastard home, when he feasts on your pussy he'll taste my dick and know you belong to someone else."

I freeze. My grip loosens as a stark realization hits.

It's another game.

He thinks I'll admit defeat and give him my heart because he caved and fucked me.

Hunter's done with the easy way. He's been patient and thoughtful. Now he's trying to manipulate me.

Your dick is magical, but it's not that good.

Hardening my gaze, I try to control the anger seeping into my veins. "I belong to no one, Hunter. Least of all *you.*"

He releases an amused chuckle, dipping to nuzzle my neck. His thumb slides over my scar with a condescending touch while his lips travel to my ear. "You're fucking beautiful when you lie. But I think I prefer when you're coming undone around my cock as you do it."

Another wave of arousal hits me—whether from his words or the feel of him as he pulls out is unclear. I jump down and smooth my skirt, calling his bluff. "You won't be able to stay away. And if you think I'll come running to you because you're pretending to be done with me, you have another thing coming."

I absolutely hate that panic edges my voice. My brain

and heart battle as he tucks himself away with a grin. "Okay. If you say so."

Hunter doesn't return my underwear, or even glance back as he unlocks the door and leaves. Part of me wants to run after him—to tell him I'm sorry and that, of course, I want to be with him. But he already knows that. Now he's trying to force my hand.

And if there's one thing I hate most in this world, it's a man who tries to control me.

Game on, Detective Dick.

Two Years Ago

"I thought they wanted pretty faces to secure private funding? If that's the case, why are you here?"

Ryan rolls his eyes and flips me off, tugging at the stiff collar of his shirt. "Fuck you, Remington."

I laugh as we enter the ballroom already in full swing—lavish decor, pompous assholes who have more money than they know what to do with—which is why a few of us were tapped to schmooze and talk them into opening their pocketbooks.

"Bet I can bring in more than you," Ryan challenges, grabbing a flute of champagne.

"You're on, fucker." I ditched my glasses and actually styled my hair tonight. Not half bad, if I say so myself, and by the way I'm already garnering looks from older ladies adorned in enough diamonds to feed the hungry for at least a month, I'd say I've got a shot.

I slide into a cluster of women and flash my best smile. "I was told I had to attend to talk to old grumpy men. I wasn't aware such lovely young ladies would be in attendance."

Inwardly, I preen as they break out in a gaggle of giggles, oohing and aahing over my attention. I may not have game with women my age—case in point: Bunny—but I can charm women my mother's age and older all night. My parents drilled manners into me.

Women my age? They want disrespect dressed as danger, not a good guy who'd do anything for them.

An hour later I've got nearly a hundred grand pledged, three invitations to hotel rooms, and a very precarious situation with an elderly—and I mean she's pushing ninety, at least—woman and her voyeur husband.

Good for them keeping the spark alive, but holy shit, I feel like I need a shower.

Her bony hands were trying to cop a feel as they tried to talk me into it for a ridiculous-sized check for the department.

I'm good with flashing a smile and flirting a little, but I'm not a freaking male escort.

"Fuck, I'd have done it," Ryan says, signaling the bartender for something stronger than champagne. "If they wrote the check to me and not the department." He laughs.

I lean on the bar, scanning the penguin suits and sequins. "What a world. If they all wrote a check that wouldn't even dent their accounts, we could clean up the whole island."

Ryan's attention drifts to a blonde. I snag the bourbon he ordered and go back to hunting my next victim... I mean...

No. "Victim" fits.

A chuckle sounds from my left, and I look over to see a set of amused hazel eyes. "Department got you working for funds? They always send the pretty ones."

He looks familiar. "Yeah. Do I know you?"

"Anderson Brooks. Used to work Narcotics in San Diego."

Recognition clicks. "You were on that case a few years back—the one NYPD tried to keep quiet. With the club, right?"

He drains the amber-colored liquid in his glass. "The club should still be kept quiet. Good to know news traveled to the Metro PD."

Aww shit, I don't wanna get in trouble for opening my big fucking mouth.

Brooks must read my expression and laughs. "Don't worry, kid. You won't get in trouble. I've heard about you—Remington, right?"

Shock spears clean through me. How?

"Relax." He waves for another drink. "Jesus, you're green. You're doing good work. Your reputation precedes you."

"Thank... you?" I fumble for words, a whirlwind of thoughts jetting through my mind, all relating to how and why a detective of his caliber would have heard of *me*.

"Don't let them work you like a dog." Whatever he's about to say next dies in his throat as a bombshell in a red dress sidles up to him, looping her arm through his.

"What about dogs?" she purrs, eyes sweeping over me, crimson lips tilting up at one corner. "Have you found a puppy?"

"Watch it, baby girl." He tucks her into his side and kisses her neck. Suddenly, I feel like I should be anywhere else. They look two seconds from tearing each other's clothes off. "Remington, this is my wife, Carmela. Cara, this is Hunter Remington, an up-and-coming *me* in the making."

Again, I'm speechless. Anderson Brooks calling me the next him—without ever working together—is an honor.

Carmela offers her hand and I kiss the back lightly. "Nice to meet you, ma'am."

"Well, aren't you charming?" she coos. Then, to her husband, she says, "I'm ready when you are, smooth guy. I've done enough ass-kissing to last all year."

Brooks laughs, unwinding his arm from her waist to reach out and slide me a card. "If you ever relocate to California, give me a call."

After we shake hands, he and his wife disappear into the crowd. Ryan finally turns around as they disappear, and I have to laugh at my good luck. Fuck securing more funding for the department, I might have just secured myself a great job opportunity.

"Who was that?" he asks, hunting for the drink I stole.

"Don't worry your pretty little—" The crowd parts just enough for me to catch a glimpse of a familiar little rabbit making her way to the bar. "What the fuck?"

"What now?" Ryan follows my stare. "Is that Jones?"

It sure the fuck is.

He snorts. "What the fuck is she wearing?"

I don't answer. I'm already moving. Her luscious locks are swept into a carefully sculpted updo with a few tendrils framing her face. The gown is shimmering, icy pink, painted on and ready to split if she makes any sudden moves.

Bunny *hates* pink.

I cage her from behind, breathing into her ear. "What the hell are you wearing, Little Rabbit?"

She whirls, eyes wide, terror stark on that beautiful face. "Hunter? What are you doing here?" Wildly, her gaze skitters over the room. She shoves my chest, creating a little distance between us.

"They sent Jacobs, me, and a few others to work. Did they ask you too? And I repeat," my gaze rakes down her body, "what the heck are you wearing?"

"You have to go." Panic threads her voice. Her chest heaves as she grabs my arm, tugging me toward the exit. "You can't be here."

Confused, I dig in and catch her wrist, drawing her into me. "Hey. What's going on? Are you okay?"

She's acting frightened, and a thick sense of dread fills my senses. I've never seen this woman afraid of anything. Tears shine in her mossy gaze, her bottom lip trembling as she tries to speak.

"I'd appreciate it if you'd unhand my wife," a man says in a deep Texan drawl.

Bunny's eyes clamp shut. Mine snap to the man in question. He's standing a few feet away, hands in his pockets, his dark gaze drilling into me.

Wife?

"Uh, I think you have the wrong woman." I look at Bunny. She's trembling. Ashen. She stares at the floor, doing anything she can to avoid eye contact. My heart stops, a sick feeling curdling in my stomach like sour milk. "Bunny?"

She lifts her left hand to peel my grip from her right wrist. Bile rises in my throat as I glimpse a large diamond ring on her dainty finger, accompanied by a smaller band. A wedding set. "Hunter..."

I stagger back as the truth punches me in the gut.

She composes herself while I just stare, horrified, as the man comes up beside her, arm locking around her waist.

"So this is the infamous *Hunter*?" He clucks his tongue, cool as ice. "I've heard a lot about you."

The tone in which he delivers his statement suggests he's not my biggest fan. Meanwhile, my little rabbit can't even look me in the eye. Silently, I urge her to raise her gaze.

That's the least you can do, after making me look like a fool for a year.

How fucking stupid am I?

Anger takes over, flooding my system like a tsunami prepared to destroy everything in its path. "That's funny. I haven't heard a word about you."

His smirk falls. He drops an irate glare to the top of Bunny's head, who refuses to look at either of us. "Yes, well. Bunny's always been careful about keeping work and home life separate. But that won't be an issue now that she'll no longer be employed with the department here soon."

I must look shocked, because he chuckles. She winces and finally lifts her gaze. Remorse shadows her face. Heavy. Palpable.

Good. Drown in it. Feel how fucking stupid I feel. What was the play here? Watch me jump? Watch me beg?

Was it amusing for her to watch me work so hard, knowing she'd never give in?

Was everything between us a lie?

"Oh, she didn't tell you? What's wrong, sweetheart?" He digs his fingers into her side and gives her a little shake. "Don't tell me you were just going to disappear on him?" Letting her go, he thrusts a hand at me. "Sorry, I'm Nathaniel, by the way. Husband of the woman you've been trying to sleep with."

"Nathaniel!" Bunny snaps, glaring at him. She tries to slip free, but he wraps a possessive arm around her tighter when it's clear I won't take his hand.

"It's okay, Little Rabbit." I'm furious, but the way he squares up—like he wants to swing—keeps me talking. "Clearly, he feels threatened if you're always talking about me at home." I wink at her, caging off my heart as I do. "Guess she's not getting the attention she needs if she's seeking it elsewhere." I shrug, sliding my hands into my pockets, aiming for a calmness I don't feel. "You won't have to worry about me anymore, Nate. You should probably worry about your marriage, though."

"It's Nathaniel," he grits.

"I don't really give a shit. Have a nice life." I give them an exaggerated bow. "Hope you enjoyed the show, Bunny."

I don't wait for a reply. I sidestep them and head for the exit. Heart stuck in my esophagus, I have to bite back the sting of tears that burn my sinuses. I'm not weak. I won't cry. No big deal—Bunny just ripped out my heart and spiked it with her stilettos.

The woman of my dreams played me.

No. She didn't. She turned you down. Every time. Flirted, sure. But never promised. Not once voiced a word to give you hope.

I run every moment back. Every look. Every line.

No ring. No mention of a husband.

Why?

I *need* to know. I need an explanation.

That need freezes my feet to the floor as my heart and head war over what to do. Both too loud to ignore.

Before Bunny, I was all about my job. I had goals and dreams, and sure, a family fit into that one day, but romance was the furthest thing from my mind. But, the second I met her, she stripped me bare and feasted on my flesh, consuming every piece of me until I was an integral part of her.

I know Bunny as well as I know myself.

And this? This doesn't sit right. At all.

<u>Bunny</u>

Fuck me.

Fuck this night.

And fuck this stupid fucking dress.

I feel like I can't breathe. The tight fabric strains across my chest as I inhale through my nose and exhale through my mouth, trying to stave off an impending panic attack. Tears cling to my lashes—mascara definitely running—and Nathaniel is gripping me so tightly I know there will be bruises on my side tomorrow.

"Go clean yourself up," he bites out through clenched teeth. "And meet me in the foyer in five. You will not embarrass me tonight more than you already have."

As soon as his fingers loosen, I race for the exit, intent on catching Hunter before he leaves.

Your lie was bound to catch up to you. You should have been honest from the start.

Silently cursing the gown I had to rush out and buy this afternoon—because I couldn't zip up the one I bought a few weeks ago—I storm through the doors, frantically scanning for Hunter.

I nearly yelp when a strong, warm hand encircles my bicep, turning me roughly just as I pass into the foyer. "What the fuck, Bunny?"

"I'm sorry!" I blurt when I realize it's Hunter.

Launching myself into his arms, I squeeze him around the middle like he'll disappear if I let go. "I never meant to hurt you."

Firmly, he pulls me off him, pushing me back. "You never meant to hurt me?" His whiskey eyes drop to my ring. "It's been almost a year, Bunny. If you never meant to hurt me, you wouldn't have acted interested. Wouldn't have led me on and let me think I had a chance with you!"

"I know! I know, and I'm so sorry." Tears line my lashes again, and I don't care that we're making a scene, or that Nathaniel could catch us at any moment. "Hunter, please believe me. I never meant for this to get so out of hand."

Reaching for him again, my heart drops when he steps back and shakes his head. "Just tell me why. Why did you let me make a fool of myself?"

"You didn't!" I plead with him to believe me. "Hunter, I swear, you weren't a fool. I *do* like you—"

"You're married!" The volume of his voice draws a few dirty looks our way. "What kind of a person does that?"

"I'm sorry." Inhaling a shaky breath, I step closer, lowering my voice. "Look, Nathaniel has affairs all the time, and I have never even entertained the thought of so much as looking at another man... but then *you* came along, and—"

"Oh, fuck that." Hunter gapes at me like I'm pathetic. Like he feels sorry for me and so damn mad at himself for falling into the trap of an unhappy, lonely, married woman. "Bunny, that's just sad. So you... what? Thought I could be your dirty little secret?"

Pinching the bridge of my nose, I look toward the ballroom. I'm running out of time before my husband comes out looking for me. "It isn't like that. Listen, can we please just talk? I'll find you on Monday, and—"

"No." Hunter's answer is resolute, shattering my heart and letting the pieces fall at his feet. I watch as he erects walls around himself, putting a barrier between us so I can't hurt him anymore. "I thought you were the woman I'd spend the rest of my life with. I thought maybe you'd been hurt in the past, and that's why you were so careful with your heart." His lip curls in disgust as he drags his gaze down my body. "Never would I have thought you were just a lonely wife who puts up with her husband cheating on her."

"Hunter..." His image grows blurry as my tears fall. If only he'd let me explain.

Yes, I'm lonely. Yes, I put up with Nathaniel's affairs.

But every second I've spent with Hunter has been real. And I want it to last forever.

"Goodbye, Bunny. Or should I say... *Mrs.* Jones."

He turns to leave, and I nearly double over in despair. Guilt and shame rack my body as I flee the opposite way down the foyer, tucking myself into a nook in the hall.

He just needs some time.

If I give him a few days, he'll cool off. Then I'll tell him I'm leaving my husband, and once the dust settles, we can try for real.

By the time my tears have stopped and I get my

breathing under control, it's been much longer than the five minutes Nathaniel gave me to clean myself up. And if anything, I'm sure my face looks like more of a disaster now.

My husband sees me coming down the hall and quickens his pace. I remain silent as he grabs my arm and pulls me into him, dragging me along until we reach the nook where I'd been hiding. Hauling me into it, Nathaniel pushes me against the wall roughly.

"What the fuck are you thinking?" he snaps. "Did you tell him to show up here tonight?"

"No!"

Fury radiates off him in waves, but we're in public, so I'm sure he'll save his worst for when we get home. As it is, his fingers dig into my arms, nails threatening to pierce my skin.

"Are you fucking him?" Leaning down, he presses his forehead to mine, forcing my head against the wall. "Huh? *Little Rabbit*?"

"You're hurting me." I squirm, trying to get away. For a second, I think about screaming. "Nathaniel, stop it!"

Suddenly, his hand is around my throat. He doesn't squeeze—wouldn't *dare* leave marks where anyone could see—but his palm crushes my trachea. Spittle flies from his mouth, dotting my cheek as he grinds out, "Are. You. Fucking. Him?"

It's time I find my backbone. I'm tired of being his punching bag. I start to squirm harder, putting more effort into getting away.

"What if I am? You fuck anything in a skirt when you're out of the house, so what's the problem, dear husband? Don't like the possibility of me taking another dick? The thought isn't so nice, is it? The possibility that I might like his hands on me more. That I might prefer the way he kisses me. Or the way he *fucks*."

I laugh in his face.

He backhands me. It's not light, either. My head whips back from the force, a sharp sting splitting my skin, spidering out as the flesh over my cheekbone parts beneath his wedding band. Stars fill my vision, the edges darken, my head swims.

"You stupid bitch. Goddammit. Now look what you made me do," Nathaniel mutters. "Your face is ruined now." He barks a dry laugh before hauling me into his arms. I'm vaguely aware he's bringing me somewhere, but the darkness keeps dragging me under, and I'm inclined to follow it.

The last thing I hear before I pass out is my husband murmuring, "No one will want to look at you now. You can kiss your pretty-boy goodbye."

"You said she fell?" A skeptical voice rouses me.

Bright white floods my eyes, and I wince, holding up a hand to block it. "Why are we at the beach?"

Nathaniel's chuckle fills the room. "We're at the hospital, sweetheart. Do you remember falling at the gala? You hit your head pretty hard on the corner of a table."

I did?

The light dims, and a soothing tenor asks, "Mrs. Jones, do you remember what happened?"

I start to shake my head, but the movement creates a wave of nausea. My stomach clenches and I reach for my zipper. "Get me out of this thing. I'm going to throw up."

Soft fingers ease the fastening. "There, there, honey. I'll get you some ice chips."

I'm guessing she's the nurse when the first voice repeats his earlier question after the door opens and closes.

"Look, how much longer is this going to take? I'd like to get my wife home to rest. She's clumsy. She tripped and fell, and if you'd like, I can give you the numbers of my work associates. They'll tell you what happened." My husband sounds irritated, and I hold my dress to my chest as I try to sit up.

"I'm fine." Though the pain screams otherwise. My face hurts like a bitch.

"Why don't you just rest a while, Mrs. Jones. We'll have someone here to stitch up your face in a moment. Unfortunately, it's going to leave a scar."

"Great, can you get me a referral for a plastic surgeon?" Nathaniel gripes.

A harsh exhale makes the doctor's mustache twitch. He narrows his eyes at my husband before softening his gaze on me. Flashes of what happened spring to life as I touch the soft bandage covering my cheek. He steps closer, lowering his voice even though Nathaniel will hear anything in a room this small.

His presence is comforting—warm blue eyes crinkling as he tries to communicate something silently. Just as he parts his lips to speak, the door opens and the nurse returns.

"Here you go, honey. Let's get you and that little one hydrated."

My world halts. My heart stops. Air refuses me. Everything sharpens to a pinpoint as my gaze meets Nathaniel's nefarious grin across the room.

"What?" I breathe.

The doctor nods, confirming I didn't mishear—confirming my worst nightmare. He offers a grim smile. "We ran some tests while you were asleep per your husband's request. It looks like you're about fourteen weeks along."

"Along?" The alarm in my voice reverberates through the room.

This can't be happening. I look back at Nathaniel, who raises his brows and tilts his head, daring me to make a scene.

"Surprise, sweetheart," he croons, pushing off the wall to take the ice chips from the nurse. "We're having a baby."

PRESENT

ANNOYANCE RIPPLES through me as I check my phone for the millionth time in the last twenty minutes.

The jury has returned with its decision.

Verdict? Hunter is absolutely ignoring me.

A few weeks ago, this man wouldn't have let an hour pass without responding to me, let alone nearly two days. Since we slept together, it seems he's sticking to his decision to stop waiting around for me.

Nausea splashes against my stomach lining, and it takes all my willpower to swallow down the sickness trying to claw its way up my throat.

Hunter's steadfast stubbornness is going to give me an ulcer.

He's cordial at work but doesn't go out of his way to include me like usual. And the other day he smiled at

Gwendolyn Cabaret... *fucking* smiled. The little hussy has been after him for months. She's even tried getting the department to pair them on assignment, even though she's been with her partner for nearly five years.

If Hunter thinks I'm going to cave, he's wrong.

Yasha and Maru perk up, their little ears twitching toward the front door as they hear Dove's keys in the lock. Seconds later, Fang bursts in to meet his friends, their yips so shrill I rub my temple to relieve the instant headache.

I must be coming down with something. Something's felt off for the last week.

"Buns? You got mail!" Dove calls out as she enters. The smell of garlic, cheese, and marinara wafts into the foyer with her arrival. As much as I wanted chicken parm earlier, the thought of food no longer sounds appealing.

It's gotta be the flu.

"Thanks, Love Dove." I take the manila envelope from her and look it over. "That's strange. I didn't even hear Teddy knock today. The boys weren't alerted either."

"Maybe he's on vacation?" She begins unpacking our takeout, placing the random containers on my small kitchen table. "I got the panzerotti dolce you like. I was at Wrenley's, so I just stopped at *Nonna Dora's*."

"Of course you were at Wrenley's. You're always with Wrenley." I'm joking, but even *I* can hear how flat my tone is.

"I know. If you're feeling neglected, I'm sorry. I

suck." She pauses in her mission to waggle her brows at me. "And speaking of sucking..."

"Oh my god, give it up, will you? I'm not telling you what happened in that bathroom." I tear into my mail and frown at the single folded paper inside. "I *will* tell you that Hunter is ignoring me."

My phone dings from its place next to the garlic knots, and Dove looks at it with a grin while I unfold the letter. "Is he now? He just texted you." She draws out the *you* like we're kids talking about silly crushes.

Even though I've been annoyed with him for not responding, the feeling pales in comparison to the violent crash of fear icing my veins.

I KNOW WHAT YOU DID.

Magazine clippings of letters spelling out the message are all that's on the paper, like an old Hollywood thriller. "Was this in the mailbox?"

"No, it was leaning against your door. Why? What is it?" She visibly cringes as I hold the paper up for her to read. "Eww. Take this in and see if they can dust it for fingerprints. What a weirdo."

I blanch at her flippant attitude. "What if it's *your* weirdo?"

"Wrenley?" Dove sets her mushroom ravioli down and spins to face me, blonde locks fanning out like a halo. "Why on Earth would you think he'd leave something like this at your door?"

"I don't know. He knows about you now. Maybe it wasn't that hard for him to figure out." My headache throbs as I think about who would send me this and why.

I grab my phone and take a screenshot, sending it to Hunter. His earlier single-word negative reply to my question about needing me for work this week is forgotten as I type.

> This was against my door when Dove got here.

Few people know about the real circumstances surrounding my husband's death—Hunter being one of them. And though the letter could be referring to my activities as the Shadow Siren, it could also be talking about Nathaniel's death, regardless of it being two years ago.

Hunter's reply comes through in less than a minute.

HUNTER

> Take it to forensics. Get it checked for prints.

I stare at my phone—at how unaffected his response is. If this had happened before the bathroom incident, Hunter would have personally gone to every house on the block to check for cameras, then bought one for my place, installed it, and had the feed streaming to his phone as well as mine.

My stomach dips as I realize how much I've come to rely on him. When I lift my gaze and find Dove staring at me, I nearly step back from the ferocious blaze in her bright blue eyes. She's only directed her dark side at me once in our year-and-a-half friendship—the night we met —and I'd rather not fight with the only real friend I have over something as stupid as a guy.

Hands on her hips, she nods to my phone. "Hunter?"

"Yeah. He said to take it to forensics." Securing the letter in the envelope, I retrieve a Ziploc bag and shove it inside.

"Great. Now can we eat and go back to discussing how Wrenley isn't the one who sent the letter and how he'd *never* do something like that? If he suspects you, I'm sure he'll just ask. We don't keep secrets anymore."

"Oh? So he knows you're planning on going to California to confront his mother?" I deadpan.

The ensuing silence is so thick I can hear my heart thumping wildly in my chest.

Just can't keep your mouth shut, can you?

Regardless of not wanting to fight with her, I can't stop the vitriol from spilling out. "Cranky" doesn't even begin to cover my mood today. You could tell me the sky is blue, and I'd argue it's green.

"Is this going to be a problem?"

"I don't know, Dove. *Is* it?"

We engage in an epic stare-down that stretches on and on, like we're about to draw guns for a good ol' fashioned Western duel.

Finally, instead of verbally producing what I'm sure would be the pinkest, sparkliest handgun in the city, my friend concedes. "What we do is a big deal. I already told you I wouldn't tell him about you until you're ready. But

Wrenley is going to be a part of my life, Buns. A big part. And there's room for you both, but you have to scoot over a little. Okay? Wrenley has demons, too. Maybe the four of us can spend a little time together so you can get to know him."

"I don't want to get to know him," I grumble. A tremor crawls up my limbs. I shake them out with a frustrated cry, trying to soften the hardened edges of my prickly temper. "I'm sorry. I know I'm being awful. I'm just in a mood. Hunter isn't really speaking to me. So the four of us hanging out isn't really in the cards."

Dove bites the inside of her cheek, her bright, watermelon-glossed lips pursing as she turns back to our food. "What are you going to do if he's decided he's truly finished pursuing you?"

Sorrow sweeps through me, rallying tears to my lashes that I hastily wipe away before she sees. Maybe after holding out for so long, the real thing didn't compare to the remembrance of what we had before I ruined everything. Hunter got what he wanted—me practically begging for his attention the second he took it away—but instead of celebrating the win, it's like he doesn't even care.

It's everything I feared and nothing I expected.

Have I turned my sweet Hunter into the type of man I despise? The one born from giving too many chances. Having his heart ripped out too many times. Have I lost him for good? And if there's even a minuscule chance that I haven't... am I ready to surrender my heart?

No.

"This is what he wants." I turn to grab plates and utensils. "For me to think he's done. And it worked. I've been messaging him every day like a needy cat in heat, when it used to be the other way around. But he doesn't get to try to pressure me into a decision."

"Well, you know I support whatever decision you make. I'm team Bunny." She pulls off a chunk of garlic knot, dips it in marinara, and pops it into her mouth. "Although, I don't support this month's book pick. It's boring as fuck. I DNF'd it."

"Oh thank god." I gladly drop the subject of Hunter and focus on our shared love. "I felt so bad that I pushed for it. It's awful. Our followers are going to question our choices after this one."

We don't like talking poorly about books on our page. If we don't like it, we don't review it. We don't need to make a post bashing the author or the book. But we've never had a book-of-the-month we didn't like, so we're in uncharted territory.

"I say we leave a rating off it and just make an aesthetic post with a few quotes. I already highlighted a few. I think that will speak for itself, and maybe we chill on that sub-genre for a while."

"Yeah. Agreed."

"By the way..." Dove waits until we've settled in the living room with our dinner. "Wrenley wants to join book club."

It takes me a moment to realize the growl rolling through the room is coming from me, not one of the dogs.

Her blonde curls bounce as she nods and grabs the remote to find a movie. "I'll take that as a maybe."

Leaning forward, I select a large garlic knot from the basket, my appetite returning full force once the first bite of pillowy, buttery, garlicky goodness hits my tongue. "Love Dove, you can take that as a *very* hard *no*."

Two Years Ago

It's been days since the night of the gala, and still my chest hurts. A proverbial wound—bloodied and raw from Bunny's betrayal—that won't fucking close, throbbing in time with my busted heart.

So this is what heartbreak feels like.

I've never experienced it before. Never thought another human could make someone feel so utterly incapacitated by the hurt they inflict. We are in charge of our emotions. We choose who can and cannot hurt us.

Only, we don't.

Not always.

Some people bury themselves so far into your marrow you don't realize that to remove them, you'll lose a piece of yourself. And that's exactly how this feels. Like Bunny took a part of me I'm not sure I'll ever get back— even if I'm still unsure about wanting it back at all.

My temples pulse with exhaustion, my brain working overtime trying to figure out my little rabbit's angle. Wondering if she really thought I'd be okay seeing her in secret, knowing she goes home every night to a man who doesn't—and can never—love her like I do.

"'Nathaniel has affairs all the time...'"

Bunny's words ricochet around and around. Her excuses. Her tears. The way he touched her. The fact that he *could*—out in the open and without consequences—because he's her fucking husband.

And I'm just the damn jerk who didn't read the signs, the red flags that would have tipped me off. I stupidly thought she wanted to take things slow—be friends first. That's something I loved about her. I could get behind building a strong foundation of friendship.

Only that wasn't it at all. She was never available to begin with.

"...Jones on the job."

My attention snaps to the front of the room when I hear a senior detective mention Bunny's last name.

A woman—I'm not sure of her official title, but I know she's who Bunny liaises with about assignments—shakes her head and releases a heavy sigh. "Jones apparently fell and messed up her face. She'll no longer be working for us. Said it's gonna be a pretty noticeable scar. Too identifiable."

It feels like all the air gets sucked from the room.

"What do you mean she fell and messed up her face?" All eyes turn to me at the harsh bite of my tone.

Uncrossing my arms, I push to my feet. "Did you actually talk to her? Or did you talk to her *husband*?"

Murmurs pop up after I bite out the word husband like it tastes bitter. It's no secret—my feelings for Bunny. But from the sounds of it, no one knew she was married. So it wasn't just me she kept it from.

The woman cocks her head. "I spoke to Bunny directly. She said she tripped this weekend and hit her face on the corner of her coffee table."

Pushing my feelings aside, I spin on my heel and stalk out, aware everyone's eyes track me as I go. Nathaniel gave off bad vibes when I met him Saturday. I don't buy that Bunny *fell*. I've seen that woman balance in nearly six-inch heels while spinning herself around a pole on a platform barely big enough to stand on. She's got the skills of a tightrope walker.

It takes longer than I'd like, but I smooth-talk my way into getting Bunny's address. Everyone knows we're friends, so all it takes is telling an HR girl I forgot her street.

It's a corner lot, with a small gated courtyard out front and a rear extension renovated for parking, edged by a garden—a rare find in the city. Bunny's never struck me as the green-thumb type, but the foliage is vibrant and blooms in bright colors bring a cheery vibe as I approach the door.

I'm taking a risk showing up. It's midday. I'm banking on her husband being at work. Bunny opens after a second round of knocking, and the sight of her has me hoping he *is* here so I have somewhere to direct my rage.

"Hunter? What are you doing here?" Her mossy eyes widen as she scans up and down the street, panic surging through her gaze and body. The left side of her face is swollen, the eye bruised, and the skin over her cheekbone is hidden behind a thin patch of gauze. Raspberry mottles her sun-kissed flesh, making her freckles pop, spreading out from under the dressing like a splatter of paint.

"What the fuck happened to you?" I step into her, one hand going to her waist to keep her from stepping back as the other hovers over the bandage. "And don't you dare say you fell."

"You need to leave." Tears spring to her eyes. Her whole body trembles as her gaze keeps searching the street. "Please, Hunter. Nathaniel is on his way home. You can't be here."

"Did he fucking do this to you?" I should have seen it that night. She was scared of him, and I was too blinded by rage to notice. "I'm going to fucking kill him."

"Hunter, stop! You're only going to make it worse than you already have!" Anger creeps into her tone, chasing away her fear if only for a moment. She sniffs back tears as I freeze, taking in what she said.

Shrugging out of my hold, she gently pushes me back a step. I keep staring, terrified by what she implies. I told her husband she was looking for attention. Told him to worry about his marriage.

I called her *Little Rabbit* in front of him.

Nausea crashes through me, settling like lead. "This is my fault, isn't it?"

Her usually glossy raven hair looks dull as it slips over one shoulder with a shake of her head. She drops her gaze to the stoop. "My problems are not your fault. But now you know why..." A shaky breath leaves her throat. "Why I can't be with you."

"Bunny, if he did this to you... You work with the fucking cops. Let's go. Right now." I reach for her again, but she retreats a step into the house, fixing me with a stern glare.

"It's not that simple, Hunter. I'm not a broken, battered woman. I can't just—"

"You're not broken and battered?" I cry incredulously, motioning to her face. "What the fuck do you call this?"

"I'm fine. I have it under control," she bites out.

Suddenly, an onslaught of memories hits me—the bruises on her neck. The time I tried to tickle her and she winced, said she'd had a hard workout, and kept clutching her side where I'd grabbed her. The time she told me she fell off a stripper pole and bit her lip—that's why it was busted and bruised.

Every single instance was a lie, rolling off her tongue so smoothly I never thought twice.

I took her at her word while her husband was beating her.

"You don't have it under control, Little Rabbit." I try to hide the pity in my voice and fail miserably. There's no way I can walk away now. No world where I stand by while she stays with a man who does this. "Let me help you."

"You don't understand." Her tone turns watery, tears lining her eyes as she shakes her head. "You can't help me."

"Yes. I can. Just come with me," I plead.

"Just stop, Hunter. Don't try to be a hero. I'll be fine." She grips the edge of the door and shrugs. "In a few months, you'll forget all about me. Go. Live your life and don't let me and my problems bring you down."

"I could never forget you, Bunny. And I don't want to. I want you to come with me. Right now. I can protect you." All it would take is one phone call and I can have her husband behind bars. I don't know why she's fighting me so hard. She has to know anyone at the department would do whatever it took to get her away from Nathaniel if they knew.

A door bangs somewhere in the house, transforming her from contemplative to terrified. "Bunny! I'm home!"

"Leave. *Now.* Don't let him see you," she hisses, then slams the door in my face.

I nearly pound on it, wanting to get his attention. The fucker must have come in through the back. I want him to open this door so I can rearrange his teeth before making sure he never sees daylight again. Rationality kicks in, though. If I stay, I'll make it worse for Bunny—or I'll end up behind bars for murder.

Instead, I go back to work. Someone needs to know what's going on, and the woman from earlier wasn't fazed when I brought up Nathaniel, which means she knew Bunny was married all along. I'll start there.

Protecting my little rabbit is at the top of my list, even if it's the last thing I do.

"WHAT DO you mean there's nothing we can do?" Anger surges through me, molten hot and crisping the edges of my self-control. "He's hurting her!"

"You don't have any proof of that, Remington. She didn't come out and say he hit her, did she?" Abigail James, the woman from earlier, arches a brow as she leans back in her chair.

"This is ridiculous. It's *obvious*. I saw them this weekend—he's a complete dick, and—"

"Look, I know you have a thing for her. Everyone in this building knows you have a thing for her. But the fact is Bunny is married, and she chose not to tell you. I get it. You're hurt, you're embarrassed, blah, blah, blah. But I've known her a while, and she's never alluded to her husband being abusive. Now, if she came in here and sat down herself to make a report, we'd be having a different conversation. But something tells me if you're here, it's because she won't. So my hands are tied, Hunter."

Disbelief bleeds into my features. At five eleven, Abigail James is the tallest woman I've ever met. Nearing seventy, she's the oldest working female in the department. She's rough-and-tumble, no-nonsense. She's seen a lot of shit within these walls.

What she doesn't understand is that Bunny is an actress of epic proportions.

And what I can't comprehend is why Bunny is choosing to stay with an abusive asshole.

Defeat must show on my face loud and clear because Abigail sighs and leans forward. "Look, Jones is a big girl. I trust she can take care of herself. Don't treat her like glass, Remington. In my experience, strong women hate it when men assume they're weak. Bunny doesn't strike me as the type to stick around and let a man beat on her. If she's staying with him—and what you're insinuating is the truth—then there's a reason."

What do I say to that?

What are my choices when there's nothing the law can do and the woman won't stand up for herself?

Pulling my phone out, I open my thread with Bunny, then pause, wondering if Nathaniel's screening her texts. Abigail follows my train of thought, shakes her head, and grabs a file folder off her desk.

"Don't do it, Remington. My best advice? Let her go. You're either going to make things worse, or you'll end up with your heart broken more than it already is. You're good at your job. Don't throw it away over a woman."

"Pretty harsh on your own sex, aren't you?" I snort, shoving my cell back in my pocket.

"Women are nothing but sirens. And what do sirens do, kid?"

I don't answer aloud, but the truth swims through my head as I leave her office.

They lead you to your death.

PRESENT

A FROWN PULLS at my lips as Hunter smiles at his phone once more, irritation racing through my veins at the speed of a cheetah going after its next meal.

Who is he texting?

Who is putting that smile on his face?

"I was thinking we should get the cupcakes decorated in green frosting with dinosaurs on top," I grumble, hands on my hips as I stare at him, trying to pull his attention from his screen. He's been preoccupied since he arrived, intrigued by whoever is on the other end of his incessant messaging.

"Yeah, sure. Whatever you want." He doesn't even look up, barely concealing a full-bodied laugh before his fingers fly over the screen again.

My eye twitches. Irritation transforms into full-on fury.

We're supposed to be finalizing last-minute prep for Dove's birthday—a task set on us by Wrenley, who apparently can't be bothered to part from my best friend long enough to do this himself.

Not that I'm upset about the party—it's her big 3-0 —but I *am* upset that her boyfriend thought Hunter and I needed to do this together, like he gave Hunter instructions I'm not privy to. Ones he seems to be disregarding, since he's not paying attention to a single detail we need to iron out. The party is tomorrow.

Detective Dick is barely speaking to me, and what little I've gotten has been distracted at best and downright rude by way of ignoring me at worst.

Finally I snap, unable to take it anymore. With a growl, I demand, "Who are you talking to?"

Since we slept together, Hunter seems determined to drive home that he's done waiting around for me. Apparently that also includes common decency. He's been a huge part of my life for so long. I don't appreciate him taking himself out of it so abruptly.

Even if—God help me—he's right.

Now that he's not up my ass all the time, I miss him. It was never a matter of wanting him, and he knows that. But I feel like I have to double down on not letting him force me into a decision I'm not, and might never be, ready for.

Whiskey eyes flick up to meet my gaze, a smirk curving his lips as he finally gives me more than a flicker of attention. "Jealous, Little Rabbit?"

"Pissed off. You're being rude. I just suggested green

frosted cupcakes with dinosaur figurines for toppers, for fuck's sake. You think Wrenley will appreciate that oversight in detail?"

Hunter exhales hard, pushing my coffee table away from the sofa as he stands. "You don't need me for this. I'm sure you can handle picking out frosting colors on your own."

"Wrenley asked us *both* to do it!" I step in front of him as he tries to leave, the air heating with my movement, heavy tension settling between us. "What is your *deal*? All of a sudden you're a hot commodity now that you're finished with me?"

A laugh bubbles from his throat, sharp and sardonic. "I never stopped being a *hot commodity,* as you so eloquently put it. Though it sure is telling how interested you are in my life now that I'm no longer interested in yours."

Okay. Ouch.

"Oh, don't kid yourself. You even said you were doing this to teach me a lesson." I step into him, our bodies nearly touching as I crane my neck and sneer. "Go ahead, Hunter. Fuck around and find out. If you want to sleep with all the fucking badge bunnies after your dick, be my guest. But if you think I won't do the same, you're dead wrong, buddy. So far, we both know neither of us has even dared, but if you cross that line? There is no going back. That'll be the end."

"I already said it was the end, so keep threatening me, baby. It makes me hard." His phone goes off again.

His eyes slide to the screen. He holds it up.

Another smile spreads across his face.

Runaway rage erupts inside me at the dismissal. Before I know what I'm doing, I snatch his phone and whip it across the room. Yasha and Maru—used to all my nefarious basement noises—don't even stir as the device smacks the wall and the screen spiders into a thousand glittering shards.

We both blink. I didn't mean to throw it that hard. He's just making me so... *furious.*

The silence that follows is deafening. Neither of us moves as our chests heave, air escaping our lungs with thick drags of anticipation. A crackle of invisible energy snaps between us, sending goosebumps across my limbs. My nipples harden against the thin material of my lavender top, and my legs clench together as warm arousal pools at the apex of my thighs.

Hunter's eyes darken, turning to molten gold as he grabs my waist and digs his fingers into my side. The other hand lifts to my face, grabbing my chin between his thumb and index finger. A cocky grin twists his lips, his voice husky as he asks, "The thought of someone else having my attention pisses you off, doesn't it? Finally got a taste of my cock after all this time and now you want it all to yourself, Little Rabbit? Tell me. Use your words and tell me how badly you want me."

His words pull a whimper from my throat and, subconsciously, my tongue darts out to wet my lips. His eyes follow the movement before he nods and lowers his head, his warm breath fanning over my face in a minty cloud. "Yeah, you do, don't you? I'll bet it's killing you, not knowing if another woman has had me in her mouth. Not knowing if I've been inside anyone else. I'll bet you're soaked at the idea of getting on your knees so you can show me what I'm missing, aren't you, Bunny? If you want to get on your knees and suck my cock, Little Rabbit, I'm not gonna stop you."

I've never given Hunter a blow job. Never had his perfectly sculpted, silky flesh in my mouth. I've seen it, admired it, had it in my pussy. I've held it and fantasized about going down on him. Envisioned him coming undone for me as I get myself off when I'm in bed alone.

He's eaten me out more times than I can count, but he's never let me go there with him, always trying to bring me pleasure instead of taking his own.

That ends right now.

Jerking my chin from his grasp, I shove him— hard. A brief flash of surprise brightens his eyes as he falls back on the sofa, but it's gone as soon as my hands are on his belt, pulling it open and unfastening his pants. Hunter sucks in a sharp breath as I fist his cock, his arms suspended at his sides, fists clenching as if wanting to grab me but unsure if he trusts himself to allow it.

"How many times have you dreamed of this, Hunter?" I demand, gaze falling to the mass of steel between my fingers. He's thick and long, precum already glistening at his tip. I drop my head and lick it off, savoring the salty taste. "How many times have you thought of fucking my face and coming down my throat?"

A heady chuckle passes through his parted lips as he

watches me with wonderment. "Fuck, Bunny," he breathes, low and raspy. "You know, all you're doing is proving me right. Proving that you're *mine*."

His hips lift slightly, pumping himself into my fist. Another wave of liquid desire leaks from me, and I rub my thighs to alleviate some of the delicious ache. "If I'm yours, stop entertaining the thought of having another woman."

Lust shudders his face. "Then make me *yours*, Little Rabbit."

Slowly, he reaches for my head, threading his fingers through the silken strands at the base of my neck. "Now open that pretty fucking mouth and suck it like it belongs to you."

I open my mouth to spit back a scathing reply, but the second my lips part, Hunter shoves my head down, lifting his hips to slide his cock against my tongue. I'm not prepared for the invasion, and I gag as he hits the back of my throat—and he's only partway in. I clutch his thighs in a not-so-silent warning, my protest sending vibrations straight down his length.

Hunter's fist tightens in my hair as he groans, holding me in place with half his cock still exposed and ready for my mouth. "No, no, no," he murmurs, rotating his hand to collar my neck, his thumb stroking down the side. "Breathe through your nose, baby." His voice dips lower, huskier. "Then hold it while I cut off your airway."

I do as I'm told, refusing to break eye contact while I focus on my breathing until it's no longer possible. After a few moments of shuddered breaths and stuttered curses, he pulls out slightly. Greedily, I gulp in air around him as tears sting my eyes while my heart thumps wildly against my ribs.

I cut my reprieve short, relaxing and hollowing my cheeks, swirling my tongue around him as I start to bob my head.

"That's my girl," he praises.

My body ignites like fireworks on the Fourth of July. Arousal dripping down my thighs, nipples trying to pierce through my shirt.

As if he knows it, Hunter tilts and drops his gaze between my legs. "Spread them, baby. Let me see how wet you are with my cock shoved down your throat. Show me how pretty your pussy looks when it's begging to be filled the way I'm filling your mouth."

Fuck. Hunter's dirty talk is enough for me to abandon all rational thought. I follow his orders, reaching down to pull my skirt up. The cool air hits my soaked pussy as I dry hump the air, searching for any sort of relief.

"Oh, fuck," he draws out the word on a moan. "Look at my perfect fucking girl. Taking my cock so well." Hunter shifts, pressing in further as he reaches down to pinch a nipple through my clothes. I shift uncomfortably as a whimper vibrates in my throat—not one of pleasure, but pain. I must be about to start my period because that fucking hurt, and I don't normally have tender breasts.

The noise sends another vibrating hum around his cock. He sucks in a breath before chuckling, pressing my head down further. "Now, suck it, Bunny. Take it all down your throat like a good girl and don't you dare leave a fucking drop."

My throat constricts around him, and he throws his head back on the sofa, releasing a shuddering groan before snapping his head forward again, desperate not to miss a moment.

I take my time, savoring every inch of him as he pulls out and pushes in again, over and over, picking up the pace. Saliva pools at the corners of my mouth, drawing another groan from Hunter.

"You asked how many times I've thought of this," he murmurs, stroking my hair encouragingly. "How many times I've imagined fucking your face."

"Mmhmm," I moan around him, eliciting a sharp gasp followed by his dark chuckle.

"I can't give you a number, Little Rabbit, because it's been too many fucking times. But I can tell you, I'm going to make it a reality right now." Hunter's grip tightens as he slams back into my mouth.

He's true to his word, holding my head down as he snaps his hips with reckless abandon. Tears stream down my cheeks as he blocks my airway, stretching my throat as he forces himself in until I'm gagging and sputtering with my nose pressed against his pelvis. My nails dig into the meat of his thighs, wanting to take everything he has to give. Wanting to show him that there's no other woman on this fucking planet who can make him feel the way I do.

"Oh yeah. Fuck yeah. Such a good fucking girl taking

my cock. That's because your throat was made for it, wasn't it, baby? This is *my* fucking throat, just like that's *my* fucking pussy that's dripping all over the floor. Isn't it?"

I'm so focused on trying to please him, and not scrape my teeth along his swollen flesh, that I don't answer him. My eyes screw shut as he picks up his pace, relentlessly using my mouth in a way I didn't think he was capable of.

I don't hate it. In fact, I love the feeling of him using me like this. I love knowing it's me that makes him feel this way. Knowing he's thought of this with me for years. Me and no one else.

"Fuck, I love that mouth. That's it. Suck my cock like the little slut you are," Hunter growls.

An orgasm hits me, and I cry out around him, partly from the pressure giving way between my legs as I tense my lower body, and partly because it catches me completely off guard.

How did I possibly come from this? There wasn't even any stimulation, just humping the air as Hunter used my mouth.

"Fuck, you just came didn't you? You dirty fucking slut." Hunter lets me go to fist his cock. "Open that pretty mouth so I can come."

I stick my tongue out, breathing harshly as he pulls out and roughly pumps himself twice before thick, white jets of his cum shoot onto my tongue.

"Fuck, yes. So. *Fucking*. Good," he moans, sliding

himself back and forth until he's coated all of it. "Now swallow."

Once more, I do as I'm told, the thick substance leaving an aftertaste that floods my mouth with saliva. Hunter grips my face, pinching my cheeks to pop it back open. I stick my tongue out at him, showing that I swallowed every last drop he gave me.

Smug satisfaction flows through me. At least, until I watch his face shift, his features softening, as if he's just now realizing what he's done. How he just treated me.

He drops his hold like touching me burns him, and quickly tucks himself away, refusing to meet my eyes. "I'm gonna go."

What?

Suddenly, the fact that my lower half is on display, sticky and swollen with need, has me super self-conscious. I scramble to my feet, pulling my skirt down. "What? Why?"

Hunter doesn't answer me. Instead, he crosses the room, still fastening his pants, before bending to grab his broken phone from the floor.

"This was a mistake," he mutters, so silently I nearly miss it.

My cheeks heat as an embarrassed flush spreads through my body. "Why was this a mistake?"

I'm genuinely confused. A few minutes ago, this man was treating my mouth like a Fleshlight, and now he looks dissatisfied, like the product didn't meet his expectations.

Tears prick my lashes. "Was it not good?"

I hate that I ask. Hate the way my voice trembles and the damn breaks, letting a single tear fall.

Hunter whips around, his face pained, as if the question physically hurt him. "Are you serious?"

I shrug, forcing my voice steady. "You're acting disappointed."

"Tch." He huffs. "You want to know why I look disappointed?" At my lifted brows, he continues, "I look disappointed because all I've ever wanted to do was give you the world, but you'd rather I treat you like trash. It's so fucking sad."

I rear back as if he struck me. "Excuse me?"

"Yeah, you heard me." He steps closer, anger creeping in. "You don't respond to me being nice—to treating you the way you deserve. You get hot and bothered when I'm an asshole who just takes what he wants."

"Well excuse the fuck out of me for wanting to suck your dick, Hunter." What the actual fuck is his problem? I thought we just had a nice fucking time there. He sure as shit looked like he was having a blast two minutes ago. Why the sudden change of heart?

His answer lands like a stone. "I'm not your husband, Bunny." Melancholy roughens his tone. "You deserve more than what he did to you. You know that, right? You deserve flowers, and chocolates, and surprise dates just because it's Wednesday."

I flinch when his thumb drifts toward my scar. I didn't sticker it since I'm in the comfort of my own home, but I wish I had with the way Hunter is staring at the spot, pity heavy in his amber eyes.

"I seriously can't believe you're complaining right now." I smack his hand away.

"I'm not complaining," he says quickly. "What just happened was... incredible."

"Then why the fuck—"

"Because you deserve better," he cuts in. "And if that's what gets you going, I'm not judging. But you need to know you can also let yourself appreciate someone taking care of you—in every way that counts. This," he touches his chest, laying a palm over his heart, "is not contingent on *that*." He motions back to the sofa.

"Well color me confused. Because you seemed to enjoy yourself just as much as I did. I don't want sunshine and rainbows right now—you know that. So why are you turning this into something it's not?"

"Whatever. Keep denying your feelings." He shakes his head and moves past me toward the door.

"Only *you* would turn a blow job into a problem, Hunter!" I shout at his back, incredulous.

"And only *you* would let someone treat you like a whore but not let them love you the way you deserve."

A second later, the door slams.

What the actual fuck just happened?

"Wait... I'm confused. You literally had her on her knees, and you walked away?"

Shame courses through me, and it's not from attempting to wrangle giant balloons, dozens of pink-and-white cupcakes, and a shit ton of Pepto-colored decorations into *The Tipsy Taco* by myself.

Where the fuck are you, Little Rabbit?

"I didn't walk away. We finished our..." I glance around to make sure no one is listening—even though multiple pairs of eyes are on me and no one offers to help. "...*activities*, and *then* I left."

Now that I say it out loud, I realize how much of a jackass I was last night. Bunny's parting words followed me like a stage-five clinger through the rest of the night and all day today. The worst part is she's right. I took something that should've been monumental—a massive step in the direction I've always wanted—and made it feel tainted.

Every part of me enjoyed what we did. So why I felt

the need to say what I did is beyond me. I want to be with Bunny, not push her away. And ever since our night in the bathroom here at the bar, she's done exactly what Wrenley said she'd do. She calls more. Texts more. Finds reasons to stop by or invite me over. It's like the second she thought she'd lose me, she woke up and realized she didn't want that.

Only she's still withholding the one part I want most. Her heart.

"Cruel, Hunt." A hint of humor touches Wren's voice. "Effective. But cruel."

"Whatever. Tell me again why *I'm* the one setting up for your girlfriend's birthday party?" Alex nods at me as I haul all the crap to the back, where Vixey is arranging a pink tablecloth on a long table.

"Isn't Bunny with you?" There's shuffling in the background, and I swear I hear Dove grumble something about cleaning up Wrenley's puke.

The fuck?

"No. She's not answering her phone either." I mouth a silent *thank you* as Vixey takes the cupcakes. She beams before turning away, catching the corner of the nearest table and nearly toppling over with all four dozen confectionaries. Smiling sheepishly over her shoulder, she gives a slight shrug, then sets the boxes on another pink-clad surface.

Wren's voice drops, like he's trying to make sure Dove doesn't overhear. "Okay, well, I have to go. Text me if you hear from her. We're likely going to be running late."

"What are you two off doing, anyway? You're the one who wanted to throw this party, remember?" The fact that just months ago Wrenley and Dove pretty much hated each other—and now can't do anything without each other—is only *slightly* annoying.

My friend comes back to the city after years away and shacks up with the bubblegum princess after months of foreplay disguised as hatred, and all it does is make me obsess over why the fuck it's been years and things *still* haven't worked out with Bunny and me.

Wrenley's response is the rustle of fabric paired with Dove's giggles before the line goes dead.

"What a way to show your appreciation, jackass." I glare at my phone and pull up my message thread with Bunny.

Still nothing.

"What else can I help with?" Vixey's dulcet tone stills my hand before my fingers can fly, ready to send a rude message to my little rabbit about her whereabouts.

Dragging my gaze from my device, I notice the honey-blonde rubbing her forearm where two small, perfectly circular red spots stand out against her tan skin. "Did you get bit by something? You should take a Benadryl."

Her cheeks flame, and she reaches up to tuck a strand of hair that isn't there—a nervous tell. Instead, she twirls the end of her long ponytail. "Oh, it's nothing. Where's Bunny, anyway? I figured she'd be the one to bring all the decorations."

"I have no fucking clue." I dump the remaining mass

of pink on a pool table and pocket my phone. "Do you mind unraveling all this while I grab a drink?"

Vixey laughs and starts separating glittery garland from an orb of pastel-pink puffballs. "Sure thing. I don't mind helping at all."

She'd do anything to get on Bunny's good side, so I leave her to it and head to where Alex is drying a rack of still-steaming glasses. "Whiskey, neat. Make it a double. Please."

"Already that kind of night, huh? The party doesn't even start for another hour." His icy-blue eyes keep darting to Vixey through the steam, a faint pink hue climbing his cheeks when he catches my smirk. "What?"

"You've got it bad, man. Why don't you just ask her out already?"

"I don't think she's interested. And I don't wanna ruin our friendship." He slides the last rack out and shuts the washer, then deflects. "Speaking of ruined friendships, where's Bunny? This isn't exactly a party I thought she'd miss."

My phone is burning a hole in my pocket, but I refuse to check it. "Who knows. But like you said, the party doesn't start for another hour. I'm sure she'll show sooner or later."

Alex raises a sandy-blond brow. "That's unlike you. Usually you know where she is at all times."

With a resigned sigh, I take my drink and slide off the stool. After last night, I might've knocked back any progress with Bunny by a few months—if not more. And I swear, if she shows up with another guy tonight, I'll be in danger of losing my badge, because I'm done watching her parade other men around to get a rise out of me.

I'm done with our games. I love her, and she loves me. It's time she owns up to the truth and stops lying to us both.

Otherwise, I don't know how much more I have left in me to keep fighting.

With her. Or for her.

<u>Bunny</u>

"Ah, ah, ah." Swinging around the pole, I whip my heel across my victim's face as he tries to grab me again. The sharp point slices his chin, just below the thick tape I secured over his mouth. "What did I say about touching women who don't want to be touched, Rick?"

The zip ties binding his wrists to the chair arms make it impossible for him to reach me, but he strains against them anyway, mumbled curses buzzing in his throat until a vein stands out along his neck.

I take another spin. The steel is warm beneath my callused palms. I should really take a class—I'm not in a club often enough anymore to keep them from forming.

Rick screams and thrashes when the tip of my stiletto catches the vein and snags before the skin gives. It's like tearing tough meat—only this lump of flesh spurts as it splits. Blood sprays in an arc, painting the table, the floor, and me.

I slide down the pole and settle on the table, stretching languidly while he flails, trying to stop the bleeding—the ends of my wig soaking up crimson the longer I lounge. I'm not usually this macabre, but I'm in a mood, and my extensive research said Rick isn't carrying anything I can catch.

Propping my head on my hand, I hold his gaze as his life starts to fade. "What is it about so many men who beat their wives also tending to cheat? Can you enlighten me?"

He tries to speak, and the blood just gurgles faster.

Yep. Definitely nicked the artery.

"I don't want to hear your excuses." I drag my gaze from his shit-brown eyes along the length of my body, drumming my fingers against my cheek while I inspect the damage. "And look what you've done. I'm a bloody mess. You've already made me late, and now I'll have to go home and shower before my best friend's surprise birthday party. She's turning thirty, you know. Isn't that the same age your wife was when you put her in the hospital with a ruptured spleen?"

I return my gaze to his, only to find his eyes are lifeless. "Well, that's just rude. I was talking to you."

Jackknifing up, I use the ends of Rick's shirt to clean my heels, then cap the sharpened tips, not bothering to clean him up. I was careful not to touch his skin except when securing him to the chair, and I already wiped him down afterward.

Besides, I'm tired. Usually an easy kill like this takes nothing out of me, but I feel winded, like I just ran a half marathon. Dove keeps trying to get me into the gym, and I've never felt the need—or desire—before, but if a few swings around a pole and a little manhandling has me stopping to catch my breath before I get ready to leave, I'm gonna need to start lifting some weights.

Securing him took way more effort than usual. My height already works against me, and Rick nearly turned the tables when he tried to cash in on the promise I made to lure him to the private room: manhandling *me*.

Age is catching up to me... and apparently it's not planning to be kind.

Some sugar pop dance mix thumps through the speakers, loud enough to muffle any sound inside the small space Rick booked. After wiggling into a black shift dress, I unclip the synthetic blonde wig—my nose scrunching at the bloodied, matted ends. Thankfully, nothing has dried on my skin, and it's relatively easy to clean up so I don't trail any of Rick's remains behind me.

Like my moniker, I stick to the shadows, making sure no one notices as I slip out the side door and down the dark hall, taking the back exit and disappearing into the inky blackness that's fallen over the city.

My cheek tingles. The special effects makeup over my scar is tight and uncomfortable, but I keep it on until I'm a few blocks away and can hail a cab. While I check my phone, I peel it off, the tacky material tugging at the delicate skin hard enough to make my eyes water—and my mascara run.

Great. Even more of a mess to clean.

Hunter is already upset I'm running late. My home screen displays a pile of missed calls and messages like, *Where the hell are you?* and *How am I the one who got stuck doing this? She's your best friend and Wrenley's girl-friend for fuck's sake.*

If I weren't still pissed at him for the way he left last night, I'd almost feel bad for leaving him to set up for Dove's party alone.

Almost.

On my way. Sorry.

I don't bother explaining. But when Hunter texts back just as I exit the car, a new spark of irritation gives me a second wind. I race into the house to double-time getting ready.

HUNTER

Don't worry about it. Vixey and I have it taken care of.

"I'M SORRY. I was only trying to help." Vixey casts her honeyed eyes downward, rubbing her forearm where it looks like she's been bitten. The tone of her voice, paired with the fact that she may be hurt, quells my anger for a hot second—until Hunter appears behind her.

Red tunnels my vision as he has the audacity to set a gentle hand at her exposed waist, just above those obnoxious hot-pink cargo pants. The little tart lives in baggy pants and crop tops that barely cover her ridiculously sized breasts.

"You don't have to apologize, Vix. I appreciate everything you did to help." He croons it in her ear, deep and husky—like a lover about to get on their knees and make you see stars. I've been on the receiving end of that lilt. It'll tighten your nipples, raise goosebumps, and soak your panties whether you like him or not.

"Hands off, Hunt!" She swats at him with a playful smirk, twirling away to tend to some of Dove and Wrenley's coworkers.

Everything goes crimson as my eye twitches. "Oh, how cute. Now you have nicknames for each other. Did you take her to the bathroom, too? You know, to show your *appreciation.*"

"You don't get to be pissed off." His tone goes flat and aggravated as he steps into my space. "So you can fuck off with the attitude."

I recoil like he slapped me, and he leans with me as I edge away, taking up so much of my air I feel near suffocation. Instinct kicks in, and I bare my teeth. "*I* can fuck off? Excuse the fuck out of me, Hunter. After the way you left me last night, *you* can fuck off."

He huffs sardonically. "Doesn't feel so great to be used, does it, Bunny?"

We're drawing a crowd, numerous people who work at *Metro Media* pretending not to stare as we battle it out next to the pool table. I catch eyes with a pair of ladies who are stuffing their faces with cupcakes while they watch the show, and they jolt, turning away when I narrow my gaze at them.

"Maybe try treating people a little better. All Vixey did was what *you* were supposed to, but you couldn't even be bothered to show up on time for your own friend's party. And as for last night, I was giving you a taste of your own medicine." His sneer is foreign to me. I've seen him use it on many deserving people, but never me.

I don't like it—any of it—especially the insinuation I don't care about Dove.

"My own... my own *medicine*?" I cry in disbelief. "Are you fucking kidding me, Hunter? Every time you've gotten me off, I've offered to reciprocate. So what kind of bullshit are you trying to feed me right now?"

His nostrils flare, his gaze darkening with heat as I mention us being intimate. The space between us spikes in temperature. My cheeks flame, gaze dipping to his mouth as his lips curl at one corner, as if the memory amuses him.

And just like that, I want to drag him to the bathroom for round two. My thighs clench, my breasts ache, my fingers itch to sink into those perfectly styled curls and yank him down for a kiss.

"...those two can't stop bickering long enough to answer their damn phones!" Wrenley's outrage splashes between us like a bucket of ice water.

Hunter whirls and the moment shatters. I find my best friend's gaze. "Shit! Happy birthday, Love Dove!" I shout, waving for everyone to join in.

Guilt crashes over me. I've been a shit friend since she and Wrenley got serious. I wish I had a decent reason, but between her having less time for me and Hunter pulling away, I've never felt lonelier.

It's the worst excuse. From this night forward, I vow to do better. Dove deserves better.

"Aww, you guys shouldn't have. Thank you!" She beams, unbothered by my lack of attention to their arrival.

As Wrenley pulls Hunter away, Dove bombards me with questions. I shake my head and paste on a smile even though I'm annoyed.

Annoyed. Horny as hell. And very pissed I just fucked up my best friend's surprise party.

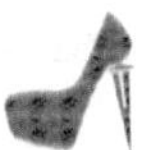

FALL IS EARLY THIS YEAR. The leaves are already turning yellow even though it's not quite September, and a cool chill rides the night breeze. Inside the bar, people laugh and clink shot glasses, merriment filtering through the open door to the sidewalk where I take a reprieve.

Dove and Wrenley look seconds away from their own bathroom sexcapades, and whether it's my earlier murderous activities or the heavy dose of irritation Hunter injected into my bloodstream, I don't feel like drinking.

I feel like taking Hunter home and having a repeat of last night. It's confusing—we haven't talked much since the birthday girl arrived—but the tension from earlier hasn't strayed far from that needy, aching place inside me.

Images of last night flash through my mind, stirring the edges of my arousal. The brick is cool against my back as I try to will away the flush creeping along my limbs.

"You're trembling." Hunter slides into my periphery, steps silent as a big cat.

I am. He mistakes my desire for being cold and sidles closer. "I'm sorry. For earlier. I shouldn't have gotten so upset, and I shouldn't have used Vixey to make you jealous."

Surprise flickers across my face as I look up at him. "I'd rather you apologize for the way you left last night."

He pivots, pressing me into the stone. His hands find my waist. His touch ignites my blood, a promise just ready for me to reach out and take for my own.

It's always been you.

It's always been us.

"I'm so sorry, Bunny. You didn't deserve that—me leaving in anger, or what I said. I should never have shamed you for wanting to feel that way during sex. I know it's your way of coping with what happened, but even if it weren't, I shouldn't have made you feel wrong. I'm truly, truly sorry."

Unbidden tears wet my eyes, a whirlwind of emotions sweeping through, leaving a disaster in its wake.

It's amazing just how much he still affects me. Nearly three years later and he still wrecks me—in the best and worst ways. Like the first night we met, when a handsome man made me feel like the most precious thing on earth after five minutes.

"Hunter..." I stop when he tenses, bracing for my inevitable pushback. Only, I don't want to push him away anymore. I'm tired of fighting my heart.

So very tired.

Tonight, I just want to exist with him. Not a serial killer and a detective. Just a man and a woman who love each other, with nothing in the way.

"I miss you." The declaration comes out a whisper. The din of the bar fades outside the bubble we make.

Surprise flickers in his whiskey eyes before he melts into me. His eyes close, forehead resting on mine, cupping my cheeks as he murmurs, "I'm right here, baby."

All it would take is for me to press up on my toes and seal our lips together. Something about the moment steals my breath as his ghosts over my freckles. A hot tear slides down my cheek and over his thumb.

"I've always been right here. I'm not going anywhere." He opens his eyes, and I drown in amber.

I don't know which of us moves first. One moment we're lost in each other's gaze, the next, we're found by each other's lips.

Hunter tastes like a future I never thought I'd get.

Like my forever.

Like home.

TWO YEARS AGO

NATHANIEL'S wild eyes blaze with palpable fury. His nostrils flare, skin flushed red with anger—likely as hot as his palm—when he strikes me across the face. My freshly healed scar stings, the skin stretching uncomfortably as my head whips to the side.

"Did you think I wouldn't find out?" My husband's tone is deadly calm, a complete contradiction to his outrage. It sets my nerves on edge, the frayed ends humming with adrenaline as I crabwalk away, even though my limbs keep giving out.

"I–I didn't—"

"No. You didn't, did you, Bunny?" he sneers, voice sardonically sweet. "You thought you'd get an abortion and I wouldn't find out? You're lucky you didn't go through with it."

"I don't want a baby." Pressing the back of my hand to my swollen cheek, I use the counter to stand. "And I want a divorce."

I'm done.

I've had enough.

The last few weeks have been hell, almost as if Nathaniel looked up how to abuse your pregnant wife without harming the baby. He's grabbed me, bruised me, pinched me, pulled my hair, and fucked me every chance he's had.

Still punishing me for Hunter. Still driving home that I'm *his* wife and there's nothing I can do to change that.

Nathaniel smirks, rubbing his thumb along his bottom lip as he turns his head and chuckles. I don't dare take my eyes off him as I run my hand along the counter, searching for anything to fend him off.

"You're so fucking ungrateful. I picked you up out of the gutter and gave you a better life."

Two strides and he's pressing me into the counter, my back bowing, his face in mine as spittle speckles my cheek. I try to push him away, but he grips my throat and forces me to look at him.

"And how do you repay me? By fucking some other guy and trying to get rid of our baby? And now you're trying to leave? What—do you think *Hunter* is going to take you in? A street rat who was *nothing* before I found her. You were nothing, Bunny!"

My neck aches under his hand. He's careful not to

cut off my airway completely, but his fingers dig in like he's trying to rip out my trachea. Panic mixes with adrenaline, giving me a last surge of strength as I struggle to get free.

I want to scream that no, I don't think Hunter will take me in. He seems to have given up after numerous attempts at begging me to leave—smart enough to know what happens within these walls. Yet he stopped reaching out two weeks ago. He never came back for me.

None of that matters. All that matters is I won't be a punching bag anymore. Since the gala it's only gotten worse. Any minuscule drop of love I had evaporated when we found out I was pregnant.

What happens if I bring his baby into this world? Will he take his anger out on them? Keep beating me? Will my child grow up in an abusive home, learning a warped definition of love—or that women are objects to be used and discarded?

No. I refuse to add to the list of statistics I've already become.

With every ounce of strength I possess, I launch my weight into Nathaniel, successfully knocking him back a few steps. He grins, laughs, tightens his fist, preparing to knock me back. "I love it when you fight. It reminds me of the feral thing you were when we met."

Using the momentum as he shoves me, I grab his arm and pivot left, bringing me closer to the dinner I'd been prepping when he got home.

Rump roast.

The knife is too far. My nails dig into the meaty top layer of the still-semi-frozen slab, threatening to break under its weight. Nathaniel realizes my intention a moment too late as I swing the marbled meat into his face, hard enough that he drops me. Before he can recover, I swing again, a war cry rumbling in my throat.

This time, I knock him off balance. I swing again. Something cracks. Euphoria floods me as I realize I have the upper hand. The roast squishes in my grip, the icy core numbing my fingertips as I drop and straddle his dazed form.

"This is for every time you put your hands on me!" I bring the meat down on his face. A satisfying crunch rewards me as blood bursts in cascading rivulets from his nose.

"This is for every time you fucked another woman while we were married!" Something gives as I strike again. A pained cry gurgles from his throat, but I give him no reprieve. I want him to feel everything—every ounce of pain, every blow, every bone as it caves. He never once gave me a break when he was beating me. He'll find no mercy here.

"This is for trying to make me carry a child I don't want!" Nausea swells violently in my stomach as the center of his facial cavity ruptures and sinks in. Blood sprays, coating me, arcing over the floor, splattering the stainless-steel appliances. Adrenaline stomps the sick feeling down for later.

"And this!"

Smash.

"This is for every—"

Smush.

"—single time you made me—"

Squelch.

"—feel like it was all my fault!"

By the time I finish, my fingers are buried to the second knuckle. Bits of roast mash away, mixing with the pulped mass of bone, blood, and cartilage that was Nathaniel's face.

My lungs burn as I gulp air around a shudder, my neck tender where he grabbed me. Falling back onto my butt between his legs, I finally let the tears come.

I cry because I just committed murder.

I cry because I'm finally free.

But most of all, I cry because pregnancy hormones suck, and I have hated every second of growing another body inside mine so far.

It must be nearly twenty minutes I sit with my fingers stabbed into the rump roast like it's a hand muff. My tears give way to hysterical laughter as I remember the criminal who chopped up bodies and broke them down in pressure cookers.

I just became like him... a killer.

Because of course Nathaniel had to take my last shred of innocence, too.

"Hey, Siri," I call. Thankfully it's close enough to hear me from the kitchen table. I wait for the soft robotic prompt. "Call Sergeant Rhodes."

Reality settles in as the line begins to ring.

I killed someone. I killed my husband. I'm a murderer.

"Bunny? Is everything okay?" Hunter's frantic voice fills my ear after the third ring, triggering fresh tears as the adrenaline ebbs.

"Hunter." His name is shaky as I try not to sob. Copper pools in my mouth, a metallic tang as my teeth dig into my bottom lip.

"Where are you? I'll be right there."

Always so in tune with my feelings. He knows with just a simple utterance of his name that I need him. That's all it takes for him to come to my rescue.

I should've left with him when I had the chance.

"Home." The single word rasps out, hoarse and wet.

"Don't move. I'm on my way."

I can't move, though I try. Shock sinks in, my blood turning cold as Nathaniel's begins to coagulate.

And that's how Hunter finds me.

Sitting on my kitchen floor, the roast still skewered on my fingers, in a pool of sticky blood and dried tears.

Hunter

Holy fuck.

Even if Bunny had told me what happened before I arrived, I don't think anything could have prepared me for this.

Blood. Is. Everywhere. And Bunny is in the middle of it, staring at Nathaniel's body, her eyes flat and haunted.

It takes far too long to realize the lump of meat

between her hands isn't part of her husband's face. I'm ashamed I have to take a few gulps of clean air before stepping into the kitchen, which smells like the inside of a butcher shop.

"Bunny?" I approach carefully, not wanting to startle her. She's in shock—her small frame trembles like she's outside in winter, stark naked. Angry purple fingerprints mar the skin around her neck, no doubt her husband's work, and her bottom lip looks busted. Mascara streaks her cheeks like coal watercolor. It makes the reddened skin of her cheek stand out, giving the surrounding flesh a charred effect.

"Bunny?" I try again, kneeling beside her, doing my best to keep clear of the blood spatter. She still doesn't respond, so I touch her chin, guiding her face toward me. "Little Rabbit?"

Awareness sparks in the depths of her forest gaze. A whoosh of breath leaves her lungs as tears spring to her eyes. "Hunter?"

"Yeah, it's me." I brush her hair off her shoulder, skimming my fingertips against the bruises. Fury rolls off me in waves. If Nathaniel weren't already dead, I'd kill him myself. "It's okay, Bunny. I've got you now."

"He... he... he," she hiccups.

"Shhh. It's okay. You don't have to explain. Come on, let's get you cleaned up." I help her off the floor since both her hands are buried inside what looks like a roast.

She must've snapped and grabbed what she could to defend herself, though the butcher knife on the counter might've been a better choice.

Her fingers are gnarled and curved, frozen from clutching the makeshift weapon so long. She stays silent, breaths shallow and shuddering as she stands at the sink and lets me clean her hands. We start with lukewarm water to coax her fingers to relax, and when I can finally massage them straight, I turn the faucet to hot and grab the soap. Blood and bits of meat dislodge from under her nails, sliding into the farmhouse-style stainless basin and whirling down the drain in orange-red swirls and white, foamy bubbles.

"You're okay. I've got you now. He can't hurt you anymore. I've got you, Little Rabbit." I repeat it over and over, trying to soothe her, trying to be as comforting as I can, considering the circumstances.

When we're done, her skin is bright pink and warm to the touch. "I'm going to make a few phone calls to get this taken care of. Okay?"

Tears spring to her eyes again, and she shakes her head vigorously. "No. Please. Don't tell anyone."

"Bunny, I have to. We can't clean this up ourselves. I don't even know the first thing about—" I cut myself off, remembering the story Keels told us about the pressure cookers.

I think about it for a second.

Only a second.

"No." I shake my head. "I'm going to call Keels and James."

My heart breaks when Bunny's face crumples in fear. "You can't!"

"It'll be okay. I promise." I turn away to make the

call, fully aware it's a promise I can't keep. Everyone loves Bunny at the department, though. Between James and me, some of the senior staff already know her situation.

So I say a prayer to whoever's listening and hope for the best.

"Fucking hell," Phillip Keels breathes, taking in the scene. "She really did a number on him, didn't she?"

"He did a fucking number on her. She looks okay, though. I don't think she needs a hospital. Unless she wants to go," Abigail James chimes in, stepping to Keels' other side.

"This'll be a mess to clean."

"Simple. Burglary gone wrong. Remington already cleaned her up—there's not much evidence she did it. We'll say she didn't know who to call."

"People know what he was doing to her, James."

I bristle just thinking about it. The fact that we knew what was going on, and that there wasn't much we could do. The fact that the harder I tried to get Bunny to leave her husband, the more she pulled away from me.

I should've stopped it.

I should've been the one to kill him.

"She's one of ours, Keels. I don't care what we have to do—she's not going away for this." James sounds ashamed—for not stepping in when I went to her, for not noticing sooner, I don't know.

"So we're going to cover it up? She'll be okay?" I exhale, relieved. I knew I could trust them. Ethically sound or not, I don't care. It was self-defense.

"I don't know if she'll be okay. You should keep a close eye on her. We'll give it a few days. She'll need therapy and probably a long-ass time to heal." James glances over her shoulder at Bunny, still immobile at the table.

"And a place to stay. We'll get guys in here to clean this up." Keels pulls out his phone to start rallying the troops, or so I assume.

"I'll take her to my place. She'll be most comfortable with me."

They hum in agreement and start making calls. Bunny lifts her gaze when I approach, terror brightening the green in her eyes. She straightens in alert, but before she can speak, I shake my head and cradle her cheeks. "Everything's okay. I told you—I got you."

"You got me," she repeats in a whisper, slumping back into the chair, relief washing over her features.

"Always, Little Rabbit. I'll always catch you when you fall. I promise."

By the time we reach my place, Bunny seems more herself. She even asks if we can grab pizza at her favorite spot down the block from my brownstone. It's not the first time she's been here in the last year, but it's the first time nothing stands in the way of us being together.

It may seem fast, but I don't give a fuck. The only obstacle to having her is gone. I don't care how long she needs to heal. I don't care how long until she's ready for a relationship.

Bunny is finally mine.

But I'd be a total asshole to treat her as anything but delicate tonight.

Even if my dick jumps when she comes downstairs post-shower in one of my old department T-shirts.

"I could live in there." She sighs dreamily as she sinks onto the sofa beside me. Not on the other side. Not even one cushion over. She sits so close our thighs press together, then leans forward to steal a pepperoni off a slice. "Seriously, you're so lucky your mom left this place to you."

My home's been in the family for generations. Long paid off, I've updated it over the years. It's more space than I need, but my mother gave it to me with hopes I'd fill the halls with another generation of Remingtons.

Another generation I want with Bunny.

"Thank you... for tonight," she whispers, settling in. My shirt rides high on her thigh, and I realize she isn't wearing the shorts I set out. Which means she's either in just underwear... or bare.

The thought sends a ripple of lust through me, and my little rabbit seems to catch the scent. Unabashed, she lays her hand on my thigh and turns to face me.

"You finally get what you want, Hunter," she rasps.

Her fingers trail toward the bulge in my sweats, her eyes dropping to my mouth. She leans in, and it takes every ounce of willpower to stop her.

As long as I've dreamed of this, I cover her hand with mine. "I want you to be okay, Bunny. What happened tonight was... *is*... a lot. When this," I gesture between us, "happens, I want it to be because you want it and you're ready. Not because you're trying to cope with a trauma."

"Hunter, please," she begs, swinging a leg to straddle my waist. "This is what I need right now. I need to stop thinking. Stop feeling."

Her hands wrap around mine, small and warm as she slides them under the shirt to the tops of her thighs where they meet her hips. Heat roars through me.

Fuck me. She's not wearing anything beneath the shirt.

My self-control is near snapping. I've kept it on a tight leash for so long where she's concerned that half of me wants to say fuck it and give her what she wants.

But I'm a better man than her husband. I won't take advantage.

As if she reads my thoughts, she dips and presses a chaste kiss to my lips.

Our *first* kiss.

I go rigid—everywhere. I'm trying to do the right thing. But then her fingers curl around my cock over my sweats and it's game over. Pitching forward, I cradle her neck, careful of the bruises, and kiss her the way I've always wanted. She mewls, and I swallow the sound, chasing her mouth, learning every inch.

She rocks against me, the movement shifting my

thumb closer to her center. "Please, Hunter. Make me numb."

"Fuck, Little Rabbit. The last thing I'm going to do is make you feel numb." I slide my hand down, finding her already slick with want. A cry flies from her throat as her head tips back.

It's the most beautiful thing I've ever seen—Bunny in the throes of pleasure—and it's all I want to see for the rest of my life.

"I'm going to make you feel *everything*."

SUNLIGHT FILTERS THROUGH THE WINDOW, casting a ray across my face and rousing me from sleep. With a groan, I stretch before reaching over for Bunny.

Her side of the bed is empty. The sheets are cold, like she's been up a while.

I snap fully awake, tug on sweats, and head downstairs. "Bunny?"

A hot cup of coffee and snuggling my girl—before burying my face between her legs—sounds like the perfect way to spend the morning. Last night was the best of my life, and by the way I made Bunny come undone again and again, I'd say she had a good time too.

Only, she isn't in the kitchen. She's not in the living room, either. Her clothes are still on my bathroom floor, so she can't be far.

I'm passing the front door to head back upstairs when I see it.

A white sheet taped to the heavy, carved wood.

My mouth pulls down, a sense of dread blossoms in my chest and limbs.

I peel the paper free and unfold it.

Two words in Bunny's neat script.

I'm sorry.

I KNOW WHAT YOU ARE.

The magazine clippings curl at the edges, not fully glued to the thin paper wedged between a flyer for a new ice cream shop and a notice about upcoming construction.

Forensics never found prints on the first letter, and I doubt this one will be any different.

"We need to invest in a doorbell camera, boys." I don't know why I haven't done that already—especially considering the things I do in the basement.

What's Dove always say about us?

Oh, right.

Worst serial killers ever.

Yasha and Maru yip in response, shaking out their freshly groomed coats. Yasha trots back into the living room, probably in search of a toy, but Maru doesn't stray from my feet, staring up with beady black eyes.

"What is it, Maru? You're not getting my sushi, buddy. Auntie Dove just brought you your own treats—this is Mommy's." He cocks his head, snowy ears flicking as he stares into my soul.

For a moment, I wonder if he senses something I don't. A smell... or a canine sixth sense about where the letters are coming from. They say animals pick up on those things, and the dogs do like to sit in the sill of the window by the front door.

Then he licks his lips, dashing my paranormal theory. He just wants my food.

I tuck the note in my bag to take to work and try my luck with prints again, shove the last piece of shrimp tempura in my mouth, and head to the back door to double-check the lock before leaving.

Part of me thinks I should take the messages more seriously. But are they even threats? Should I cool it on the killing until I figure out who's sending them? My sense of self-preservation is clearly lacking because I'm more preoccupied with the fact that my pants feel tight today than with someone possibly playing a prank—or worse... having found me out.

Sabrina in forensics gives me a look as I hand over the newest letter. "Is everything alright, Bunny? Are you receiving threats?"

"It's a friend who's getting them." I purse my lips and stare at a random spot behind her like I'm solving a complicated case, when really I'm trying to keep my lunch from reappearing all over her workstation.

Note to self: no more sushi for a while.

Even cooked, my stomach rejects my favorite shellfish. A lump forms in my esophagus and heartburn spiders through my chest. Nausea rolls like I'm about to yeet my food back out, whole and undigested.

Apparently it's written all over my face.

Hunter nudges me gently as I enter the briefing room. "You okay? You look sick."

I meet his whiskey gaze and swallow. Warmth encompasses me as concern brightens his features, chasing away the queasiness when he brushes my hair over my shoulder.

"I'm okay. I think I just ate some bad sushi." Leaning into his touch, I soak up the affection, uncaring who sees.

For some reason, my eyes sting, and Hunter's narrow in suspicion before he pulls me into a hug. "What's wrong, Little Rabbit?"

I wish I knew.

I almost laugh at the absurdity. This isn't me. I don't randomly cry—certainly not at work. And while everyone knows Hunter and I are close, I've never let him touch me like this in front of anyone here.

My hands clench into his sides as I focus on my breathing, forehead pressed to his chest. He runs his fingers lightly down my back and jokes, "Where did you get sushi from? Remind me never to eat there if it makes you cry."

This time, I do laugh.

Settling into his warmth, I simply enjoy the feeling of his arms around me. Dove and Wrenley interrupted our kiss right when it was getting good at her birthday party, and Hunter's been busy on a new case, so I've barely seen him.

I don't even feel weird about the PDA. I'm not sure what exactly changed for me all of a sudden, but I want everyone to know he's mine. It's like a light switch clicked in my chest, turning fear and unease about our situation into a desire to move full-speed-ahead.

A feral need to claim him—publicly and thoroughly —so all the badge bunnies know exactly who holds his heart.

"I have to brief the team on a new case. But after work, we can hang out if you want? Spend some time together... *uninterrupted.*" His voice heats on the last word, the insinuation as clear as the way he presses into me, desire pouring off the hard planes of his body in fiery waves.

Sweat beads at the base of my neck and trickles down my spine, leaving goosebumps in its wake. Letting him go with a nod, I lift my hair and fan myself, relishing his smirk as he swipes a thumb along my cheek before heading to the front.

I love watching Hunter work.

Eighteen months ago, when I returned to the department after disappearing for half a year, I was excited to see my friend again—the skinny Narcotics detective who knew exactly how to make me laugh and who'd given me the single most incredible night of my life.

But the guy I found in his place was different. Instead, I found him in the Homicide department, nearly doubled in size, his thick, muscled form filling out his suit in ways it hadn't before. Curls combed and styled into submission, a hint of stubble on his jaw, glasses nowhere in sight. Hunter had been handsome when I left. What I came back to was criminal—and the worst part is he knew it.

No, scratch that.

The worst part is that I threw it all away because of my trust issues.

Only, judging by the way he's looking at me now, it was never thrown out—just stored away until I was ready.

Which I am.

So ready, that I—

A cold sweat breaks across my face. It sweeps down my limbs as saliva pools in my mouth. My stomach cramps. My hand flies to cover it.

You will not throw up right now. You will not throw up right now.

I scan for a trash can. No time to sprint to the bathroom. My insides are done being tamped down.

Hunter stops briefing, eyes locking on me. "You okay, Bunny?"

Everyone turns.

Two seconds later, my cheeks puff and my lunch hits the floor between my feet.

Not-so-fun fact: shrimp tempura does not feel great coming back up. It also does not taste the same the second time.

"Fuck!"

"Gross, Bunny!"

"Dude, seriously?"

Geez, you'd think a bunch of Homicide detectives could handle a little puke. Hunter's rich tenor rises above the assholes. "Hey, you're okay. It's okay."

His warm fingers brush my nape as he pulls my hair out of my face. "Someone get a trash can!" he snaps, then goes soft again. "I got you. Bad sushi, hmm, Little Rabbit?"

My only response is a groan before another swell of rice and seaweed erupts from my mouth.

"HAVE I mentioned how much I hate that you still live here?" Hunter unlocks the back door and immediately drops to greet the dogs with a sugary baby voice that makes him sound like Ryan Reynolds doing Deadpool. "Hiya, boys. Who's such good doggies? You are! That's right. You are!"

Yasha and Maru ignore me completely, barking and pogoing on Hunter's legs like he's their owner. "What am I? Chopped liver?"

I follow him in, rubbing my stomach, still sore from the violent retching. By the time I've locked up and turned around, Hunter is holding both dogs like babies, cooing at them in an unintelligible language.

"For fuck's sake, you'd think you're the one who feeds them and walks them and makes sure they always have their favorite toys and treats," I deadpan.

He ignores me, still crooning like a proud papa. "Mommy is just grumpy because she doesn't feel good. No, she doesn't. We're gonna help her get into comfy clothes, put on her favorite show, and snuggle with crackers and ginger ale, aren't we, boys?"

"You don't have to do any of that. But by all means, since they love you more than me, take them when you go. Don't let the door hit you on your way out." I head to my room, desperate to get out of my tight black pants and into something less constrictive.

I need a shower and a good teeth cleaning before I lie down. And for some reason, chicken noodle soup sounds delicious—even though I just expelled lunch at work. The kind with thick egg noodles and creamy broth.

"How about you clean up, and I'll run out to grab some things and take the boys with me? You always like the soup from that place when you're not feeling well. That sound good?"

I don't know why my eyes flood as a surge of emotion hits—just because he knows exactly what I need. I hum noncommittally, wiping at my eyes as he grabs the leashes and ushers the dogs out without another word.

Under the warm spray, memories bombard me. Hunter and I work together so well—like an oiled machine—whether it be at work or in life. We're so in tune it's remarkable I've lasted this long without giving in to my feelings—giving in to him.

Everything about us is already established. Maybe that's what makes us different from Nathaniel and me. Hunter and I took years to *know* each other. Nathaniel and I bonded over shared childhood trauma and fell in love fast. I didn't truly know who I was marrying... not until the papers were signed and I was legally bound to the monster.

But with Hunter, whatever haze has been clouding my decision to keep my heart locked away has lifted. My rationale has evaporated. I want to skip the early stages of romantically pursuing someone. We're way past that point.

Hunter's mine and I am his—and why the hell have I been holding back when he's all I've ever wanted? I mean... besides the part where I'm a serial killer and he's actively trying to figure out who I am.

The questions persist as the steam fills my bathroom. By the time I've changed into black Soffe shorts and an oversized tee—the same one Hunter lent me *that* night—he's back, emptying soup into a bowl, crackers fanned around it, pouring ginger ale into my lavender Stanley.

Gratitude blooms as he lifts the ottoman tray and nods toward the living room. "Scoot, Little Rabbit. I queued up where you left off on *Inuyasha*. How many times have you rewatched that now? Ten? Twelve?"

My cheeks heat as I mumble, "Twenty-three."

Hunter's brows shoot up. "Jesus. I can't imagine loving a show that much."

It's my comfort show, I inwardly pout. Outwardly, I snap, "Don't shame me."

"I'm not shaming you!" he protests as I climb onto the sofa and tug a rolled throw from the wall holder. "I *am* thinking about slapping your ass right now, though, not gonna lie. It's like a juicy peach staring at me, begging me to take a bite."

Laughter bubbles up as I get comfortable. "Shut up and give me my food." I make grabby hands, mouth watering as he sets the tray on the ottoman and slides it toward me.

While he's still bent over, I grab his shirt and pull him down for a quick kiss. He freezes, shocked, and I just smile like it's the most normal thing. "Thank you for taking care of me. Did *you* get food? You'll stay, right?"

A slow smile spreads across his face, making my heart flutter. "Yeah, I'll stay."

<u>Hunter</u>

"Bokutachi waaaaa..."

I startle awake to the end of an episode blaring over the TV. The character Maru is named after stares into the distance, his long, fluffy tail-cape thing drifting behind him as the credits roll.

My sudden movement doesn't so much as disturb Bunny, who slumbers peacefully at my side with her legs kicked out over the cushions and her head propped on the pillow I grabbed from her bed earlier.

Her long raven locks spill over my lap, and I realize that at some point while we were sleeping, we must have reached for each other, because our fingers are laced together, resting at the curve of her waist.

A sense of completeness settles in my chest. I love this woman so much, and it seems like she's finally coming around to the idea of letting me in. I don't know what changed, but I'm not going to look a gift horse in the mouth.

This feels right. It feels like home. It feels like all my patience has finally paid off, and for once, the nice guy isn't finishing last.

I run my free fingers through her silky strands, relishing the scent of raspberries and jasmine that consumes my senses as I play with her hair. A contented sigh leaves her parted lips, and she snuggles deeper into her pillow.

"Hunter…" she murmurs in her sleep.

"Shh. I'm right here, baby. I'm not going anywhere."

Except at that exact moment, Maru's ears flick forward and his head whips toward the front door. In a split second he goes from splooting next to his brother—who remains unbothered—to alert and on his feet.

A low growl rolls out of his tiny chest, raising the hair on my arms.

Gently, I untangle myself from Bunny and rise. "What is it, boy?"

Maru looks up at me, his little body shaking as he

immediately steps to my side and herds me out of the room. I pause at the threshold, looking back at Bunny to see that Yasha is now on the couch in the spot I just occupied, alert and rigid, as if protecting her.

Slowly, I creep into the kitchen to grab my gun. Maru continues to the front door, sniffing along the bottom while his ears swivel back and forth. His growl deepens.

My heart jumps into my throat when a rustle outside makes him bark. Small or not, he sounds like he means business and begins scratching at the door, alternating between growls and short, sharp barks.

The glass on the heavy wooden door is rippled, distorting the image of the outside. With the impending night growing darker, I can't make anything out, but the noise on the other side grows louder with each step I take.

"I swear... if you're making all this racket over a squirrel, we're gonna have words." I meet his gaze. His investigation ceases and he plops into a sit, head tilting in that ridiculous, adorable way only dogs manage.

Suddenly, the noise on the other side stops, and the thud of heavy footsteps running away fills the air. I lunge for the door and curse when I have to stop and unlock both the deadbolt and the regular lock before I can throw it open and sprint down the stoop.

By the time I make it to the street, there's no one around.

"Note to self: install a doorbell camera." I've had

Bunny's place under surveillance for a while now—unbeknownst to her.

A good hunter must also be an excellent stalker.

And I am one of the very best when it comes to my little rabbit. But it seems she's now the subject of a trespasser—one who keeps leaving her notes—and I'd bet my badge he was just outside her door.

I spin to see Maru sniffing the bushes next to the stoop. He lunges beneath them to inspect something, and a nagging feeling twists in my gut. "Maru! No!"

Surprisingly, he jumps back and trots to my side as I approach the greenery warily. "Go in the house, boy." I motion to the door and wait until he's safe inside, his little head peeking out to watch me, before I duck down to see what caught his interest.

Below the bush sits a heaping pile of cherries, and if my memory serves me, cherry pits are toxic to dogs.

Motherfucker.

He's targeting them—to make it easier to break in later.

With as much shit as I've installed in Bunny's house, I'm an absolute idiot for not doing anything to the outside. It should've been the first thing I did when she told me about the letters, even if I've spent more time casing her place than I've been at my own home.

I can't always be with her, and I have to keep her safe. That's always been my number one priority... especially since she has a habit of getting herself into precarious situations.

As soon as I gather the toxic fruit in a bag and toss it

in the trash, I double-check all the doors are locked before heading back to the living room. Yasha is curled on Bunny's stomach, watching me with his beady little eyes, while Maru happily gnaws a yak-milk chew.

"Come on, little guy. Let's get your mom to bed."

Yasha's black tufted ears flatten, and he lunges for my hand when I try to remove him, sharp teeth sinking into the flesh between my thumb and index finger. His high-pitched snarl startles Bunny, and she springs up, sending him tumbling to the floor.

She nearly topples back onto the couch as the movement puts us close. "Did he just try to bite you?" Her voice is laced with sleep, eyes half-open as she stares between me and the black ball of fur.

"Yeah, he's never done that before. I was just going to move you to your bedroom." Yasha stares, unblinking, as if I'm a threat.

"What's wrong, boy? Did Daddy scare you?" Bunny coos, bending to scoop him up.

For the second time tonight, surprise flicks across my face, seizing my heart in a vise grip. If she realizes what she called me, she doesn't correct herself as she nuzzles Yasha's fur.

He remains steadfast in his mission to keep me from her. I reach to scratch his head and he nips at me again.

What the hell happened between me going outside and now?

I've known the dogs their whole lives, and neither has ever so much as growled at me.

"I'm starting to take personal offense here, bud. What did I do to piss you off in the last ten minutes?"

"They've both been moody lately," she mutters through a yawn, setting him down. "Very yappy and very snarly toward men when we're out on walks."

She leans into me, lays her head on my chest, and wraps her arms around my waist. "I'm so tired. I'm going to go back to bed."

I press a kiss to the top of her head, holding her to me, breathing her in—trying to hold on to any piece of her I can in case she wakes tomorrow and her feelings revert to normal. "See you tomorrow?"

Her fingers dance along my waist and down my arm, then lace with mine. Gold-flecked pine gazes up at me as a rosy hue breaks over her cheeks, highlighting her freckles and the shimmering silver of her scar. "Stay the night?"

"Are you sure?" My free hand drifts along her cheekbone, the barest touch against her soft skin as I search her face for any sign she'll regret this tomorrow.

"Yes," she breathes, pulling me down. The kiss starts soft and sweet before turning into an inferno I fully intend to pour gasoline on once we get to the bedroom.

I lift her and head upstairs. She wraps her legs around my waist, intentions clearly aligned with mine as she shifts and shoves my hand down the waistband of her shorts.

That went from zero to sixty real fast, but who am I to deny my horny rabbit?

She cries out—the sweetest sound—and I swallow it

with my tongue as I swipe my fingers through her soaked center. "Hunter," she mewls against my lips.

"That's right, baby. Who's making you feel this way?" I growl, dragging my mouth down her neck to nip at her flesh.

"You are." She sinks her fingers into my hair, pulling me closer as I work her skin between my lips and teeth, sucking the sensitive spot that has her grinding against me.

"And who's the only one who can make you feel this way?" I kick open her door, sinking my fingers into her as I lay her on the bed.

"You," she whines, legs spreading as her hips chase my hand.

Bunny thrashing in the throes of pleasure is the prettiest thing I've ever seen. I want to commit each second to memory as the heavy reality of her waking tomorrow and changing her mind lingers in the air, trying to suffocate my hope that things have shifted between us for good.

My little rabbit lifts her hips and I tear her shorts down with one hand, the other fucking her as I work my pants open. She grabs at me with desperate, needy sounds, using her feet to usher me forward while she frees my cock and aligns it beside my arousal-covered fingers.

I pull them from her, fisting my cock and notching myself at her entrance, pushing in enough to bow her back—then stop.

"And who does this pretty pussy belong to, Little

Rabbit?" I rasp, gathering her wrists above her head. Heavy, ragged breaths shudder my lungs as I wait for her answer.

Bunny struggles against my hold, feet locking at my backside and digging in to slide me farther inside. My dark chuckle fills the room as I resist, savoring her impatient whimpers.

"Who does it belong to, Little Rabbit?" I repeat, jaw clenched, keeping a hold on my instincts. I want to claim her. Thoroughly wreck her and make her mine.

"You!" she finally cries, head digging into the mattress as I sink into her to the root before she even finishes the word. "You, Hunter. I've always belonged to you."

Abandoning her wrists, I hitch her legs into the crooks of my arms to thrust deeper, and her body welcomes me like a snug winter jacket. Soft and warm and comfortable. As soon as her hands are free, she's pulling at me everywhere, hips rolling to meet mine, tugging my shirt to yank me down to her.

"Always," she whispers before kissing me. "There's never been anyone but you."

I've always known it, but hearing her say it means more than spying on her to find it out. I don't say it back because she already knows. I've been proving myself to her since the moment we met. With my words. My actions. With the way I worship her body and never ask for anything in return. And now she's finally opening up to me, blossoming like a rare flower after so much care, devotion, and nurturing.

"I'm so close," she warns. "Come with me."

I don't tell her she never has to ask. I'll follow her anywhere—as many times as she wants me to.

And I plan on there being many, many times tonight.

I don't tell her about the intruder at her door. Or the pile of cherries left for the dogs. I don't want to cause her stress, and I selfishly want to enjoy our time.

I can tell her everything in the morning.

After I wake her with my head between her legs.

Once I'm sure her feelings haven't changed.

WARM FINGERS BRUSH *my hair off my face. A gentle touch of lips to my forehead. "I have to go, baby."*

I don't want him to leave.

His chuckle is a throaty rumble that sends electric pulses through my body as it remembers all the things he whispered the night before: all the promises he made and all the plans he laid bare before me.

His map for our future.

So why is he leaving me?

"No, don't leave. Come back to bed," I whine. Between my legs is warm and wet and waiting for him to sink back into the space where he fits so perfectly.

"Something came up. Trust me, if I could stay, I would." Another kiss. This time on my lips. "Call me when you wake up."

"Please don't go..." My words trail off as exhaustion fights my consciousness and wins, dragging me back under the watery waves of slumber.

"Goodbye, Little Rabbit. I love you."

"Goodbye? Why are you saying goodbye?"

"You know why."

"No I don't."

Silence.

"Hunter?"

Darkness creeps into the edges of the room, swirling ominously as whispers begin to echo off the tightening walls.

"I know what you did."

"I know what you are."

"Time's up, Little Rabbit."

"Time's up."

"Time's—"

"No!" My eyes snap open to see two sets of shiny black eyes staring at me. Maru barks as Yasha lays his head over my racing heart with a whine.

It was just a dream.

Fuck, it felt so real.

The dogs both nudge my hands, and with a smile and a yawn, I scratch behind their ears. "Good morning to you, too, boys. What gives?"

Usually, the sun has barely begun to filter into my room when I wake up, but the thick, buttery shafts are nowhere to be found. Frowning, I stretch and look outside before glancing at the alarm clock on my nightstand.

Shit. It's raining and it's nearly noon.

Well... Hunter did keep me up for most of the night and early morning.

A giddy smile takes over as I roll onto my side, hiding

my flushed face in the pillow beside me. It smells like him. The scent of his CK One clings to every part of the bed—and to me—like he ingrained himself in one night.

"Hunter?" I call out. Maybe he's downstairs making food. Then again, if he were, I doubt the dogs would be here with me. His side of the bed is cold, but since it's mid-afternoon, that doesn't surprise me. I can't believe I slept so long, even after last night's activities.

I listen for a reply, but only the faint sound of rain filters through my cracked window. My heart sinks with the realization that he must have left.

Mindlessly, I go through the routine of getting dressed, feed the dogs, then search for my phone. It's where I left it on the ottoman the night before, a note next to it with Hunter's chicken scratch scrawled across the paper.

Fed the dogs this morning. Couldn't stay. Something came up. I'm sorry.

Dread claws at my throat, chasing away the high I've been riding since Hunter told me he'd stay yesterday.

I'm sorry.

It doesn't escape me that it's the same thing I wrote to him the morning I left. And Hunter is too calculating —too clever—to miss the irony.

I call him anyway. He doesn't answer, and a fresh wave of apprehension ripples through me.

Did I dream about him leaving this morning? Or did that really happen?

The remnants of my dream cling to the edges of my memory, as they tend to do when it's one of those really good ones—or one of the nightmares that keeps your heart pounding long after you've woken.

Aside from the nightmarish voices whispering the things from the letters, Hunter's declaration rings clear through the reminiscence.

I love you.

He's said he loves me before. At one point, he said it so often it almost started sounding disingenuous. I don't throw that word around lightly, even if I do feel the same. It's been a while, though, and I wish he'd said it to my face when I was fully awake—if he even said it for real at all.

Melancholy drapes over me like a cape, blanketing my soul with wistful longing. Between us coming home together, hanging out, and everything else that happened over the past nearly twenty-four hours, it was starting to feel real, like a normal relationship.

A glimpse of how it could be all the time.

I'm sorry.

"Why the hell would you write that, you dick?" I ask the air with tears in my eyes, which only irritates me further. Tipping my head back, I yell, "And why the fuck am I so emotional?"

Hunter has drawn more tears from me in the past few months than the last three years combined. I'm not an overly emotive person. I do my best to keep that shit tamped down so no one ever knows what really goes on in my brain.

It's why I'm good at my job. It's how I survived Nathaniel. And it's how I kept the truth from Hunter for so long.

So what the fuck is happening, and why am I a blubbering mess?

Vaguely, I recall reading somewhere that shit like this happens to women once we hit our thirties. Just another thing to add to the list of why it sucks to be a woman. I've never been super regular, but I grab my phone to check my period tracker app to see if I'm about to start. That would explain the crying.

Wrenley's name flashes across my screen with an incoming call before I get the chance, causing my heart to seize for a moment. Why would *he* be calling me? Unless something bad has happened to Hunter or Dove.

"Hey, is everything okay?" I answer, returning to the kitchen to find something to eat.

"Of course, why wouldn't it be? What? I can't call to see how you are?" His silky-smooth baritone rolls through the speaker like decadent, melted chocolate—warm and inviting without a hint of bitterness, even though I haven't been the nicest to him lately.

It's not that I don't like him—I do. It's just that now, with him knowing about Dove's real identity, it puts me at risk. To my knowledge, he still doesn't know I'm the Shadow Siren, and all feelings about the things he's said about my alter ego aside, I'd like to keep it that way.

All it would take is one big blowout fight between the two, and Dove and I could find ourselves in a world of trouble. I'd rather he be a threat to only her. It will be easier for me to eliminate him if he doesn't see me coming.

"I'm fine." I draw the word out suspiciously as I pull out a yogurt. "Did Hunter ask you to check up on me?"

"No?" Genuine confusion shades his voice. "I haven't talked to Hunt in a few days. Should I be checking up on you?"

Disappointment floods my chest like bad heartburn. I rub my sternum, trying to ease the ache. "No. What's up?"

There's a heavy pause before Wrenley blows out a long breath. "I was wondering if you'd go ring shopping with me today, for Dove."

"Thanks for clearing up who we'd be shopping for," I deadpan.

I knew this was coming. I'm happy for my friend, I truly, honestly am.

I guess I just hate the fact that he's privy to our little club now... even though he doesn't know about me. It's like a joke he gets to be in on, but he's not even fully in on it. For some reason, it bothers the shit out of me.

Irritation ripples through me as he laughs. "Bad day, Bunny? Come on, this should cheer you up. I want your help. No one knows Dove like you do."

I do feel a sense of satisfaction that he's even bothering to ask. They've been lost in their own little world lately, while I'm over here struggling to make sense of mine. Wrenley and Dove are settling into this blissful life together while Hunter and I keep blowing ours up every time we make any progress.

It's frustrating, but I know I have no one to be disappointed in except myself.

Glaring at my unopened yogurt, I decide to return it to the fridge. If I have to leave the house today, the least he can do is feed me.

"Yeah. Okay. Come pick me up. But you owe me lunch." And I suppose the least *I* can do is stop acting like such a bitch to him. "And froyo."

"Deal. Headed your way now. And Bunny?"

"Hmm?"

"Thank you."

The line goes dead, and my home screen lights up. A picture of Maru, Yasha, and Fang stares back as though trying to remind me of something.

Wasn't I going to check something before Wrenley called?

I sift through my brain fog and come up empty.

"Well, boys, I guess Mommy is spending the afternoon with your soon-to-be uncle. Oh, joy."

Their responding yips and tail wags indicate they clearly don't catch the sarcasm in my tone.

"WHAT DO YOU THINK?" Wrenley nervously shows me what he's already picked out.

Apparently, he's been working with a jeweler in the diamond district for over two weeks now, and I have to admit, the time and thought he's putting into this is adorable. Dove deserves it, and his choice is honestly perfect for her.

But, because I'm me, I have to give him shit.

"I don't know, Wrenley. What do *you* think?" I scoop another spoonful of froyo into my mouth, compliments of the tall, dark blond who's about to be the newest member of my little found family.

I don't even look at the ring as he stares at me, anxiety dripping from his pores and flushing his skin, even though the mid-September weather is unusually chilly today.

The edges of his rich brown eyes crinkle as his gaze swings back to the sparkling pink diamond. It's a very light shade of pink with what the jeweler calls a purplish tint, though I only see my best friend's favorite color reflected in the facets of the oval. The setting is white gold, the band twisting near the top and peppered with small round pavé diamonds that hug the larger stone in the center. It's big, but not so gaudy that it will take over her dainty finger.

All in all, I think it's perfect.

"I think it's classically Dove," Wrenley says reverently. "Shines bright, but not overpowering. The oval is said to represent life and rebirth, and I feel like that symbolizes us perfectly. She helped me lay my past to rest, and we're starting a fresh life together. The shape is never-ending, just like my promise to her." He smiles, no doubt thinking about their relationship and everything they've already been through in the short time they've been together.

Dove told me everything that happened in California with Wrenley's mother, so hearing him speak makes my heart clench. I can't imagine the horrors they endured while growing up.

As it is, I remember my first murder and what I felt like after I killed my husband. I remember the numbing pain and the terror at what my future would hold. It was easy to get lost in Hunter that night, and the hardest thing I'd ever done to leave him the next morning.

I'm being too hard on the man before me. All he wants is to be happy, and he makes my best friend happy.

Why am I the only one so *unhappy*?

"I think it's perfect, Wrenley." I slide a hand over the glass to tilt the small cushion in my direction. "And I think you'd be stupid not to write all that nonsense into your vows."

He laughs, nodding to the attendant, who beams and informs us she'll be right back with the rest of the paperwork. "I haven't even asked her yet. Let me tackle one thing at a time."

Once he's secured the ring in his pocket, we wait outside under the awning as the rain sprinkles down around us like a misty haze. It's late afternoon, and I still haven't heard a word from Hunter.

I try to call him again, but he still doesn't answer.

"Do you want me to try?" Wrenley asks after catching me frowning at my phone.

My mouth twitches to the side, and I shrug, wishing I'd worn something other than my leather jacket over the maxi dress I picked out for today. The air is sticky and heavy. Balling my hair in a fist to gather it off my neck, I nod. "Yeah, will you try?"

Hunter doesn't pick up for Wrenley either.

"Sometimes he just gets caught up in work and doesn't check his phone," Wrenley informs, as if I don't already know that. "Let me check his location."

I blink in surprise.

"You have his location?" *That* I didn't know. *I* don't even have his location. Though for good reason—if he shared it with me, he'd want me to share mine with him, and obviously, that isn't a good idea.

Like a tropical Florida shower, the rain passes with a swath of thick gray clouds. The sky brightens a smidge, and passersby shake out their umbrellas as we wait for Wrenley's phone to load.

"He's at home. Probably just poring over his new case. You know how he gets."

I do. I also know that when he hyper-focuses, he tends to forget to eat. A plan forms as I part ways with Dove's soon-to-be fiancé and head home to take care of the dogs before proceeding to his place. I'll bring Hunter an early dinner and then, hopefully, we can have a repeat of last night.

We have a lot to discuss, and it's time we sit down and figure out exactly what we're going to do moving forward.

But first, food. And orgasms. Lots and lots of orgasms.

Then we'll figure out the hard stuff.

THE RAIN PICKS up again as I approach Hunter's door. His family has owned this home for generations, and even though he could sell the place for millions, he still chooses to live in the massive structure by himself.

I'm ready to strip down by the time I make it to the top step, shrugging out of my jacket and draping it over the bag of Indian food I grabbed on my way here as I ring the doorbell a million times in succession.

Impatient? Who, me?

It seems like hours before I finally hear footsteps and... is that... a *chicken*?

One side of the heavy black wood opens, and I oscillate between salivating at the sight before me and curling my lips inward to suppress a disbelieving laugh.

Hunter stares back in surprise wearing deliciously revealing gray sweats. Water drips down his sinfully bare abs, his curls are mussed, and he's wearing his glasses like he's gearing up for some sort of photoshoot—with a chicken in his arms.

A chicken that looks like it's seen better days, with rumpled, greasy-looking feathers and a foot that looks mangled, like something once tried to chew it off. A cloth wraps around its bottom half, secured with a large plastic safety pin.

"Bunny, what are you doing here?" He switches the chicken to his other arm, and it squawks, eyeing me like it's daring me to say something about its appearance.

In the end, my laughter wins out. "What are *you* doing?"

I try to enter his house, but the chicken puffs up and begins making the most god-awful sounds I've ever heard from an animal.

"Calm down, Pepper. Shh. That's it, pretty girl. It's okay. You're okay," Hunter coos as he gently strokes the black plume on top of her head. He moves aside, and she aggressively snaps at me as I pass.

Affronted, I glare at her. "Watch it, you spicy nugget."

I've never been a fan of chickens. They are dirty and loud, and I'm a cereal-over-eggs-for-breakfast girlie anyway.

"Sorry, she doesn't like anyone except Mom and me. That's what the emergency was this morning. My parents are heading on vacation, and their usual house sitter wasn't available." He leans over, keeping the chicken far away from me as he plants a soft kiss on my lips.

I melt under his attention, and it's almost enough to make me forget that I'm upset about the way he left this morning.

Almost.

"That doesn't explain why you haven't answered your phone all day. Or why you left the way you did. And don't your parents have a whole farm upstate? Who's watching that?" I follow him into the kitchen and set the food on the white-and-gray marbled granite island.

Hunter sets *Pepper* in a small wire pen in the dining room. The second he lets go of her, she stomps her foot and continues her screeching.

"Their vet is going to keep an eye on things, but Pepper is nearly impossible for anyone else to deal with. She tolerates their usual sitter, but I think she hates their vet more than you hate the color pink, if that helps you understand her any better."

He steps toward me, and I retreat a step. "Nuh-uh. You were just holding that dirty, mangy thing to your body." His very toned, very delicious-looking, very wet body. "Why are you dripping wet?"

"I was just about to give '*that dirty, mangy thing*' a bath. And she's not mangy. She's a frizzle silkie. They just look like that."

"Well, that's unfortunate."

"Don't be mean."

Pepper clucks angrily as if agreeing.

"Why did you write what you did on the note this morning?"

My sudden change of topic draws his brows together. But instead of asking what I'm talking about, his jaw ticks as his whiskey gaze hardens. "It didn't feel good... did it?"

Swiftly, my emotions swing from reasonable to irrational. "Are you fucking kidding me, Hunter? You wanted me to know what it *felt* like?"

I push him away as he draws near, Pepper growing louder in the background and adding to my increasing aggravation.

Remorse shines in his gaze as he reaches for me again, and this time, I don't fight him. "Admittedly, it was a dick move. I'm sorry, Bunny. I regretted it the moment my cab pulled away this morning and—"

"And what? I thought we were in a good place, and you wanted to what, Hunter? Teach me a lesson?"

Why are we like this? Every single time we move forward a step, one of us fucks something up and falls back two.

Okay, to be fair, up until this point it's been mainly me who fucks things up, and Hunter's given me more passes than I can count. I should let this one go.

Only I can't.

Rationally, I know I need to calm down, but with every word that comes out of his mouth, I fall deeper and deeper down a chasm of rage toward an impending lava pit of doom. My skin heats, tears prick my eyes as my nails dig into his arms.

He lifts my chin gently and wipes at the purple foil paw print stickers over my scar. "I'm sorry. I shouldn't have written it. I'll admit, though, I wanted you to know what it felt like to wake up alone after spending an incredible night together. I wanted you to know what I went through and why I don't ever want to experience it again. You seem like you're finally ready to give this a chance, but I want you to know what that means, Little Rabbit. You can't run again. I won't survive it a second time."

His words are earnest, and he swallows my answering sob with a gentle kiss. Once again, I don't even know why I'm crying, other than from intense frustration. It's fair that he wants me to understand what I put him through, so it's only fair that I'm willing to do the same for him.

Hunter has been through hell and back for me.

"You didn't have to be such a dick about it." I wipe at my eyes before leaning into his embrace.

"You're right, and I'm sorry I haven't answered your calls all day. Gwen has been blowing up my phone over this new case, so I put it on silent—"

"Why is *Gwendolyn* contacting you about the case?" I bristle, pulling away as a new wave of anger incinerates my tears. "Are you fucking working together?"

"Yes. I thought you knew that." Hunter shakes his head, a frown curving his lips. "Miller just had surgery—"

"I don't give a shit what's going on with her partner, why is she working with *you*?"

"It's their case, Bunny."

"I don't care, I don't want her near you."

An erupting laugh launches into the air, his face crumpling until it mirrors my rage. "You made me watch you date guy after guy. Taunted me while you flirted with them."

"I was never planning on bringing any of them home! You said yourself you knew that!"

"I have no intention of bringing Gwen home!"

"Work *is* your second home, Hunter! And stop calling her *Gwen*!" My voice spikes into a shrill shriek, and even *my* eyes widen at my outburst.

"Did you start your period this morning or something? Jesus Christ." Hunter drags a hand through his curls and turns his back on me, like he's stopping himself from saying more.

Another bitchy comment is on the tip of my tongue when I suddenly remember that's what I was doing when Wrenley called this morning. I was trying to check my tracker app to see how many months it's been since I had my period. I'm irregular, but I usually don't skip more than one, and I can't remember the last time I rode the crimson wave.

I stare at my screen as I go through the dates.

Jesus Christ is right. It's been months.

Quickly, I calculate the timing, details and facts flying through my brain as fast as I can process them.

"Bunny? What is it?" Hunter's voice sounds far away, like there's a wall between us, siphoning all sound out except for the blood rushing through my ears.

In a stunned stupor, I turn, walking out of the house and into the rain, uncaring that it soaks through my dress or turns my hair into a mass that weighs heavily on my back.

He yells after me, cursing the farther I get. I don't expect him to follow, knowing he can't just leave the chicken in the pen. I walk mindlessly for blocks until I find what I'm looking for, then head back.

By the time I return, I already know what the outcome will be, but I still need to see tangible proof.

"What the hell, Bunny? What was that about?" Hunter demands as I walk past him to the bathroom, dripping water all over his hardwood floor.

Our future.

The fact that we're about to become irrevocably entwined, whether we're ready or not.

The mood swings, the tight clothing, the sudden necessity for the affection and the sex and the feral ownership I feel over Hunter—mostly normal things when it comes to *us,* but lately they've all been height-ened needs.

That night in the bathroom at *The Tipsy Taco*—the night we gave in to our baser desires and took everything we've wanted from each other—we never used a condom.

We never used a condom.

"Bunny!" Hunter pounds on the door. "What is going on?"

I can hear the frenzied worry in his tone, feel his rest-lessness through the door. It mirrors my own as I stare at the sticks on the counter and count down the minutes.

Three.

Two.

One.

Two pink lines.

A plus sign.

With a resigned sigh, I open the door and meet Hunter's distressed stare. "I'm pregnant."

"You're *what*?" His molten-amber gaze flicks past me to the multiple tests on the vanity.

I swallow the lump in my throat as his eyes meet mine again. His Adam's apple bobs thickly as I repeat myself. "I'm pregnant."

My heart aches when his eyes harden and he takes a step back. I see his walls rising as he voices the question I know is coming, but it still hurts to hear how much he feels the need to ask it.

"Is it..." He blows out a shaky breath, gaze dropping to the floor as his voice cracks. "Is it mine?"

How are we supposed to do this? How do you raise a child with someone you don't trust?

Do I even want a baby? Does he? He's on the rise at work—this will ruin all the progress he's made in the department.

My lips curl inward, my teeth sinking into the bottom one to quell another onslaught of tears. "Yes, it's yours."

A relieved sigh spills past his lips, a nervous chuckle racking his body as he runs a hand through his hair again. "Bunny..."

I can picture Hunter as a dad so easily. See these halls filled with the pitter-patter of tiny feet. T-ball games and team snack runs for a toddler with another strapped to his chest. He'll want to be a coach, of course, and spend weekends upstate on his family's farm.

It's everything I never imagined I'd have with a man who loves me as profoundly as Hunter does.

How will it work, though, when this man doesn't trust me?

"I've never slept with anyone else, Hunter." His eyes lift, so much longing and uncertainty in their glistening depths. "After Nathaniel, it's only ever been you."

How will it work when he's the detective actively looking for a serial killer?

And that serial killer happens to be me?

Bunny sucks in a breath as the physician squirts gel on her bare belly. Her head turns to the ultrasound machine, so I can't see her face, but I'd give anything to catch a glimpse of her emotions right now.

"Sorry about that, it's a little cold at first," the woman apologizes, sliding the transducer through the goo.

My fingers twitch, desperate to touch her—hold her, anchor her, remind her I'm not going anywhere.

I'm pregnant.

Two words I never thought I'd hear from Bunny's lips—especially not where I'm concerned. But here we are... and I hate that I can't allow myself the slightest bit of happiness.

She's been distant since we found out, and for once, I'm at a complete loss. I want to scream it from the rooftops that I'm having a baby with the woman I love. But Bunny isn't happy about it at all. She doesn't seem angry, just... neutral.

Which almost feels worse. I'd rather she yell and pound on my chest for forgetting to use a condom that night—and all the times after—than have her stare blankly like she's gone catatonic.

A whooshing reverberates off the walls, followed by a rhythmic pulsing, reminiscent of a gallop. "There we go. See?" The doctor points to a space on the screen that, in my inexperienced opinion, looks like a kidney bean. "We have a strong heartbeat."

Baby bean blurs as my eyes go glassy. Pain anchors me as I dig my nails into my arms, trying to keep from getting emotional—attached—to this tiny thing we created. Ultimately, it's Bunny's decision, and she may want to terminate the pregnancy. I don't need a reason to resent her, so I keep my gaze on my loafers.

"...nose, there's the arms and a leg." The doctor keeps rambling, and I close my eyes, imagining what a kid of ours might look like. Would it have her soft hazel eyes? My sharp jaw? One thing's for sure: it would definitely have fantastic hair because that's a trait we've both been blessed with.

Utter helplessness pours through me as I press my back to the wall and silently repeat, *don't look up, don't look up.*

This is all I've ever wanted—right here in this room —and I'm terrified Bunny won't just take it away from me, she'll rip it from my grasp and disappear again. When the going gets tough, my little rabbit runs. And now there's another life in the mix... what does this mean for us?

Whatever choice she makes, we'll never be the same after today.

The doctor's laugh cuts through my mantra. "Mommy is reaching for you, Daddy."

I blink, tears slipping down my cheeks as I drag my gaze from the speckled blue tile. She's right. Bunny isn't looking at me, but her hand is outstretched, waiting for me to take it.

An unsteady breath pushes past my lips. I rush to her side, lace our fingers, and bring her hand to my mouth. "I'm right here."

"That's ours," she whispers shakily. "That's our baby."

"That's our baby, Little Rabbit." My tears fall freely now, and I don't bother to hide them. Not even when Bunny turns to me, silver clinging to her lashes as her mossy eyes gleam with her own unshed emotions.

"That's your baby," the doctor repeats, soft and motherly. "You look like you're measuring at about twelve weeks."

"That tracks." Bunny laughs, and it's like music to my ears—the first sign she's not as miserable about this as I feared. Giggles bubble out of her, shaking the bed as she pulls our joined hands to rest on her stomach. "We baked a baby in a bar."

A deep rumble spills from my chest as I join her, roughly wiping my face before raking my fingers through my hair, uncaring that I'm headed back to work after this and probably just messed it up. "Taco-bout the timing."

We pause, grinning at each other, before erupting into hysterics.

The doctor cants her head, amused. "I'll let you two have a moment. Bunny, you can get dressed now, and we'll discuss next steps when I return."

Bunny manages to quell her laughter until we're alone, but this time it sounds forced. My merriment dies as we lock eyes and her joy pivots back to tears. "Hunter, what are we going to do?"

"What do *you want* to do?" I ask quietly, rubbing my thumb over her knuckles. With each silent breath she takes, I start to harden my heart, preparing for her to lash out and tell me this is my fault.

She sniffs, her bottom lip trembling as she releases my hand to grab the towel the doctor left, rubbing the gel off her stomach. "I want to scream and rage because the timing sucks."

Drawing up my walls, I step back and turn to give her privacy while she dresses. "If you don't want to keep it…"

I'm not prepared for her arms to wrap around my waist or the press of her cheek against my back. "We're keeping it. Why would you even say such a thing?"

Indescribable.

There isn't a word for the way my anxiety pops like a water balloon, relief flooding my chest—heavy and over-whelming. Blowing out a breath, I bow my head and tug her arms around me tighter. "I just want you to know I support whatever decision you make, Little Rabbit."

"We were just getting to a good place," she murmurs. "Like I said, the timing just sucks. I would've liked to have you to myself for a few years before I have to share you."

Her warmth chases the cold lingering in my ribs. Maybe it's the hormones, maybe she's finally ready to commit. Either way, her admission makes me the happiest man alive.

Gently, I turn, cupping her cheek as she tilts her face up to me. There's no doubt in her gaze—only trust and acceptance. "Usually it's the man saying that to the woman."

"Don't be misogynistic, Hunter. We both know how feral I get over you now." Her fingers thread into my hair and tug me down.

"Now? Try always," I laugh. "*Now*, I'm just afraid I'll have to keep you from murdering any woman who looks at me sideways."

Moss darkens to deep forest pine, and her nails catch in my curls. "Then you'd better tell *Gwendolyn* to watch herself."

She lets go and spins toward her clothes. I ask the same question I always dread. "Does this mean you're ready to give your heart to me, Little Rabbit?"

Silence hangs between us, my gaze locked on a watercolor print of a famous painting hanging on the wall while she dresses. When she's finished, she startles me by grabbing my hand, turning me to face her. "Come on. I want a bacon maple milkshake and fries. And—"

"Bacon maple milkshake? That sounds... absolutely disgus—"

Her glare kills the word, and I lift my hands in surrender. "My apologies. Carry on, baby mama."

Her gaze softens, lashes fluttering—like a butterfly testing its wings. As if I've just reminded her we created a tiny human currently residing in her belly.

"And *then* I have something I need to tell you," she says softly.

Fuck. Nothing good ever comes from a woman saying those words.

Well, shit. It was nice while it lasted.

I LOVE that Bunny has an appetite. She's never been afraid to eat in front of anyone, and I find that highly attractive.

What I don't find attractive is the way she gnaws on the crystallized bacon that came with her milkshake like it's a dildo for her mouth. Give me food porn all day—I don't judge. But there's something that has always inherently grossed me out about bacon.

Gooey maple drips from the slab of crisped meat, glazing her lips in burnt-gold sap. All of it *should* have my dick hard and ready to pour *my* milky sap into her mouth, however, I can't help picturing the poor piggy who died to make that milkshake.

I don't realize my drink is gone—and that the loud slurp of an empty straw belongs to me—until her annoyed gaze snaps to mine. "What is your problem?"

"Are you planning on feeding our kid pig often? Or is this topic up for debate? Because I don't eat pork, as you well know."

"You will have to pry bacon from my cold, dead hands. There's no way I'm giving it up. I can do without most other pork products, but bacon? Hard no. So yeah, our kid is going to eat bacon." She makes a show of licking the syrup from bottom to top before aggressively crunching the end between her teeth, smirking as she chews.

Pepper clucks in her pen in my dining room. Yasha and Maru sit on the other side of the wire, cocking their heads every time she makes a sound. Yasha's tail wags excitedly as he watches his new friend, but Maru and Pepper *despise* each other, so we keep them separated unless we're watching closely.

When we introduced the dogs to the chicken a few days ago, I wasn't sure what to expect. Yasha sniffed her and barked playfully while Pepper didn't mind his curiosity. Maru, however, put her at the top of his shit list when she snapped at Bunny for trying to pet her. Poor Pepper is two tail feathers short now, and Maru won't let his mother near the pen.

"Adding pork to the list of things to talk about, then. Noted." I pop a fry in my mouth before hesitantly venturing into territory I'm not sure I want to explore. "So, what did you need to tell me?"

Pink blooms across her cheeks, popping her freckles and the rainbow foil hearts over her scar. Nervousness rolls off her as she swallows hard and sets the bacon down.

"Hunter, I—"

"Little Rabbit, you don't have to be worried about telling me whatever it is." I swivel on my stool to face her, tugging hers closer until she has no choice but to face me, too. Gathering her sticky hands, I kiss her knuckles and drop our entwined fingers to my thighs.

"You might feel differently when you hear it." She drags in a breath, eyes fixed on my chest, then exhales slowly. After another breath, her gaze meets mine. "I was pregnant... before... when I was with Nathaniel."

An ice pick lodges in my heart, but I keep my face neutral even as the shock hits. "What, uh..." I clear my throat around the words. "What happened?"

Her fingers tense. Silver rims her lashes. "I never wanted a baby with him. Maybe at first, before I knew who he really was. But when it happened, I knew it wasn't what I wanted."

She pauses, and I take the opportunity to inhale my own deep breath. Ever since she started talking, I've been holding it in, bracing for the part that breaks whatever piece of me feels responsible for what she endured.

"The night I killed him, he was angry because he'd found out I was thinking of having an abortion."

Slowly, my eyes close as my soul clenches. If she was pregnant when she killed her husband, then that means—

"I was pregnant when we slept together, Hunter. It's

why I left afterward. And why—" A cry fractures her reasoning, her body convulsing with deep, soul-shattering sobs. "I couldn't handle the thought of having a part of him inside me." I stand and pull her to me, my body absorbing the emotional onslaught. "I didn't want to bring any part of him into this world... I couldn't... I—"

"Shh. It's okay, Bunny. It's okay." I kiss her hair and hold her tighter as she falls apart.

She clings to me like I'm a lifeline, and my heart breaks for her. For everything she went through. Before me. *Because* of me. I fucking wish I could turn back time and erase her pain. Save her from that jackass. I knew something was wrong. I *knew* it, and I didn't stop it.

I could have saved her.

When her cries subside, she sniffs and pushes back to look up at me, still leaning into my chest for support. "I never wanted to hurt you. I just couldn't stay here. I needed space and... time to deal with everything."

Smoothing her tears, I cradle her face and shake my head. "You could have told me, Bunny. I would've been there for you."

"How could I ask that of you? How could I ask you to support me while I was carrying another man's child?"

"We're friends. That's how. Do you really think so little of me that you thought I'd abandon you in your greatest time of need? Give me a little more credit than that." Her dark brows pinch, the remaining tears drying up in a swell of anger. She tries to pull back, but I tighten my hold. "Don't mistake my frustration for anger, Little Rabbit."

"You don't get to be angry, Hunter." She struggles harder, and I let go so I don't hurt her. "I didn't have to tell you, but I wanted to. I left and found a place where I could settle down and think without anyone clouding my judgment. I got the help I needed, and when I had clarity, I made the conscious decision to do what was right for *me*."

Hysteria threads her tone, even though I never asked her to explain. It sounds like she's defending her actions to herself more than to me.

"I'm not angry. I said, 'Don't mistake my frustration for anger.' I *do* get to be frustrated here, Bunny."

"Why do you think you get that? What gives you the right?" Wild outrage flares as she crosses the room, putting distance between us.

Yasha and Maru abandon Pepper—whose clucks have turned into squawks at Bunny's rising pitch—to circle their mother with concerned whines. Vaguely, I know I shouldn't be putting undue stress on her. From what little I've gathered about timelines for pregnancy, we're still on the cusp of there being a greater risk for complications.

So when I speak, it's with a gentle, pleading tone, urging her to understand where I'm coming from. "I'm trying really hard here, Bunny. I've always given you so much of me... all of me, honestly. But all you do is lie to me. Can you really not understand why I'd be discouraged? You slept with me while carrying another man's child, then didn't give me the agency to prove I'd be there for you in the aftermath. Didn't I deserve that? After all we went through?"

Her silence speaks volumes. The things she wants to say are written all over her face, in the way her gaze grows glassy again and how her bottom lip begins to tremble— she's frightened. Whether by my reaction or of what she's feeling, I don't know.

Always a mystery, my little rabbit. I never fully know what's going on in that beautiful head of hers.

"Come here."

Bunny obeys, melting into me as I wrap my arms around her. "I'm scared, Hunter."

"I know, baby. I am, too." I huff a dry laugh against her hair. "You keep everything so close to your chest. I'm just asking you to let me in. This is bigger than you and me now. I need to know you won't take off on me at a moment's notice."

"I want to give in." She releases a harsh breath, pressing her forehead to my chest. "Fuck, I want to open up to you so badly."

"Why do you feel like you can't? What have I done to make you so hesitant about me—about us?" Discontent swirls around the questions, but I tamp it down. She's trying. That's all I can ask.

Only, I'm not prepared for her answer.

"It isn't you, Hunter. I mean, it is, but not in the way you think." Her sigh heats my shirt before she tilts her head back and meets my eyes. "What I feel for you... it's *too* much. It's the type of all-consuming, earth-shattering, life-altering *love* you never recover from. And it scares the shit out of me. It gives you too much power over me, and I don't know if I can do that again—give myself to a man who has that kind of hold on me. I know you're nothing like Nathaniel, but what I felt for him doesn't come close to the way I feel about you. I *know* you're going to break me."

I press my lips to hers, telling her without words how fucking happy she's just made me. We cling to each other, a maelstrom of emotion swirling in the wake of her confession. I've waited so long to hear the depth of her feelings, when all she's ever offered is surface-level hope.

Now, I can spend the rest of our lives proving I'd drown to keep her afloat. That she—and this baby—are my entire world, and absolutely nothing will ever change that.

"That's where you're wrong, Little Rabbit. I've spent too long piecing you back together. You're a masterpiece. *My* masterpiece. And I will never... *ever* break you."

BUNNY

"Don't ask me why there are so many boxes. I think I blacked out from the joy of finding them in bulk." Dove leans on three giant packing boxes that tower nearly to her height, each stuffed with mini boxes of my favorite food in the world—Lucky Charms.

Unfortunately, my stomach roils at the thought of all that toasted, sugary oat and marshmallowy goodness. Baby bean, as Hunter has so affectionately taken to calling our child, has decided they are not a fan of my treasured cereal.

Cereal has a long shelf life if it's unopened, right?

She high-fives the random teenager she grabbed from the sidewalk to carry them in and slips him a twenty. "Thanks, my man."

In a nasally tone, with an expression that suggests he's adding her to his mental spank bank, he flashes a grin around a mouthful of braces. "No problem, Miss. Anytime."

He lingers, staring dreamily, until finally her smile

drops and she jerks her head toward the door. "Okay, kid. Off you go."

Once the door shuts behind him, she spins back to me. "Aren't you excited? These are *all* Lucky Charms! I got the haul for, like, I don't know—less than fifty bucks."

"Thank you. What a steal." I force a smile and bite back a wave of nausea. It's lessened lately—the sudden need to vomit if a smell or the sight of a particular food doesn't agree with my stomach's definition of appetizing —but the sickness always lingers in the deep trenches of my belly, ready to rear its ugly head whenever it wants.

Have I mentioned how much I hate throwing up?

My best friend beams, utterly unaffected by my less-thrilled-than-I-should-be composure. "I know, right?" She flips her long blonde waves over her shoulder and starts unpacking her Barbie pink tote. "Let's crack one of these bad boys open and get to picture-taking for the book club."

Shrugging—though her attention is on the haul of faux greenery she brought—I place the mini cereal box back in the bigger one and move to the cabinets to see where I have space to store them. My first thought is the basement, but all those stairs...

And it's not like I can ask Hunter to take them down there. I want him as far away from my basement as possible.

"I'm okay for right now. I'm not that hungry, and I don't want it to go to waste."

Silence permeates the room like an onion as soon as

you peel back the skin. Suffocating, with an in-your-face aroma that clogs your airway and makes your eyes burn —only instead of a foul odor doing the choking, it's that eerie, icy feeling people talk about when they think a presence is haunting them. The kind that smothers you and steals the breath from your lungs.

Looking over my shoulder, I yelp when I find my best friend directly behind me. I didn't even hear her cross the kitchen. "Jesus, Love Dove! Are you trying to scare the shit out of me?"

Her brilliant blue eyes narrow as she appraises me head to toe. "Something is different about you."

If a sweatdrop could form on my forehead in real life, it would—*it's an anime thing.*

Heaving a nervous chuckle, I edge around her. "What are you talking about?"

Why is this so hard? Just tell her already. Hunter is telling Wrenley, and she's going to be pissed if her boyfriend finds out before she does.

Hands on her hips, she pivots with me, keeping us face to face as we step in a half circle.

"I know we haven't been spending as much time together, but don't think I haven't noticed, Buns. You're wearing less leather, you're no longer participating in our extracurriculars as frequently, and I saw the box from *Aux Merveilleux de Fred* in your trash. Hunter's been here. And you haven't been filling me in on all the juicy, dirty details!"

Shit.

Sometimes I forget how perceptive Dove is.

"Are you two fucking? I swear to god, if you've been holding back—"

"I'm pregnant." The words tumble out in a rushed, muddled phrase that's barely intelligible. We both freeze in our face-off.

The bright white bow holding up half her hair bounces as she snaps straight, gaping. "I'm sorry, can you say that again? I think I misheard you."

Sighing, I pop my hip as a hand drops to my newly distended belly. Hunter says it's getting more noticeable, which is why we finally decided to break the news to our friends. I'm now unsure why we decided to do it separately instead of telling them together. Yes, Dove and I have serial-killer things to discuss but having Hunter's support while announcing our news for the first time is something I'm craving at the moment.

"I'm pregnant."

Bubblegum-pink lips pop open in surprise once more. "I thought that's what you said."

A pregnant pause—*pun intended*—hangs between us before she shouts, "You've been Peter poisoned!"

The fuck?

My confusion must show because she sticks a finger in the air like a walking dictionary and recites, "Symptoms last nine months, after-effects for a lifetime."

"I'm... so... huh?" I cant my head—then my bewilderment dissolves as she launches herself into my arms.

"I'm going to be a godmother! Oh my goodness, this

is so exciting! Hunter is the father, right? I *knew* you two were fucking! You dirty bitch, holding out on me. How did this happen?"

Laughing, I pat the top of her head. "Well, sweet girl, when a man and a woman—"

"Don't make me hurt you," she jests, poking my belly softly. "What are we having?"

"You're really okay with this?" I guess I thought… well, I don't know what I thought. Some part of me felt like Dove would be upset I didn't tell her sooner. Now I feel like she's taking it *too* well.

A delicate blonde brow arches as her lips purse. "What do you mean?"

We abandon the book-club aesthetics and move to the living room, where the dogs happily gnaw on a new batch of dick jerky Dove brought. Fang's once rainbow mane has faded back to pristine white, sandwiching Yasha between him and Maru, making them look like a reverse Oreo cookie.

Why do Lucky Charms sound bad but cookies sound great right now?

As we settle on the couch, my phone dings, and Dove snatches it up before I can grab it. "Oooh. Daddy wants to know if you need him to grab you snacks while he's out with Wren."

How does he always know what I need?

"Oh my god, don't call him that." I laugh as she gives my phone back, and I type out a quick request before setting it screen down. "As for earlier, I just meant that… I don't know. This is a big change."

My hands drift down absentmindedly, and I watch a smile spread across her pink lips before she leans over to place her strawberry-tipped fingers over mine. "Are *you* okay with this, Bunny?"

"Yes." The answer is immediate, and her lips twitch knowingly. "Hunter is going to be an amazing dad. I just... I guess I wish we could've had some time together before *this*." I gesture to my belly.

"Haven't you? I know your relationship has been all sorts of unconventional since you met, but you've had time. You just spent it in secret with a lot of pent-up sexual tension. But neither of you has been with anyone else. You may as well have been in a relationship this whole time."

"I guess. I don't know—I'm having a hard time with the idea of being under a man's control again. I still have issues with how stubborn he is about needing to hear me say I'll give him my heart. It's his way or the highway, and that scares me."

"I don't think Hunter means for it to be that way, Buns. I think he's just as scared of you hurting him. He's guarding his heart, too. Maybe if you both let down your walls, you'll find you've already built a strong foundation that won't crumble."

Hearing it from her perspective solidifies my intention to move things forward with Hunter. It's strange how sometimes we hear things from other people—even if they're the things we've been telling ourselves all along—and it changes our entire outlook.

"Yeah, you're right. But I'm telling you now, we

aren't disappearing into the relationship abyss like you and Wrenley. You two have been neglecting your friendship duties, and while I admit I fucked up your birthday surprise, I refuse to let my life become all about Hunter. I don't want to be dick-whipped."

Playful shock dances across Dove's face as she presses a hand to her chest. "I'm not dick-whipped! How dare you, missy."

Canting my head, I flash a teasing smirk. "You spent months not publishing Wren's articles because you didn't want him romanticizing the Doll and then literally caved and published an article where he thanks her for your relationship like she's some sort of serial-killer matchmaker."

She grins and waggles her brows. "Wasn't she? Or me? It was I... You know what, never mind. The point is it's okay to get lost in him for a while. You and Hunter have been heading down this path for a long time. Maybe the baby part came early, but you were close to giving in. You know you were. Hasn't Hunter proven himself by now? I know you love him, Buns. And I know why you're holding back, but don't you deserve to be happy? Nathaniel's been gone for a while. It's time to move on. Just because one man hurt you doesn't mean they're all like that. It's okay to be guarded, but it's also okay to be vulnerable."

"No, you're right. And I'm sorry. I'm just now realizing how rude that sounded about you and Wrenley." They've gone through so much—they deserve to be happy. And once again, I'm dashing that happiness for no reason other than deflection.

"It's okay. I know what you meant. I'm sorry I haven't been there for you lately. But look at it this way… it pushed you and Hunter closer together?" Her shoulders hitch suggestively as her inflection ticks upward.

"Are you and Wrenley thinking about having—"

"No." The word is sharp, flying from her lips before I can finish my question. She rises and heads back toward the kitchen. "We're both in strong agreement that we don't want children. Our pasts are too sordid, and we don't want that leaking into our parenting. We're fine being fur parents."

Following, I help her sort through our book-club aesthetic, then we bring everything back to a spot in front of one of the giant living-room windows that gets a lot of natural sunlight. While we piece it together, she says, "I have new video footage for you whenever you have time to rip it apart and piece it back together. There's no rush, and it will be the last video I send in for a while."

This piques my interest. "Did Wrenley go with you again?"

"We're working on a way to make the operation run smoother—as in, what he can take care of without watching all the gruesome, bloody bits. I think California was a one-off for him. It was personal, so it was easier. If I have to keep cleaning up his puke, it might be enough to send me into early retirement."

Grabbing a silk rose, I hum in response, my mind

drifting to my situation with Hunter as far as the Siren goes.

As if Dove can read my thoughts, she asks, "What are you going to do about the Siren?"

It's a question I've been wondering myself. "Obviously, I can't keep going while pregnant. However, I do have one more name on the list I'd like to terminate before taking a break. Only thing is, he's not back in town until close to Christmas. By then, if Hunter and I make a go of this, I don't know how I'm going to keep it from him."

"Do you even want to keep going? I can't imagine it'll be easy to sustain if you and Hunter move in together. Get married. Have more kids." She sits back on her knees. "Not that I'm saying you have to do any of those things—it's just something to think about."

"No, I know. As far as those things go, I have no clue. Hunter's never been in a hurry to find the Siren or the Doll. We do what we do for a reason, and I don't know if it's something I can just give up." I touch my stomach again—something I've been doing often since finding out about baby bean. "Baby comes first, obviously. I just think about the women I've helped and how many more there are out there."

Dove lays a hand on my forearm. "It's not your burden to shoulder, Bunny. It's okay to put your family first."

All three dogs' heads perk up moments before I hear the front door open. "Daddy's home!" Hunter's silky voice rings out.

Wrenley's deeper baritone follows. "Oh, god. Make it stop. He's been referring to himself as *Daddy* all day."

Dove and I share a knowing look before getting up to greet them. Our conversation will have to resume later, and I'm more than happy to shelf the bitter discussion for another day.

Because right now, I want cookies.

BUNNY

SILKY SMOOTH SAX notes blare as Hunter opens the door to one of his favorite jazz clubs. Ushering me in, he slides his hand from the small of my back around my waist to rest on my stomach as he introduces me to an elderly man named Sammy.

"Well, it's very nice to meet you, young lady. Hunter's never brought a woman in before, you must be pretty special," Sammy croons with a wink. His powder-white hair is gelled in a combover, and his thick, wiry mustache is peppered with gray. Cigar smoke and the scent of bourbon cling to him like a second skin, but he has a warm smile and an obvious fondness for Hunter, which makes me like him immediately.

"It's nice to meet you, too." I shake his hand, and Sammy lifts my knuckles to his lips with another wink.

"If he gives you any trouble, you let me know and I'll take care of him."

Genuine laughter bubbles from my throat as Hunter waves him off and steers me away. "Laying it on a little thick, aren't ya? If you're not careful, she'll leave me for you and then you'll be on my shit list."

Sammy's full-bodied chuckles bellow after us as Hunter winds through a sea of small, black-lacquered tables in front of a stage where a band plays a slow jazz number. Pleated red silk drapes adorn the walls, with golden embellishments and antique frames of famous singers and jazz players—signatures and all—giving the club a timeless, prestigious vibe.

You wouldn't know it just by looking at him, but I can see why Hunter loves this place. It's undoubtedly *him*. He's all cool charm and suave smiles as he shakes hands with multiple people, introducing me as his *girl-friend* as we move to our booth along the back wall.

Several men and women break into knowing smiles as soon as he says my name. It makes me nervous and exalted, all at once. Clearly, he talks about me here, and now that we've sort of slapped a label on what we are—still having a hard time with that one—they're treating him like he's come back from a treasure hunt with a chest full of gold.

They're happy for him—for us. My moods may swing on a dime, but there's no room here for anything other than delightfully happy and perfectly content.

"I told you I'd get you here one day." His lips ghost the shell of my ear before pressing a kiss to my temple as he helps me up into the booth, which is situated on a platform nearly a foot higher than the main floor. Even in my favorite pair of Louboutins, it's quite a step up.

"What on earth kind of design is this?"

Hunter lets out an excited laugh, and I swear if he'd worn his glasses tonight, he'd be pushing them up the bridge of his nose right now. "It's actually a neat concept. When they built the club it was just open space, and over time, they added the tables. Years later, when they started doing dinner, they realized people along the back couldn't see much through the crowd up front. So they added the platform so the dinner patrons could enjoy the show, too."

Pure joy lights his face as he gestures, reminding me a little of when we first met and were just getting to know each other.

"I suppose that makes sense." Picking up my menu, I browse the selections, noticing Hunter isn't bothering to look at his. "Already know what you want?"

"I get the same thing every time. The roasted chicken is the best in the city. The chef uses a balsamic glaze that is to die for." Hunter watches the stage like a kid seeing theme-park characters for the first time.

"Interesting. Perhaps Pepper and I should discuss your preferences regarding her species when we get home. As for my dinner, I think I'll get the pork chop," I razz with a playful lilt.

His whiskey gaze swings my way, full of devilish heat. "When we get *home*, huh?"

Warmth bleeds into my cheeks. "I was expecting to stay at your place tonight. I didn't even think when I said it."

"Don't apologize, Little Rabbit. I love that you're carrying my child and now calling my place home. I feel like I've won the lottery." He flashes the sexy grin that always wrecks me, and I have to press my thighs together to relieve some of the mounting tension.

Would it be wrong to ask for another bathroom trip? Maybe that can be our thing—bathroom sex. That's gonna be a great story to tell the baby. "Hey kid, you were created in a bathroom at a bar and unfortunately had a front-row seat to your parents desecrating more of them during your stay in your mom's belly."

At nearly sixteen weeks now, I'm horny as hell and Hunter is more than happy to oblige. I'm about to suggest it when a pretty red-headed waitress sashays up with bedroom eyes aimed squarely at my man.

"Hey, Hunt. Long time, no see. How've you been, handsome?" She flashes me the briefest smile before angling her body toward him, and a hot surge of anger zips down my esophagus like a cannonball into a pool of lava.

My insides go molten as she brushes a hand down his arm, cooling only slightly when he shifts deeper into his seat to create distance between them. Reaching across the table for my hand, he smooths his thumb over my knuckles as he introduces us.

"Sophie, this is my girlfriend, Bunny. Bunny, Sophie." His eyes stay on me, warm smile, relaxed posture. And yet, I can't help feeling he's relishing this a little.

How many times did he show up and interrupt my dates? How many times did I mention loudly, within his vicinity, where I'd be? It was always a game between us, but the game was never fair. I held all the pieces and Hunter just played by my rules.

Fuck, I'm such a selfish bitch.

Sophie straightens and steps back, umber eyes wide as her head whips my way, tight red curls flying. She laughs nervously. "Bunny! Wow, I almost didn't think you existed. It's nice to meet you."

Turning my hand in Hunter's, I lace our fingers together, my other hand drifting to my stomach the way pregnant women absentmindedly do. Flashing her a sweet-but-derisive smile, I reply, "Jazz really isn't my thing, but the baby is fond of Daddy's favorite music, so I figured I'd oblige them both tonight."

I may as well be a dog pissing on its territory—bared fangs, raised hackles—as the blood drains from Sophie's face. For a brief second I wonder if something ever happened between her and Hunter.

One look at him tells me that's an irrevocable *no*.

"*Oh!* C–congratulations!" Sophie looks mortified. "I need to go check on my other tables, but, uh, I'll have Katie come take your order."

As she scurries off, I angle a brow at Hunter, who's failing miserably to keep his laughter contained. "Oh, how the tables have turned. Was I this amusing when I'd interrupt your dates?"

"Comical," I say dryly before dropping my voice to a purr. "But I much preferred when you'd have your way with me afterward."

"Oh, trust me, Bunny. I plan on doing very naughty things to you when we get home. But first, you're going to sit there like a good little rabbit and enjoy the music and the food—even if you do get the pork chop. Then we're going to dance, and you're going to be lit up like a goddamn Christmas tree with lust the entire night just thinking about all the ways I'm going to make you come later."

He says it so nonchalantly, like he's detailing our work itinerary instead of getting me hot and bothered.

"Or you could fuck me in the bathroom again." I flash my best, most enticing smile. It doesn't work.

Hunter's eyes go wide with mock astonishment as he presses a hand to his chest. "These are hallowed halls! How dare you suggest such a thing, you harlot."

A stab of disappointment pierces my gut, even as I laugh.

Another waitress—this one far more respectful—takes our order, and gratitude sweeps through me when he orders mocktails for both of us instead of just me.

"If you can't drink, then I won't either. Simple." Hunter shrugs like it's nothing.

We keep it light for a while—work (I'm banned from any undercover assignments), and holiday plans (Thanksgiving upstate at his parents' with Dove and Wrenley).

When our food arrives—*yes, I did order the pork chop*—the tension shifts to a topic we've avoided, though it should be at the top of our list.

"Have you received any more letters?" he asks after a bite of perfectly succulent chicken breast. I've eaten more off his plate than he has. He wasn't lying when he said it's the best. He even offered to switch when my meal didn't compare, even though he won't touch the pork.

"No." I swirl my fork through the mashed potatoes. "I think whoever's sending them noticed the new addition to the security system."

It's been radio silence since Hunter installed a Ring camera the night we found out I was pregnant. And I've been funneling all my stabby tendencies into whatever meat I'm cooking for dinner instead of any new victims.

I meant what I told Dove. One more big kill, and then I'll be done. The Shadow Siren will retire, and I'll focus on being the best mother I can be... something I never had growing up.

Eventually, once baby bean is in school, I'll look into other ways to help domestically abused women.

"I swear that thing goes off every five seconds." Hunter pushes his plate back, jerking his chin at the rest of the chicken and giving me a silent okay to finish. "My battery keeps draining from how many times it alerts me any time there's so much as a breeze."

"You don't have to have the alerts on your phone, you know. It is *my* house."

"And you're *my* girl carrying *my* child."

Our conversation dies as a beautiful woman with old-Hollywood starlet hair and bright red lipstick appears from the curtain behind the stage. As the band starts a song, Hunter's hand appears in my line of sight.

"Dance with me."

Heat envelops me as he curls his fingers around mine

and helps me down. My heels close the height gap a little, but I still have to crane my neck to look up at him as we wind our arms around each other. Only a few seconds into the song and I settle for pressing my cheek against his chest.

It feels nice. Normal. Everything we could have started so long ago if we weren't so stubborn. Being in Hunter's arms makes me feel safe, but I still ask, "Do you think someone at the department could have found out about Nathaniel?"

"No, Little Rabbit. Keels and James kept that shit locked up tight." He kisses the top of my head and squeezes me reassuringly.

"Who is sending the letters then? And why?" I muse out loud, more to myself than to him.

He shushes me gently. "Can we just enjoy this moment, please?"

"Sure. It's not like a stalker is sending you letters," I deadpan.

Hunter stops moving, abandoning my waist to lift my chin. "If you think I'm going to let anything happen to you, you're dead wrong, Little Rabbit." His voice drops to a husky timbre—gravelly and intense—and I feel it all the way to my toes. "Anyone who tries to hurt you or our baby will find themselves in a world of pain, because I don't take kindly to others threatening my family. And that's what you are, Bunny. *My family.* If anyone tries to take you from me, I'll rip them apart with my bare hands."

I should be bothered by the ferocity in his statement,

but I am so incredibly turned on I'm pretty sure my arousal is starting to smear on my thighs.

"Now be a good girl and dance with me. Because as soon as the song is over, I'm going to take you home, bend you over, and eat my dessert from between your thighs."

A whimper slips between my parted lips, an inferno blazing low as he guides my head back to his chest and I try to think about anything other than the promise of what another hour will bring. I'm hot, needy, and desperate to get out of this tight dress, to the point I can barely focus on the song.

Hunter hums along, the notes reverberating against my ear like he's trying to fuse the lyrics to my soul. I pay closer attention, listening to the singer croon about her ex-lover wanting her back—about crying her a river like she did for him. I pull my head away, narrowing my eyes. "Seriously?" I deadpan.

He chuckles, asking innocently, "What?"

"You're lucky you're cute and that I'm too horny to care about the lyrics."

"Feeling guilty for the way you treated me, Little Rabbit?"

Why does everything he says have to sound so damn sexual? "No. I am, however, feeling highly sensitive to literally everything you do right now. And I swear to god, if you don't touch me soon, I might explode."

Irritation sparks—then fizzles when he grips my chin. "I think this is my favorite thing about you being pregnant. Alright. Let's get you home, my little sex goddess."

<u>Hunter</u>

Sighing heavily, I turn from where Bunny's passed out on the couch, snoring softly.

At the club and during the cab ride back to my place, she was insatiable. As soon as we get home? Out cold after a few minutes while I check on Pepper.

Hunter Jr. deflates from the hard-on he's been sporting since she expressed her displeasure at the familiarity with which Sophie greeted me. "Well, that didn't exactly go as planned."

Should've left when she wanted to.

Sex isn't the only reason I wanted to take her out tonight, though. Sure, it's been great that she's horny all the time—it's like we're making up for all the time we could've actually been fucking instead of just fucking around. But nothing compares to holding her in my arms in front of a crowd and saying she's mine.

It's been hard for her to bind herself to a title, but she's trying for me, which is all I can ask.

Intending to put her in my bed, I step into the living room, but Yasha lifts his head from where he's perched next to her and lets out a soft, warning growl.

Instead of focusing on her, I bend to pet Maru so Yasha doesn't feel threatened. "So that's what this is about, hmm? I appreciate you protecting your mom and all, but that's *my* baby in there, buddy."

Once he settles, I scratch behind his ears, then cradle Bunny in my arms. She snuggles into my chest and steals the breath from my lungs with how beautiful she is—even in sleep.

Part of me feels bad for dismissing her worry about the letters earlier. It isn't that I'm not worried about her safety. I just don't want her stressing over something we can't control. The less paranoid she is, the more at ease her stalker will be.

And when he slips up—and he will slip up—I'll be there, ready to put an end to his miserable life.

A BREATHY MOAN fills the air as silk glides against my skin.

Warm.

Wet.

Lower and lower, until fevered lips wrap around my cock.

Sucking.

Licking.

Turning me into her personal Hunter-flavored lollipop.

My fingers tangle in her silken strands, careful not to tug too hard as I lift her off me, groaning at the pop of her mouth and the string of saliva connecting her tongue to my steel-hard length.

Slowly, she crawls up my body and sinks onto me like her pussy is the lock and my cock is the key to our shared pleasure. "Fuck me, Hunter."

My hips roll, one hand anchoring her hip while the other smooths over her swollen belly. Her breasts heave, dusky nipples tight and begging to be kissed.

"Doesn't that feel good?" She bucks, grinding down as her pussy swallows my length.

It feels too fucking real to be a dream.

Am I dreaming?

Or is this—

The lust-fueled haze of what I thought was a lucid dream lifts as my eyes snap open. Bunny is riding me, clenching around my cock with every salacious pass of her hips. She's even more perfect now that I'm fully awake—head tipped back, mouth open in bliss.

"What are you doing, Little Rabbit?"

She must've woken up and slipped out of her undergarments. Before I put her to bed, I peeled the dress from her body but left her partially covered so she wouldn't wake thinking I took advantage. She knows I'd never do that, but I won't risk her feeling uncomfortable. And there's something just plain weird about a man stripping his girlfriend completely bare while she's passed out.

"Milking your cock for your cum. Don't you like that? Isn't my pussy nice and tight? And wet? And warm?" Each sleepy question is punctuated with a thrust, the swell of her belly turning my insides feral at the vision she makes.

Fuck, I'm so in love with this woman.

Bunny's always had a dirty mouth, but lately there are no boundaries to her inhibitions when we're intimate. I've heard her say shit that nearly made *me* blush.

"Oh yeah? Does my greedy girl want to be filled up?" Her responding moan is music to my ears as I gently rotate us, laying her back against the pillows.

Staying on my knees, I push into her and lift her legs around my waist. Raven strands fan over my sheets like a dark halo as her head thrashes. I thumb her clit and thrust slow and deep, making sure she feels every solid inch I have to give.

"Fuck, baby, you're so fucking tight."

"Hunter," she cries my name like worship. Half-lidded pine watches me through the dark, moonlight casting her in a resplendent glow like a true goddess receiving my offering.

"You're mine, Bunny." I hook her legs higher, hitting a new angle, then return to strumming her like a guitar string. "This pussy is mine. This swollen little clit is mine. These perky breasts? All mine." Shallow breaths make her chest heave as her walls flutter. "Your mouth and that sinfully wicked tongue."

"Claim them all, Hunter. I want to feel you every-where." She's fully awake now, earthy pine brightening to golden moss as it catches the silvered light. "Remind me who I belong to. I've been a bad girl, and I think I've forgotten."

A growl rumbles from my chest and I flex inside her. "Well then, Little Rabbit, I'll make sure that by the end of the night you're so thoroughly wrecked you'll never forget again."

Sweat slicks our skin, shining where we meet as I lean

down and capture her mouth in a searing kiss. Picking up my pace, I snap my hips, branding her pussy with my cock. Electric tension coils at the base of my spine, slithering into my balls as she cries out.

Without warning, she clamps down—trapping me in a vise grip, pulsing around me as she comes on my cock. She's everywhere, pulling me in with her nails and her heels and her fucking tight pussy, milking me until I'm spilling inside her in thick, hot bursts.

"Keep going," she begs, and it sounds so fucking pretty it drags another climax out of me.

I obey, fucking her through another release—her warmth flooding me until I've got nothing left to give. I slip from her searing walls and kiss down her sweat-slicked skin to the apex of her thighs.

"No, I can't take any more. I need a break." Bunny pushes at my head, whimpering as I lick through her center to clean up our mess.

Gathering her wrists in one hand, I pin them to her chest while I scoop the cum leaking from her pussy and push it back inside with two fingers. "Oh, baby, there are no breaks tonight. You had your rest earlier. And you just said you forgot who you belong to."

"You. I belong to you. It was a figure of speech in the heat of the moment." She gasps, struggling against my hold as I lick a path up her center and seal my mouth over her clit. "Fuck, I'm too sensitive. Hunter, I can't."

"You can, Little Rabbit. There's nowhere to run. You're trapped." I suck her sweet and steady, fingers pumping in rhythm with my mouth, building a pace that has her keening like an animal in heat. "And now, it's time for the hunter to devour his prey."

OVER THE NEXT TWO WEEKS, my baby bump pops. Thankfully, I'm on extended leave. Otherwise, work would be difficult since Hunter and I still haven't told anyone besides Dove, Wrenley, and Hunter's parents. Now that it's impossible to hide baby bean, we've been debating *how* exactly to tell people who know us that we're having a baby.

Surprise! All that "will they/won't they?" tension culminated in another living being, and now we're basically all in together.

Telling his parents was hard enough. I stressed myself out thinking his mother hated me to the point that I made myself sick. Turns out, Carla was just relieved to hear that "I finally got my shit together."

Needless to say, I think we're going to get along just fine. We've met before, but it was always in passing, so spending Thanksgiving at their farm upstate will be... insightful, as to how the rest of my life is going to go.

Tonight, however, is about celebrating Dove and Wrenley's engagement and—if Hunter has anything to say about it—telling Alex and Vixey, who is apparently now part of our little group, much to my chagrin. I'm not sure when exactly that happened, but I guess me spending less time at the bar resulted in her and Dove spending more time together.

"It's so pretty!" The tall blonde squeals, gawking at Dove's ring for the umpteenth time since we arrived at *The Tipsy Taco* five minutes ago.

"I'm still pissed he didn't bother having any of us there," I grumble. I've had a while to sit with the news and process that Wrenley didn't include us.

His reply when I brought it up the first moment I could get him alone was, *"Should I be upset that you and Hunter didn't invite us to join when you made a baby?"*

Touché, California Dreamin'.

Not that I'm trying to make it about me, but Wrenley could have at least asked me to hide and record the whole thing. I wanted to be there when Dove saw her new pink sparkly.

"But he put the ring on Fang's collar, and how cute is that?" Vixey coos like she's talking to a baby. Her tone has my face tightening in disgust.

Hunter has been working overtime with that bleach-blonde bimbo, Gwendolyn, so I'm particularly moody tonight. It's starting to grate on my nerves how much time they're spending together, to the point where I'm ready to walk into the department—big belly and all—

and plant one right on Hunter to publicly claim him as mine.

Alex preemptively sets a round of tequila shots in front of us, breaking me from my reverie. "Vixey, why don't you take the rest of the night off and celebrate with the girls?"

"Can she?" Dove squeals, which only further exacerbates my bad mood. "I've been wanting to go dancing. We should have a girls' night!"

She spins toward me and visibly flinches when she sees my face. Erasing all irritability as quickly as I can, I flash her a tight smile, not wanting to ruin her mood. "Sure thing. Whatever you want, Love Dove."

My best friend looks between me, the shots, Alex, and back again. "Bunny has news, too."

A devilish smirk stretches her rosy lips as Alex and Vixey turn to look at me, but before I can say anything, Hunter and Wrenley appear behind us. The crib Hunter ordered arrived early, and Wrenley went to help him get it upstairs to the nursery, which is why we arrived separately. If Dove gets her way, we might not be leaving together tonight, either.

Girls' night used to end with pizza and a bottle of tequila at one of our houses, but now that I can't drink, I can only imagine she and Vixey getting crazy while I'm forced to babysit.

"Whoa there, Little Rabbit. That better be water in that shot glass." Hunter reaches around me, picks one up, and sniffs it before frowning. "Do I need to be worried about something?"

"Ew. Just because you're, like, dating now or something doesn't mean you get to control her," Vixey snaps.

I like her a little bit more for her defensive outburst.

"Settle down, Vix," Hunter cajoles.

I like her a little less now that his nickname for her has apparently stuck.

He checks his watch as Alex congratulates Wrenley, trying to diffuse the situation.

"You haven't told them *our* news?" Hunter looks momentarily offended before I nod toward Dove. "Oh, I get it. You wanted to let Dove shine." He nudges her with his elbow. "Well, doll. You had your moment. I kind of want to be a bastard and steal some of the spotlight."

"Oh, please, it's *our* moment. You know I'm not one of those girls. Tonight is about you two as much as it's about us." Dove leans back into Wrenley, who puts a protective arm around her while looking at Hunter like he wants to shove one of Dove's daggers between his eyes.

Hunter and Wrenley may be best friends, but Wrenley is still holding a grudge for that kiss, and I don't blame him in the slightest.

"What are we missing here?" Alex asks, leaning his elbows on the bar top as he peers between us all.

"Oh my god, are you pregnant?" Vixey blurts. Both she and Alex drop their gazes to my stomach. It's hidden beneath the lip of the bar, and even then, I wore a trench tonight to hide my bump until we told them.

Hunter points at her. "Ding, ding, ding! What gave it away? My comment about the tequila? See, Vix, I'm not an overbearing asshole." He wraps an arm around my waist and squeezes as if to drive that comment home.

"Wow," Alex muses. "That went from zero to sixty real fast."

"We figured it was time to tell you. After all, we did make the baby in the women's bathroom." Hunter reaches for the shot, lifting it to his lips. "Points for cleanliness in there."

"Are you serious?" Alex deadpans.

"Congratulations," Vixey offers, looking at me timidly. "Do you know what you're having yet?"

She's tiptoeing the line of getting too personal, and she knows it, but I decide to oblige her. If Dove is already friends with her, I'm going to have no choice but to accept the honey-blonde ditz.

With a sigh, I shrug out of my coat, prepared to settle in. Hunter and Wrenley shift over and take the seats next to us, leaving us girls to chat on our own.

"We're not telling."

"Is this because Wrenley didn't include you in the proposal?" Dove flashes me a good-natured look of annoyance. "You better tell me the gender of that baby, Buns. I'm the godmother—I get to know these things."

"Sorry. My lips are sealed. Hunter said not to tell."

If I'm being honest, we don't even know yet.

Even though I'm cooking a literal human inside me, there's something so surreal about the whole thing—it's like my motherly instincts haven't really kicked in yet. There's a connection there, but I haven't nurtured it the way some expecting mothers do as soon as they know they're pregnant. A part of me is still waiting for something to happen. To wake up one morning and realize it was all a dream, or find that I'm losing the baby.

It's been hard for me to allow myself to get attached.

"Oh, and you listen to everything Hunter says?" Dove snaps sardonically.

"Only in the bedroom," I reply with a saccharine tone. "Sort of like you and your songbird, wouldn't you agree?" Silently, I mouth *dick-whipped*.

"You're one to talk! Hunter poisons you with his peter, and all of a sudden he's completely in charge of your pickled peppers!"

"What?"

She blinks, then shakes her head and tosses back a shot. "I don't even know. It just came out."

We erupt into giggles before Vixey's wistful voice cuts in, "You guys are so cool."

I don't think she meant to say it out loud. Her cheeks flare red as she stands. "I should get back to work."

"I thought Alex said you could have the night off?" I ask. She stops and looks at me like she's not sure she heard me correctly. "Didn't you and Dove say you wanted to go dancing?"

Taking the small olive branch I'm offering, she beams. "Really?"

Fuck, am I really that horrible?

Suddenly, I'm overcome with emotion. I don't want to be one of those females who goes out of their way to make another woman feel like shit. Not unless they're trying to go after my man—looking at you, Gwendolyn. The least I can do is *try*, I guess.

"Of course, really! Let's do this! Girls' night!" Dove chimes in.

"I know a place we can go," Vixey proposes, still watching me for a sign I'm not being genuine.

"I'm going to need to go home and change. I don't want to go out in this." Dove gestures to her hot-pink skirt suit. "I had an interview with Tripp Kennedy today. Nice guy. Much nicer than Jackson Tailor."

I swear Wrenley visibly shudders on the other side of her at the mention of the billionaire's name.

"Why don't I give you both the address, and we can just meet there in a little while? I'll go home and get ready, too," Vixey suggests.

"Where are you ladies going?" Hunter interrupts, leaning around Wrenley.

"To this nightclub in the East Village. It's safe, I promise," Vixey replies with a roll of her eyes. Sometimes I wonder if she flips him sass to get on my good side. The more I watch them interact, the more I get a big-brother/little-sister vibe. For some reason, that puts me a little more at ease about the woman who's moved her way into my circle.

Hunter flashes me a look that very much says he doesn't want me to go, but also doesn't want to be controlling. He's been so careful not to act like Nathaniel. Still, it's been hard navigating boundaries without my ugly past rearing its head at least once a day.

"It's fine, Hunter. We'll take good care of your girl."

Dove picks up on the tension, leans over, and pokes his cheek. She snaps back quickly, shaking her hand as if touching him burned her. "Jesus, who has jaw muscles that firm? What the hell do you do to—"

She trails off as he swings a devilish grin her way.

"Oh yeah, you're a world-class Bunny kitty eater. I forgot." She pokes her fiancé's cheek. "Why aren't yours that firm?"

"Are you saying you want me to do more kitty eating, Turtle Dove? That can be arranged." Wrenley buries his face in her neck, and she breaks into squeals and giggles.

"Aaaand I'm going to take that as my cue to go. Dove, I'll text you!" Vixey bounces behind the bar and kisses Alex on the cheek. Pink blooms along the bridge of his nose as she hugs him from behind. "Thank you for the night off!"

"No problem. Have fun, ladies." He manages it through a cough. The poor man is so smitten, and Vixey doesn't seem interested in him in any remotely romantic way. I wonder if she knows he's carrying a torch for her?

"Do you wanna go home and grab a dress and meet me at my place?" I ask, interrupting Dove and Wrenley. Their PDA doesn't faze me one bit.

"Okay. I'll text you when I leave. Why don't you come home with me, and you can come back later?" she suggests to Wrenley, who's out of his seat before she finishes.

Hunter chuckles, sliding over as soon as they disappear. "I'll keep my phone on if you need anything. Or, if you'd like me to come over afterward. I haven't gotten my *kitty eating* in today." He waggles his brows, then presses a chaste kiss to my lips.

Turning in my seat, I lean against his chest to kiss him harder. Hunter's love language is physical touch, and I've been doing my best lately to ensure he knows I want him around. I'm not the best at showing my feelings, but this is something I can do for him. Not because I feel like I have to, but because I genuinely want to be there for Hunter the same way he's been there for me.

Our moment is cut short when Alex taps on the bar in front of us. "Hey, Buns. Thanks for inviting Vixey out. She really needs this, and she really wants to be your friend."

"God, I don't know why. I've been awful to her." I snort and pull back from Hunter, picking up the glass of water Alex set down after our announcement.

Neither guy replies, and my gaze slides from the lime wedge floating atop the ice to Hunter, then to Alex. Both men are staring at me with worried expressions, like I just said something completely out of pocket.

"You kind of have..." Alex says carefully.

"Are you feeling okay, Little Rabbit? You just willingly admitted you're not very nice to Vixey."

Huh. I guess I did.

"Whatever. If she's here to stay, I might as well try to get used to her. Seems like she and Dove have gotten pretty friendly in my absence."

"Dove isn't going to abandon you just because we're having a kid and they don't want any, Bunny." Hunter wraps an arm around my shoulders and kisses the top of my head. "Don't worry. Your friend isn't going to replace you with Vix."

My brows flatten, and I pull back. "Call her that one more time, Hunter, and there will be no *kitty eating* for a week."

He smirks. "Baby, you can't go that long without me on my knees."

I flash him a wide, sweet smile. "You're right. Let me rephrase. There will be no *Hunter Jr. sucking* for a week."

His smirk drops as he pulls away. "Okay. Geez. You're so mean, Little Rabbit."

Alex groans. "I swear I need a shower after listening to you four talk about your sex lives."

"Don't be so vanilla, Alex!" Hunter shouts at his retreating back, then drops his mouth to my ear. "How about we rush home and get in a workout before you go out?"

"We don't have time," I laugh. "Dove is coming over."

"Oh, please. You don't think they aren't going to do their own adult gymnastics before spending a night apart?" He slaps money on the bar, grabs my hand, and helps me down from the stool. "Come on, your chariot awaits."

I don't recall seeing him grab his phone, and with it being the weekend, I'm sure it will take forever to get a car. "Did you already order a ride?"

"My face, Little Rabbit. Your chariot is my face."

As we step out of our cab, Dove squeals the moment she sees Vixey waiting for us on the sidewalk. "We look like we're straight out of *Romy and Michele's High School Reunion!*"

She's not wrong. While she's decked out in her signature pink, with five-inch platforms and a metallic sheen to her bubblegum-colored dress, Vixey is wearing a short sequined mini in the color of the Pine Green crayon from the old Crayola box. Meanwhile, I chose a glittering lavender bodycon—just because I'm pregnant doesn't mean I can't dress cute.

"I don't know what that is, but I'm happy to be a part of it." Vixey wobbles in her kitten heels, hands flying out to catch nothing but air as she steadies herself. She's clumsy enough on flat feet, it's a wonder she hasn't broken an ankle in the sixty seconds since we arrived.

"You don't know *Romy and Michele?*" Dove asks incredulously, as if it's a crime.

"How old *are* you?" I ask.

"She just turned twenty-six," Dove answers for her. "Which, okay, I guess that makes sense, but still... we're going to need to watch it!"

That explains a lot.

There's a six-year age gap between us, and that makes all the difference. I remember how I was at twenty-six, and the amount of shit that's jaded me since.

I ignore the fact that Dove knew she just had a birthday.

"Vixey!" We all turn toward the sound of one of the bouncers shouting the tall girl's name and waving us over. He's built like a pro wrestler, with a buzz cut and a scar running through his upper lip that hitches the right side up.

"Hey, Daniel! I brought some friends tonight, is that okay?" She greets the man with a tight hug and a kiss on the cheek. He gives us a friendly once-over, gracious enough not to linger on my bulging belly—thank god, because I was a little worried we might have a *Knocked Up* moment.

"Anything for you, V. You ladies have a nice time tonight." He unclasps the rope and moves aside to let us through. It doesn't surprise me, the hearts in his eyes while looking at her. The girl's a bombshell... even if she is graceless.

A chorus of frustrated cries rises from the long line waiting to get in, but one mean mug from Dove has a good portion of them shutting their mouths mid-complaint.

"You can check your coat there if you want." Vixey motions to a space once we reach the end of the long, dark hallway. Even though it's cold outside, I'm the only one who wore a jacket. I don't particularly want to part with my old leather, but a few minutes inside tells me if I keep it on, I'll be a sweaty, sticky mess within a couple of dances.

"So, how long have you two been friends?" Vixey asks while they wait for me off to the side.

"Gosh, almost two years now, I think? I actually knew Hunter before I knew Bunny." I hear Dove explain. "Remember Ryan? I met him at a gala and met Hunter through him. Then it was like fate when Bunny and I ran into each other one night while we were—"

My head whips around just as she stops herself from saying more, stretching the word and finishing with, "—both at the department waiting on the guys. We hit it off instantly."

"Whatever happened to Ryan? I noticed he hasn't been around since he and Wrenley got in that fight." Vixey leads us to the bar, practically yelling over the music.

For as packed as it is, the bartender notices her quickly—another cute guy she greets by name, who seems to have a hard-on for her. I have a feeling Vixey is one of those girls who gets along easily with men, so other women make assumptions about her. It explains why she doesn't have any female friends.

While she's distracted, Dove and I share a look before I reply, "He moved out of state. Got transferred somewhere west."

"Oh. I always liked him—he was nice. Well, I guess to me anyway," she muses, handing Dove some sort of tequila cocktail and me a soda water with lime.

"Of course he was nice to you, you're hot. I'm surprised he didn't try to sleep with you. Unless he did, and you just haven't told me. You can be honest if you slept with him, though—we were never exclusive. We knew each other forever before we even slept together."

"I would *never* do something like that!" Vixey vehemently waves her hands, her long, balayaged mane flying.

Dove waves her off. "Relax, Vix. I'm just saying it's okay if you did. You're definitely his type."

"*Was* his type," I mumble loud enough for only Dove to hear.

Vixey is too tall to catch the joke and downs two shots before spinning toward the dance floor. "Well, I didn't. Fucking guys my friends have fucked is not my jam."

"Great rule to live by." I hold up my glass in a *cheers to that* motion.

Loud remixed pop thumps through the space. The main floor is packed, so Vixey leads us up a few steps to a roped-off level, where there's a smaller, less-crowded dance floor adjacent to the VIP area. A group of guys instantly hone in on her and Dove, passing me by the second they see my stomach.

Once upon a time, it might have upset me to be dismissed so easily. But all that goes through my mind is how, when I tell Hunter about the night's events, he will undoubtedly make a joke about how no one better think they're too good for his girl. It brings a smile to my face, and I *nearly* grab my phone to text him.

Tonight is about us girls. And I am *not* dick-whipped.

It honestly feels good to let go for the night. Dancing with Dove and Vixey is freeing. For as much attention as they pull, neither strays from my side—we're celebrating each other and couldn't care less about the men trying to steal their attention.

Nearly an hour later, Vixey goes to the bathroom while Dove and I settle into a booth along the wall as a younger group of girls abandons it to return to the floor.

"See, she's not so bad, is she?" Dove asks while texting Wrenley.

The guys decided to have their own night out and went back to the bar to hang with Alex. Even though Hunter and I haven't spent a night apart in a while, Dove and I decided we're going to see if Vixey wants to stay at my place tonight.

I'm trying.

"Okay, she's not that bad. You're right."

Vixey is honestly a lot of fun, and I feel like a total brat for not accepting her into our group sooner. But I also feel like I'm just a moody bitch who happens to be having a good time tonight. Tomorrow, I might wake up and regret it when I find her still in my house.

Dove's phone lights up with an incoming call. "Oh, my sweet songbird. He knows we're in a club. I'll be right back—I'm gonna find a quieter place to take this."

I have no idea where she plans to do that. She'll have to go outside if she hopes to hear him over the music. We practically have to yell at each other as it is.

As she leaves, a flash of green catches my eye, and I turn to see Vixey approaching from the other side of the room. She only makes it a few feet from the bathroom before she trips, and I suppress a groan when she falls face-first into the crotch of a man sitting in a plush armchair with a group of guys.

A friend would rush over and rescue her. However, from where I'm sitting, it looks like that might embarrass her more. The only thing worse than head-butting a man's dick is the position Vixey finds herself in—with her ass in the air and her hair caught in either the belt or zipper of his pants.

Vixey's hair is teased and fluffed to high heaven. It's that sexy-waves style where it almost looks like it hasn't been washed in days and stands up on its own, so I imagine when it caught on her way down, it tangled pretty badly.

Her short dress is nearly flashing the rest of the room her underwear, but if she's embarrassed, it doesn't show. She brackets his legs with her arms, trying to push up, only to yelp and lower herself again.

Sitting back against the leather, I sip my soda water, entertained by the soft-core porn show they're putting on. Whoever the men are with him, they're wolves dressed in sharp suits, chuckling into their whiskey as they watch the scene unfold.

The man cups her chin and says something that makes Vixey stiffen, eyes wide. He goes to work untangling her strands, his mouth moving with words that hold her in a trance. Once she's freed, he grips her chin again, and this time I squint to read his lips.

Good girl.

Well, hot damn. Get it, Vixey. He's gorgeous.

For a moment I feel bad for having the thoughts,

knowing Alex likes her. But if the way Vixey is staring at this man is any indication of the type she prefers, poor Alex never stood a chance.

She climbs to her feet slowly, using his thighs for leverage. Their locked gazes don't waver as she rises to her full height, then she's the one towering over him since he remains seated. The lights pulse with the music, oscillating between casting them in shadow and highlighting their frames as he stands, buttoning his suit jacket while he speaks to her. Just when I think we might lose her for the night, she turns abruptly and heads back to the booth.

A few steps away, her honeyed eyes snap up to mine. "Did you see that?"

"Oh, I sure did." I keep sipping my soda water. "What are you doing back over here? That man looks like he wants to eat you alive."

"It's girls' night." She sounds so young and innocent as she says it, almost pouty, her shoulders slumping slightly.

"Don't worry, I'm not trying to get rid of you. Just saying—I'd understand. He's hot." My gaze tracks across the room. The man is still standing, watching Vixey with a determination I often see in Hunter's face when he looks at me. "How's your scalp? That looked like it hurt."

Her hand drifts up to rub the spot absentmindedly. "I'm pretty sure I lost a chunk of hair."

"But maybe gained a phone number?" I push,

because I'm invested now. The guy still hasn't taken his eyes off her.

"What? No!" She slides into the booth just as Dove reappears.

"Did he or did he not call you a good girl?" I press.

Dove's head snaps up from her phone, ping-ponging between us. "What did I miss? Who called her a good girl?"

Vixey groans. "It's nothing."

"She fell into that guy's lap over there." I nod across the room, but he's finally sat back down, attention elsewhere. "Got her hair caught in his zipper."

"It was his belt," Vixey grumbles, slouching over her drink. "So fucking embarrassing."

"You really are so clumsy." Dove cocks her head, studying his side profile. "But hey, if it works. He's hot."

"That's what *I* said!"

"Girls'. Night." Vixey stresses. "Do you know how long I've waited for you to invite me to do something? I'm not ruining it by running off with a guy I don't know."

"We're just saying..." I start.

"That we'd completely understand," Dove finishes.

"Besides. Don't knock the rushed, have to take you in a bathroom because I need you now sex. One of the best orgasms I've ever had."

"There's something about public places. Wrenley and I did it in a storm once, next to a body." Dove tosses back her remaining shot.

Panic surges as Vixey stiffens and swings her head

toward Dove, grotesque confusion twisting her tone as she repeats, "A *body*?"

My best friend coughs and pounds her chest. "Of water. A body of water. We were on the beach. You know, a public place." She laughs nervously as I refrain from slapping my forehead.

Her answer seems to mollify Vixey, who only pauses a moment before sliding back out of the booth. "Let's dance!"

Dove and I share a look as we follow, both of us whispering, "Worst serial killers ever."

"Where did Vixey disappear to?" Dove scans the club, which has only gotten busier as the night wears on.

Exhaustion hit me like a freight train ten minutes ago. I'm ready for pajamas, bed, and to scrub off this makeup. As the weeks pass and the baby grows, my will to complete the whole getting-ready routine has evaporated. It takes as much energy to paint my face as it does to wash it off.

"Maybe she decided to go fuck *belt guy* after all?"

Annoyance creeps into my bones. Dove won't leave without the other blonde, but Vixey's been gone nearly twenty minutes.

"Or maybe the line for the bathroom is just really long? She did take a lot of shots. I feel bad for challenging her to drink me under the table. I thought her tolerance would be better." Dove pushes onto her toes even though that does nothing for her height. "I'm going to text her again."

As she pulls her phone from between her breasts, Vixey breaks through the crowd with a sheepish look. "Hey, sorry. That took way longer than expected."

"You're fine! We're ready to go, though. Is that okay?" Dove asks, already turning toward the exit.

Even with the lights casting everyone in blue, pink, and purple, I can tell Vixey's pallor is off. She looks spooked, and she's trembling.

Alarm bells go off. My hackles rise, and I pivot into a protective mode I never thought I'd have where she's concerned. "What happened? What's wrong?"

Her head snaps to me—and instantly she relaxes. All signs of distress melts away, replaced by fatigued contentment. "Nothing's wrong. I'm just tired. Ready when you are."

She takes off after Dove, who's grabbing my jacket at coat check and misses our exchange. Suspicion needles me, but I drop it after one last glance at the raised level. The nameless man from earlier stands at the railing, watching Vixey with intrigue.

Wherever she was, I'd bet he was there too.

For some reason, instead of giving me a bad feeling—especially after how she looked coming back—a sense of relief washes over me, almost like foreshadowing.

Whoever he is, I have a notion he's someone she wants in her corner, and this won't be the last time we see him.

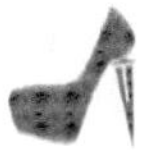

"I REMEMBER when I was that age. I could stay up till four and wake at six, ready for work. I didn't take her for such a lightweight." Dove points her slice of pizza toward the living room, where Vixey is dead asleep on my sofa. She didn't even stay awake long enough to enjoy the pie we grabbed on the way to my place. Dove held the food under her nose to try to rouse her, but the girl was gone the instant her head hit the pillow.

Checking the oven clock, I nod and pluck a crispy pepperoni to pop into my mouth. "Yeah, she's not what I expected at all."

"Told you. She's a sweetheart." Dove kicks off her platforms and sinks into a chair at the kitchen table. "I'm not saying you have to be best friends, but we had fun tonight, didn't we?"

"Yeah, yeah." I wave her off. "She's more tolerable after Hunter gives me an orgasm."

"And the dogs love her." Dove keeps ticking off reasons to keep Vixey around.

It surprised us both when all three dogs curled up on the sofa with her like she wasn't a stranger. Our animals usually have more stranger-danger sense, but then again, Fang fell in love with Wrenley instantly. Yasha and Maru, however, don't typically take to people they don't know.

"I get it, Love Dove. I'll stop being a bitch to her."

Silence settles between us as we finish our pizza. Dove's phone pings every few seconds, and she stares at it with a giddy grin. Wild to think six months ago she and Wrenley couldn't stand each other—now they're engaged, he knows about her extracurriculars, and they're still in the honeymoon phase.

"Let me guess, Wrenley wants you home?" I tap my screen to see if Hunter messaged.

Nothing.

Disappointment trickles in—along with the possibility he got called in because Gwendolyn wanted to see him. The little tart beckons him at all hours, and I don't understand why he puts up with it. He says it's because she has seniority over him, but if that's the case, then he should file a sexual harassment claim.

"No." She flicks her gaze to mine. "He knows we need girl time. He just got home and said Hunter left when he did. Hunt wanted him to tell you his phone died."

I don't know why that doesn't make me feel better.

"Have you done any more recon on the Christmas guy?" Dove slides her phone away and gives me her full attention.

My hand drifts to my bump. In six weeks, baby bean will be even bigger. How am I supposed to kill a man with a stomach the size of a soccer ball?

"There's not much to do. He's a bastard who made his wife have three kids she never wanted and abused her through each pregnancy. I was already working on him before his trip. The belly will be a turn-on for him. It'll be easy."

Tiny taps click across the kitchen as Maru pads in and settles behind Dove's chair, ears swiveling toward the front door, then the living room. I check the door cam, but the street is empty, greenery swaying in the courtyard.

"Want help with this one? I worry about you. I know you can handle yourself, but you'll be farther along and…" She trails off, her big blue eyes glistening.

"You think I'm putting the baby in danger." Not a question. "Come on, Dove. Let the Shadow Siren go out with a bang. It's not like I'll keep killing after the baby is born."

Maru barks sharply, startling us both. He isn't sitting anymore. He's standing, shaking with the force of his wag, staring at the threshold where the kitchen meets the living room. Dove keeps talking, but my attention locks on the dark opening.

"Maybe I should retire the Doll, too. Can you imagine that headline? The Baby Doll Killer and Shadow Siren disappear from Manhattan?"

"Dove, stop talking." Slowly, I step out of my stilettos and rise, keeping one heel in my hand, the point outward. Maru's tail keeps wagging as he watches whatever has him rapt.

Flashes of the letters that keep appearing strobe through my head as I creep toward the hall that leads into the other side of the living room. Dove's brows pinch as she swivels. Whoever is in my house is trapped with two very pissed-off serial killers.

Someone broke into my house.

Anger spikes when I think about my baby. Mama bear energy surges, fueling me with adrenaline as Yasha and Fang join Maru's delayed alerts. I hear the scraping of Dove's chair against the kitchen tile. Whoever is in the living room starts moving toward my end in hurried steps.

Raising my shoe, I get ready to slash the intruder's throat. A flash of green darts under my swing, nearly slamming into me as it runs from Dove. The lights snap on.

"Vixey?" Dove and I shout together, and the tall blonde's eyes go wide with fear.

Well, fuck. I was just beginning to like her, too.

"I swear, I won't say anything!" The dark-blonde girl shakes her head frantically, wide honey eyes ping-ponging between Dove and me.

"You're damn right you won't." My snarl is more annoyed than dangerous.

To her credit, Vixey walked herself down to the basement without us having to manhandle her, willingly sat in a chair, and even said Dove could zip-tie her, if we wanted.

Either she has a death wish or she's really desperate for friends.

"Why were you eavesdropping?" Dove asks. Her tone goes flat, all the cotton-candy sweetness melts into something poisonous as the Baby Doll Killer surfaces.

"I'm sorry. I woke up and heard you talking, so I was

going to join you, then I overheard what you said about the Siren and stopped to listen." Vixey trembles, mascara tears streaking her golden cheeks. "Dove, I swear I won't rat you out. I've always admired the Siren and the Doll."

Dove sighs, and I know this is taking a toll on her. She really likes Vixey, and if it comes down to it, I'm not sure she can take her out. "Anyone in your position would say that, Vix."

The stairs took it out of me, so I pull another chair over and sit, fiddling with the heel cap of my stiletto. Once it's loose, the tiny dagger springs free, newly sharpened. Vixey squeaks and shakes harder as I meet her gaze.

"As much as I'm sure you won't believe me, I'm not going to enjoy this like I once might have."

We only have one option: eliminate the witness.

Yesterday, I might've been happy to press my blade to her throat and wallow in the gurgles as her life bled out.

Today, the thought upsets me. My stomach roils at the thought of spilling her blood.

Or is that baby bean moving?

Whatever it is, it's swimming around in my stomach and threatening to send my pizza back up.

"You don't have to do this. You can trust me." For how scared she is, Vixey's voice is firm, determined to change our minds even as her tears keep falling.

"And why would we do that?" Dove unsheathes a black-steel dagger, testing the point against her finger.

Vixey heaves a sigh, casting her gaze to the ceiling. Shaking her head before she speaks. "Because I'm a killer too."

Silence follows.

One second.

Two.

Three.

Vixey watches us with wide, pleading eyes. Dove and I look at each other.

Four.

Five.

Six.

We both burst into laughter. Not the Doll's childlike giggles or the Siren's sultry chuckles—pure, uncontrollable amusement.

"*You*? A killer? Of what? Coordination?" I double over, clutching my stomach.

"Grace?" Dove belts between guffaws.

"All the glasses at the bar?" I wipe a tear.

Vixey scowls. "You are both so rude," she spits like a petulant child. "You want to know why I was gone so long tonight? A guy tried to take me out back and have his way with me by the dumpsters. He manhandled me out the door, so I handled him right back. He tripped and fell and hit his head. I left him for dead... at least I *think* he was dead."

She crosses her arms and slouches, bottom lip jutting as we roll over the information she's divulged.

"You killed someone tonight?" Dove arches a delicate brow and glances at me, looking for a tell that I believe Vixey.

"Yes. I mean... I didn't *mean* to. It was an accident.

But it happened." Her head wobbles, sass peeking through.

"Down, killer. You understand why we're skeptical?" Stroking my stomach absentmindedly, I think back to how shaken she looked coming back. "Was it one of the guys you knew?"

"No. Just some random guy I've hung out with there before. He was trying to make out with me at the bar, and then he dragged me out the side door before I knew what was happening."

"How'd you get back in without anyone seeing?" Dove asks.

"I pounded on the door until someone opened it. Usually there's a bouncer, but he wasn't at his post. The dumpster's out of the door's line of sight." Her voice drops. "Plus, I kinda dragged him behind it."

"So your DNA is all over him?" Dove sighs. "Rule number one, you never leave DNA."

"No. Rule number one is never get caught," I correct, eyes still on Vixey. She doesn't seem to be lying, but I barely know the girl—no way to tell how good an actress she is.

"Right. Rule number one: never get caught. Rule number two: never leave DNA." Dove ticks them off on her fingers.

"What's rule number three?" Vixey asks, like a scolded baby bird trying to fly too soon.

"Rule number three: you never kill without a purpose. Some guy trying to take advantage of you is purpose enough for me. Though I'm still not sure I believe you." My stomach swims again.

If you could chill right now, baby bean, that would be great.

I haven't been sick in weeks. If it comes back, I swear bitterness will be my only feeling toward this child. I hate throwing up, and morning, afternoon, and night sickness already ruled too much of my first trimester.

"I'll prove it! The body has to still be there!" Vixey jumps up, only to be shoved back down by Dove, who taps a palm to her forehead.

"Rule number four—which should probably rank higher and," she whirls toward me, exasperated, "we should *really* rearrange the rules. Now that I'm saying them out loud, I feel like they need to be updated." Swinging back toward Vixey, she sucks in a deep breath. "Never, and I mean *ever*, go back to the scene of the crime!"

"Can I write this down, or is there a handbook or something?"

Jesus fucking christ.

"No, there isn't a handbook," I mimic, acerbic. Breathing through my nose, I try to quell the climb of nausea.

"We'll have to keep an eye on the news. That alley isn't exactly high-traffic, but as soon as trash goes out, someone will find him... if you're telling the truth." Dove crosses her arms. "I have half a mind to keep you tied up until then."

"Don't put me on babysitting duty. I'll kill her before

you make it back." Racking my brain for a solution, I come up empty, unable to focus on anything other than trying not to get sick.

"Bunny? You don't look so good," Vixey says softly.

Gee, what gave it away? The sweat rolling down my temple or the way I'm clutching my stomach and breathing through my mouth?

Ignoring her, I focus on Dove. "If the body's found, like you said, her DNA will be all over it. Why don't you stay here and I'll go? I need fresh air, and I'm well acquainted with the shadows."

I don't give her a chance to reply, climbing the stairs as she calls, "Are you sure?"

"Yes, I'm sure, Love Dove. Don't let the vicious vixen out of your sight."

"Oooh, unless you're lying, you're in the club now. You've been graced with a moniker," I hear Dove tell Vixey.

Inwardly, I curse, only now realizing what I did. I lock eyes with Dove. "We are the worst serial killers ever."

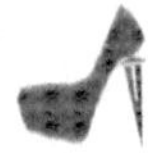

IT'S EARLY ENOUGH that the club is closed. The sky is lightening—its midnight ink turning violet as the stars blink out one by one.

Soon, there will be no shadows to hide me.

But it doesn't take long to find what I'm looking for.

Behind the dumpster, just where she said, lies a dead

man with a good chunk missing from his face. Blood drips down the corner of the bin. The pool on the ground still gleams.

Slowly, I creep closer to Vixey's "kill." His face must've caught a sharp edge. A horizontal gash splits his lips and one eye, the orb pooling from the socket. A bit of frontal lobe has puddled onto the concrete.

But something feels… off.

Shit—she must *have put serious force behind that.*

This doesn't look like a simple push-and-fall. It looks like someone smashed his face into the dumpster repeatedly, and Vixey doesn't seem like the strong type. She's willowy with giant boobs—no real arm muscle. So either adrenaline did the trick, or—

A resounding boom makes me jump, the hair on my arms standing on end as the side door crashes open. Silently, I press to the wall, rising onto my toes until shadow swallows me.

Curiosity edges into intrigue as a familiar figure steps around the dumpster, wiping his hands with a white rag.

His bloody hands.

Belt guy.

He's on the phone, voice hushed but clear enough to catch.

"It needs to be a quick cleanup. It'll be light soon."

He pauses, listening. His eyes sweep both ends of the alley. I press flatter to the stone and angle my bump away from view. He doesn't clock me—just returns his glare to the body.

"His identity is of no concern to me. He assaulted a woman tonight. He got what he deserved."

Well, well, well.

Looks like Vixey wasn't lying.

Pulling out my phone, I text Dove. Vixey isn't a serial killer, but she'll keep our secret as long as we keep hers.

Looks like the serial killer book club just grew by one more beast.

CRUNCH.

Crunch.

Slurp.

Crunch.

A bead of sweat rolls down Hunter's temple in time with my cup's condensation as it drips over my fingers. His dress shirt is damp, sleeves rolled to the elbows, stretching taut over corded forearms. My pussy flexes, wet and ready, just watching him work.

I pop another carrot into my mouth, then take a sip of the pineapple smoothie I picked up on the way to his place.

Slurp.

Crunch.

Crunch.

"Enjoying the show, Little Rabbit?" Hunter grins over his shoulder, catching me staring.

"Yes. Carry on, baby daddy." I wave a carrot at the

crib he's almost finished assembling. "What other manual labor can I get you to do after this?"

His chuckle fills the air as he fits the last piece and steps back to admire his work. "I can think of a few things that require my hands. Some that require my mouth."

My heart kicks as he prowls toward me, bracketing the rocking chair with his arms and leaning down to steal a gulp of my smoothie straight from the straw. Heat zips from my spine to that aching spot between my legs. I clench again as his scent wraps around me.

Sex has become a two or three-times-a-day situation for us. I'm always horny, and Hunter is always willing. I can't get my fill. As soon as the post-orgasm haze fades, I want him again.

The need to give him the affection he craves has become a necessity for me. I want to be touching him at all times—fusing some part of ourselves together in order for me to function.

But with the high sex drive comes the mood swings, and I never know what will set me off—especially now that Vixey knows mine and Dove's secret.

So when the doorbell rings just as Hunter is about to kiss me, irrational ire floods my bloodstream like a dam breaking.

"No," I whine. "Don't answer it."

I'm about to thread my fingers through his hair when he kisses the tip of my nose, then stands. "I'm waiting on a package of Pepper's diapers. It'll just be a moment."

"I hate that damn chicken," I grumble, crossing my arms.

As if she hears me, Pepper squawks from her pen downstairs.

"You know what I love, though? Chicken nuggets!" I shout.

Hunter's chuckles fade as he leaves, and like we're attached by an invisible tether, the need to follow him grows with every second he's gone.

Gathering my snacks, I head downstairs. In the kitchen, he's glaring at a sheet of paper with a manila envelope on the island in front of him.

Slowly, his gaze lifts to mine. His amber eyes are lit like someone set a whiskey barrel on fire. "Hunter? What's wrong?"

Silently, he flips the paper around. My breath catches.

YOU'LL GO DOWN TOO, DETECTIVE.

It's been a few weeks since a letter appeared, but the fact that it's at Hunter's house is wildly confusing. "What the hell is that?"

"What do you think?" Hunter snaps.

I know he's not upset with me, but his anger still feels directed my way, and I don't appreciate it. "Don't snap at me. *Clearly* someone knows about Nathaniel. Now they're targeting you?"

Which is odd. The only people who supposedly know what happened that night are Abigail James, Phillip Keels, and *us*.

"I'm getting real pissed at whoever keeps leaving these letters. Why now? Why this long after his death?"

"Didn't the letters start when we started spending more time together?" Hunter asks, sliding the paper back into the envelope.

Mulling it over, I realize: they started when Hunter and I had our night in the bathroom... when he told me he was letting me go.

An icy thought crawls along the edges of my mind. *What if* Hunter *is doing this—herding me closer to him?*

It shakes me to my core, just the very idea of it. It's never crossed my mind, but now it flashes like a neon warning over his head as he watches me.

Maybe he was tired of waiting for me. Maybe the letters are his way of forcing my hand. At first I thought they were Siren-related, but now that he's received one, all signs point to Nathaniel's death.

"No," I say slowly, watching for any sign that might lead me in the right direction with my conjecture. "They started after our night at the bar."

Hunter's brows screw together, his gaze dragging over the marbled granite. "Didn't Nathaniel have a brother?"

Neil. I haven't thought about the brother-in-law I never met in years. "He'd been in prison long before Nathaniel and I got together."

Are you trying to throw me off your trail, Hunter?

Would he really go through these lengths to keep me close? My hormones are making it hard to tell if that's absolutely crazy—or a little endearing.

It's fucking crazy. There's nothing cute about being threatened into someone's arms.

On the other hand... have I driven him to this?

He wasn't even worried when the first letter arrived.

"I don't know, Bunny. This screams stalker, and I don't know who else would fit the profile. Didn't you say he contested the will?"

I move around him and sit by Pepper's pen. To my surprise, she wobbles over, softly clucking at the wire.

"Yes, but I never heard from him again after they ruled in my favor."

Pepper stares up with inky beads for eyes, and I find myself reaching over to stroke her mangy-looking feathers. Neil doesn't make sense. He's in prison. He wanted Nathaniel's money for lawyers, but if my late husband had wanted to help, he would have. And I had no desire to stay tied to that family beyond the name—and that's only because changing it is a pain in the ass.

"Well, look at you two." I snap out of my reverie to see Hunter leaning on the island, arms crossed, a smile stretched wide across his handsome face.

Only then do I realize Pepper is leaning into my hand, letting me pet her. It's the first time she's allowed it.

What changed, you spicy nugget?

"I think you should move in." Hunter's abrupt statement ricochets off the walls.

Logically, I know he wants to keep me and the baby safe. But a large part of me is now stuck on this theory that perhaps it's him sending the letters and trying to spook me into his arms for good. I don't know why I can't let it go—like the moment I thought it into existence, the idea latched on with spindly, hooked fingers and embedded in my chest.

"I don't want to give up my place." Pushing to my feet after one last head scratch, I head for the door. I need space to think, and time to convince myself that I'm going crazy. I want an answer, so I'm clinging to the most hair-brained theory I can concoct.

"Bunny." Hunter catches my hand as I pass, pulling me back to him carefully. "It makes sense. We're together. We're having a baby. I don't want to raise our child in separate homes."

Frustration tinges his cadence, and his body is tense—gearing up for a fight, no doubt—because he knows he's about to piss me off. Yet he barges on anyway. "I'm not asking you to wear a ring. Take your own room if you want. I just want you nearby. And to know you're safe. Is that so bad?"

"Why do I have to give up my home for that?" My words are so sharp, I can feel their bite. And yet, I can't seem to stop. "Why are you trying to isolate me, Hunter?"

"Isolate you?" He rears back like I slapped him. "Bunny, I'm not trying to isolate you. I love you, and I'm trying to keep our family safe." He steps in, splaying his large palm over my stomach. "I'd never forgive myself if something happened to either of you."

His earnestness bleeds into my marrow. However, my walls remain high and impenetrable. "This is moving too fast. I told you—I didn't want strings, and yet here we are, practically living together with a baby on the way. I just... need space."

"And I need you to get over your insecurities. This isn't a game anymore, Little Rabbit. There's another life involved. I don't see the point in keeping the house your abusive piece of shit husband beat you in. I don't want my child raised in a place where their mother lived with another man," Hunter bites out.

He's close to losing his temper, as I so often push him to do. Since we found out about the baby, he's reined it in, but I can feel the angry heat radiating off him. It's suffocating, and my heart clenches as it brings me back to a time when that same energy was a staple in my life.

With a choked breath, I step back. I try to bite my tongue to keep the nasty words from flying between my lips, but they force themselves out anyway. "At least it gives me a place to go when I don't want to see your face. You're acting just like *him*."

Tears prick my eyes as I spin on my heel.

"Bunny! Wait! Please don't go. I'm sorry." A vortex of panic and regret swirls in Hunter's words.

It pulls at my heartstrings, but Nathaniel's face is all I can see. "Too late, Hunter."

"Bunny! Please!"

"What, are you going to get on your knees and beg?" I don't know why I say it. I'm certainly not prepared for him to do it.

But when I glance back, Hunter sinks to his knees. "If that's what it takes, yes. I'll beg."

The image breaks me. This man—who has done so much for me and only asked for love in return—is on his knees, ready to beg, even though I keep handing him nothing but heartache over and over.

Heat floods my cheeks. I stride back, gripping his shoulders as all the guilt I feel pushes out any suspicion that remains. "Get up. I'm sorry. I'm so sorry. I don't know what came over me."

Instead of rising, he wraps his arms around my middle, resting his cheek between my breasts. "I'm doing the best I can. I'm sorry you feel like I'm pushing you to do something you don't want."

He sounds so sad, and I realize this is our theme song, playing again and again like a broken record.

This is how it's always going to be with us—me hurting him, time and time again, going around in circles because of my stupid trust issues. It's weighing on him, and he's so damn undeserving of it.

Cradling his cheeks, I lift his head. "I do want it." Tears stream down my face as all thoughts of him sending the letters evaporate—Hunter would never do something like that. "I promise I do. It's just... hard."

"I know, baby. That's why I'm trying to be patient." Melancholy softens his delivery, and we cling to each other like we need the other to breathe. "You have to start letting me in, Little Rabbit. I thought we were making progress."

"We are." I sniff. "We are, I promise. I'm sorry. Can we... table this until after the holidays?"

After I kill my last victim and retire the Shadow Siren —for a while, at least. And after I figure out who's stalking us.

"Okay." He stands, thumbs smoothing beneath my eyes. "I hate it when you cry. I hate it more when I'm the cause of your tears. It breaks something inside me every time."

I rise on my toes to kiss him, but he pulls back with a small smile, unlocking his phone. After a few taps, *Pony* by Ginuwine pours through the speakers.

"I *was* going to save this for after we finished setting up the nursery," he says, grinning. "But I want those tears erased from that beautiful face."

Lust instantly heats my body, vaporizing any lingering embers of unhappiness. Whatever tears clung to my lashes dry as he unbuttons his shirt, intent on erasing our fight.

"Sit down, Little Rabbit. It occurred to me the other day that while you gave me a lap dance the night we met. I've never returned the favor."

Hunter drags the chair I previously occupied over. My mouth waters at the ripple of muscle. Every trace of anything but desire vanishes as he guides me to sit.

"Now let big daddy show you his moves," he whispers, rolling his hips against mine.

"As long as you never call yourself 'big daddy' again." My fingers find his waistband, and the second his cock is free, I'm a goner.

Stupid fucking hormones.

Pepper lets me check on her while Hunter sleeps, strangely enough, even allows me to touch her again. Maybe it's because the dogs are at Dove's and the house is calmer, despite our earlier argument.

"Have we formed a truce, you spicy thing?"

She clucks softly as I pour a glass of water. Hunter exhausted me. If the color of the sky is any indication, we slept through the afternoon and into the early evening after he gave me three glorious orgasms.

His phone lights up on the island, dragging my gaze from the bay window that overlooks the street.

Fucking Gwendolyn.

> I could really use your help tonight. We could order dinner and go over the files at my place?

> Or we can go to one of your jazz bars? Fit in some dancing between work.

> One of these days, I'm going to wear you down, Remington. 😉

"Yeah, and I'm going to put you in your place the next time I see you, you little tart." I set the glass down harder than necessary, earning a sharp squawk from Pepper.

It enrages me that she even knows he likes jazz. Or

dares talk about dancing with him. Hunter swears he's been clear he doesn't see her that way. So if she keeps pushing, we'll have problems.

Movement flickers at the edge of my vision. I turn back to the window.

Like a spilled drink, adrenaline races through my veins, goosebumps breaking out along my flesh as I take in the shadow standing outside, peering in with a blank expression.

Dark eyes. Sandy blond hair.

Nathaniel.

Blinking, I scrub my eyes, trying to wipe the image imprinted on the backs of my lids.

It can't be.

It had to be a trick of the light.

Opening them again, the shadow is gone.

Like the stupid girl in a horror movie—the one who dies first because she does all the wrong things—I rush to the window. Hands splayed on the glass, I scan up and down the street.

Nothing.

My heart slows, inching back toward normal.

"Now you're seeing things. Get out of your head, girl," I whisper. Pepper clucks behind me, like she agrees.

"Bunny?" Hunter's voice rings from upstairs, threaded with panic.

"In the kitchen!" I call back. I swear I hear his audible sigh of relief, and I wonder if he'll ever stop expecting to wake and find me gone.

Tugging down the hem of his old gym shirt to cover

my backside, I take my water and head for the stairs, giving Pepper one last head pat.

Note to self: check if paranoia intensifies during pregnancy.

"GET your sticky claws off the cake!"

Dove jumps and whirls as I enter Hunter's kitchen, caught with her fingers tucked under the plastic lid of the gender-reveal cake.

"I was just checking to make sure the lid was secure!" she cries, hopping onto a stool and kicking her feet like she thinks that makes her look innocent.

"Uh-huh." I take the seat beside her and watch the guys puzzle over loading Hunter's car through the bay window.

"Do you really think Hunter is the one behind the letters?" Dove blurts, a pinprick of anxiety needling my chest.

I've tried not to think about it, but the idea still prowls the back of my mind like a big cat at night, waiting to make a kill.

I take too long to answer, because she hums—a soft, neutral sound. "I don't know, Buns. I don't think it's him."

I don't get the chance to reply. The guys trod back inside, looking exasperated.

"Is there a reason you both need to bring two bags for a weekend away?" Wrenley asks, peering between us like we're lunatics.

"Duh, Songbird. We're reading a cowboy romance right now. We're going to a farm. We needed farm outfits for aesthetic photos," Dove explains, vexed, like she's said this a hundred times.

"What are *farm outfits*, and why does this sound kinky?" Hunter waggles his brows at me. "Does it include boots and Daisy Dukes? Please tell me it does, Little Rabbit."

"Maybe if you're a good boy," I purr with a wink. Though, I have zero intention of having sexy time in his parents' house. He swears they won't hear us, but the thought alone is a lust-killer—no matter how hot Hunter on a farm will be.

"You both know we have to bring all the dogs and the chicken. Can't you consolidate the bags? Even getting rid of one helps," Wrenley says, staring at Dove like they're having a silent conversation.

Whatever passes between them has her hopping off the stool. "Fine. Fine. Bring our bags upstairs and we'll work on them."

"We will?"

Dove grabs my hand. "If I'm a good girl, I get a spanking later, and I do love those."

"Oh god."

"If Wrenley is getting lucky tonight, I better be too, Bunny!" Hunter's chuckles follow us up the stairs.

As soon as the guys drop our bags on Hunter's bed, Dove shoos them out and shuts the door. "Okay, now that we're *alone*-alone, we can talk."

At my quirked brow, she sighs. "We should tell Vixey about belt guy."

"I told you I want to keep something else over her besides the fact that she *killed that guy*." I make little air quotes. "I'm almost certain he wasn't dead when she left. You didn't see him. I think belt guy finished the job—he had blood on his hands when he came outside."

"Okay, but she's part of the club now. That's not something we keep from each other," Dove says, already excavating our bags and tossing out what we don't need.

"She's not a serial killer," I whisper, even though the door's shut and the guys are downstairs. "She made a mistake and told us because she found out our secret. I don't fully trust her yet."

"So you're saying there's a chance?" Dove stills, looking at me like a puppy when someone says *walk*.

"I'm *saying* I want to keep something on her stashed away in case things go sideways." I haven't talked to the new third of our little club in a few days, and for some reason, I'm just now wondering if we should have invited her with us for the weekend.

"What's Vixey doing for Thanksgiving?" I assume Dove knows—they talk daily. It used to bug me. Now I've accepted it.

"She's in Connecticut with her parents," Dove says, flinging a third pair of pink cowboy boots on the bed.

Of course she has a nice family who wants her around for the holidays.

Sighing, I rub my belly as baby bean shifts. I'm still not used to another life moving inside me. As Dove pulls out a stack of pink-and-white shorts, I shake my head. "Okay, I think Wrenley is right, Love Dove. You don't need this much. And it's cold. Why the shorts?"

"Listen, missy. It's not every day we go to a farm—"

"Hunter's parents will let you visit whenever you want."

"And I want to take lots of photos—"

"We're literally going back for Christmas in a month."

"And I want enough photos that we don't have to do this again at Christmas when it's colder. I want options! Why can't a girl have options?" She stomps and glares.

Holding my hands up in surrender, I start sorting through her outfits and props. Picking up a stuffed chicken, I toss it aside. "There will be real chickens, Dove."

A low growl rumbles from my best friend, and I hold in a laugh while she shoves everything back in her bag and mutters, "Fuck it." Yanking the door open, she yells, "Make it work, Songbird. I'm not unpacking anything."

"No spankings for you then," Wrenley calls up, completely unbothered like this is just their daily conversation.

She snorts and looks over her shoulder. "That's what he thinks. I'll just tie *him* up and give *him* the spankings."

THE AUDIOBOOK'S narrator purrs through the car's speakers: *"I release a whimper as the rope cuts into my wrists, the pain as deep and mind-numbing as the length of Orson's cock rubbing against my walls. His piercing adds a sense of heightened pleasure, the tickler on the ball of the ring making me see stars..."*

"Oooh. Tickler? That's new. I don't think we've read anything like that," Dove chirps, delighted.

I sneak a glance at Hunter, quietly laughing when I see he's white-knuckling the wheel, eyes locked on the road.

"Shut that pretty mouth before I stick something in it and shut it for you. Unless you want the town to hear your screams. Is that it, city girl?"

He presses harder on my lower back, forcing me down further. My wrists hang above my head, chapped and raw, and I wonder how I'm going to be able to hide the marks when we return to the party happening just on the other side of the barn.

Hunter adjusts himself discreetly. I hear Wrenley whisper, "What the actual hell are you two reading?"

"Don't you dare judge, Songbird. We like our word

porn. Besides, you *know* how much I like listening to the dirty stuff," Dove says primly.

"Is this the kind of shit you want me to do to you, Little Rabbit?" Hunter murmurs for my ears only.

The thought of someone catching us only lights my body up with excitement, and that—paired with the fact Orson is currently trying to penetrate my stomach—sends an unfurling wave of electricity zipping down my legs to make my toes curl.

"Yeah, that's it, isn't it? You city girls always like to be roughed up and fucked good and hard. You like taking the cowboys out for a ride for the weekend and returning to your concrete jungle where the suits are selfish and can't figure out how to pleasure a woman even if they treat it like a business deal."

"Hey!" Hunter and Wrenley bark in unison, faces morphing into offended indignation.

"We are not selfish!" Wrenley argues.

"I am the most unselfish man ever," Hunter huffs, shooting me a worried look. "Right? You don't think I'm selfish, do you?"

"Oh my god, just because it's in a book doesn't make it true!" Dove cries, leaning over the center console to turn down the volume and pause it.

"Exactly—and it's not like we want everything that happens in these books. Rope burns? No thanks," I add. "Besides, he means the big-corporate millionaire types."

"Which—yes, he's talking shit about her cheating fiancé, but honestly, something tells me men like Jackson

Tailor are absolutely *not* clueless about the female form," Dove segues.

Holding my fist back for her to bump it, I nod. "I hear that."

"Can we not talk about Mr. Tailor? Like... ever... again?" Wrenley groans, flopping back to stare out the window.

"Wow, he really did a number on you, didn't he, Wren?" I glance at him in the side mirror. "What happened at that work lunch with his wife?"

"Aww, buddy, Brooks says he's not that bad," Hunter teases. Plastic crinkles. I look over to see him fishing out a bag of—oh god—jerky.

All my humor evaporates. The scent hits. "Hunter, where did you get that?"

Please say you packed it from home. Please say you packed it from home.

"Grabbed it from the back when Wrenley wasn't looking. Bastard's holding out on road snacks." He grins and lifts a strip to his mouth.

"NO!" Dove, Wrenley, and I shout together.

Everything slows. I lean across to smack the jerky from his lips at the same time Wrenley lunges for the bag. Dove squeals as Hunter slams the brakes and swerves. Adrenaline zips through me as my fingers clamp the *oh-shit* handle.

It takes a few seconds to get the vehicle under control, and he pulls over hard, shoves it in park, and twists around to pin Wrenley with a look. All traces of humor are gone, sucked out of the car. Heat radiates off Hunter.

"Do not ever—and I mean *ever*—pull that shit again while they're in the car." He jabs a finger at me. "If you want to put your princess in danger, be my guest, but I will fucking kill you if you harm my queen or my child. Do you understand, Wrenley?"

This side of Hunter doesn't come out often: dark, broody protector who only appears when he thinks I'm in danger. His voice drops, amber eyes molten. If our friends weren't here, I'd climb into his lap because this version of him turns me on immensely. Goosebumps pebble my skin, my breaths go shallow, and my thighs flex, trying to relieve some of the pressure between them.

A soft cluck from Pepper, who's in a pen at my feet, cuts the silence, followed by the dogs' whimpers from their kennel in the back.

Wrenley releases a long breath before apologizing. "I'm sorry. You're right. But that's the dogs' jerky. Sorry —I didn't want you eating whatever shit they put in this."

My eyes find Dove, who's biting back laughter, eyes sparkling with mirth.

Hunter mutters under his breath and turns to me. "You okay?" His hand spreads over my stomach, and a tiny flutter blooms beneath his palm.

"Yeah, I'm fine." Warmth floods me—gratitude and lust swirling like eddies.

Danger and sex might make strange bedfellows, but holy hell are they a delicious combination.

Then it hits me. By shouting with our friends, and trying to stop Hunter from eating Dove's dick jerky, I might've given myself away to Wrenley—if Dove isn't lying and hasn't already told him. He's an investigative journalist, it wouldn't be hard to piece it together, considering how close Dove and I are.

Looking at him through the side mirror, I inwardly sigh. His eyes catch mine, a knowing spark in them that serves as an answer to whether he already knows.

Looks like we have another name to add to the list of people who know about the Siren.

Fantastic.

HUNTER'S PARENTS live just under three hours north of the city near the Massachusetts border. When he said "farm," I pictured acres of corn, cows, and a big red barn. Instead, their farmhouse sits on an acre and a half, and while they do have a barn, there are no sprawling corn fields or cows.

Well, they have *two* cows. Along with chickens, some turkeys, four goats, and two of the fattest pigs I've ever seen.

Carla gives me a tour while Hunter's dad, David, and the guys bring our bags in. Dove goes with them so Hunter's mom and I can *get to know each other*, and if looks could kill, Wrenley would be digging her a shallow grave right now.

It's not that I don't want to spend time with Carla, but I didn't have parents growing up. Not ones who gave a shit about me. I'm terrible with parents. It's part of why Nathaniel and I worked so well together—we both had trauma caused by the people who were supposed to take care of us.

But a few minutes into our walk, I'm doing better than expected. Hunter's mom radiates a warmth that beats back the November chill—kind and accepting.

"I just want my boy to be happy," she says. "You've been making him happy for a long time. I'm glad you're letting him do the same for you now."

Shockingly, I can see myself living here. There's something about the vast area that calls to me. I don't know if it's the sense of owning something that seems larger than life, or maybe having a place where I could dispose of my victims more easily—or how free the dogs are as they venture ahead of us, sniffing all the animals curiously.

Bessie, a milk cow, moos from behind a fence, eyeing the dogs as their winter coats rustle with each excited wiggle. It reminds me of that scene in *101 Dalmatians* when the puppies hide in a barn.

Pepper clucks happily in Carla's arms as she gushes about how elated she is that the mangy chicken and I bonded while they were on vacation.

"It really is a miracle. When she was a chick, Doc told us there was no hope and to put her down, but Hunter insisted she just needed extra love. He drove up every weekend to help. Now look at her." She pets Pepper's head gently. "Our girl is nearly eleven. That's longer than the average life span for a chicken, you know."

"No wonder you're such a spicy nugget—you're a wise old lady, aren't you?" I reach to stroke her, but a flutter blooms in my belly. A breath whooshes from my lungs, nausea rolls through me, and I rub my stomach. "I think the bean is excited to see the animals."

"Is the baby kicking?" Carla's dark eyes light up, and she leans forward before catching herself, as though she doesn't want to overstep.

"Yeah, I think? It's like a bunch of bubbles popping at once. I thought it was gas, but now I think it's the baby." A rush of frosty air envelops me as I unzip my jacket and grab her hand, placing it where the baby keeps moving. "You might not feel it yet, but if this is a preview, I'll be lucky to have all my ribs intact by eviction day."

She releases a watery laugh, tears shimmering. "Hunter was a rowdy baby, too. His father always said he'd grow up to be a pro wrestler."

"Really? David seems more like the baseball type than wrestling." I've known him all of five minutes, but he's tall and lean, and I thought Hunter once said he could've gone pro if not for a shoulder injury.

"Oh—David is Hunter's stepfather," Carla explains. "Hunter's biological dad left when he was younger." She turns back toward the house—a gentle cue to head in.

"C'mon, boys," I call the dogs. Zipping up, I fall into step beside her. "Hunter never mentioned that."

"He doesn't like to talk about it." Carla's tone turns melancholy. "Logan—his father—cared enough to leave.

He couldn't clean up his act. Drinking. Gambling. He divorced me before he got into enough trouble that we'd lose the house. Kindest thing he could've done for Hunter."

My heart aches for the father of my child, for my friend who carried so much of my pain and never spoke of his own.

"It's what the boys bonded over," she adds, nodding toward the house. Frosted grass crunches under our boots as we grow closer to the white, ranch-style home. "Their fathers leaving. Even years later, Hunter was deeply affected when Wrenley's mother moved him across the country. He's always feared the people he loves most abandoning him." Her tone is leading. I hear it.

Wispy clouds form from my breath as I process what she's saying. Leaving, the way I did last time, hasn't crossed my mind since we found out about the baby. There's only one instance in which I can imagine needing to flee the city, and that's if Hunter finds out I'm the Shadow Siren.

If that happens... everything will change. Hunter is thrilled about this baby. What if he decides their mother is a monster? What if he thinks they need protecting— from me?

Carla's gentle cadence pulls me back. "Thank you for letting him do the gender-reveal cake," she says, laughing as she strokes Pepper. "That boy has dreamed of having a family of his own for as long as I can remember. He used to say he'd name his first daughter Faline, from *Bambi*."

Laughter bubbles from me at the image of a young

Hunter scribbling baby names. As if conjured, present-day Hunter steps onto the wrap-around porch as the dogs bound up the stairs. He bends and somehow gathers all three in his arms. I take the chance to drink him in, trying to imagine him as a child—precocious and certain. It's just like him to already have names picked out even though he hasn't mentioned it. I don't want him swallowing joy to avoid my reactions. He deserves to be happy. He deserves a real family.

"Admittedly, I feel bad I haven't been more excited. It's just hard, you know? It was a surprise after all, and kids weren't really on my radar if I'm being honest." Absentmindedly, my hand smoothes over my stomach. "Thank *you* for welcoming me into your family. I know this baby will be so loved, and I never had that growing up."

Carla squeezes my shoulder. "It takes a village, dear. We're yours now."

My eyes sting at her offering. The cold cools the tears on my lashes, and I swipe them away before Hunter looks over, a wide smile breaking across his chiseled features.

I *want* the village she promises. Holidays on the farm. Birthdays in the city. More kids filling the halls of Hunter's home. Baseball games and picnics in the park.

Little lavender bows and an unusual name—like her mother.

Something prickles in my chest. Fierce protectiveness wrapped in unyielding devotion. For the first time since finding out... I *feel* like a mother.

"Thank you, Carla. I'd really like that."

"YOU SHAVED YOUR BEARD!"

Water drips from Hunter's half-naked form as he appears in the doorway from the en suite. A towel hangs loosely around his waist, curls lying haphazardly across his forehead, brushing the tops of his glasses—the old pair he's been wearing more because he knows what they do to me.

"Mom wants photos tomorrow, so I figured I'd clean it up. Forgot my moisturizer, though—guess I'll have to get some from between your thighs." He chuckles and waggles his brows.

I bite my lip to hold back the rush of need that sluices through me like a water-park slide.

The walls here are paper-thin, and I am a loud lover —that's one of Hunter's favorite things about me—so deciding to withhold until we're back in the city wasn't hard... for me.

Hunter seems determined to change my mind. Grinning, like he knows exactly where my thoughts have gone, he asks, "Like what you see, Little Rabbit?"

"Don't tease me." I relish the way his eyes track my fingers as I trail them down the valley of my breasts. I used to want a boob job, now I can't wait for these monsters to deflate post-bean. "This morning was supposed to hold us over until we get back home."

"Well I'm absolutely ravenous for you *now*." He prowls to the end of the bed, climbs up, and slides between my legs with catlike grace, gently kissing up my stomach to claim my mouth with an urgency that heats my skin and soaks me through.

As if baby bean knows this is a bad idea, the strongest flutter yet hits just as his hand passes over their home. The force steals my breath like a bucket of ice water.

"You okay?" He nudges my nose, shifts to his side, and props up on an elbow. Irritation vanishes as he lowers his head and kisses my belly. "Stop being feisty, will you? Your mom is fragile."

A laugh bubbles from my throat as he wraps his arm around my middle and lays his head on my stomach. If only he knew how wrong he was. I may be little, but I can still tie a man up *and* lift my weight on a pole while I slash his throat open. It's the constant flutters tipping me toward nausea that'll take me out.

Idly, I run my fingers through his curls as they air-dry —frizz be damned. "Hunter?"

"Hmm?" He nuzzles my skin, hugging me closer.

"I kinda like the name Faline. If the baby's a girl." I've been rolling it around my tongue since Carla mentioned it. Saying it out loud, I realize how much I love it.

Hunter barks a laugh, then looks at me, amber eyes lit with amusement. "Oh god. What else did my mother tell you?"

"I'm serious! I love it. It fits our little family."

Something shifts in his gaze—from warm and playful to guarded yet vulnerable. "It does, doesn't it?"

He gathers me in his arms, pulling my softness to his hardness as he sinks against the pillows. "Faline Remington," he tests. "People are going to think we're *those* parents who don't let their kids eat sugar and don't own a TV."

"No way. Our kids will be the cool ones who get along with everyone."

"And what about a boy's name?"

"Okay, hear me out, I don't *hate* Forest." Craning my neck to look at him, I smile when I find him trying—and failing—not to grin.

"Forest and Faline, huh?" He nudges my nose and kisses me lightly. "Planning a future with me, Bunny?"

"I think I am." The words come out soft and a little broken. He kisses me like the glue that's been holding me together for longer than I care to admit.

"It's about damn time, Little Rabbit."

"Why me?" I ask the question that's been burning at the back of my mind for as long as I can remember. "You've always been so sure of me. Of *us*. Your mother even mentioned that she was happy I finally came around. What is it about me that attracts you?"

"Well, besides your good looks and stunning personality?" he teases, sobering when I level him a look. "Since this is apparently a weekend for sharing, I guess it won't hurt to show you. But if you laugh, I promise you punishment will be swift when we get home."

Curious, I sit up as he pads over to retrieve something from an old, distressed desk. "When I was a teenager, we were up here for the weekend and my mom picked *Practical Magic* for movie night. Have you seen it?"

"Of course. It's a classic. Not to mention, I've seen everything with Nicole Kidman."

He smirks, climbing back onto the bed. "Remember when the girl writes down everything about her perfect guy? I guess I was inspired, because I came up here and figured it couldn't hurt to try the same thing. Minus the flowers and herbs and spell and all that." He hands me a weathered piece of paper that's yellowed at the edges. "I was always a hopeless romantic. Even then."

His thumb sweeps my cheek, vulnerability bright in his whiskey eyes. Jerking a chin at the paper, he bites his lower lip, and drops his gaze. Threading our fingers together, I read it silently.

> Unique name.
> Dark hair.
> Green eyes.
> Short.
> Stubborn but kind.
> Loves a hobby as much as I love jazz.
> Playful.
> Loves animals.
> Has quirky interests, like liking cartoons, even as an adult.
> Sees the bad in the world and wants to make it right.

My hand flies to my mouth, eyes brimming with tears.

Written on the paper, like a *Practical Magic* recipe, is *me*.

"Hunter..."

Brushing my hair over my shoulder, he nuzzles my neck, pressing a chaste kiss to my flesh. "I knew I loved you long before I met you, Little Rabbit. You've been my dream for a long, long time."

THAT FEELING Leo had when he boarded the Titanic and shouted, *"I'm the king of the world"*? Yeah—that. That's me.

Bunny is deep in my bones, my soul, the nuclei of every cell. And this time she isn't going anywhere. I'm sure of it.

She's making plans with my mother, settling on baby names, and currently helping my dad feed the chickens— well, *he's* doing the feeding. Dove and Bunny are playing dress-up and posing with Bessie.

"Thank you for helping with winter prep, Wrenley," Mom says from the kitchen. "It gets harder the older we get."

"It's no problem at all, Carla. You know you can always ask me to help out." Wrenley and I turn from where we watch our girls through the large back window in the dining room.

The house smells like the winter holidays—pine and

cinnamon, roasted meat, spiced gravy, with the warm sweetness of pecan pie. Mom stands at the little rolling butcher block island David built her last Christmas, pouring sweet potato filling into a crust.

"I can't believe you told Bunny about Faline," I murmur into my coffee.

Her eyes crinkle over the rim, full of festive mischief. "She's my future daughter-in-law. I plan to tell her *all* your childhood stories, even the embarrassing ones."

"What's a Faline?" Wren asks, popping an olive from a charcuterie board into his mouth as he turns back to the window.

"Haven't you seen *Bambi,* dear? She's the doe."

Realization dawns over his features as he looks at me. "That's right. You wanted to name your kid that, didn't you? What did Bunny say?"

"She actually likes it."

"Of course she does." He claps my shoulder. "Have I told you how happy I am for you? Seriously, Hunt—long time coming. You two deserve it."

A timer dings and Mom swaps pies: pecan out, sweet potato and pumpkin in.

"Why are you making so many pies, Mom? Isn't it just us?"

"Well, I wanted to send you both home with left-overs, but no, Todd is joining us. He needs David to sign some papers, and I plan to make him stay to eat. I'll need to send him home with an extra plate or two."

Todd, or Theodore, Langston is the youngest managing partner at *Metropolis Investments Group,* a rapidly growing real estate enterprise. He's an absolute shark, and the fact he's bringing work all the way from the city for David to go over is a testament to that.

He's bought more commercial real estate in the Meatpacking District than *Tailor Industries* has in Manhattan this year. Rumor is Jackson Tailor—multi-billionaire and owner of the illustrious conglomerate—has been side-eyeing M.I.G., ready to poach Todd for his own nefarious ambitions of world-domination.

"He couldn't wait until after the holiday? I know the guy's a workaholic, but e-sign exists," I mutter.

David's been holding onto some warehouses he acquired from an old shady business partner. The guy tried leaving him high and dry during their startup's first year, but luckily, my dad has a knack for business—and a legal team that forced the guy to pay up in real estate when he couldn't cough up cash. Since he has no use for them and he knows Todd's father, he's all too happy to sell.

"I don't think he has any family to spend the day with, and the more the merrier—you know we don't turn anyone away."

My mother, the ultimate bleeding heart. Of course she'd feel sorry for a businessman who probably wants to be in his office more than at family dinner. Growing up, she always invited people who had nowhere to go for the holidays, saying, *"When we take care of each other, that's when the community thrives, Hunter. Always give back more than you take."*

My attention drifts out the window as a flash of purple and pink catches my eye.

Even though the barn is warm and well insulated, I don't know why the girls would brave the chill in Daisy Dukes and crop tops just to get photos for their Iconic profiles.

Okay—well, *Dove* is in Daisy Dukes and a crop top.

Bunny is in a pretty lavender dress that hugs her bump and makes the word *mine* thrum through my chest like a growl from some primal beast.

"Oh my goodness. Everything smells delicious!" Dove cries as she steps through the back door. "I'm starving!"

She makes a beeline for Wrenley, who's already made her a plate of appetizers.

"Same. I swear this child can't go more than an hour without snacks." Bunny rubs her belly, heading for my mom instead of the food table. "Do you need any help with anything, Carla?"

Arrows of pride, appreciation, and gratitude hit my heart like a bullseye. I know it's hard for her—being around my parents when she grew up with none, doing the whole "loving family" thing when Nathaniel was anything but loving. The fact that she's offering to help and willingly spending time with them makes my chest swell.

"No, sweetheart. I made those cranberry brie bites you suggested. Go try them and tell me if I got the recipe right."

My gaze drops to the table as Bunny reaches for a

puff pastry filled with red and white and topped with rosemary. I quirk a brow as she pops it into her mouth.

"Sharing recipes with my mom? I didn't even know you cooked anymore, Little Rabbit."

Bunny's mossy eyes flutter closed as she hums. "Carla, these are perfect." Then, to me, she snarks, "I'm a great cook, I'll have you know. It's just harder to cook for one, so I don't do it often."

Leaning in, I wipe a smear of cranberry from the corner of her lips, relishing the way her eyes track my thumb as I lick it off. "Well, soon it'll be three of us. So you'll have to show me your skills."

A flicker of heat ignites her gaze at my double entendre, but she shakes it off as the front door opens and my dad's voice rings out. "Todd! Happy you could make it. I hope you're hungry—you know Carla's making you stay for dinner."

Whatever Todd says is drowned out by Dove's hand slapping the table until Bunny looks at her.

"Buns! It's *belt guy*!" she squeaks.

Bunny's head whips around, her long raven locks slapping against my face in a curtain of jasmine and raspberry. Her body tenses, hand flying protectively to her stomach, instantly sending me into defensive mode.

"Holy shit," she breathes. "What's *he* doing here?"

Wrenley and I lock gazes with matching *what the fuck* expressions.

"How do you know Todd, Bunny?"

If he was one of her old dates I didn't get to crash—

Spinning, she pushes me toward the end of the table

while Dove does the same to Wrenley until all four of us are corralled together.

"That's the guy Vixey fell into at the club the other night!"

Relief floods my veins while Wrenley asks, "Okay... and why is that a big deal?"

The girls share a look I can't decipher, a silent conversation passing between them they clearly don't want us guys to be privy to. Bunny told me briefly about what she saw between Vixey and the guy—who, apparently, is Todd—but it just sounded like another Vixey being clumsy moment.

"Are you sure? I can't really see Todd in a nightclub." Wrapping an arm around her midsection, I pull Bunny against me. "Besides, who cares?"

The idea of her attention being focused on another guy irritates me.

"They just seemed to hit it off and didn't exchange numbers," Dove replies. "How exciting that we get to play matchmaker now!"

"He can sit between us at the table," Bunny adds, sounding weirdly excited about playing Cupid.

It's completely out of character for her. Since when is she close enough to Vixey to care about setting her up?

Not that I mind. It's just the overprotective beast that's taken over since I found out Bunny's pregnant is not amused at the idea of her entertaining another man all night.

Before I can interject, Dad appears with Todd in tow.

If the real estate mogul recognizes the girls, he doesn't show it.

"Todd Langston." Bunny rolls his name with a sly smile as she shakes his hand after Dad introduces them. "You don't know us, but you were at *Allegro* a few weeks ago. Our friend fell into your lap."

Intrigue sparks in his greige eyes like an ember, and Dove's next sentence fans it to a blaze.

"How lucky we are to run into you. I'm sure Vixey will be thrilled to see you again. She's not here today, but we'll have to all get together when we're back in the city."

"Vixey," Todd repeats, his rich tenor only a fraction less dry than usual. "So that's the blonde in the green dress." Lifting his sand-colored eyes, he acknowledges me. "Hunter."

"Todd. Good to see you."

I introduce him to Wrenley, then—unfortunately— the girls make good on their plan to seat him between them, leaving us to sit across the table.

It's going to be a long night.

IF LOOKS COULD KILL, Todd would be dead twice over by the time dinner concludes.

While he spends most of the meal talking to David about work, Dove keeps steering the conversation back to him—asking about his life, his goals, and whether he's looking for anything serious—as if they're on a date.

His gaze keeps flicking between me and Wrenley, silently begging us with his trademark deadpan stare to rescue him from her relentless interrogation.

Finally, Wrenley intervenes.

"Turtle Dove, are you writing a novel on commercial real estate I don't know about? You sound like you're gathering enough information to write his biography."

"Oh, hush, Songbird. I am not," Dove huffs, turning her attention back to her fiancé.

Todd's shoulders visibly loosen. Meanwhile, mine are wound as tight as brand-new bowstrings as Bunny picks up where Dove left off—less direct, but far more calculating with her questions about his life.

Pushing my *"slutty little glasses,"* as Bunny likes to call them, up the bridge of my nose, I rake a hand through my unruly hair, vexed and unsure how to intervene.

Her approach keeps his interest. And while there's nothing remotely sexual about it, I don't miss the way his gaze assesses her when she isn't looking—like a predator trying to decide if the creature it's just stumbled upon is prey or another predator. Bunny confuses him, as she always does when meeting powerful men, throwing off his instincts with a well-placed touch on the arm or a demure laugh in place of a snarl.

With every minute that drags on, the urge to claim my little rabbit coils tighter inside me, a venomous viper sinking its fangs into that dark, primal part of me that always hungers for her.

The fact that she's all but ignored me all night only

heightens it. I know Bunny is mine, and I know she's not doing it to play games. But with my child growing in her belly, whatever rationale I once had when it comes to her and other men has flown out the window. In its place is razor-edged possessiveness.

It's an authority I can't exert over her. Otherwise, I'm no better than Nathaniel.

But that doesn't mean I can't remind her in other ways—like getting her so drunk on my dick she remembers exactly why there's been no one else in her bed all this time. And that's exactly what I intend to do.

Can I wait until later when everyone's gone to bed?

Yes.

But where's the fun in that?

Besides, I draw the line when the possibility of exchanging numbers comes up—even if it's just to set him and Vixey up. He's been asking questions about the blonde all night. Questions her friends are unwilling, or perhaps unable, to answer. They seem much more interested in him asking her himself.

"Babe, why don't we get the gender reveal cake?" I don't give Bunny the chance to answer, pushing my chair back and rounding the table to help her from her seat.

"Gender reveal?" Though it's a question, Todd's inflection is as dull as a blunt knife. I really don't see what the appeal is—or why the girls think Vixey would be interested in Todd the robot when she has Alex, who looks like he could be a movie star.

"Didn't you notice? We're expecting." Placing a hand over Bunny's stomach protectively, I flash him a smile—

though by the way Wrenley's shoulders shake with suppressed laughter, I have a feeling it looks more like I'm baring my teeth.

"Congratulations." Another forced sentiment, delivered with dry wit.

I pull Bunny into the kitchen and around the corner to the walk-in pantry where the cake is. "Enjoying yourself, Little Rabbit?"

"As a matter of fact, I am enjoying myself," Bunny says with a sly grin. "Don't be jealous. He's into Vixey, I know it. You should've seen them—"

Her words cut off on a surprised squeal when I push her against the pantry door as soon as we're inside and crash my mouth to hers.

"I don't care," I growl against her lips. "All I care about is being inside you right fucking now."

Earlier, I slipped upstairs to retrieve her AirPods under the guise of using the bathroom. Now, I slide one into her ear and the other into mine, then pull up the audiobook she and Dove made us listen to on the drive.

"Hunter," she laughs breathlessly, cheeks flushed, "you can't be serious."

"Deadly." I lift her onto the counter and shove her skirt up around her waist. "Now press play, Little Rabbit."

Pink colors her cheeks as I drag her blue lace panties down, pocketing them before unzipping my pants. The sound is loud in the enclosed space, mingling with her ragged breathing.

"Hunter," she whispers, though her eyes are already

half-lidded with lust. "Everyone is right on the other side of the door—"

Her gaze drops as my cock springs free, and her tongue darts out to wet her lips. She swipes her thumb across the bead of precum at the tip, and my restraint frays. I don't step out of my pants all the way, pushing them down far enough that I can get the job done with precision.

"Then you'd better be quiet." I grip her thighs and pull her to the edge. "Now press play and open up for me, Bunny."

She obeys, and the husky voices of the audiobook curl between us. I sink into her in one slow, punishing stroke until I'm buried to the hilt.

From the speakers, a woman pants, *"Orson's palm strikes my ass, and I bite my lower lip to swallow the scream. Everything he's saying is the truth. I've never had a man fuck me this thoroughly, let alone hold out until he's made sure I've come at least twice.*

Bunny's nails sink into my back, her teeth worrying her bottom lip. Slowly—so fucking slowly—I pull out, shift her, then press back into her tight heat. "Fuck, you always feel so fucking incredible."

Reaching around to thumb my clit, he picks up his pace just as the music dies. I try to muffle my squeals as he thrusts against my backside,—sharp and deep—like he's trying to destroy my insides—like he's trying to brand me just as he does his cattle.

"Is that what you want, city girl? Do you want me to

fuck your dripping pussy while I burn my brand into your body?"

Shit. I must have said that part out loud.

"You branded me the day we met," I whisper against Bunny's mouth. "Seared yourself into my skin, my brain, my bones."

She answers with a whimper. I lick the seam of her lips, trying to get her to open them before she bloodies the already swollen flesh.

He stops balls deep inside me, rolling his hips in a way that has his cock rubbing against that sweet spot inside that makes me melt.

"I'll take you to the field and spread you wide for the whole herd to see before I devour you. And once you've left your mark all over my face, I'll make you see those stars you're so desperate for. Then, when you're nothing but a puddle of pleasure only I can give you, I'll burn my brand into you so deep, you'll never forget your sordid weekend out here."

The counter shifts under the force of my next thrust, the wall of canned goods rattling as I drive into her harder.

If our friends know what's good for them, they'll keep my parents—and Todd fucking Langston—distracted.

"Is that what you do with your cows, Orson? A little bestiality before you brand them?"

I don't know why I give him sass when he's being the nicest he's been since I arrived.

Yes, I do, it's because I crave the punishment that comes with it.

Smack.

Bunny's whimpers turn to moans. I hook my thumb into her mouth to keep it open. "So fucking wet for me, Little Rabbit. Or is it because you're listening to your beloved characters getting fucked at the same time?"

"Hunter," she breathes, wrecked and reverent, fisting my hair while digging her heels into my ass.

I let go of her jaw and devour her mouth.

A sharp cry flies from my lips before he grips my thighs and lifts them until I'm suspended in the air between him and the beam. My breasts dangle and sway as I scramble to grip the rope so it doesn't cut deeper into my wrists, while Orson pounds into me like a rutting steed.

"Orson!" I cry. He's fucking me in the closest to a wheelbarrow position I've ever been in, and the rope is dangerously close to breaking my skin. His balls slap against my pussy with every drive home, and his grunts sound so loud in the barn that I'm sure people will hear us—until the music kicks back in and drowns our rough coupling.

"Such a fucking. Dirty. Girl," he moans. His fingers dig into my thighs with a force that will leave marks, and I don't know why the thought of that turns me on even more, but it does.

Not that I could be more turned on My pussy leaks all over his cock, so wet I can hear it every time he pushes inside.

Bunny leans back, grasping for anything to anchor herself as she rolls her hips against me, completely giving into the moment. A startled cry falls from her lips as she ends up placing her hand directly into the cake, smashing the entire thing.

"I'm going to come!" I try to whisper, but the words are strangled and hoarse.

Orson picks up his pace until he's jackhammering into me, and my vision bursts with white dots as I explode all over him—my walls contract, gushing and squirting and trying to push him out.

"Fuck yeah, city girl. Such a goddamn filthy whore, aren't you?"

With one final thrust, I feel his warm cum splashing my insides and coating me with his essence.

Branding me—just like he promised.

Thoroughly wrecking me for the six feet of disappointment that is Jordan when I inevitably have to return home to the man who hasn't made me feel in three years what this asshole cowboy did in three days.

Bunny's breasts heave and I ache to pull one out and suck on it, but I know she's too sensitive. I miss her nipples, and though pregnancy's filled her chest out more, I couldn't care less—I'm counting the days until I can bury my face between those perfect globes and clamp the rosy buds between my teeth.

I expect Orson to lower me, but he doesn't. Instead, he shifts his hands beneath my thighs, his cock slipping from my pussy, before he raises me in the air.

"What are you doing?" I squeal as my head tips toward the ground, bound wrists stretching above me.

Orson hooks my legs over his shoulders and licks

between my legs, humming with contentment. "There's something so sweet about you big city sluts."

Before I can yell at him for bringing up other women with his face buried in my pussy, he begins lapping at me, cleaning our mess and flicking his tongue against my sensitive, swollen clit. My legs tighten around his head as he clamps his teeth down on it and sucks like he's trying to eat my very soul.

Moving my hand between us, I thumb her clit while she rides my dick again—taking what she needs, leaving me at her mercy. Each sweep of her hips grinds her against my pelvic bone, swallowing me to the hilt.

Vaguely, I'm aware my asshole is shoved against his nose in this position, but I can't bring myself to care, undulating my hips like the dirty slut I am until I'm coming again and he swallows me down like he's been lost in the desert and I'm the first drink of water he's had in days.

"Hunter, I'm gonna come," Bunny mewls, clawing at my neck, smearing cake and frosting everywhere before erupting all over my cock. Just like *listening* to the spice turns her on, *watching* does the same for me. I take over the pace as she rides out her orgasm, and the sight of her creamy release streaking my cock has my balls tensing just moments before my own climax steals my breath.

This time, while I'm coming down from my high, Orson gently lowers me before releasing my wrists from their bindings.

I don't know why I expect pretty words or a soothing kindness from him, but I'm still disappointed when he throws my dress at me before pulling on his pants.

"You'll want to put some salve on those." He nods at my *wrists.*

The audiobook cuts off as I hit pause. Without the sound in my ears, I realize just how loud our ragged breathing is—and I can only imagine how much worse the counter slamming into the wall must've sounded.

"Holy fuck, Hunter." Bunny holds me close, burying her face against my neck. "That was amazing."

Sweat slicks our skin, and I keep shallowly thrusting as we come down from the high. My gaze drifts past her shoulder to the ruined dessert, and blissful contentment thrums through my veins when I catch the color inside.

Unhurriedly, I still my hips, my cock still pulsing inside her as I gently coax her face from my neck.

"Well... would you look at that?"

Lifting her frosting-smeared hand between us, I let Bunny see the color of the cake crushed between her fingers. Pure, unfiltered joy floods my system at the sight of tears glittering in her mossy eyes as they flick between mine and the bright pink confectionary crumbs.

"Looks like we're having a girl."

Sticking her fingers into my mouth to clean off the mess, I can't help but think it's not nearly as sweet as watching that last piece of the puzzle to motherhood click into place in her eyes.

As Bunny drops her gaze to her belly, that connection she's been so afraid of settles over her—sure and unwavering.

Her clean hand drifts down to the gentle curve of her

stomach, and her voice trembles on a laugh. "Mommy and Daddy can't wait to meet you, baby girl."

For the first time since I met Bunny, I don't need to ask for assurance from her. Don't need to ask for her heart, or hear her make me promises of forever.

I *feel* it.

Right here, right now, in this pantry, with cake smeared across us and our little girl on the way. I know—undoubtedly—that Bunny is mine, just as I'm hers.

Finally, after all this time, my world feels complete.

BUNNY

"My child hates me. She *hates* me, I'm telling you. While I love *K-Pop Demon Hunters* as much as the next person, we've watched it four times today. She won't let me watch anything else—or else she starts somersaulting so hard I want to vomit."

Dove blows a raspberry on the other end of the line. "She does not. And besides, KPDH is amazing. I don't even like cartoons, and *I'm* obsessed with it. You know those demons were *not* singing about soda pop, Buns. I like 'em spicy."

"Am I allowed to buy baby fawn something pink?" Vixey interjects, the third part of our little conference call.

"No," Dove and I respond simultaneously, before I add, "And her name is Faline. Not Fawn."

"I *know* that, silly. But Faline from the movie is a doe, and a baby doe is a fawn."

"She has a point," Dove declares.

Per Hunter and Wrenley's request, we didn't

exchange numbers with Todd on Thanksgiving, but we did tell him where to find our tall friend. It's been a few weeks, and so far, if he's gone to see her, she hasn't said anything.

Then again, I'm still not sure I trust her entirely. She could just be keeping it from us.

"Well, I haven't watched it yet." Hangers clink in the background as Vixey speaks. "But if it's that good, I'll give it a try. I'll bet it's driving Hunter nuts, huh?"

Anger sparks like an ember stoked from the smoldering ashes of my jealousy.

"Hunter has been working nonstop. I swear it's like Gwendolyn thinks the more she demands of him, the more likely he is to one day wake up and realize *it was her all along.*" The whimsy in my voice flattens. "Get real. Everyone knows it was always going to be me. Hunter would never."

I don't add that this is most likely—and that's giving the woman a lot of credit—still happening because we haven't announced that we're having a baby yet. Every time it comes up, something interrupts. It's not like no one knows—Hunter told his chain of command since he'll need time off when the baby arrives—but people like Gwendolyn don't *need* to know.

Still, the longer we go without saying it, the more intense my *need* gets to march up to her face and tell her to back off.

Hunter and I have been playing our little games very publicly for long enough that she should already understand he's never going to choose her.

"Wait. I'm sorry, who are we talking about? Does she have Iconic? I need to look her up." Vixey's words taper off and muffle before growing louder like she put us on speakerphone.

"I forgot Iconic rolled out to everyone," I say.

"Yeah, she's on there. The department got access to it months ago, like we did at *Metro Media*. Gwendolyn Cabaret." Shuffling sounds on Dove's end and a muffled order for burgers and fries filters through the line before she returns. "She's been after Hunter's dick for years."

"Hold on. I'm looking her up."

I wait patiently, watching the Saja Boys perform *Soda Pop* for the umpteenth time. Baby girl has calmed down on the gymnastics since I turned the movie back on, and my stomach is grateful for the reprieve.

"I'm sorry, who does this bitch think she is? Bunny, babe, go to work and get your man." Vixey's switch from *bubbly and sweet* to *I'm going to whittle your fingers into shanks and stab you with them* throws me.

Never mind that she's never called me an affectionate nickname before, and I'm not entirely sure we're on that wavelength yet, but I don't think I've ever heard her utter a single violent thing.

I'm honestly liking her more and more as time goes on.

"Uh, what the fuck?" Dove cuts in, stunned.

"What happened?"

Slapping the speaker button, I pull up the app in a panic. Anxiety ripples through me like a stone dropped in still water, the nervous electric energy skittering down my limbs with a tingling ferocity.

Before either of them can answer, I see it.

A photo of Hunter's desk, with an array of food laid out on it.

No her. No him.

Only his thick-framed glasses, the food, and the caption: Dinner date. #workhusband.

Bubbles of air catch in my throat, expanding through my chest until it feels like I might burst. "Excuse the fuck outta me?"

Oh, hell no.

Vixey sounds like an eager puppy ready to play. "Do we do teamwork? Dove can hold her down, and I'll have Nibbles bite her."

"Who is Nibbles?" Dove asks.

Meanwhile, I'm already on my feet, digging for something other than the sweats I've lived in for two days.

Hunter wouldn't have dinner with her... right?

And he sure as hell wouldn't let Gwendolyn post something like that, which means he doesn't know.

"He's my black flame centipede. His bite hurts like a bitch. And I'd like to help hurt this one."

I freeze halfway up the stairs, one foot hovering over the hand-scraped walnut, unsure if I heard her correctly. "What?"

"Uhhh..." Dove trails off.

Someone shouts at her to keep walking, and she tells him to go fuck himself in her signature sugary-sweet lilt.

Long silken strands of my hair fall forward as I shake

my head, tamping down the hundred questions clawing at my tongue. Surely we're misunderstanding our ditzy friend.

"Okay, but like... you're *joking*, right?" Dove finally asks, the question spurring me to keep moving up the stairs in a stupor.

"No? Why would I be joking?" Vixey's usual innocence bleeds back into her tone.

She doesn't strike me as someone who would own a pet centipede—but then, I wouldn't have pegged her as someone who would severely injure a guy, and look how that turned out.

"You have a creepy crawly pet who has a painful bite, and you named him *Nibbles*?" Dove giggles. "Well, you know what we're going to have to call you now, don't you, darlin'?"

I'm only half listening as I wriggle into leather skinnies, but I know what's coming.

"Now I'm crowning you the Venomous Vixen."

"No offense, but I don't even understand why she's getting a name," I huff. "Is she planning on killing any more people? Are you planning on killing more people, Vixey?"

Nervous giggles bubble through the line from both girls.

"I don't know what you're talking about, *Bunny*," Vixey grits.

"Bad Bunny! Down, girl!" Dove teases.

Admittedly, I shouldn't be speaking like that over the phone, unsecured network and all.

But it's not like Vixey even killed anyone. From what I saw, Todd took care of the guy for her.

Whether Vixey knows that is an entirely different story.

"Whatever. *I'm* crowning you *Vexing Vixey*."

IN HINDSIGHT... could I have messaged Hunter and asked what the hell was up?

Yes.

Instead, I march my cute, pregnant butt down to the department to make sure everyone—and by everyone, I mean Gwendolyn—knows that he is very much mine, I am his, and we are a family not to be fucked with.

But first, I have to pee.

Also, he hasn't responded to any of my messages since this afternoon, which is unnerving in itself.

Hunter rarely goes long stretches without replying to me.

Voices echo off the cream porcelain tiles of the second-floor bathrooms just as I flush and start wrestling my pants back up.

I thought only my ankles would swell. Why is my whole body bloating like a hot air balloon?

Agitation creeps up my spine as Gwendolyn's light rasp suddenly reverberates off the walls.

"It's only a matter of time. I mean, I heard she's pregnant. What, is he going to stick around and raise another man's baby? It's tragic."

Tugging carefully, quietly, I fasten my pants as I listen.

"Have you ever considered that Hunter might be the dad?" A voice I don't recognize cuts in over the sink's running water. "He's pined after her for years. And anyone who's seen them together knows she's got it just as bad. I think you're barking up the wrong tree. Don't be a homewrecker, Gwennie."

Note to self: find out who that is and get her a nice gift basket filled with coffee cards and chocolate.

Gotta love a woman who looks out for other women.

Gwennie barks a harsh laugh.

Peering through the crack in the stall, I see her primping in the mirror—fluffing her over-bleached hair, checking that her ridiculous red lipstick isn't all over her teeth.

How about I knock your teeth out so you don't have to worry about it?

"Bunny Jones is a little tart who tramps around in too much leather and self-assuredness. She probably got knocked up by one of the guys she's always dating. Hunter deserves better."

Flicking the lock, I relish the way she jumps at the crash of the door. Our eyes meet in the mirror, and her shit-brown gaze goes wide.

"Bunny. I didn't know you were coming in tonight," she remarks snidely, her sour expression scrunching like she just ate a lemon.

Without a word, I stalk toward her, not sparing the other woman a glance. Gwendolyn spins as I come up behind her.

"Let me fill you in on a little secret, Gwendolyn." Points for keeping my voice level, because my fury could fuel a rocket to Pluto and back.

And yes, Pluto *is* a planet. I didn't memorize *my very elegant mother just served us nine pizzas* in fifth grade for nothing.

Stepping into her space, I force her to retreat or risk getting bitch-slapped by my baby bump. "You keep begging Hunter to take you on a date. He begs me to keep his cock warm at night. We are not the same."

All the color drains from her already pasty face as her muddy gaze drops to my stomach.

Her mouth parts, the question forming—but I don't let her speak.

"That's right. Hunter *is* the father of my child, and he's *mine*. He always has been. He always will be. And if you know what's good for you, you'll find someone else to harass from here on out. Do you understand?"

Bloodlust screams through my veins like a banshee. I've never wanted to harm an innocent person, especially another woman—but after hearing all the nasty things she said, I'm seriously considering luring her to a club just to slit her throat and watch the light die in her eyes as I reveal myself in her last few moments.

Even though I'm severely shorter than she is, and I have to crane my neck to look her in the eye, I hold her gaze and repeat, low and lethal. "I said, do you understand?"

Gathering whatever aplomb she still has after that demonic takedown (*see what I did there, baby girl? Mommy is going to teach you how to be hilarious*), Gwendolyn nods curtly and spins on her heels.

Shifting my gaze to the other woman, I allow my feralness to leech back into the inky black compartment reserved for my victims. Offering a small smile, she waves awkwardly before sprinting out of the bathroom behind her friend.

Once we're alone, I stare at my reflection, rubbing my stomach protectively.

An odd sense of satisfaction swells through me from finally giving her a piece of my mind—but as quickly as it hits, pinpricks of annoyance follow.

"Daddy has some explaining to do."

<u>Hunter</u>

Bang!

Startled, I spin in my chair as Bunny storms into my office, slams the door, and locks it.

"Brooks, I gotta go. I have an angry baby momma who looks like she's out for blood."

Anderson Brooks's chuckle filters through the speaker. "Hi, Bunny."

"Bye, Anders," she croons sweetly before reaching over and disconnecting the call. She drops the receiver beside the cradle and fixes me with a displeased stare, lips pursed, arms crossed.

She's obviously pissed. Don't look at her breasts. Don't look at her—

"Hunter!"

Shit. She caught me.

They're just getting so big, though.

"Yes, my gorgeous little rabbit?" Spinning my chair, I pat my lap as she rounds the desk in a huff. "What's wrong? I thought you didn't want to leave the house today?"

"Yeah, well, your *work wife* pissed me off."

For a second I think she might actually smack me. Instead, her hands fly to the button of my pants, unfastening them and attempting to wrangle my dick out of its confines like it personally offended her.

"Seriously, Hunter? Dinner with Gwendolyn?"

"I have no idea what you're talking about." Strangely, the jealousy rolling off her in thick waves is a total turn-on—even though we're in the middle of the damn police department. "I didn't have dinner with Gwendolyn."

"Really? Because she posted a photo on Iconic—dinner on *your* desk with *your* glasses—and captioned it, 'dinner date with my work husband.'"

She steps back and yanks her pants down, nearly tripping when they catch around her ankles.

"Bunny, what are you—" Pleasure zips up my spine as she climbs into my lap and sinks onto me, already soaked. "*Oh, fuck.*"

"I figured it was time to stake my claim publicly."

Sharp, pointed nails dig into my cheeks as she clutches my jaw, forcing my eyes to hers. Rolling her hips with feral vigor, she rides me like she's training for the rodeo.

"We had a little run-in just now in the bathroom. She better not bother you again."

God, the way she moves is sin personified. And the way she feels—slick and hot and so fucking mine. So very fucking mine.

Reaching between us, I languidly rub her clit, pulling her down to swallow her moans. If she keeps this pace, I'm not going to last. Our tongues tangle, her teeth scraping my bottom lip, tugging it between us with a sharp nip.

"Why aren't you denying it?" she demands, using my shoulders for leverage as she rocks in my lap.

"I don't know what you're talking about, baby. But shut the fuck up about it and drench my cock already— I'm about to come."

Sultry laughter bubbles from her lips as she spins the chair to lean back over my desk. Her pace slows to a grind, the new angle stretching me as her walls strangle my cock when she arches back.

Reaching for my hand, she places my fingers back on her clit, encouraging me to stroke her as she widens her legs around my thighs. Slickness pours from her pussy, drenching my cock and my lap, and it takes everything not to dig my fingers into her hips and slam into her.

"Do you know how many times I've imagined you fucking me on your desk?"

"Probably not as many as *I've* imagined fucking you on it. Now be a good girl and come for me." I give her pussy a light slap and savor the squeal that spills from those pink lips.

"Fuck, Hunter," she rasps, keeping her voice low. Her fingers dig into my forearms, and her pussy clamps down around me.

"Yeah, baby. That's it." Wrapping my arms around her thighs, I push her farther onto the desk as I stand and spread her wide. "Look how soaked you are for me, you greedy little slut."

"There!" she cries when I lean over and angle deeper. "Right there. Harder!"

I give her exactly what she wants, taking pleasure in the sight of her clawing at me—pushing me away and pulling me closer—like she can't decide how powerful she wants her orgasm to be.

I decide for her.

Her mouth opens in a silent scream as I piston in and out. When her pussy chokes me again, I empty inside her while she bathes my cock in her release.

Breathless giggles float in the air as I slow. Golden-pine eyes blink up at me, sated. "That was so worth leaving home for."

"Glad I could be of service." Brushing a chaste kiss to her lips, I help her sit. I'm still lodged inside her, and her legs cinch around my waist when I try to step back.

I smooth my thumb over her naked scar. She's been leaving the house more without the foil stickers, and it

wrecks me—in the best way—that she's finally comfortable showing it or not caring who sees.

"Now, about your accusation… I didn't have dinner
with Gwendolyn. I was in a meeting up until right before
you stormed in. I'd barely gotten Brooks on the phone."

Bunny frowns. "I know it was your desk. Your glasses
were in the photo. And she made it sound true when we
spoke."

This time she lets me pull back. I grab tissues, clean
us up, and help her down as she chews her thumbnail.

"Did you ask her straight up if we had dinner
together?"

"No," she grumbles.

After I tuck myself away, I help her into her pants,
steadying her hips as I tug them up. "Okay, well. I hate to
tell you this, but we've been here before with the whole
social media thing. It wasn't me. If she used my desk for a
photo, it was while I was in the meeting—which means
she's fucking crazy, and I'll be talking to someone about
getting transferred off her case." I kiss the tip of her nose
and straighten. "Now, I'd say you owe me an apology for
the dramatic entrance, but honestly the only thing I'm
upset about is that you felt like you had to leave the
house when you didn't want to."

She lifts a shoulder, a pink flush blooming over her
freckles. "I think it's time everyone knew anyway, don't
you?"

The hope on her face turns my insides to goo. "What
my little rabbit wants, she gets."

A sharp laugh escapes as she pushes me back playfully. "Remember, all this happened because you started denying me. Once I pop the baby out, you'll probably revert to depriving me."

"We'll cross that bridge when we come to it."

It's meant as a joke—riffing off hers, because she knows I'd never deny her anything. But the humor drains from her face in an instant. Suddenly, the air goes thick, and I know I fucked up.

"Yeah, I guess we will." Without waiting for a reply, she storms for the door.

"Bunny, wait! I was kidding." Hastily fastening my pants and hurry after her.

But she's already sailing out with a sharp, "Cool joke, Hunter."

"Bunny!" Ignoring the stares thrown my way, I decide against running after her. If I've learned anything these past months, it's that when she's angry, she wants space.

Pregnancy hormones are a bitch.

"I THINK one of us should go with you." Dove grabs my hand and squeezes, pouring her worry into the touch as much as I hear it in her voice. "I'm not saying you're not capable, Buns. I just don't think it's a good idea. It's New Year's Eve. Places are packed. This isn't just a hard kill, it's nearly impossible to pull off without getting caught."

"That's why it's perfect to do it tonight. People are shit-faced, and it's easier to slip back into a crowd."

The Tipsy Taco is already alive with the bustle of partygoers. Glittery confetti, shiny streamers, and shimmering balloons have transformed the space for the evening.

Instead of sitting at the bar like usual, Dove and I have a back-corner table, talking in hushed tones so no one overhears—even though we can barely hear each other over the music.

Wrenley gave us a moment alone, making up a reason to talk to Alex. Things have been awkward since Thanksgiving when I all but outed myself to my best friend's fiancé, but he graciously hasn't brought it up, and for that, I'm thankful. I know he supports Dove and likely doesn't have an issue with me, but asking him to keep it from Hunter doesn't sit right with me. Dove is Wrenley's world, and Hunter is his best friend. He's already carrying her secret, he doesn't need to be burdened with mine as well. And if I remain silent on the matter, it's like he doesn't know.

Girl math... or reasoning... or whatever.

Vixey flounces around in a sparkly rust-colored dress that looks like a shorter version of something you'd see in the 20s. With it being a holiday, it's busier than usual, and she's working so hard a thin sheen of sweat glistens on her skin. Alex keeps barking orders, his whole vibe dripping bitterness and apoplectic energy.

She scoops her curtain of honey hair up—teased and fluffed like the night we went dancing—fanning her neck while she waits for Alex to finish a round of drinks. He says something that screws her features in displeasure, lips pursing as if to hold in her words. Even Wrenley looks taken aback.

"Is Alex still not over the whole Todd thing?"

The *Todd thing* would be Todd Langston bursting into Vixey's life like a wildfire—quick, all-consuming, and blazing with the heat of a thousand suns. I can barely stand to be in the same room with them for fear of getting scorched by their sexual tension. I'm horny enough as it is, I don't need a catalyst.

They haven't officially labeled their relationship, but Todd made it pretty damn clear to Alex that Vixey is off-limits.

"Don't change the subject, missy!" Dove smacks my hand to regain my attention. But when my hazel eyes meet her cerulean blues, she rolls them and shrugs. "No, he's not. And I feel bad because I'm team Tixey."

"Please don't tell me that's what we're calling them. Sounds like a pair of bloodsucking beasties."

"Yep," she pops her p. "Wren and I are team Dovely, you're Hunny, and they're Tixey."

Dovely, Hunny, and Tixey.

"No, Dove. Just... no." I sip my soda water and check my phone for a text from Hunter. Fortunately, he's working tonight. So I won't have to worry about him wondering where I am.

I have less than an hour before my meeting with Matthew Price at a seedy strip club in Midtown West. I'm going to get in, get slashy, and get back to Hunter's before he notices I'm out doing murdery things.

"Uhhh, yes. Anyway, don't change the subject. Are you sure you don't want me to come?" Her attention flicks to Wrenley, and I use the opening to gather my things.

Pushing my chair back, I kiss her cheek and stand.

"I'll be fine. I'll text you later. I don't want to explain to your man why he can't kiss you at midnight."

"He could always come with?" she squeaks, barely audible over Pitbull's "*Tonight.*"

"No, Love Dove. Now stop it. You've never been worried about me before." My hand settles on my stomach as I give her a look. "Baby and I will be fine. I'll call you later."

"Fine." Her shoulders slump, pink satin frills fluttering with her sigh at losing this round. "Love you."

"Love you." I wave to Vixey weaving through the crowd with a tray of drinks, turn—and nearly plow into Wrenley's chest.

His hands on my shoulders steady me, and he bends to whisper, "Be safe. And for the love of god, please let Dove know you're okay later."

Standing to his full height, he bestows me with a wink—his perfectly styled dirty-blond locks making him look like some sort of Prince Charming—then steps around me. "Happy New Year, Bunny."

As soon as I finish my mission, it will be.

New year. New me.

Tonight, the Shadow Siren sings her last song.

Heels?

Check.

Fit?

Appraising myself in the full-length mirror, I can't help but think I look pretty damn cute. It echoes the outfit I wore the night Hunter and I met and proudly showcases my bump. I shrug into a long black leather trench and tuck my signature stilettos in my bag.

Check.

Scar putty?

In the en suite, I open the cosmetics organizer where I keep my special effects makeup. It holds a singular tub —scraped clean—of the stuff I use to make my cheek appear normal.

Shit.

"Well, fuck. What are we gonna do, baby girl?" Rubbing my stomach, I think through my options.

I could go without. It's late and dark. People will be intoxicated and occupied. One night without hiding it won't kill us. My foil stickers are more noticeable anyway and even though I've been going without them lately, they are still an identifiable mark. Plus, they'll catch the light.

"Guess we're going naked."

I pack the rest and head downstairs to check on Yasha and Maru. Even though we're a decent distance from the fireworks, sometimes the sound still carries, so I keep the boys sedated and comfy. Their ears barely flick from the giant donut bed in the living room.

Turning the TV on, I cue *Inuyasha* where I left off, sucking in a harsh breath when Faline kicks the second she hears the theme *One Day, One Dream*. "Rude, little girl, that's one of Mommy's favorites."

If *this child grows up hating this show, we'll have problems.*

Mentally running through my murder checklist, I double-check the lock and head down the stoop.

One step.

Two.

Wait.

Slowly turning, I frown at the piece of paper taped to my door. I didn't see the white parchment when I opened it because I was distracted, but subconsciously, I must have glimpsed it when I turned away.

Odd. The camera never went off.

Goosebumps ripple my skin.

I peel the tape from the black wood, icy dread clawing down my throat as I unfold the letter.

TICK TOCK. 14 WEEKS. TIME'S ALMOST UP, LITTLE RABBIT.

This time, the cut-out letters are joined by a crayon drawing: a rabbit in a pool of blood, X's for eyes.

Fear rattles my bones, filleting my flesh with razor-sharp revulsion.

Fourteen weeks. My due date.

No one knows that except Hunter, the girls, and Wrenley.

While Vixey and I got off to a shaky start, I consider her a friend now. There's no way any of them did this.

A whoosh of air expels past my lips.

Breathe in. And out. In, in, out.

I haven't started birthing class, but isn't that how you control your anxiety about pushing a watermelon out of your vagina?

Shoving the letter in my bag, I check the camera, only

to see it's been smashed off the side of my house. Bits of hardware cling to the stone, but the unit's gone.

No wonder the app didn't notify me. Whoever left the letter must have come from the side and dismantled the device before taping the paper to my door.

Instinct says call Hunter, but I have a mission, and I don't need his attention on me.

Just a few more hours and I'll be free.

I'll be free. And so will Monica Price.

MATTHEW PRICE LIVES in a well-to-do Jersey suburb full of husbands who tell their wives they're working late in the city so they can party and fuck random women.

The difference between him and them, though, is he's calculated and paranoid, which not only makes him a hard kill, it makes him dangerous.

But his paranoia is my gain. The strip club he picked is big, packed, and takes money for private dances that end in "happy endings" for the patrons and a bundle of cash for the strippers.

Directions wait for me in the encrypted app he insisted on when I put myself in his path and started this whole mission. It makes it easier, because all I have to do is go in and go straight to the room, no questions asked.

For an abusive asshole, Matthew is charming and handsome. But then again, most of them are.

Tall, thick chestnut hair, eyes like the underside of

arctic glaciers. When I step in, his gaze goes straight to my stomach. He bites his bottom lip, deep chuckles filling the room over a house dance mix.

"Look at you," he croons, crossing the room in slow strides. "You're a vision."

I resist flinching as he smooths a thumb over my scar. It's an intimate trail I've come to associate with Hunter, and I hate that this man is tracing the same line.

A shudder racks me when Matthew's thumb dips to stretch my bottom lip. "Fuck, I missed you."

I let the Siren take over and melt into seduction mode. I was working Matthew before he left, and I know what he needs to drop his guard.

Smoothing my hands up his chest, I pout. "You were gone so long. I was getting lonely."

Bile catapults up my esophagus as I push him toward the big booth circled around a platform with a gleaming pole. The light is dim, casting golden shafts over the black interior.

"Why don't you get comfortable and I'll get you a drink."

He loves the doting-wife scene—the *"it's his right"* fantasy. No surprise he willingly agrees.

"Lose the jacket. I want to see your stomach," he says, loosening his tie. For someone with a breeding kink, it baffles me he hit his pregnant wife.

Regardless, I do as asked, setting my bag on the bar cart. I take my time, giving him a show while I slide my trench down my arms, looking over my shoulder demurely as I retrieve my stilettos and step into them.

Balancing on these bitches gets harder every day.

"What are you having?" His voice booms as he sprawls his arms along the back of the booth, eyes tracking me.

"I'm not sure yet," I lie, reaching for a bottle of whiskey. It's rare for a club to let you have your own mini bar, but I'm sure he paid extra for discretion. "I'm debating waiting until the baby is born to find out."

He's none the wiser when I slip a vial from my top and pour it into his drink—not enough to knock him out, just enough to make him easier to steer. I want him fully aware of what I do to him tonight. A devilish grin stretches across his plump lips as I turn with the glass, twirling a pair of black fuzzy handcuffs.

"Those better be for you." He takes a gulp, his cool gaze drifting down my body, leaving a chill in its wake.

"I was thinking we start with *you* tied up." Climbing onto his lap, I stretch over him, slowly sliding my hand down to his and pulling it above his head. "You must be so tired after such a long day of working hard. Why don't you sit back and relax?" He tosses back the rest of his drink and raises his other arm, crossing his wrists. I clip the cuffs to the rail edging the booth and whisper, "Relax."

My stomach roils at being this close to another man. Before, even if Hunter and I cared for each other, rubbing my body against a victim while I lured them into a false sense of security never bothered me.

Now it feels like cheating.

And I am not a cheater.

Matthew is rock hard beneath me, extending his neck to reach my lips, but I jerk back as Faline kicks—twice—like she disapproves. He feels it. His eyes drop to my belly, pressed against him so tight he can't miss it.

Wistfulness threads his voice, "Let me feel."

Hazy contentment slips into his cadence. His eyes droop as I slide off his lap to the floor and pull out the zip-ties I shoved into my top, binding his feet fast.

Matthew doesn't even notice as he shakes his head. "Fuck, that drink was strong."

"You know what else is strong?" Reaching behind me, I uncap my heels. The blades retract as I stand, but when I press my foot between his legs, the moment my weight leaves the shoe, the hidden weapon springs out. "Your wife."

Dark brows notch together in confusion, but I can see Matthew swimming against the fog like a man drowning in a riptide. The cuffs bang the rail, but the music swallows the sound.

"What?" His question is alert, but heavy. "What did you do to me?"

Smug satisfaction widens my lips into a feline grin as he continues to struggle against his bindings. He tries to kick, but zip-tied and drugged, he can barely lift his feet.

This is what I live for. Watching the fight flare to life in evil men's eyes when they realize their own poor choices walked them into a she-devil's arms.

"I drugged you, Matthew. And now I'm going to kill you." Simple and matter-of-fact.

With a jerk, I lift my foot and sink the blade into his stomach.

His cry is music to my ears.

Blood spurts, dribbling down his crisp white shirt in a crimson bloom.

"You fucking bitch!" he snarls. Adrenaline eats away at the drug, and he thrashes harder.

I pull away and drive the blade into his crotch. Another painful howl mixes with my laughter and P!nk's *Raise Your Glass*. "I'm sorry, what was that? You want me to stop?"

"Yes! Please! I'll do anything!" Matthew freezes, trying not to move because every flinch drives the steel deeper into his privates.

"Why didn't you stop when Monica asked you to stop?" I slide onto the platform in front of the booth, resting my feet between his legs. "I'll bet she'd have done anything for you to stop taking your frustrations out on her with your fists. And while she was carrying kids she didn't want? Forced breeding. Domestic violence. Child endangerment." I cluck my tongue. "Your list of indiscretions is long, Mr. Price."

"Did she put you up to this?" Sweat gleams on ashen skin. His head drops, chest heaving.

Pressing the toe of my stiletto to his chin, I shove until the blade kisses his Adam's apple. His body goes rigid and he pushes back, trying to get away. But the strain of his retreat causes the blood to pool faster from the wound in his stomach.

Faline kicks twice again, the last one stealing my

breath and rolling nausea through me. I settle a hand over my stomach without breaking eye contact. "Mommy is working, sweet girl. You should be sleeping, not helping."

Crystal blue narrows as his lip curls. "You're psychotic."

I lift my shoulder with a nonchalant shrug, dragging my heel shallowly across his throat. "I've been called worse."

Blood beads, trickling down. I kick my other leg up and skim the heel over his cheek, relishing the pained groan he tries to swallow.

His cries turn garbled as I flutter-kick, slicing through his collar and leaving shallow lines along his collarbone, throat, face. Death by a thousand paper cuts can hurt more than a stab.

"Hush, little baby, don't you cry, Mommy's little victim's about to die." I giggle the lullaby—pausing abruptly as a shudder racks me.

Now I sound like Dove when she makes her videos.

"I'll give you anything. Please. Just stop," Matthew pleads.

I'm about to tell him no when a loud knock thuds at the door. "Open up! This is the police!"

The music muddies it, but I could have sworn—

"Metro PD! Open up!"

Hunter.

Fuck.

Why is he here?

Fear grips my insides as Matthew opens his mouth to

scream. Before a single sound comes out, I drive my heel through his throat, cutting off his airway. Blood sprays my legs in a scarlet arc, and the last remnants of his strangled moans die fast.

Hurriedly, I hop down, cap my heels, and grab a handful of napkins. Cracking open a mini bottle of water, I sluice my legs, wipe them down and toss everything in my bag.

One of the serial-killer rules: never meet anywhere without an exit strategy. I cross the room, shrug on my trench, and slip through the other door. I'm halfway down the hall when a door slams open.

Don't look back. Don't look back. You're almost there.

The glaring red EXIT sign calls like a lighthouse in a storm. The countdown to midnight starts, the club vibrating with hundreds of voices ready to ring in the new year.

Just a few more steps.

"Hey! You! Stop!" An all-too-familiar voice shouts behind me.

I don't stop.

I pick up the pace as the countdown hits seven.

"I said stop!" Footfalls pound the thin, worn carpet of the hall.

Bile rises as the crowd shouts, "Four!"

Hunter is too close. Right on my ass.

The push bar is cool under my fingers as I frantically fling the door open.

"Two!"

Don't look back. Don't look back.

"Wait!" Hunter's command is thick with frustration.

Like a fucking magnet with no choice but to pull toward its opposite pole, my eyes swing over my shoulder just as the air fills with an emphatic "Happy New Year!"

Mossy green meets molten gold.

I'm so sorry, Hunter.

And then I run for my life.

IN MY HURRY TO FLEE, I make one of the stupidest mistakes I could possibly make.

I go the wrong fucking way.

With how close Hunter is, though, I have no choice but to pray to whoever's listening that there's a way out of this alley—a way to escape, even though he undoubtedly recognized me.

You can spin it. This is how you met. Undercover work. Stop running and just fucking spin it, Bunny!

The door crashes open behind me. No hurried shouts. No demands to halt. Just slow, calculating steps.

He knows.

He knows.

He knows.

The words replay in my head like Chopin's *Marche Funèbre.*

Faline squirms, and my already-turmoiled insides pitch like a small ship in rogue waves. Cold steals my breath as I reach the chain-link fence that cages me in.

Before, I'd have just climbed it. Now, at twenty-six weeks pregnant, there's no fucking way.

Spinning, I search frantically for anywhere to hide, even as Hunter draws closer—shrouded in shadows, while the light on the other side of the fence beams down on me like a spotlight.

Here she is! The killer you've been looking for!

I focus on my breathing as tears prick my eyes. No matter what I do, I lose. I could try to convince him I was just bored staying home, but he knows better.

Pivoting back to the fence, I try to gauge if I could make it, but he's already reached me.

"There's nowhere to go." Hunter's amused drawl resonates down the alley.

Flinching, I spin to face him, guarded and unsure what to expect.

"It's over." Every step he takes forward, I take one back.

He wouldn't really hurt me... would he?

Hunter loves me.

And I'm pregnant with his child.

My back hits the fence. The chain rattles behind me like a crescendo to my death march.

Deep chuckles fill the air, and finally, he steps out of the shadows until we're face to face.

"Time's up, Little Rabbit. Looks like I've finally caught you."

Dread fills my chest as I think back to the letter taped to my door earlier.

Time's almost up, little rabbit.

A nervous laugh escapes my throat, surprising us both.

"I'm sorry I didn't tell you. I took on some extra work," I lie through my teeth. "I was getting sick of just sitting at home while you got to have all the fun."

Hunter shoves his hands in his pockets, his expression going dark. "Don't do that, Bunny. Don't fucking lie to my face."

"Hunter—"

He stalks forward until his abs press against my bump, reaching above my head to curl his fingers into the fence. I can feel the heat of his rage pulsing off him in waves, wrapping around me like a warm blanket to stave off the cold midnight air. Warmth, however, is the last thing that imbues his words.

"There's a fucking dead man in that room with wounds matching the Siren's victims." His voice comes hushed but lethal. When I drop my gaze, unable to withstand the way he's looking at me, he grips my chin and forces my face back up. "So do not fucking lie to me, Little Rabbit. You are damn lucky it's me here and not someone else. But your man—Matthew Price? He had a hunch he'd been speaking to the Siren. He contacted me at the department. I kept that to myself and got here later than I should've. So—do you want to tell me the fucking truth?"

It's crazy how fast you can lose everything.

One second is all it takes for your world to come crashing down.

One second where you have to decide what you're going to do about it.

And in that second, my survival instincts devour the terror until there's nothing left but a will to survive and crumbs of a lost future.

"You know the truth," I snarl, jerking my face out of his grip. "So what are you going to do about it, Hunter? Huh? Throw me in prison while I'm pregnant with your kid?"

In all the time I've known him, I've never seen Hunter this angry. His nostrils flare, the chain rattling under the pressure of his grip. His shallow breaths shudder with ire.

"Was it worth it?" The question catches me off guard. Amber glazes over as tears line his lashes, though there's no ounce of sadness in his eyes, only blazing fury, sharp and pointed directly at me.

Without waiting for a reply, he pushes off the fence and snatches my wrist. Snarling like a feral cat, I claw at him as he drags me down the alley. We pass the club's side door, and I scratch at his forearms, ready to uncap a heel and injure him to get away if I have to.

"Hunter, let me go!"

I'm not going to prison.

Was it worth it?

No. It wasn't fucking worth it.

The man I love looks at me with pure disdain. Everything I feared is manifesting at once, as if my dread conjured it into reality.

He's going to take away my baby.

I'll be locked up.

I'll never see her again.

"Hunter, I'm serious, let me go!"

"Shut up, Bunny. I can't fucking *think* straight right now, I'm so fucking mad at you."

"Hey!" a voice calls behind us, halting Hunter mid-step.

As he turns, I wrench my wrist, putting enough force behind it that, in his distracted state, he lets me go.

It happens in slow motion. A metaphorical action that symbolizes the death of our relationship.

Before my heart can interject, my mind makes the decision. Pivoting, I race toward the main street, thankful for the adrenaline rushing through my veins and the confidence I have in myself to not fall flat on my face.

Hunter calls my name behind me, his voice swallowed by the crowd and the gridlocked cars.

Every part of me wants to turn back.

Every instinct screams at me to run.

I can't stay.

Not now that Hunter knows the truth and will be forced to punish me for my crimes.

Tears blur my vision as I race through the crowded streets. Block by block, I run until traffic thins.

It was always too good to be true. Just when I was finally happy.

You couldn't just let it go, could you, Bunny?

By trying to save Monica Price, I condemned myself —and my child.

Faline can't grow up without a mother. She can't

grow up without a father either... but she *needs* her mother.

She needs *me*.

When my feet ache and I can't go anymore, I hail a cab and collapse into the backseat, giving the driver my address.

I have to move quickly. There's no telling if Hunter is behind me or racing home to intercept me.

A sob tears from my throat, my chest burning from the cold air, my stomach fluttering with Faline's tiny feet.

"Rough night?" a familiar raspy voice asks.

Choking on another cry, I glance at the rearview mirror—and see the same cabbie who picked me up the night Hunter kissed Dove at *The Tipsy Taco*. His bushy mustache twitches when our eyes meet.

"You okay, little miss?" His fatherly demeanor invokes a fresh batch of tears.

"I just ruined my entire life. I'm the complete opposite of okay." Sniffing, I wipe under my eyes, smearing my makeup until black coats my fingers. My face probably looks like a panda, but I couldn't care less.

"Well, it's a new year. You know what they say—new year, new you. Whatever you did, I'm sure it's not that bad. There's always a way to correct our mistakes." He coughs into a napkin balled in his hand.

I'm sure he doesn't mean for me to see, but the bright red flecks on the white tissue are hard to miss. Remorse blankets my lungs like scratchy wool.

Everyone has problems. Mine aren't worse than anyone else's.

"What you need is some rest and relaxation. Don't get yourself too worked up or you'll stress out the little one," he continues.

"You're really kind, you know that, sir?"

"Oh, it's nothing, little miss. And you can call me Hank."

Surprisingly, Hunter isn't blowing up my phone. When we're close to my house, I pull up Dove's contact.

"Hank? Could you please wait here? I won't be long, and I need to go to the airport."

"Sure thing, little miss."

He stops his meter. This sweet old man is getting an envelope full of cash when I return.

Yasha and Maru barely lift their heads when I walk in. Guilt pierces my chest as I give them kisses. "Mommy has to go away for a little bit, you guys. Auntie Dove will take care of you. I promise I'll be back."

It's easier while they're still groggy. If they were their usual excited selves, I don't know that I'd be able to leave.

Dove's phone rings and rings until it goes to voicemail. Placing it on speaker, I set it next to my suitcase while I pack.

"Hey, Love Dove. I hate to do this, but I have to go away for a little while. The dogs are at my house. Please take care of them while I'm gone." Emotion clogs my throat, suffocating my words with cloying melancholy.

That's as far as I get before Dove rings in on the other line. Steadying myself with a shaky inhale, I switch over. "Hey."

"What's wrong?" My best friend instantly goes into

protective mode, no doubt hearing the waver in my voice. "Buns, what happened?"

"Listen, I need you to come get the dogs." I grit my teeth, flinging clothes and whatever essential items I have in close range into my suitcase.

"Bunny, what happened?" she presses. Wrenley's voice echoes faintly behind her.

Sniffling, I admit, "Hunter found out, Dove. He knows."

"Don't run," she orders. "That's what you're doing, isn't it? Bunny, don't. Please." Panic frays her usually bubbly demeanor, souring my friend's sweet tone. "We can work this out. Just come here, I'll protect you."

"I'm not dragging you into this, Dove. It's bad enough he'll come looking for me there." Zipping my suitcase, I head to the safe, grab two pouches, and throw as much cash as I can fit in them. "I'm not going to prison. I'm not having my baby in a cell and then having her ripped away from me."

Keys jingle on her end as another call beeps in on mine.

Hunter.

"I'm sorry, Dove. I'll be back for the dogs after Faline is born. After I figure out what I'm going to do."

"What about *me*, Bunny?" Her voice cracks. "If this panic is anything like what Hunter felt last time... I can't—"

Dove is my best friend. My family. Doubt claws at me, but then Faline kicks, as if sensing my distress, reminding me that she's the only one that matters at the moment.

"I'm sorry. I love you. This isn't goodbye. Just see you later."

"Bunny—"

"I have to go." It takes everything in me to hang up.

As soon as the call disconnects, Hunter's name flashes across my screen, the photo of him asleep with both dogs curled on his chest stabbing grief through me.

You're never going to forgive me. And I will hate myself until the end of time for this.

Minutes later, Hank loads my suitcase and we speed toward JFK.

"Which airline, little miss?"

His question jolts me—I didn't realize I'd fallen asleep.

"Um..." I glance at the signs, strangely calm despite having no plan. No idea where to go. "Here is fine, I guess."

Hank pulls over but doesn't get out. "It can be hard to stay sensible in the heat of a moment. Sometimes it's best just to take a few days. Cool off. I hear Jacksonville is lovely this time of year—not too warm, not too cold. Not too far away, should you choose to return sooner rather than later." He pulls a card out of his visor and hands it back to me. "When you come back, give me a call. If I'm still around. I'll come get you."

"I didn't think I could cry more tonight, Hank, but thank you. I'm Bunny." I give him a zippered pouch in exchange. I left my phone behind so Hunter can't track me, but I'll get a burner once I land.

"What's this for?" His caterpillar brows draw together as he looks at the pouch.

"For being kind. Kindness to a stranger in crisis is rare these days."

Hank gets out slowly, retrieving my suitcase from the trunk before sticking out his hand for me to shake. He has to balance his weight on the back of the car, and I imagine it might be uncomfortable for him to walk. Now that I'm truly looking at him, his pallor is gray, and his hair isn't as thick as it was months ago, when we first met.

If he's getting treatment for whatever ails him, it must be wreaking havoc on his body.

"It was a pleasure to see you again. You're a good girl. I'm sure whatever trouble you're in will work itself out."

You're a good girl.

"Oh, Hank. If only you knew the things I've done." Leaving it at that, I grab my bag and turn to go.

I'm halfway to the doors when he calls, "Little miss!"

I glance back. He leans over the top of his car, too weak to stand straight. "Whatever you're running from, I hope it doesn't catch up with you."

Me too, Hank. Me too.

From the second she runs, barbed wire snares my heart. Twining. Twisting. Bleeding me dry as I clean up her mess while my chest rips to shreds.

Oh, Little Rabbit. What have you done?

She's lucky the bouncer didn't see her. He did, however, demand to know why I locked the door back up after crashing through it. Luckily, he buys my excuse about "suspicious activity" the police need to handle and agrees to keep everyone out of the room.

A few well-timed calls and a bit of serendipity let me leave the club and the scene in someone else's hands, feigning an emergency.

Only there's nothing fake about it.

Cursing, I tap my foot impatiently against the cab floor. Bunny isn't answering her phone, but a quick trace tells me she's at home. She thinks I don't have her location—but she's insane if she thought I wouldn't turn it on the second I found out she was pregnant.

Everything changes when you become a parent.

People say fathers don't truly become fathers until the baby is born, while a mother becomes a mother the moment she finds out she's with child.

Me? I became a father the second I saw those two little pink lines.

And the thought of my child being withheld from me...

I try her phone again.

Please answer, Bunny.

An icy foreboding lances through my chest with each unanswered call. Brick by brick, my subconscious starts building a wall—a shield—to brace for the fallout of tonight.

She probably thinks I'm going to slap cuffs on her and read her Miranda rights. I almost laugh at how absurd that is. I *would* laugh if the threat of her leaving wasn't hanging over me like a heavy cloud.

This isn't how I wanted to catch her.

This isn't how I wanted tonight to go.

If that damn bouncer hadn't interrupted, she'd be laid out on her bed right now with my head between her thighs in reassurance.

I know I was harsh. Stressing her out is bad for the baby. I didn't intend for things to get physical. But the rage at her putting herself in danger—putting Faline in danger—burned away all rational thought.

I don't bother knocking when I arrive at her house.

Even worse—Yasha and Maru don't greet me. That has my heart plummeting.

"Bunny?" I yell, panic spiking as I storm up the stairs

—only pausing when a faint *woof* comes from the living room.

"What's going on, boys?"

They're curled in their giant donut bed like a yin-yang symbol. Maru barely twitches in acknowledgement, and Yasha's tail lazily thumps against his brother's head as I crouch down to pet them. "Where's your mom?"

She wouldn't have just *left* them.

I vaguely remember her saying she might knock them out with meds because of the fireworks—that explains their dazed behavior—but still. They're her babies, just as much as Faline.

Rising, I take the stairs two at a time, calling her name once more, stopping short as I reach her room. My lungs burn, forgetting their job, as I freeze in the doorway.

Her room's a disaster. Clothes thrown everywhere, the short neon-blue wig on the floor next to her stilettos, and there, in the middle of her bed, is her phone.

Frantic, I tear through her en suite. Hair and makeup products litter the vanity, lying in small puddles of water. Her staples are gone—her prenatals, the foil stickers she wears over her scar.

Desperation claws up the brick wall I've been building around my heart.

I call Dove as I fly back outside to hail another cab, anguish cinching my lungs until I can't breathe. Over and over, I told her I wouldn't survive it if she left again. We've come so far over these last few months.

How could she do this?

Maybe if you'd assured her you wouldn't put her in prison, this night would have gone a lot differently.

Wrenley answers, somber and guarded. "Hunter."

I rattle off Dove's address to the driver before I've even shut the door, then bring the phone back to my ear. "Is she there?"

"No." Simple. Straight to the point. Accompanied by a frustrated sigh.

"Let me speak to Dove." My own annoyance sharpens my tone.

"You're on your way here. You can talk face-to-face." Even though his tone is naturally deep, it can't hide Dove crying in the background.

"Wrenley, I swear to god—"

"Do you think I appreciate being dragged into this? The only thing I care about in this whole fucking world is currently beside herself because her best friend just decided to up and fuck off," he snaps.

So Bunny *did* leave.

Steeling my anger, I deliver a parting shot. "I'm your best friend, Wrenley. And the only fucking thing *I* care about in this whole world just broke my heart. *Again.* Have a little fucking compassion."

I hit the back of the seat.

"Hey, man! Watch it!" the driver shouts, glaring over his shoulder.

Flashing my badge, I glare back. He shuts up and spins back around rigidly. "Step on it, would you? I'm on official police business."

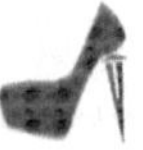

"W‍here is she?"

Dove has calmed by the time I arrive, but tears instantly fill her big blue eyes at the sound of my voice. "I don't know. She asked me to take care of the dogs and—"

"Don't lie to me, Dove. Where. Did. She. *Go*?" I jab a finger toward her, stepping into her space before curling my hand into a fist and dropping it to my side. "If you don't tell me, we're going to have problems."

All the sorrow vaporizes from Dove's countenance, eaten up by flames of her fury. "Oh yeah? And what are you going to do, Hunter? *You're* the one who drove her away!"

She takes a step toward me, all five feet of her puffed up like a rabid pomeranian, but I meet her anger with my size, though it seems to do nothing to deter her.

Wrenley steps between us, palm to my chest. "Back the fuck up, Hunt."

Ignoring him, I glare over his shoulder at her. "Do you think I don't know who the fuck you are? You two aren't as good as you think. You know that? You're fucking lucky I've saved your asses so many times. I'm the *only* reason the Doll and the Siren haven't been put behind bars!"

Silence suffocates the air.

My best friend doesn't so much as flinch as I tell him his fiancée is the serial killer he's been obsessed with catching.

And *that* says everything.

Taking a step back, I search his face to find no trace of surprise.

Astonishment spikes through my anger. "You knew. Didn't you? You knew and you never said anything."

Wrenley shakes his head, calm and level-headed amidst the rolling waves of mine and Dove's rage. "I could say the same. You clearly thought she was good enough for me to be with, Hunter. And you knew about Bunny, yet you still pursued her. I knew you weren't trying to catch them. Not really. They were getting rid of the bad guys. But I've suspected it was more than that for a while now. You're too smart not to have pieced it together."

"I had an inkling you knew too," Dove admits softly, stepping up behind him. "I just never said anything to Bunny about it."

"Why?" I scoff. "If you thought I knew, why not face me?"

"Because when it became obvious you were protecting her, I knew as long as she was safe, so was I." Dove narrows her cerulean gaze, lashes still wet from her tears. "So why did she feel the need to run, Hunter? What happened tonight?"

All my turmoil slams back into my chest like a gunshot. I may as well be suffering from a wound just as fatal. "I fucked everything up."

"What did you *do*?" Dove's face twists into something unrecognizable. A ruthless, caramelized version of herself that has to be cracked to get to the sweet filling beneath.

"I was angry! I *am* angry!" My voice carries through their condo. Fang, her Chinese Crested, jumps off the couch and growls at me. "I thought when she found out she was pregnant she'd be done. That she wouldn't possibly put our baby in danger. I kept a close eye on her, monitored her house and her phone, and I was content she was staying out of trouble until her latest victim called my line at the department, saying he thought he'd been in contact with the Shadow Siren."

Dove's eyes widen as the color drains from her face. Wrenley curses quietly, rubbing her back as she crumbles. "He was going to be her last one. She'd already put in so much work..."

"It doesn't fucking matter." I fix her with a pointed look. "We were free. It was over. And she had to go and fuck it all up."

I don't mention that I didn't make things better. I didn't have to yell through the door. I could have picked the lock or gotten keys from security. But I *wanted* to scare her. To give her time to run.

"I tried going with her. I—"

"Should have stopped her!"

"Hunter, I'm not telling you again—this isn't Dove's fault," Wrenley warns, tension thickening around us.

"It might as well be!" My rationality shatters. "She could have talked her out of it!"

"You know as well as I do that once Bunny gets something in her mind, there's no talking her out of it!" Dove screams back, voice cracking.

"I know she'll contact you if she asked you to keep the dogs—which won't be happening. *I* will take them. Find her, Dove. Or there will be consequences."

A growl rumbles from Wrenley. "Do *not* fucking threaten my fiancée."

We square off as he shoves her behind him. "Then tell her to find out where the fuck the mother of my child went."

Dove speaks around him. "Hunter, I know you're hurting. I know you're angry—with her, with me, with the situation. Believe me, I'm upset too, but—"

"Do you know what happened last time she left?" I cut her off.

Pain breaks down the wall I've tried so hard to erect in the past hour. All my fears manifest into shallow breaths as tears prick my eyes, and my hopeless distress clogs my throat and strangles my words.

"She was pregnant with her husband's child, and she had an abortion. And all I can think about is if she'd rather try to get rid of our baby than put her through what she *thinks* is coming."

My knees buckle. Wrenley catches me. I don't care that I'm a grown man sobbing in the middle of what looks like Barbie's playhouse. I let it all out, trembling as Dove falls to her knees to hold me too.

"I fucked it all up, Dove. I was so angry with her. I let her think I'd turn her in. I let her think—"

"Shh. Shh." Dove combs her fingers through my hair.

"It's too late for that, Hunter. She's too far along. And Bunny wouldn't do that. She loves Faline. And she loves you. All we can do is wait for her to come home."

"If I—"

"No," she cuts me off gently. "This is what she does, right? She runs. But she always comes back. We're her home, Hunter. When she returns, we have to remind her of that. And trust me," she pulls back to look at me, "I'm so angry with her. But, for as strong as she pretends to be, Bunny is sensitive. So when she reaches out, and she will, because I can't see her just up and leaving the boys for that long without a word, we have to tamp down our anger and surround her with support."

"And we're here to support you, too," Wrenley adds quietly. "I'd be at a loss as well."

Pushing back from them, I swing my legs around, propping my arms on my knees, rubbing my face. I don't understand how life went from perfect to ruin in twenty-four hours.

Fuck, Little Rabbit. I'm so sorry. I never meant for you to run again.

The thought of her out there, scared and alone, consumes me. The loss of her and Faline feels like someone swung a wrecking ball into my chest.

"Didn't you install a security camera by her door?" Dove asks, pulling me from my miserable cloud of self-pity.

A renewed sense of hope bursts through me. I don't know why I didn't think to check the cameras—the one outside *and* the ones inside. Yanking my phone from my pocket, I pull up the security app... only to find the last video from the outside camera was yesterday afternoon.

"What the hell..."

Confusion coils in my gut as I play it. A lone figure walks up to Bunny's house.

Why wasn't I notified? The app never went off.

"What is it?" Wrenley asks, leaning in with Dove to look over my shoulder.

Little by little, the man comes into focus, eyes locked on the camera.

"Who is that?" Dove questions.

Every synapse in my body fires off in shocked disbelief as he leans into the lens—grinning.

I'd know that face anywhere. The first time I saw it, I wanted to break his nose. That smarmy smile. That cocksure vibe as he announced he was Bunny's husband.

And I remember how Bunny reduced it to a mound of meat and bone and sinew.

Nathaniel.

THREE MONTHS LATER

"WE NEVER SHOULD HAVE LEFT, baby girl. I'm sorry I took you away from your daddy, but if you can please just wait a little longer..." A sharp pain blooms low in my belly, effectively cutting off my words.

Faline's displeasure has been obvious since I vanished in the middle of the night three months ago. This last trimester has been the worst, and now she's trying to make her appearance a couple of weeks early.

I broke.

It's been hard enough—leaving the way I did, having no contact with Hunter or even Dove, leaving Yasha and Maru in their care. I'm the worst dog mom ever. How am I supposed to be a good mother to an actual baby?

Gripping the railing, I haul myself up another stair. I don't remember there being so many leading up to Hunter's door—or maybe it's because I'm now toting around a melon-sized human. My vagina throbs, the pressure nearly unbearable, but I power through the urge to sit and breathe.

Faline is coming, and my need to have Hunter with me outweighs my need to go to the hospital.

It was a mistake to flee. I knew it when I left, and I've had an angry little reminder every day since.

The last three months have been agonizing—never staying anywhere long enough to get caught, never roaming too far in case something happened with the baby. Not only will Hunter be furious, but when he finds out I've never been more than a few hours away...

Focusing on my breathing, I tackle the last four steps and pause on the stoop, leaning into the railing. It feels like Faline is about to explode out of my lower body. My kitty will be absolutely destroyed after this. How do women do this multiple times?

A soft growl filters through the door, followed by a deeper one. I'd know them anywhere. Why does Hunter have the dogs? I asked Dove to take them.

Praying they don't cause a commotion, I slip my key into the lock and open the door.

Warnings flip to excited yips. I hush them, not wanting to wake Hunter this way—if he's even asleep at all. It's the middle of the night, but who knows with him...

He might not even be here.

Thoughts of him spending late nights at work with Gwendolyn slam through my mind, sluicing icy-hot rage through my veins. He's well within his rights. I fucked everything up by leaving.

Even if I regretted it the second I landed in another state.

Valid reasons or not, what I did was bad. I killed people. Sure, they might have deserved it, but it's still murder. I can't cherry-pick bad behavior. I don't know what would have happened if I'd stayed, but I know Hunter wouldn't have put me behind bars until after Faline was born.

As much as I don't want to face the consequences, I have to. Hunter deserves better. Faline deserves better.

And I'm so stupid for letting fear keep me away again. I can't imagine what Hunter's been through—the turmoil, the disappointment, the hopelessness of losing his child.

I don't know how I'll ever earn his forgiveness. I can only hope he'll let me be part of Faline's life through letters and photos once he puts me away.

"I missed you, too, my good boys. Mommy is so sorry she left you." I try to bend to pet them, but there's no way that's happening. I can barely balance on my cankles as it is.

Another contraction hits. A screech fills the foyer as I bump the little table that holds Hunter's keys and other random stuff. It quiets the dogs, but my breathing takes over their whimpering. The contractions are coming quicker, lasting longer, and I can confidently say I will not ever be giving birth again.

My poor vagina.

Measured breaths help slow my heart rate—until my gaze drops to a pair of golden, glittery heels next to Hunter's shoes.

A scorpion of despair pinches my heart, tearing out a chunk as tears prick my eyes.

What did you expect, Bunny? That he'd wait for you again? After everything you put him through?

Even though I know it's irrational, it's true. In the deepest part of my heart, I did think Hunter would wait. But who can blame him for moving on?

A sob rips from my throat, catching on a gasp as pain bursts between my legs while I start up the stairs to Hunter's bedroom. I push past it—past the physical pain, the emotional turmoil, and my own stubbornness at not wanting to see him with another woman.

You have no right to be upset. And he has every right to be there when his daughter is born.

Anguish stutters my steps. Hunter's name ghosts my lips just as I hear a door open above. Heavy steps accompany the click of the safety on Hunter's standard-issue pistol. Through my tears, his form appears at the top of the stairs. My knuckles go white on the banister.

"Where the fuck have you been?"

There's no warmth in his question—no relief, no concern, not even surprise. His hardened whiskey gaze spears my soul, thick with outrage. He looks like an angry Greek god carved from cold, golden marble, unmoving as he fixes his prey—me—with a disgusted curl of his lip.

"Hunter, I'm sorry... I'm so sorry," I manage, before another nausea-inducing wave rips through me.

Why can't I be one of those women who breeze through labor and come out glowing like a goddess? At this rate, I'll be lucky to survive looking like a haggard raccoon that got locked in a dumpster for days.

He's descended a few steps now, worry and apprehension warring across his face. Shaking my head, I fight the pain and climb another stair. "I was wrong to run. I'm not expecting you to forgive me, but the baby is coming, and—"

"It's too early," he interrupts.

"Nope," I pop the p, gritting my teeth as annoyance rakes through me at his unbothered state. It is so unfair that men don't suffer during labor. "She's considered early-term, but she's ready to make her appearance now."

"Is that why you came back?" I hate that his tone is rough and guarded. I hate that I did that to him.

Most of all, I hate that I've never deserved him, and he's finally seeing that.

Self-preservation kicks in, my feet backpedal on their own. I open my mouth to retort, the words dying on my lips as a familiar feminine voice calls his name.

"Hunter?"

Ice trickles through every fiber of my being, every muscle tensing as Hunter flinches.

No. He wouldn't have. Please tell me he didn't.

Soft steps on hardwood, and a massive mane of honeyed blonde hair appears behind him, mussed like she was fucked before bed. Surprised golden eyes meet mine over his shoulder, belonging to the last person I expected to find in Hunter's home in the middle of the night—

especially wearing nothing but one of his old, ratty college shirts.

Vixey.

"Bunny?" Her excited cry snaps me out of it.

With a jolt, I turn and bolt, Hunter's heavy steps snapping into action behind me.

"Bunny! Wait!" he growls.

Tears blur my vision as I try to breathe. Anxiety swells. Betrayal, thick and viscous, churns in my gut. Distress fills my body fuller and fuller... and then warmth gushes from between my legs, releasing the pressure.

Shock sinks into my bones as I stare at the puddle at my feet. Vaguely, I hear Hunter racing up the stairs, shouting something about his phone.

Delicate hands grip my shoulders, Vixey's elated face filling my vision. "Bunny! Your water just broke!"

No shit, Sherlock.

Shoving my bitterness toward one of the only two women I never expected to betray me aside, I let her help me toward the door.

Here we fucking go.

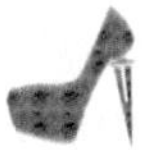

"Alright, Mama, you got this. Give me another big push."

Ignoring the doctor, I fix Hunter with my most furious glare. "I hate you. You're seriously the worst for doing this to me."

To his credit, Hunter just shakes his head and allows me to continue my mission in breaking every bone in his hand.

"There's the head!" Vixey crows, shoving her phone toward my vagina.

"I hate *you* even more! Why are you still here, you homewrecker?"

The doctor shoots her an annoyed look at her antics and my accusation.

Prickles of awareness, both painful and distressing, creep back into my lower body as the epidural begins to wear off. "I need more drugs."

"Can someone *help* her?" Hunter asks, frantic—unaware it's up to us to press the button that administers another dose of the only thing getting me through this.

"I'm not a homewrecker," Vixey pouts. "I told you, it's not what it looks like."

"She's right, it's my fault," Dove chimes in from the phone screen, crunching on a bag of popcorn. "We went out of town for the weekend and... No, Songbird, you can't look yet, I'm still watching Bunny's vagina in high definition. Anyway, Vixey called me first, I wasn't available, so she went to Hunter instead. She had a bad night."

The distraction is helping, so I glare at Vixey and demand, "What happened tonight?" She's in a glittering gold gown now, having changed while we waited for Hunter to pull the car around—too formal for a casual date unless it was a gala. "Where's Todd?"

A darkness I've never seen shutters her gaze. "We're not... together... anymore," she says tightly.

"What—"

"I don't want to talk about it," she snaps—then lifts her phone back toward my privates, voice reverting to her usual, cheerful manner. "Would you look at that head of hair? She's gonna be a looker like her mama."

"I need you to push, Bunny," the doctor orders, her brows pinching with concern.

My shoulders slump. We've been at this for hours. I'm exhausted. I just want to sleep.

Hunter's lips warm my temple. "You got this, Little Rabbit. I'm right here. Squeeze as hard as you need. Give me your pain. I've got you."

His reassurance breaks something inside me. Tears spill as I turn my face to him, taking in his messy curls and his slutty little glasses, knowing that this is the man I'm utterly in love with, and I messed it all up. However, he's still here, supporting me, calling me the affectionate nickname I've missed so much these last months. He's still here, holding my hand, encouraging me.

Because at the end of the day, Hunter's always been more than a lover—he's my best friend.

"I'm so sorry," I whisper, pouring every ounce of sincerity into the words, repeating them over and over.

"Don't worry about that right now." He nods toward the end of the bed. "Focus on saying hello to our little girl."

His words fill me with pride. Filling my lungs with air, I grit my teeth and push. I literally grew a human and am evicting her through my vagina. I am tearing my body so this tiny person can live.

Women are resilient. This is a battle wound I'll be proud to bear for the rest of my life.

"You got this, Buns!" Dove shouts from the phone as Vixey cheers.

Through all the victims I've claimed as the Shadow Siren—every man I've killed and every woman I've saved—*this* is my greatest accomplishment.

"Okay, Bunny, one more big push and you can meet your little girl."

If you'd told me two years ago this is where I'd be today, I would've laughed. I was too hurt, the wounds Nathaniel left were too raw. Even when I came back because I missed Hunter, I never wanted to be a mother.

Why would I want to raise a child in today's world? A world that hurts and breaks and takes from people who don't deserve it.

Yet even with all those big feelings, they wash away when the doctor lifts Faline. A sob tears free—part joy, because Hunter and I created this tiny little thing, and part sorrow, because she'll have to grow up without a mother.

Hunter's soft laugh mixes with his tears and Faline's loud cries. He leaves my side to take the scissors and snip the umbilical cord, severing the last thread tying Faline to me.

Vixey comes to the head of the bed, sweeping sweaty hair from my eyes while she and Dove murmur soothing nonsense. The doctor massages my belly, working on the placenta, while Hunter follows the nurse. It all happens so fast it feels like I barely breathe before Hunter returns and places our bundled baby on my chest.

"Say hello to your momma, Faline," he coos.

"Hi, baby girl," I whisper, cuddling her close.

Most babies are ugly as shit when they're born—discolored, wrinkly, covered in the slimy goo of their mother's insides. Our baby, however, is the most beautiful thing I've ever seen.

"She's perfect," I tell Hunter as he wraps an arm around my shoulders.

"Of course she is, she's got you for a mother." He kisses my temple, his thumb stroking my skin.

Our gazes lock. So many unspoken things crowd the space between us. Slowly, our smiles fade in unison. We know there's so much to discuss. So many questions. So many hard things ahead.

A quiet understanding passes between us.

We can worry about it later.

For now, we're going to enjoy our new little family.

HUNTER'S soft humming pulls me from consciousness.

Bland walls greet me as I open my eyes, sunlight filtering through the partially closed blinds to bathe the room in a dim beige glow. The clock above the hospital door reads four in the afternoon.

An ache in my lower body drags a groan from my throat when I try to stretch—and am painfully reminded I just pushed a whole-ass baby out of my kitty.

"How are you feeling?" Hunter's question is quiet. I turn my head to find him stretched out in a reclining chair, Faline nestled on his chest, sleeping peacefully.

"Like someone shoved their fists up my vagina and stretched it wide enough to fit a watermelon in there." I huff a laugh and use the buttons to raise the bed into a sitting position. "I don't kink shame, but I don't think I'll ever understand fisting."

Hunter doesn't laugh. Instead, he huffs a noncommittal hum, gaze never leaving the baby.

A subdued silence blankets the room, weighted by the last three months of my absence.

"She's so beautiful," he says at last, gently pushing the soft purple baby blanket—a gift from Carla—back from Faline's face. "It's crazy to think we created something so small. So fragile. And now we're responsible for her for the rest of her life."

The rest of her life.

Tears line my lashes, emotion clogging my throat. "Promise you'll tell her about me? All the good things—none of the bad, of course," I croak, forcing a laugh. "And promise me you'll send photos. Lots of photos." Winding the edge of the scratchy blanket around my fingers, I drop my gaze to my lap, unwilling to look at Hunter while I babble about accepting my punishment.

"Bunny," he sighs—tiredly, aggravatingly—but I barrel on.

"I don't want her to ever see me behind bars. So it's okay if you tell her I died in childbirth or somethi—" I cut myself off. "No, don't tell her that. I don't want her growing up with a complex. I'm sure Dove will think of something."

"Bunny."

"Promise you'll let Dove be the main female presence in her life—besides your mother. I don't want Gwendolyn anywhere near her. Or *Vixey*, for that matter." I don't care what the story is there, the blonde is lucky I'm sore and wearing an adult diaper, or I'd go hunt her down for throwing away the friendship she fought so hard for.

"Little Rabbit, *stop*." Hunter sighs again, places Faline in the bassinet, and comes to sit on the edge of the bed.

I can't stop, though. Can't stop crying even when he takes my hand and rubs his thumb across my knuckles. Can't stop the sobs wracking my body as I picture the motherless future our child will have.

His palm is heavy and warm as he cups my cheek, guiding my face up. "As pissed as I am with you right now, Bunny, I would never do that—and I never *planned* on doing that."

Surprise flickers through me. "What?"

He scrubs a hand down his face, and now that I'm seeing him in the light of day I catch the sunken cheeks and dark circles. The chiseled perfection is gaunt, rife with stress and exhaustion.

Guilt slams into me, another apology forming—though at this point, I'm sure they're meaningless. Before I can speak, a soft knock pulls our attention to the door.

"Hey," Vixey greets sheepishly. She's changed into a pair of flare jeans and a white crop top, hair piled messily on her head. An oversized rust-colored cardigan engulfs her tall frame.

The vision of her coming up behind Hunter last night flashes through my mind. My gaze hardens as I look between them. As if it's a shield, she pulls the cardigan tighter, eyes bouncing between us before landing on the bassinet. A sweet smile tugs at her mouth, a heavy breath follows. "Care to hear my explanation for being at Hunter's last night?"

"*I* don't care to be here for this." Hunter stands, gracing her with a warm smile he hasn't given me. The man who praised and guided me through birth with whispered encouragement and affectionate touches has retreated. In his place—the jaded shell I left behind, the one who is very much sick of my shit.

"And you're always welcome in my home, Vix. You don't have to apologize for it. To anyone."

Direct, and landing exactly as intended, his statement stuns me.

Always welcome.

My home.

Vix.

You don't have to apologize.

I have no right to be upset. But fuck if it doesn't hurt hearing him accept her into his home when I know I'm not exactly welcome.

Vixey groans, muttering, "Hunter, don't make things worse. Go get us something hot to drink, will you? And a bowl of Lucky Charms."

Gratitude bubbles up despite my best efforts. I've missed real coffee *and* my favorite cereal. Shockingly, my appetite perks at the mention of my once staple food, instead of souring my stomach.

Hunter looks between us, shakes his head, and disappears without a word.

Despite what I saw last night, there's zero sexual tension between them. It's not like when he kissed Dove to rile Wrenley. Their aura gives off a sibling vibe that I felt long before I even left. It only sharpens my curiosity about why she went to him for comfort—and what happened with Todd.

Vixey wastes no time, throwing her crocheted bag into the chair by my bed and sinks into it, locking her bright golden gaze with mine. "Look, I'm just going to come out and say it. Todd and I got into a fight last night. We were at a party and..." She bites her lip, weighing how much to tell me. "Let's just say he turned out to be a huge dick."

Surging forward, she grabs my hand. "What Dove said is true. She and Wrenley aren't in town—though they're racing back now. It's the only reason I went to Hunter's. Things with Alex are *strained*, to say the least. And I... I didn't want to be alone." Her voice tapers off. She shrugs, the movement causing a lock of honey hair to slip from the loose bun into her face. "I didn't have siblings growing up. Hunter feels like the big brother I never had. That's it. I swear. And I know I've never been your favorite person, so I probably can't lose more points than I already have by saying this, but Hunter has been a fucking mess since you left. He's not eating, not sleeping. Dove, Wrenley, and I have been making sure he doesn't drown himself in a bottle of whiskey. I've kind of assumed a little-sister role. Especially because things are strained between him and Dove... He doesn't know I know why, but it's obvious."

Sympathy floods me. I know what it's like to grow up lonely. The foster kids I grew up with were solitary, keeping to themselves. I never had true siblings. Hunter's often said how much it sucked to grow up without them.

He and Vixey are only children, so it makes sense they'd gravitate to each other. Especially if they were all hanging out a lot over the last few months.

I never want Faline to feel alone. Never want her to feel like she has nowhere to turn if she needs a shoulder to cry on. Friends matter, but family—the ones you choose—is priceless.

And everything she says about Hunter... it's nothing I don't already know, but the guilt threatens to swallow me anyway.

"I'm sorry about Todd. And about my anger. I'm sure you can imagine how it looked..."

"Oh, I'm sure it looked awful. But I promise, it's not like that." She trails off as Hunter reappears, then continues as if he's already heard her story. "I have a past that's... less than savory, let's just say. One day I'll tell you about it. But last night I found out Todd is tied to the singular most awful experience I've ever had. I just didn't want to be alone."

Curiosity piqued, I arch a brow and squeeze her hand before taking the Lucky Charms, bowl, and milk Hunter hands me. "Consider it water under the bridge."

A sigh escapes her lips. "Thank you. Now," she claps, then winces when I glare and point the milk carton toward Faline, "sorry. *Where* have you been the last few months?"

"I think that's a conversation she and I need to have alone, Vix." Hunter passes her a cup with a tea tag sticking out of the lid. "If you don't mind."

She glares at him, clearly wanting the juicy details of

my disappearance. But Hunter's right—he deserves to hear it first, and we have other things to discuss.

Like how he alluded to not planning on putting me in prison before Vixey interrupted us.

"We can talk later." I don't bother looking at either of them as I busy myself making my cereal.

Blowing out a breath, she acquiesces, holding her hands up as Hunter shoots her a look. "I'm going! I'm going. Geesh."

When her footsteps fade, Hunter closes the door, pausing before turning to me. I assume—hope—he'll pick up where he left off, but he pivots into detective mode instead.

"I'm getting the letters now." He checks on Faline, then drops into the chair Vixey vacated. "And I know who's sending them."

Disappointment gives way to a desperate need to know. "Who?"

The anticipation is crippling. How did he figure it out? Have they caught the person? Do we know them?

"Nathaniel's brother was released from prison around the same time you got the first letter." His tone is all business, like he's briefing a colleague, not the woman who just gave birth to his baby. My annoyance about it fades as he continues, "I saw him on one of the security cameras before he disabled it. At first I thought it was Nathaniel, but there was obviously no way that was possible, so I did some digging. Turns out Neil was exceptionally pissed when he found out about

Nathaniel's death. I guess they'd been in contact. Nathaniel told him you were cheating on him."

"Excuse me?" Disgust and astonishment lace my tone. The sugared oats and marshmallows turn to ash in my mouth. I curse my late husband for ruining my most anticipated treat.

"It took a while to get the correspondence, but Nathaniel had Neil believing you and I were having an affair. He told him he suspected we were plotting against him. He had a file on me and knew you were lying about working undercover. How the fuck he found any of that out without tipping off someone in the department, I'll never know." Hunter growls, raking a hand through his wayward curls.

If Nathaniel knew, it explains why he got more aggressive whenever I mentioned Hunter. Explains the push for a family—his desire for me not to work. Why he tried harder to isolate me.

Frowning down at my cereal, my stomach churns. Dejectedly, I set the bowl on the rolling table on the side of the bed, pushing it away before turning my attention back toward Hunter. "Nathaniel once told me Neil would be behind bars for life. How did he get out?"

"He'd been helping him apply for early release. For whatever reason, he was all too happy to leave his brother in prison—until..." His jaw muscle ticks as his gaze flicks to Faline. "Until I came into the picture."

"So, what? You think he intended to get Neil out and send him after you?"

"I don't know. What I *do* know is Neil is after *you*.

While you were gone, he kept leaving letters about finding you before I could." A shudder rolls through him, and he stands, pacing for a moment before retrieving Faline and curling her into his chest.

I watch him—how gently he moves so he doesn't wake her, how he whispers promises that he'll never let anyone hurt her.

It hits me—how hard it must've been not knowing where I was, or where his child was, while someone threatened our lives. If the roles were reversed, I don't know how I would have managed.

"I'm sorry, Hunter. For getting you into this mess." I could say it a million times and it would never be enough. All I can do is keep repeating it like a broken record and hope he hears it isn't meaningless.

He shakes his head and returns to my side. "You know, Bunny—for all the books you read, you're sure as shit the worst at communicating, aren't you?"

As if sensing the anger creeping into his tone, Faline stirs. Wordlessly, he hands her to me to feed her before taking a seat. Every passing second, his frame grows more tense, knees bouncing, fists clenching, jaw ticking.

"I never claimed to be perfect, Hunter. I have issues —that's not a secret. And after everything that happened —" I stop as he stands abruptly.

"I admit that was my fault. I never should've made you think... never thought you'd believe I would do that to you." His voice is quiet, but the meaning behind them speaks volumes.

"Hunter..."

"You two really are the worst, you know that?" He huffs a laugh and goes to the window.

Confusion swirls as I get Faline to latch, but before I can look up, he laughs again.

"God, this is so fucking stupid. I can't even rage at you the way I want—not with you holding her." He drops to his haunches, fingers threading into his hair. "How could you do it? I guess *that* is what I don't understand."

Sighing, I shake my head. "There's not a lot to understand. You know the motive. It's obvious *why* I created the Shadow Siren."

"That isn't what I meant. I meant, how could you keep doing it while you were carrying *her*?" He motions to the baby suckling my breast.

It feels like all the air gets sucked from the room as I mull over his reaction and his words. My heart skips a beat, stumbling to keep a normal pace as it picks up.

Hunter laughs incredulously as he stands. From the sound of it, he's not angry that I *am* the Shadow Siren— he's angry I kept at it while pregnant.

"Come on, Bunny. Did you really never suspect I knew?" He comes closer, a crazed look in his eyes. "Do you really think I'm *that* bad at my job?"

"Hunter... I... what?"

Suddenly, he lunges, causing me to startle. Pressing further into the bed, I try to keep my breathing even as he clasps my face between his hands, careful not to jostle our daughter. A whimper escapes me, but it only seems to spur him on.

"Oh, Little Rabbit. How could you not know? I've been obsessed with you for so long. How could you not figure it out? Didn't you ever wonder how I knew exactly where you were? Exactly where your dates were located?" His voice drops, strangely amused and skirting deranged. "Didn't you ever wonder how I knew you never took them home? How I knew you came every night with *my* name on your lips? Bunny, I knew when I met you, I wanted you. Nathaniel was a momentary obstacle, but then you took care of him, and you were mine for the taking." His thumbs smooth over my cheekbones, wiping away the tears that I'm trying desperately—and failing miserably—to hold back.

"Hunter..." I'm not afraid of him, but I fear he might be close to having some sort of psychotic break. I've never seen him like this, and if what Vixey said is true— and judging by his appearance, I wouldn't doubt it—he's suffering from a major lack of sleep.

"Then you left me. And I won't lie—as angry as I was, I knew you'd come back eventually. So I set a trap. I wasn't going to let you slip away again. After all, I dreamed you up, remember? You were always meant to be mine. I wanted to know the moment you returned, so I put up cameras in your house."

Shock spears through me, stealing my breath and plunging into my gut. "Wh—*what*?"

Whatever jagged joy he's getting from confessing bleeds out of his face. He releases me like my skin burns and backs up. His gaze drops to Faline and softens, chasing away the crazy.

After a beat, he goes on, composed again. "That's right, Bunny. I broke a handful of laws to have front-row access to your life. I almost felt bad about it when you returned. But then you fought so hard against me... against the idea of us... that I decided it was worth it." He huffs a dry laugh. "Imagine my surprise when I found out about your extracurriculars."

Hunter knew. He's *always* known I was the Shadow Siren.

Nausea worms its way through me, threatening to expel the few bites of Lucky Charms I managed.

"The first time you brought a man home, I was furious enough to burst in and kill him myself," Hunter muses, a faraway look glazing his eyes. "But then you took him to the basement and came back alone. I was confused—I hadn't set anything up down there—so I snuck in and added more surveillance."

Images flood me—Yasha and Maru always greeting him like they knew him, even the "first" time. "The dogs—"

"Oh, yes. The boys and I were well acquainted long before you introduced us." He smirks.

"All this time, *you knew*?" Astonishment—and maybe a sick sort of awe—edges out the panic swelling in my chest.

"I knew. I helped keep it secret. I fought to keep your case, even when my boss was pissed I wasn't producing results." He steps closer, glare hardening. "I've kept you and Dove from getting caught all this time, Bunny. And while I should've been clear about my intentions on New

Year's—and you leaving again is largely my fault—you should *never* have gone after a target while you were pregnant."

"I know! And I'm sorry! I can't take it back, Hunter." I shove everything else he said into a mental box to unpack later. Part of me is convinced this is a fever dream, and that the last ten minutes have been a figment of my imagination. A product of the drugs they gave me during labor, and I'm still asleep.

"I can't take it back either. Not the way things happened. Not the part of me that wants to hate you now. And that part hates *me* for allowing it to happen again. But at the end of the day," he nods at Faline, "you're the mother of my child. And I'll be damned if I ever give you the chance to take her from me again."

Tears prick my eyes, and I try my damnedest to hold them back. "So where do we go from here, Hunter? I don't know how to get back to where we were. I don't know how things can ever be the same."

"No, Little Rabbit." He shakes his head, taking Faline and turning toward the bassinet—though it feels more like he's turning his back on *me*. "Things will never be the same."

SOME SLEEP-DEPRIVED PART of me wonders if Hunter sending me to prison would be better than the self-induced hell I've put myself in.

For as long as I've known him, Hunter has been in love with me. Sure, we've had our spats, thrown temper tantrums and played our games. But in the end we always end up back in each other's arms—whether for an hour or an evening.

I don't know how to exist in this new world where Hunter treats me like I'm just another woman in his life. One he's kind to, but not overly so. One he tolerates because I'm the mother of his child, but not one he wants around more than necessary.

He's passive-aggressive and infuriatingly overbearing. It was like pulling teeth to get him to agree to let me take Faline to *my* home instead of his once we left the hospital. With everything Hunter admitted to, and the fact that I can't set foot in his house without picturing Vixey behind him—even though I *know* nothing happened—it's the last place I want to be.

Not to mention he almost didn't let me have Yasha and Maru back. I know I deserve the award for Most Horrible Dog Mom, but at that point I nearly threw fists.

Hunter is punishing me, and I don't blame him. With hormones riding shotgun through my veins, I oscillate between wanting to punch him, wanting him to speak to me like a normal person, and wanting to fuck his brains out—though my kitty protests that last one loudly.

Research says most women want nothing to do with sex after delivery, but my brain is hardwired to conflate Hunter and sex, so I'm short-circuiting because of how he's acting.

Maru, the loyal boy he is, sticks close to my side as we head down the hall toward the soft notes of a saxophone drifting from the open nursery door. Yasha, happy I'm home but still pissed at me, lifts his head from his place at Hunter's feet as I enter.

Hunter has a sleeping Faline on his chest, swaying gently in the rocking chair Carla brought—after I insisted on coming home, he moved most of the setup he had at his place to mine. A globe on the dresser emits a soft glow, casting stars that crawl along the walls and ceiling as it turns.

"Hey, are you—"

"Shh." He nods to his phone, where the music is playing. "This is the best part."

A flicker of annoyance sparks in me, then dies. I edge

further into the room and sit in the recliner in the corner, adjusting a few times until I find a comfortable spot and listen.

I've never been a huge jazz fan, but it's grown on me since Hunter and I got serious—the soft stuff, anyway, like whatever he's playing now. The rhythmic notes carry me back to a happier time only a handful of months ago, when things were simpler, even with my psycho brother-in-law sending me threatening notes.

It's another reason Hunter doesn't want Faline and me staying here. Which I can't blame him for, but he's been present nearly every moment. And when he's not, Dove usually is—even though Hunter's said that never comforts him.

When the song ends, Hunter pauses the playlist. Neither of us speaks for a long while until I can no longer stand the silence. There were three months of it—my fault, I know—so the least I can do is *try*. Hunter tried for years. Now it's my turn.

"You know, I never asked you where your love of jazz comes from." It's an olive branch—delicate and spindly, but a peace offering nonetheless. A chance to regain some normalcy. A moment for him to look at me with something other than anger and disappointment.

Hunter smiles fondly without breaking his sway or loosening his hold on our daughter. "When I was a kid, my mom and dad took me to SeaWorld. We saw the whale show, and they played *Forever in Love*—the song that just played—while the trainer danced with an orca. I remember being so moved by the music—feeling warm and... *right*. So when we got home, I begged for a Kenny G album. It all went downhill from there." His gaze drops to Faline then meets mine, full of a sorrow I helped make. "I thought it was beautiful because I was too young to understand animals don't belong in cages. They should roam free, untamed, like they were meant to be."

It isn't lost on me that the story carries a double meaning. It reads like the saddest goodbye I can imagine, even though we're bound together forever through our child.

I can't fathom life without the man across from me, and I don't understand how we got here—how we keep finding ourselves at this impasse.

Tears sting and I hastily wipe them away. "You know I never meant to hurt you, Hunter."

He doesn't answer, but his eyes turn glassy and my heart splinters as he holds my gaze. "I once said you were my masterpiece and that I'd never break you. But you've been breaking me, Bunny. Over and over. I told you I wouldn't survive if you left again, and you did it anyway. You're not selfish—you need to protect your heart, I get it. Maybe if I'd protected mine better, you wouldn't have gotten so far under my skin that I don't know how to be me without you anymore."

A sob tears from me. I clamp my hand over my mouth to muffle it so I don't wake the baby. Hunter's chest shudders like he's holding back his own. Gracefully, he stands and settles Faline into her bed. Making sure one of the baby monitors is on, he picks up the other one and motions for me to follow.

In the hall he keeps talking as I trail him downstairs. "It's my fault. Everything. From letting you consume me so thoroughly to being so angry that I let you think I'd actually turn you in. I had a lot of time to reflect on our relationship, Little Rabbit, and I realized we do nothing but make the stupidest mistakes and hurt each other."

I know where this is going and brace for the blow. Our crash and burn was always inevitable. Now that it's here, I scramble for any way to extinguish the flames.

"I've always chosen you. Always. But you've never really chosen me, and I think I finally understand you likely never will."

"Hunter." I reach for him, but he steps away, dabbing at his own cheeks. "No. Bunny, I can't do this anymore. Pushing you away is the only self-defense I have. You'll always be in my life because of our amazing little girl upstairs, but I can't do it anymore."

Hearing him say it out loud shatters a piece of me I never thought could break—the piece he built up with promises that we were endgame and nothing could make him stay away.

He turns for the door, muttering that he can't be here.

What's left of my broken heart hammers against my ribs, blood rushing in my ears like an angry ocean crashing against the shore. Racing after him, I pull at his arm, not caring how desperate I sound. Fair or not, all I want is for him not to leave me the way I left him.

"Please, don't go, Hunter!"

Gently, he shakes me off, ignoring my pleas. Panic

claws my insides. Somewhere in my head I wonder if this is how he felt when I left.

Karma is a fucking bitch, Bunny.

"Hunter!"

"Just stop!" he roars, turning to face me, eyes wild as if surprised by his own outburst.

He still hasn't really slept. I don't know how he's holding it together. The man standing over me is unrecognizable.

And it's all my fault.

If there's ever a time to do what's best for him, it's now. Let him go.

This time, when he turns, I don't stop him. I watch him leave, warm, silent tears tracking down my face as I try to hold in my sobs. Yasha and Maru whine, following him to the door, probably thinking they're going with him.

None of it matters. Hunter throws the door open and disappears into the night, taking half of my fractured soul with him.

While the other half sleeps upstairs, blissfully unaware of how badly her mother fucked her life up.

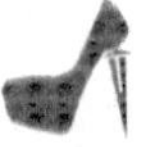

SOFT DOG WHINES WAKE ME.

My phone says I wasn't out more than twenty minutes after crying myself to sleep on the couch when Hunter left.

Checking the monitor, I relax—Faline is still sleeping —before a prickling awareness makes my skin break out in goosebumps.

Yasha and Maru stand at the living room threshold, fixated on the front door.

Did Hunter come back?

My gut says no.

But someone *is* here.

Maru's ears lay flat, his whole body trembles as he growls at whoever's entered my home. He wouldn't act that way with Dove. Yasha goes full attack mode—barking, feigning advances with his sharp teeth bared. Maru joins in, snarling and trying to look vicious.

Footsteps shuffle across the hardwood causing my heart to jump into my throat. It sounds like someone dragging their feet down the hall. Alarm spikes when I realize I forgot to lock the door in the chaos of Hunter leaving.

A sharp clicking of a tongue emulating the ticking of a clock accompanies the steps, making the hairs on my arms rise. Hastily, I put myself between the intruder and the stairs and shout, "Get the fuck out of my house!"

Deep chuckles roll off the walls as a tall, dark figure emerges from the shadows. It takes a beat for my eyes to adjust, the moon the only thing illuminating the room. A voice rings out, a familiar face coming into view.

"Technically, *Little Rabbit*, this should be *my* house."

Neil.

He has the same deep Texan drawl Nathaniel had. The same dark blond hair and ordinary brown eyes. If I didn't know better, I'd swear I was staring at the ghost of my late husband.

Neil laughs—a loud, guffawing sound that drowns the dogs and makes my body jolt. Upstairs Faline cries. I watch, horrified, as his eyes travel up the staircase behind me.

"You know, my brother always wanted a baby girl." He slides his hands into his pockets. He's dressed head-to-toe in black business attire, looking like a man going to an office rather than breaking into a house. "He was so sure you'd give him his happily ever after. Shame you became his demise instead."

"Your brother wasn't a good man, Neil. I don't know what he told you—"

"He told me enough!" Neil snarls. "Did he tell you why I went to jail? Did he tell you it was to protect him? Did he tell you there's nothing I wouldn't do for my little brother? Including getting revenge?"

Everything stills—the dogs, Faline, my heart. Two seconds stretch like an eternity. I see the night I killed Nathaniel flash through my head.

Then Neil lunges.

Fight-or-flight kicks in. The urge to protect my baby sends adrenaline roaring through me, smothering my grief and the lingering threads of physical pain left from giving birth.

I sprint up the stairs and trip, barely catching myself on the edge of a step as Neil grabs my ankle and yanks me down. I kick and squirm while both Yasha and Maru bite at his legs.

One must get a good hold because he howls. I hear a sickening squeal as he flings them away. Taking the opportunity while he's distracted, I try to climb but don't make it two steps before he drags me back.

Neil's weight pins me across the stairs. "I see why he liked you. We always loved women who put up a good fight."

Disgust coils through me as I fight to break free. In the back of my mind, I think about what will happen if Neil succeeds at whatever it is he's trying to do. Kill me? Rape me? Beat me?

What will happen to my daughter once he finishes what he's come to do?

"You know, I told him never to get married." He shoves his leg between mine and hauls me up by my wrists, tossing me over his shoulder. "But he promised you were worth it. Said you had a golden pussy and once I was out I'd get to see for myself. We always did share everything."

"Let me go!" I batter his back, panic choking me.

Faline's crying spikes. Motherly instincts drive my anxiety, the need to get to my baby and comfort her outweighing the pain of my wounds. Adrenaline eats at every ache, blanketing my discomfort like a cape.

Neil drops me on the sofa and I fight like a feral cat, becoming a flurry of limbs and nails and teeth. Hissing and biting and fighting against his superior strength.

All the while, he laughs. "Do you know how fun it's been to watch you?"

He wedges his leg between mine again, hips pressing

down until I feel the hard length of his cock against my thigh. He pins my shoulders and my teeth find the skin above his wrist. I clamp down until I taste blood.

A cry of pain accompanied by spittle flies from his lips before he yanks his arm away. I spit out a chunk of flesh when it comes free.

Bony knuckles smash my cheek over my scar. Another blow to my jaw knocks my head sideways. White bursts in my vision, a dizzying haze fogging up my brain until the fight bleeds from me.

"I'm going to have so much fun tearing you apart until you are *begging* to die." Neil's words are filled with grit and giddiness as he speaks against my ear. "Then I'll paint your detective's world crimson with the blood of your illegitimate spawn."

The weight on my upper body lifts, settling on my thighs as his palms skim down my chest, roughly groping my breasts. I can feel them leaking, the sweet, milky odor rising to my nostrils as Neil laughs in crazed delight. Nausea causes my head to spin, the sound of my top ripping fills the air, before a warm wetness slicks my nipples.

Tears sting my lashes. I lie there gathering whatever strength is left, thinking about how whatever happens to Faline will be my fault, just like everything else that's happened is a product of all my bad choices.

"So fucking sweet." Neil smacks his lips against my chest. "I think I'll—"

Suddenly his weight jerks—and vanishes. I wait, muscles coiled, listening for him to return. The buzzing in my ears clears and I hear ragged breathing—then a voice that makes the room tilt.

"Fucking die is what you'll do, you fucking bastard."

It takes a moment to focus on the form standing above me. If fury could manifest physically, I'm certain it would have dark hair and eyes of the purest amber, the fires of hell glowing in their depths as they hone in on Neil.

Hunter.

RAGE like I've never known flows through me, giving me the strength of a thousand men—all of them insisting on the most gruesome death for the bastard who's been harassing us for months.

"Are you okay, Bunny?" I try to keep my tone level, but it wavers with my ire. My attention stays locked on Neil, stunned on the floor from the blow to the side of his head.

Fuck no, she's not okay. You just walked in on her being sexually assaulted by this piece of shit.

A fresh, fevered wave of wrath brushes my insides. Rough bristles paint my thoughts with a madness I can't quell—one I'm ready to unleash on the monster before me.

"How fucking dare you," I seethe, driving my butt of my pistol into his face before holstering it. Chest heaving, I collect Neil by the ankles and drag him toward the basement stairs. "You made a mistake thinking you could have my girl."

"He threatened to kill Faline." Bunny's voice shakes, and even though I try not to look, I do. She clutches what's left of her top to her chest, dried tears smearing her cheeks, raven flyaways stuck to her face.

Seeing her exposed and violated wakes a beast I've only ever shaken hands with but never let out of its cage. One that manifested when I realized what her husband was doing to her.

Thank fuck I turned around after only a few blocks. The farther I got from Bunny, the more the barbed wire around my heart twisted, leaving bloody chunks of me on the sidewalk.

It doesn't matter that she hurt me. I'd suffer more without her.

The thought that it could've become a reality tonight if I hadn't turned back makes me sick.

"Go upstairs, Bunny. I'll take care of him."

Without another word, I head to the basement. A grunt rips out of Neil every time his head knocks against a stair as I descend into what's about to become his personal hell. By the time we reach the room beyond the main basement, blood slicks the back of his head.

When Bunny was gone, I scoured her basement—learned every nook and cranny. Pieced together what she did to the men she brought down here. My old cameras never went beyond the main room. When I learned she was the Shadow Siren, I could've pushed further—but something about that chamber felt sacred to her.

Tonight marks my commencement into her world.

Tonight, the space beyond the door becomes my altar. Tonight, I become a murderer.

Neil barely struggles, too dazed to fight, as I secure him to a chair draped in chains. I set my gun on a table littered with tools like something you'd see on a thriller flick.

Grabbing a pair of bolt cutters, I sink to my haunches in front of him, taking my time straightening each of his fingers as they dangle over the arm of the chair.

"You know, I never imagined I'd find joy in something so fucking depraved. But I guess we have that in common, don't we?"

The image of him on top of Bunny floods in—his mouth on her body, her helpless beneath him, frozen as if she'd accepted her fate. My little rabbit is anything but helpless. Seeing her reduced to a near catatonic state boiled my blood.

"What the fuck are you doing?" Neil coughs, spitting blood at my feet as he fully comes to.

I don't give him a reprieve, snipping off the tips of his fingers to the first knuckle. His screams tear the air as he thrashes against the chains and I take them one by one.

"This is to teach you not to touch what isn't yours."

Surprisingly, he stays conscious—barely—by the time I finish.

"Fuck you!" he spits as the blood drips to the floor. He won't bleed out, which is precisely the point.

Neil deserves as much pain as I can possibly inflict.

"No, fuck you, you piece of shit!" Bunny's voice

rings out behind me, alive with anger, malice, and a deep-seated need for revenge.

Turning, I see she's replaced her ruined shirt, baby monitor clutched in her hand like a lifeline. I rise and go to her. Without looking away from Neil, she hands me the screen to show that Faline is no longer crying. The sound of Kenny G hums through Bunny's phone by the bassinet. If it were a better time, I'd kiss her for that.

"I almost had you, you fucking bitch. You fucking whore!" Neil screams.

Bunny surges past me. I didn't see it at first, but she's holding one of her stilettos—the heel pointed outward, a slim blade protruding from it. Forcefully, she slashes across his face, carving a long gash through his cheek. As his brother marked her, she marks him.

"You want to be like Nathaniel, Neil? I smashed his brain in with a rump roast. Maybe you should suffer the same fate." She drops the shoe and flexes her hands, fingers curling into claws. It's how I found her that night —with them curled into the meat like rigor had set in and caused them to stick that way.

A sick sense of pride rolls through me. I know how wrong this is, but the monster in me doesn't care—he's relishing finally getting to see this side of her, knowing she's harbored it in secret for so long.

"There's a nice set of turkey legs in the freezer," I supply darkly, chuckling when disgust twists his face. "I can think of a few places to shove those to make it hurt."

"No need to ruin good meat—there's an old rack of ribs I don't mind sacrificing. I could smash his face in with those. After all, Neil, you said you and your brother liked to share. Seems fitting you die the same way."

Empathy takes over my reasoning for a split second. "I know the piggies are already dead, but don't desecrate their memory that way. Let them keep their honorable death."

Bunny goes to the table and grabs the soldering iron, turning it on. "Maybe I'll take a page from the Baby Doll Killer's book."

"That's my girl."

Our eyes meet. Understanding passes between us.

That's right, Little Rabbit. You're mine. I'm yours. We're okay.

Neil jerks against the chains, his ruined fingers bleeding again. "You're fucking crazy!"

"Says the psycho who drank my baby's milk, then said he'd kill her." Bunny's words are ragged with the weight of her exhaustion and a feral need to match the energy he brought into our home.

"What can I do, Little Rabbit?" This is her revenge. Her *choose-your-ending* to this vein of her past. But she needs to know I'm here. She needs to know I support her in any way she needs me.

"Get the water ready," she instructs before leaning over him, lowering the iron toward his dick. "I'm going to have so much fun tearing you apart until you are *begging* to die."

His eyes widen, his screams fill the basement as she digs the iron into his crotch. The stench of burnt cloth and flesh permeates the air. Fire catches on his lap, nearly singeing the ends of Bunny's long locks. He passes out from what I assume is excruciating pain.

Quickly, I toss the water over his lap before gathering Bunny's hair out of her way, holding it back as she slaps Neil's cheek to rouse him. "No, no, no, my dear brother-in-law. Wake the fuck up. I'm not finished with you yet."

"Is it weird this is making me hard?" It's an ill-timed joke, especially given what I walked in on, but before shame can chart a course through me, Bunny's light laughter extinguishes it.

"Is it weird I like that it's making you hard?" She flashes a devilish grin over her shoulder and lowers the iron as soon as Neil groans awake.

She makes quick work of what's left of his dick, and we work in tandem to keep him conscious. His skin goes ashen and slick as she holds the iron to his face.

"Did you know I'm actually a serial killer, Neil?" Bunny muses, tapping the iron against his nose. Flesh sizzles. The grotesque smell of cooked meat wafting into my sinuses.

He wheezes through clenched teeth, refusing to answer. There's still an edge in his gaze—dark and deadly, like he thinks he's getting out of this predicament alive and planning how to make us pay.

I shift all Bunny's hair into one hand—no easy feat with the amount she has—and shove my fingers between his lips, hauling his tongue forward before he can bite me.

"My girl asked you a question. It's rude not to answer."

Neil whips his head side to side, snarling, but Bunny is precise. She drops the iron onto his tongue and holds until it's fully cleaved from his mouth.

High-pitched shrieks split the room. I glance at the baby monitor. Faline sleeps on, blissfully unaware, while her uncle sings his death lullaby below her.

Bunny burns his lips into a bubbling mass, then drives the iron through his eye.

That one nearly makes me puke when it bursts across what's left of his face.

Her wrath fuels her, even though Neil has long since passed out again, but I can tell the Shadow Siren starts to recede when her limbs begin to shake as the adrenaline wears off.

"Bunny, it's okay. You don't need to keep going," I tell her gently.

Surprisingly, she steps back. Dropping the iron, she spins out of my hold. I let her go, grab my pistol, and end it.

A second later, Neil Jones is dead.

"That's more than you deserve, you bastard."

Soft whimpers draw my attention to Bunny. She's huddled against the wall, breathing ragged as she watches. Now I take her in—*really* take in the damage he did before I got here. A bruise is blooming over her scar, smaller ones peppering her skin, while a trickle of blood dries at the corner of her mouth.

If I'd gone to her first, I might've given him time to recover and get away. Even though every instinct screamed to hold her, I had to fight the urge.

My little rabbit is strong and resilient, but she looks ready to break.

"Bunny—" She launches into my arms with a sob.

Her frame is so much smaller than I remember. I hug her tight and bury my face in her hair, inhaling her scent, savoring the feel of her in my arms.

I missed this. *Missed* her. All the anger and resentment from her absence washes away with the realization I could've lost her tonight.

"You're okay. I've got you, baby. Shh. I've got you," I murmur.

"I'll never leave you again. I promise. I'm so sorry." The words hitch with shuddered breaths and hiccups from crying. I do my best to convey with my touch and whispered reassurances that everything is okay now we're together again.

As if sensing we're done mutilating the monster, Faline's cries rise through the monitor, pitching higher the longer she wails.

We both turn toward the door at the same time, pausing to share a watery laugh before ascending the stairs. With every step, the future I thought I'd lost draws closer. Now that the threat is eliminated, and my girls are back home, I'm not letting anything else get in our way of happiness.

I once wrote Bunny into my future. Now I'm ready to write our happily ever after.

"WHAT WILL HAPPEN to the Baby Doll Killer and the Shadow Siren?"

Bunny's question startles me. Turning, I see her standing a few feet behind me, oversized sweats hanging from her frame as she pulls her massive mane of hair into a bun on top of her head.

"What do you mean, Little Rabbit? Good morning, by the way. How are you feeling?" I finish rinsing the mug in my hand before facing her.

Waking her earlier to feed Faline almost sent me into a tailspin when she broke down from sheer exhaustion. I can't even imagine how she's feeling. It's been a little over two hours since she fell back asleep. I've checked on her periodically. Every time I open the door, I'm afraid I'll find her gone again—something I know I'll have to work through.

"Like I got hit by a Mack truck. Is there any more coffee?"

She takes a seat at the table as I get her some,

preparing it how she likes—two sugars and a dollop of cream—and answer her earlier question. "As far as the vigilantes go, I have no intention of doing anything about Dove. But stop sending in videos—command isn't going to look the other way forever."

"I keep telling her that..." Bunny sips, eyes closing as she inhales the steam of roasted French-vanilla. "I think I'm going to retire—at least for now."

"I can't tell you what to do, Bunny. It's just not about—"

"Just me anymore, I know."

Reaching over, she lays her hand over mine. After everything, that simple touch still kicks my heart off-beat. I was so angry when she left, now I can't imagine staying mad for more than a few minutes.

"I'm just not sure I can give it up for good."

"I'm not asking you to. From now on, though, can it at least be a discussion?"

She smiles at my casual claim on our future. "I promise that when I'm ready to pick it back up, it'll be a discussion."

Silence settles between us, but those mossy eyes I've missed so much keep darting from me to her cup, like she wants to ask something and can't find the way in. It makes her look small and fragile—even though she's anything but—and it spikes the feral need in me to protect her from everything.

"Out with it, Little Rabbit."

"Were you with anyone... you know, while I was

gone?" She nibbles her lower lip, gaze dropping to the table.

"Of course I wasn't." I keep my tone soft as I reach for her. "Come here."

There's no hesitation— she abandons her chair for my lap, wraps her arms around my neck, and sits sideways. It takes a few moments to adjust and find a comfortable spot, and I silently curse Neil for marring her skin with bruises that keep reminding me of last night.

If I hadn't left, she wouldn't have been attacked. I would've been here to protect her. To protect the dogs, though, they bounced back fine—Wrenley and Dove have them out for a walk with Fang, and Wrenley keeps sending photos of the three of them chasing squirrels in the park.

"I know I don't have a right to ask, I just—"

"Hush." Cupping her cheeks, I press a chaste kiss to her lips, savoring her familiar taste. "You have every right to ask—though it hurts that you feel you need to."

Silver rims her lashes as she presses her forehead to mine. "I wouldn't blame you if you did. I've been so terrible to you. You've been waiting for me for so long, and I've been utterly awful."

"I waited because you're worth waiting for, Bunny. I had little to no experience dating or loving anyone when we met, but I knew what we had—what we *have*—is once in a lifetime. It was instant for me, Little Rabbit. The second you climbed on that stage, you stole my heart, and you've had it ever since. Every piece of me belongs to you. You know that."

"I do. I'm just... afraid." Her small frame shakes as the tears multiply. "Afraid I'm too late. That I hurt you too much. How do we come back from everything I've done?"

"Twenty-four hours ago, I admit, I didn't know how to get past the anger. You've been the center of my world for a long time. Now that world includes our beautiful little girl and, baby, I want better for her than this. I don't want her growing up watching her parents play *will-they/won't-they*. That means you have to *let* me love you. I want Faline to grow up believing in love—not think it only hurts. One day I want her to lock eyes with a man... or a woman... or whoever—and know *instantly* they're her person. I want her to know *that* kind of love exists and it's worth fighting for. Even when the other person hasn't figured it out yet. Even when they fight against it. You don't give up when it's hard. You look your partner's demons in the eye and say, 'I *dare* you,' because there's no way in hell you'll let anything hurt them."

"And what happens when your partner is the one who keeps hurting you? You've always given me so much, Hunter. So much. And I've given you nothing—"

"You're wrong." I cut her off. "You've given me more than you know, Little Rabbit. After all, I spent more time with you than you realize."

Grinning, I capture her mouth. This time nothing is chaste about the kiss. She opens for me, tongue sliding to meet mine, hands in my hair. I'm halfway to trying to crawl down her throat when she yanks back, laughing at the pathetic whine that escapes me.

"You sound like a stalker. Don't teach our daughter it's okay to stalk people. She needs to know bugging people's homes isn't normal and that no means no."

Nudging her nose with mine, I nip her bottom lip, careful with the tender skin. "You've never told me no, Bunny. Not once. If you ever uttered the word to me, I would've left you alone. You may be too damn stubborn for your own good, but you know what's best for you, don't you?"

She nods, then fuses our mouths again. I shift her, wrapping her legs around my waist. Her tongue conquers mine as she tries to take control.

"I love you, Hunter. I always have," she murmurs against my lips.

I've always known it, but hearing her finally say the words after so long makes me pause to take it in. Her hair's mussed from the fallen bun, eyes puffy from crying, lips swollen from my attention. She's the most beautiful thing I've ever seen.

And she loves me.

She loves *me*.

Hunter Jr. decides to announce himself, poking Bunny's butt to say hello. She hisses softly, arching her back, then drops her forehead to my shoulder.

"You know we can't have sex yet, right?" she groans.

"We may not be able to have sex, Little Rabbit, but I can sure as fuck make you come. Besides, you're due three months' worth of punishments." I lift her chin, thumb stroking her lower lip. "I've been dreaming about punishing this mouth since you left."

Color blooms over her cheeks and nose, highlighting her freckles, creating one of my favorite sights. A devilish smirk curves her lips as she unwinds from my lap and sinks to her knees.

"Normally it's the guy who has to grovel in the books, but I think it's high time I did some groveling of my own." Reaching for my zipper, she keeps her gaze locked with mine as she undoes my pants and pulls my cock out.

"You never have to get on your knees for me, Little Rabbit. I'm not the kind of man who expects favors while you're out of commission."

But fuck if the silken wetness of her tongue isn't in-fucking-credible as she licks up my shaft, swirling around my head, sucking the tip into her mouth like a popsicle.

"Hunter, you've proven yourself for years. It's my turn to prove myself to you."

I'm about to tell her she has nothing to prove when she takes me so deep I almost blow.

"Oh, fuck, baby, I missed that mouth."

She hums appreciatively as she licks and sucks, bobbing slow, never breaking eye contact. Flexing her throat around me, she grabs my hands and pulls them to her head as the sound of her choking on me fills the kitchen. Sloppy wet kisses, my rough breathing, helpless moans—it's a carnal symphony that grows louder with every glide, as she works me into delirium.

"Bunny, I'm not going to last."

She hums again. Three months without her touch, without her mouth, and I'm about to nut faster than the first time I opened a *Playboy*.

"Baby, I'm going to come." I slide my fingers from her hair, stroke her cheeks, and lift her until only my tip rests on her tongue. My cock twitches, releasing months of pent-up frustration.

She opens wide and lets me watch as I coat her tongue in thick bursts.

"Fuck, you are so fucking beauti—"

Suddenly, the door opens. Dogs yip. Dove and Wrenley yap. We both startle.

I grab for my pants at the same time Bunny lunges to stand—her mouth clamping down just as I move and drive myself forward again.

We freeze.

A high-pitched scream knifes the air, aaaand I'm pretty sure it's mine.

Holy fucking shit... the pain. It hurts. This is definitely how I die: death by my little rabbit chomping my dick off.

"Oh my god." Bunny releases me and falls back on her butt, eyes wide with horror.

"What was that god-awful sound?" Dove's saccharine lilt floats into the kitchen.

Covering my bits so the tiny blonde doesn't see more than she should, I slide off the chair and curl into the fetal position while Bunny scrambles to the freezer for ice.

"She bit me!"

"I guess the Bunny really does like her carrots!" Wrenley's boisterous laughter fills the living room.

Slowly, I swivel my head and glare, repositioning the ice pack in my lap. "Fuck. You."

"At least it's still in one piece, buddy. Imagine if you'd lost any. Can't afford to get much smaller. Bunny would need a toy." He slaps his thighs like he's headlining a comedy tour.

"Oh, fuck off. You know that isn't true. I'm bigger than you are." Though I have no insecurities about my size, heat still hits my cheeks as my gaze flicks to Bunny.

She's glaring at Wrenley, and if that doesn't comfort me, the fact that her breath smells like my cum does.

Wrenley stops laughing. "Hey, that's just rude."

"I happen to think Wrenley is perfectly sized," Dove chimes in.

"Can we stop talking about this!" Bunny screeches. She snuggles into my side, trying to be comforting while being careful not to disturb Faline sleeping in her arms.

Babies are kind of boring at this age. Not gonna lie.

"I'm so sorry," she apologizes for the millionth time.

"You're fine, Little Rabbit. It's just a little bruised, that's all." Wrapping my arm around her shoulders, I kiss her temple.

"Hopefully you're not too injured to help haul that piece of shit out of the basement." Wrenley tucks Dove close, mirroring us. He looks away when Faline fusses and Bunny pulls her top down to feed her, though Dove watches with open fascination.

Wrenley's eyes flick back, then away quickly when a growl rumbles in my throat. "Breastfeeding is natural, Wrenley. It's not an invitation to stare—especially not in her own home."

"Honestly, it doesn't bother me. I didn't even think to grab the cover. I'm sorry, Dove," Bunny groans. "They're kind of just... out all the time now."

"It's fine," Dove says, gaze glued to Bunny's chest. "You're hot, and your boobs are *massive* right now. Poor Wrenley can't help himself around her, Hunter. Neither can I, for that matter. Consider his sneak peek payback for that kiss you planted on me." She finally drags her eyes away and pats his thigh. "As for the body, I can help you, Songbird."

"You don't have to worry about it. We already took care of it," Bunny tells them. "Also, thanks for the compliment. I think."

They trade a skeptical look. "What do you mean? What did you do with the body?" Wrenley asks.

A laugh rumbles in my chest, joining Bunny's sultry chuckles. My little rabbit and I share our own knowing look before answering them in unison. "Pressure cookers."

"You have a baby! In a bar!" Dove flashes Hunter and me a wide, saccharine smile, nodding and waggling her brows. Her tone has a Southern twang—albeit a poor one—as she grabs a pool cue, stomping her platform-clad heel like an exclamation point.

Hunter and I share a confused look. She knew we were coming. We made plans to meet for lunch a few days ago.

Her joy falls flat. She tosses the stick back onto the pool table and lets her arms flop. "*Sweet Home Alabama*?"

Wrenley, on the other side of Hunter, leans over, hiding his mouth from her as he whispers, "We're coming off a Reese Witherspoon marathon."

"Oooh." Hunter turns to me, making grabby hands for the baby. "How are my girls today?"

"Well, our little princess was less than thrilled about her shots, but she's good." Lifting Faline out of the Baby-Björn, I hand her over, inwardly melting as Hunter cradles her to his chest and coos in an unintelligible language.

He looks around, brows notching together. "Where's the car seat?"

"With Hank. I told him to come in for lunch, but he has a doctor's appointment, so he'll be back when he's finished."

Yes, Hank is still alive.

The old cabbie took the money I gave him and immediately went to a better doctor for a better treatment, which couldn't have made me happier. Though it's still too early to tell if he'll beat it, he's looking and feeling better. Now he's *Uncle* Hank. He and Hunter took an immediate liking to each other, and Carla and David welcomed him into our little family with open arms.

Our family.

Finally, after being on my own for so long, I feel like I have an actual home. Somewhere I belong. I never had that before, even when I was married to Nathaniel.

It's truly the best feeling in the world.

"Vixey!" Dove shouts through the bar even though it's the middle of the afternoon and not very busy.

Turning, I see our honey-blonde friend walking in... Todd right on her heels.

They look like the oddest pair, and I'm not sure I'll ever get used to it. Where Vixey is all baggy pants, crop tops, and a wild mane of hair Serena van der Woodsen would envy, Todd is crisp suits, watches that probably cost more than her rent, and a perfectly styled coif that always looks freshly cut.

My gaze flicks to Alex behind the bar, watching them with thinly veiled annoyance. He, like us, was skeptical when they got back together. But whatever Todd did, Vixey seems to have completely forgiven him, and now they're insufferable.

I thought Hunter and I were bad. Vixey and Todd take PDA to a whole other level.

"I didn't think you were going to make it." Dove stretches on her tiptoes to hug her as they reach us.

"Todd pushed a meeting so we could come." Vixey shrugs like it's the most normal thing in the world.

Oh yeah, they don't go anywhere without each other.

"So glad you could make time for us with your busy schedule," I deadpan, eyes locked on Todd.

Just because she's forgiven him doesn't mean I will.

Hunter laughs as Todd fixes me with a dry stare. There's no love lost between us, and everyone knows it. Vixey is like my unofficial little sister now, and as far as I'm concerned, he has a lot more groveling to do after what he did to her.

Vixey hugs me from behind, her woodsy-vanilla scent engulfing my senses as she leans down to whisper, "Just give him a break today, okay? I promise, he deserves forgiveness."

She straightens and heads toward Hunter. "Now let me see my niece!"

"Come with me," I whisper to Hunter, grabbing his hand and pulling him up from the table.

No one pays us any attention. The girls are busy fawning over the baby while Wrenley and Todd talk in a corner about real estate investments. And I'm glad for it, because I've been wanting to get Hunter alone since I left the doctor's office earlier.

"Where are you taking me, Little Rabbit?" Hunter laughs as I tug him toward the bathrooms.

"I know you have to go back to work soon, so I want to talk before you leave." I make him wait in the hall while I ensure no one's in the women's room, then pull him in and lock the door.

Instant arousal floods me as I spin and jump into his arms. Hunter catches me effortlessly, groaning when I smash my lips to his. "Well, this is a nice surprise."

"I got cleared today for sex, and I didn't want to wait until tonight." I work his belt open as he sets me on the vanity.

Hunter chuckles, smoothing my hair off my shoulder before kissing my neck. "Is my little rabbit horny?"

"*Very*," I moan, freeing his cock from its confines. "I need you *now*."

Stroking him, I relish the shuddering gasp that flies from his mouth as he grips my hips, dragging me to the edge and shoving my dress up. "I did not imagine our first time after you were cleared would go like this."

My body sparks to life as his fingers dance along my skin, skimming between my legs to pull my underwear to the side. I notch him at my entrance. "I don't care, Hunter. I can't wait any longer."

Electricity crackles between us. Everywhere he touches feels on fire, and the proof is in the wetness pooling between my thighs. Hunter takes over, swiping the swollen head of his cock through my center while we watch our bodies join for the first time in nearly half a year.

"Fuck, I missed your pussy." Hunter swallows my loud groan as he pushes all the way in.

There's no waiting for me to adjust, no whispered sweet nothings or declarations of love—just our shared feral hunger and an insatiable appetite for each other. He stretches me, filling me again and again. Muscle memory kicks in, and our bodies crash in a tidal wave of fevered starvation.

"*Mine*," Hunter growls, nipping my lower lip.

One hand anchors my hip while the other strums my clit. My feet dig into his ass, helping him thrust as I cry his name over and over, our voices ricocheting off the tile.

"All yours, baby. Always." I slide my hand up to cup his cheek, pulling his gaze from where he watches us to meet mine. "Show me who I belong to."

It's probably my overactive imagination, but I swear Hunter swells inside me, angling my body back to hit deeper. We fit so tightly that I feel every ridge and vein of his cock, and I kiss the air with a curse, wondering how the fuck I survived so long without him.

"This pussy belongs to *me*." Hunter jerks his hips, spearing me with deep strokes like he's trying to imprint himself as one of my vital organs. "This body belongs to *me*." His fingers pinch my clit, then trail upward—over my stomach, through the valley of my breasts—before encircling my throat. "*You* belong to *me*, Little Rabbit, and I'm going to make sure you *never* fucking forget it."

Each word lands with a thrust. His mouth maps my neck, teeth sinking in to leave love bites before his tongue laves the tender skin. Our wet flesh slapping together reverberates through the small space, mixing with our ragged breaths and murmured encouragements as he drags us higher and higher until we're on the edge together.

"I love you," I whisper.

"Fuck, baby. I *revere* you. You're the only divine thing I'll get on my knees for, and I'm going to spend every day for the rest of our lives worshipping at your altar."

My pussy flutters. His fingers tighten at my throat—firm but gentle—pulling me impossibly closer as he presses our foreheads together. "Come for me, Little Rabbit."

We jump off that precipice at the same time, our orgasms washing through us. Our muscles flexing, groans mingling as our open mouths seal again, licking and sucking and biting to savor every morsel of each other.

"Fuck, I'm so obsessed with you," Hunter breathes into my mouth as we come down from our highs.

"Obsessed doesn't even begin to describe what I feel

for you." I exhale a shaky laugh, rolling my hips slowly, loving the way his eyes roll back and his cock flexes inside me.

I'm about to suggest we stay joined until he's ready for round two when pounding rattles the door. I squeak as he slips out of me, and I feel so fucking empty as our releases begin to spill down my thighs.

"You two better not be fucking in there again!" Alex roars from the other side.

Hunter's deep, amused chuckle vibrates against me as he scoops our cum and slowly pushes it back inside. I'm sensitive, my hips jerking as he toys with me. I bite my bottom lip and lean back, angling my legs wider so he has a glorious view of his ministrations.

"One day soon I'm going to fuck another baby into you." He steps away, grabs paper towels, and wets them at the sink so we can clean up.

It's then I realize, in my haste to have him, I completely forgot a condom.

You can't get pregnant again this soon... right?

Swinging my keys around my fingers, I shake my head and click my tongue as I venture farther into the house. Crimson covers nearly every inch of the living room of Dove's target. The girls are in the middle of it in their suits, hacking away at the man while carrying on a conversation about a new bakery that just opened on Dove's street. Meanwhile, Wrenley's in the kitchen with his head shoved into a trash bag, puking his guts out.

I feel like a dad who just rolled up on his kids while they're making a mess of their toys.

"Wrenley, for fuck's sake, man. Why do you come if you can't stomach it?" I frown as my best friend keeps dispelling his lunch.

As far as I know, he's been helping Dove with her *hard kills,* as she and Bunny call them. But if this is what he does at every crime scene, he's just making it harder for the little pink princess to clean up.

Wrenley glares over his shoulder. "Listen, for the

most part, I can handle it. It's when she goes overboard that—"

"I don't think there is such a thing as overboard when it comes to these fuckers," Dove cuts in, bubbly as if we aren't discussing dismemberment.

I swing my gaze to where she and Bunny are doing precisely that. Dove's got a line of intestines strung between her hands and is winding them around her elbow like she's putting away Christmas lights. Blood and organ chunks freckle the white suits the girls are wearing, and that's when I spot Bunny setting body parts off to the side.

"Whoa, Little Rabbit. The freezer is already stocked. I thought we talked about cooling it on the human fertilizer."

Bunny grins sheepishly, her lips curling inward as she peers up at me. "I know... but... well..."

"No buts, baby. We're walking a thin line as it is. Vivian next door keeps trying to convince me to enter the garden in some big magazine contest—says we'd surely win. We don't need anyone poking around asking how the hydrangeas got so vibrant."

Bunny pushes to her knees and starts toward me, reaching for my hand.

"Little Rabbit, this is the *only* time I'll say this, but keep those grimy paws off me." I flash a grin, mirth lacing my tone.

Her sultry laugh fills the room as she remembers she's covered in another man's bodily fluids. Stripping quickly, she leads me out of earshot of Dove and Wren. "I figured maybe we could use just a little more... because this will be my last time helping Dove for a while."

I can tell by the way she says it there's a hidden meaning tucked into her words. I mull it over for a beat. Bunny's smile widens—unable to wait for me to decipher it. "I'm pregnant!"

Shock spears through me—both at her statement and the fact she seems so happy about it. Excitement pours off her as she bounces on her toes and reaches for my shoulders. "Hunter, did you hear me? I just confirmed it this morning. I'm twelve weeks."

My hands find her hips, blood roaring in my ears. Quietly, I ask, "How on earth are you pregnant again?"

I won't pretend to know how the human body works. Faline is only five months old. If she's already three months along... My brain spins while Bunny laughs at my puzzled expression.

"We made another baby in the bathroom at the bar." She giggles, lacing her fingers into my hair. "We're having another baby, Hunter."

A dam breaks inside me, giddiness and elation flooding my veins. "And you're... happy? You're okay with being pregnant again?"

Her gaze softens as one hand slides down to cup my cheek. "Yes, baby. I'm so happy. I love you."

"I love you too." Hugging her to me, I nuzzle her ear. "But I know you wanted to wait a while. So if—"

"Hunter, stop. I'm excited to be growing another part of our little family. I couldn't be happier, okay?" She cups both my cheeks and lays a chaste kiss on my lips. "It's okay to be happy."

"Well, in that case..." I grin, release her, and pump my fists in the air as I shout to Dove and Wrenley, "We're having another baby!"

<u>Three Months Later</u>

Kenny G filters softly through the house as I get home from work. It's late. The case I'm on is eating up too much time, and with Bunny on bed rest as she nears her last trimester, I hate missing chances to take care of her.

Yasha and Maru yip excitedly as I toe off my shoes. "Shh. You don't want to wake your mom and sister, do you?"

Something tells me Bunny isn't asleep, though. Something soft cushions my feet as I head upstairs.

Roses?

Ruby petals blanket the steps, leading down the hall to our bedroom, where a soft glow spills from the open doorway.

"Bunny?" I call.

No answer.

Quietly, I continue, and when I step into our room, I see why.

My little rabbit is sleeping peacefully on our bed. Rose petals coat the floor. At least a hundred candles flicker as *Forever in Love* plays on her phone. Warmth blooms in my chest, my heart skipping a beat as I grow closer.

Next to her, the petals spell out a message.

Two words. A question mark.

Marry me?

I was already the happiest man on earth, now I feel like the luckiest in the universe. After everything, Bunny keeps proving she chooses me, chooses our family, and that she's not going anywhere.

But fuck if she doesn't still surprise me from time to time.

A laugh escapes me, stirring her awake.

"Hunter?"

Kneeling beside her, I smooth the hair from her face. "Yes, Little Rabbit."

She bolts upright, petals flying as she swings her legs off the bed. "Oh my god, I fell asleep!" Her forest gaze drops to the message, half-slid to the floor. "Shit! It's ruined."

Chuckling, I ease her back and climb onto the bed, bracing over her. "It's okay, Bunny. I saw it. And my answer is yes—though I can't believe you beat me to asking."

Nuzzling my nose, she grasps my face. "It's my turn to make the big, grand gestures, Hunter."

"You've given me a beautiful baby girl. You're growing my son. And now you want my last name. I'd say you've more than made up for the hell you put me through, Little Rabbit," I joke, then pause. "You *are* taking my name, right? I know it sounds antiquated, but

I hate that you still use *his*. I want our names to match—and our kids', too."

"That was never a question, baby. I love you. I always have, and I always will."

Fuck, I never get tired of hearing her say it.

I knew the moment I laid eyes on her that she was meant to be mine. But hearing Bunny say the words always sends my heart galloping.

My little rabbit *loves* me.

Our story couldn't have a more perfect ending.

Want to know what was said between Vixey and Todd at the club?

Sign up for an exclusive bonus chapter and sneak peek into book three of the Serial Killer Book Club.

AFTERWORD

For not being a huge fan of the pregnancy trope myself, I really do love the way Bunny and Hunter's story came to fruition.

I agonized over this book for months. Wondering if taking the time gap would be okay—would readers be upset? Would they have wanted to see what happened in those three months? But at the end of the day, I felt like the backstory was more relevant to the book than Bunny's last trimester.

This book came in at over thirty thousand words more than Dolls & Daggers did. Bunny and Hunter would have kept going, too—as a matter of fact, they did, I'm pretty sure Sam and I got rid of like twelve thousand words. They were talkative and vulnerable and could have gone on and on about their lives forever if I'd let them.

That's what bonus scenes and extra content are for, though, right?

I can't wait to dive into Vixey and Todd's story now. These two are yelling at me and even helped come up with a fun new project that I can't wait to announce.

Even though they might be the worst serial killers ever, they are truly the best in my eyes, and I can't wait to see them grow.

ACKNOWLEDGMENTS

Forever grateful to my team: Jessica, Ashley, Lauren, and Heather. My mom squad. Since my kids have fur, there were many, many, MANY questions about pregnancy and mom stuff. And, of course, it's always Lauren's fault in some aspect, because Pepper McChicken wouldn't exist without you and your furry farm.

Victoria, with Cruel Ink, my blurb queen. Thank you for making the absolute worst part of the job the easiest on me.

My editor, Sam. I'm forever asking "what would Sam do," and still learning the answer to this question, but I'm so thankful that you're always willing to voice message me about my ridiculous questions and talk about "positions" and slutty dumplings.

Charly, my cover designer, I love the purple so much and the HEELS! The heels are everything. These are going to look so good together. Thank you for always putting up with my crazy.

My very own golden retriever, Mr. Darby. Thanks for not being too concerned when I filled my browser with questions about how aquamation works and how to break down a body. Also, for putting up with my ridiculous mood swings—I was really trying to channel Bunny in this one.

Last but never least, thank you to my readers who continue to love and share our terrible vigilante serial killers. You've changed my life with this series and I will be forever grateful to each and every one of you. Keep sliding in those DMs with your messages because they make my day!

Xo

ABOUT THE AUTHOR

D.L. Darby lives in Anchorage, Alaska, with her husband and two fur babies.

By day, she's a hairstylist, and by night, she's continuously drafting new ideas on her "murder board" at home. While she writes across multiple romance sub-genres, you can always expect to find spicy alpha males and strong-willed women with a flair for dramatics in her stories.

www.ingramcontent.com/pod-product-compliance
Lightning Source LLC
Chambersburg PA
CBHW022018110726
47901CB00006B/1574